THE
PHYSICIAN
OF
NINEVEH

GLENN
COOPER

Goddess of love, mistress of desire,
Shine your light upon my heart.
I long for the one my soul adores,
Bring us together as you unite heaven and earth.

— ANCIENT ASSYRIAN PRAYER TO ISHTAR,
GODDESS OF LOVE

PROLOGUE

KATE HAS NEVER BEEN ONE TO LOSE HER BEARINGS, BUT NOTHING about the day seems real, not even this drab interview room at the Tottenham Police Station. She has passed the drab, red-brick Neo-Georgian police headquarters on the High Road countless times, never giving thought to what went on inside. The airless room was exceedingly basic—a table bolted to the concrete floor, two chairs on one side, hers on the other, and cameras high on plain green walls.

The interview pauses when Detective Constable Hayes, a man young enough for acne, excuses himself. Kate isn't sure why he is suddenly on the move, but she sees him taking a phone from his pocket. She guesses it vibrated, and he was summoned. She is unsurprised when an older woman takes his place.

"Miss Mayne, I'm Detective Sergeant Warrington from the Metropolitan Police in Richmond."

Kate takes a sip of cold tea from a paper cup. "Dr. Mayne," she says.

"Sorry, I didn't know you were a doctor. What kind?"

"Professor kind. University College London."

"Oh, right."

The detective sergeant is a bottle-redhead whose most prominent features on a wholly ordinary face are deep, geographic crow's feet branching from the corners of her eyes. Her clothes smell of cigarettes.

She lays a tablet computer on the table. "DC Hayes and I are collaborating with our colleagues in Tottenham on this matter. DC Hayes has filled me in. I thought I'd carry on with some questions."

There hasn't been enough time for a briefing, so Kate knows her new inquisitor has been watching.

"I've been here for hours."

"Yes, well. This *is* a murder investigation, and you *were* an eyewitness."

Kate is annoyed by the officiously exaggerated emphasis on the verbs but doesn't show it.

"I'm sorry. I'm very tired."

"We'll move this along just as quickly as we can. Tell us again about the men you were with last night."

Kate repeats her previous narrative. She knows one of them, having met him a few days earlier. She believes he is a visiting Iraqi scholar. The other two were strangers. She suspects they, too, are Iraqis.

"How could you tell?"

"They spoke Arabic. Specifically, the Mesopotamian dialect of Arabic."

"And you know this how?"

"I know the country well. Ancient Mesopotamia is my subject area."

"This scholar—what was his name again?"

"Dr. Ashur."

"And Dr. Ashur knew these two men?"

"It appeared so."

"Were you expecting them to arrive as they did?"

"No."

"What were you and Dr. Ashur doing there last night, considerably after visiting hours?"

"We were locked in, I'm afraid. Alcohol might have been involved."

"I see. An afternoon of heavy drinking? Where?"

"Heavy enough, apparently. At my flat."

"So, after an afternoon of heavy drinking at your flat, you decided to accompany this Iraqi scholar to Kew."

"Yes."

"Why?"

"He had never been. He had heard about it."

"And once there, you were sufficiently inebriated to become locked in."

"We might have dozed off in a quiet spot."

"And after dark, two more Iraqis appeared out of thin air."

"I don't know about thin air—we must have been followed. We awoke, greatly surprised by them."

"Your Dr. Ashur—he knew these gentlemen?"

"He seemed to, yes. They exchanged words. There was an argument. It became heated."

"What were they arguing about?"

DC Hayes hadn't asked that question, and Kate invents an answer. "It sounded like a dispute about money. Money owed on a property sale."

"Then, what happened?"

"One of them, a large man, attacked Dr. Ashur. Dr. Ashur fought back and struck him."

"How did this large man attack him?"

"With his fists, I think. Maybe a rock."

"Maybe a rock?"

"No, a rock.

"Did Dr. Ashur hit the other man back?"

"I think so, yes. He might have taken the rock away."

"How many times did Dr. Ashur hit him?"

"Once, I think."

"With this rock? Once?"

3

"Yes."

"I see. The other man—what was his involvement?"

"None that I can recall."

"He had no physical contact with Dr. Ashur of any kind?"

"I don't think so."

"What about you? Did you have any physical contact with either of these men?"

"No."

"What were you doing during the altercation?"

"I was shocked. I was standing aside."

"After the fight was over, what happened?"

"We were in a panic. We broke a window and ran to my car."

"What about the third man?"

"I don't know what happened to him."

"He didn't leave with you."

"No."

The detective sergeant shakes her head sharply. She uses enough spray that her hair doesn't move.

"You're not telling the truth, are you, Dr. Mayne?"

Kate protests but watches nervously as the detective props the tablet on its stand. She should have known there were cameras. The microphone didn't pick up low conversations, but the shouting was audible. She watches for a minute or so, feeling sick to her stomach.

"I'll grant you there was a scuffle, "the detective says. "But you were hardly a non-involved bystander. Your Dr. Ashur hits the deceased with a rock repeatedly until the man's face was gone. A bloody rock was found at the scene. Then, you, Dr. Ashur, and the third man run off. And we had one of our officers, who's Egyptian, listen to this. He says it's not Arabic. He doesn't recognize it."

Kate spews words. "It all happened very fast. It's a blur. I think I was in shock. I didn't remember what I did. I didn't watch the fight, so I didn't know Dr. Ashur hit him repeatedly. I only know that he was struck first. I believe what's spoken is a local dialect."

"Where is Dr. Ashur?"

"I don't know," Kate says. That isn't a lie.

"We have a witness who states he was in your flat late last night."

Kate makes a fist under the table. She knows who the witness is. "We drove back to my flat. Dr. Ashur collected his things and left. We hardly spoke after the incident. I was in shock. He didn't say where he was going, and given what had happened, I didn't want to know."

"What about the other man?"

"I didn't remember that he left with us. I don't know what happened to him. I swear."

"What was in the bag?"

"What bag?"

"The full Tesco carrier bag we can see right there in the video."

"I don't know," Kate says unconvincingly. She is a terrible liar. She had lived the kind of life where lying had never been necessary. "Do I need a lawyer?"

"You're attending this voluntary interview as a witness. DC Hayes informed you of your rights. Witnesses don't usually require solicitors. However, if you believe you might have committed a crime, you are entitled to have one present during questioning."

Kate blinks helplessly. "I don't know what to think. Out of an abundance of caution—"

That's all the detective needs to hear. She picks up her tablet and rises.

"This interview is terminated until you can arrange for a solicitor to attend. If you do not wish to or cannot afford to retain counsel, the duty solicitor will assist you. While you're having a think, we'll have your tea freshened up. And I should mention, we have received approval from a magistrate for a warrant to search your flat on Langham Road. That search will take place presently."

Alone, Kate looks into the interrogation room camera, stiffening her lips, refusing to cry.

CHAPTER ONE

THE BOY, MANNU, IS RUNNING ALONG THE MIGHTY INNER WALLS OF Nineveh, his bare feet making shallow impressions in the alluvial soil, his small hands brushing against stiff river reeds and soft feather grass. He is eight, poised between childhood and adulthood, free to disappear from his father's house for hours, unencumbered by the demands society will soon place on him. He senses that this period of his life is drawing to an end and is determined to extract sweet juice from every precious day. He loves the impossibly chaotic city, which constantly serves up new treats for his senses, and he freely roams its vastness, scampering through majestic public squares, ornate gardens, bustling marketplaces, and residential alleyways. His natural curiosity knows no bounds. He asks gardeners the names of flowers and bushes, merchants the price of sesame and barley, soldiers how much the king pays for their service, and craftsmen why they make some weapons with bronze, others iron. Many know him by name. Others simply call him *aplu ša iš'alu ša'aṭa* —the boy who asks questions.

Today, he has a rudimentary plan to loop through his favorite parts of the city. He lives on the outskirts of the palace district near the Nergal Gate with its massive stone guardian sculptures that humble visitors to the royal city. His father's villa is to the north of the River Khosr, a tributary of the mighty River Idigna, which, in time, will come to be known as the Tigris. From his house, he will run along the city wall toward the lesser Sin Gate, then wander through a maze of small streets toward the walled compound of the king's palace. He will pass by the house of one of his father's subordinates in the grain kisru, the office that administers the king's grain storehouses, and he will see if his friend, Ninurta, can join his romp. On their way to the palace district, they will pass through the main market in the prosperous residential area, inhaling aromas of freshly cut flowers and bushels of eastern spices. They will stop at the stall of the date merchant, who likes Mannu and respects his father. The boy will cup his hands and, in exchange for a bright smile, will receive a free handful of ripe fruit. Then, they will approach the terraced palace walls and sit on their haunches to munch dates and watch yoked oxen turn the screws that drive buckets of water from the moat to the top of the wall to irrigate the lush gardens of King Ashurbanipal. Mannu has never seen the gardens inside the palace walls, but his father says they are a paradise on Earth. He marvels at the vegetation that cascades down the terraced walls. The vines of ripe purple grapes, scented jasmine, flowering morning glories, and carpets of green ivy set against the glazed blue, yellow, and white bricks of the palace walls are a feast for the eyes. Mannu and Ninurta will dreamingly stare at the ziggurats of the Temples of Nabu and Ishtar rising within the palace complex toward the gods in the heavens, and the friends will speak of the future as they often do.

Neither wants to be grain merchants like their fathers. Ninurta's grandfather was a soldier bitterly disappointed that his son's withered arm prevented him from joining the army. He insisted his grandson be given an auspicious name, a bow to Ninurta, the warrior god. The boy is called Ninurta-sharru, which means Ninurta is king, and Mannu's friend believes that becoming a soldier is his destiny. Mannu likes to play fight and can better Ninurta on a good day, but he has no desire to kill and maim. He has a deep reverence for life and an insatiable curiosity about the natural world. His dream is to become a healer. When they finish their dates, they will go to the artisan district and watch the armorers bang out bronze shields.

But that day, Mannu never makes it to Ninurta's house, for as he runs along the mudbrick city walls, he spies a pair of soldiers high atop a sentry post, shooting arrows into the grass. As he gets closer, he sees a black-and-white patch at the base of the wall and hears the distinctive cry of a goat.

"Hey, you, boy!" one of the soldiers shouts. "Away with you. That is our supper!"

Mannu is close enough to see the creature's pleading brown eyes and a splash of blood on the reeds.

"He is hurt," Mannu shouts into the sky. "He is in pain."

"This will finish him," the other soldier shouts back, drawing his bow.

"Move away, or you too will be hurt."

Mannu is defiant. He moves closer to the frightened creature. "No! Let him be! Only brutes kill an animal so cruelly."

"I will come down and show you the back of my hand," the first soldier yells.

"You will not!" Mannu bellows back. "My father is Nabû-bēl-uṣur, the *Rab Karāni*, chief of the king's grain houses, and you will be flogged for striking me."

Mannu sees the soldier relax his bowstring and confer with his compatriot.

The two men say no more to him and resume their duties on the wall.

As the boy bends, the animal tries to flee but is too injured to go far. It is only a kid, maybe a couple of months old, and one of its hind legs has been flayed to the muscle by the barbed arrow embedded in the mud.

"Come, little one," Mannu says, scooping it into his arms. "I will not harm you," and as he carries the kid toward the Nergal

Gate, he feels a powerful urge to show it that not all men are cruel.

His father's house is large, befitting a man of his position. Its whitewashed mudbrick walls reflect the sun's rays. Five rooms surround a central courtyard, and its heavy wooden door has fancy bronze fittings. Mannu's mother, Zabītu, hears loud bleating and rushes to the door, veiling her head at the threshold.

"What is this, my son?" she asks.

"It is a sweet kid, cruelly shot by a wall sentry."

"I hope the blood on your tunic is but the blood of a goat."

"It is, Mother."

"Why have you brought it here?"

Her tone is inquisitive, not scolding. She is tall for a woman and has a kind and gentle way about her.

"I would like to heal it," the boy says.

"And then, what?"

"Then I will keep her, and she will give us milk when she is older."

"Ah, you possess a clear plan," she says. "But behold her wound. I think she is beyond saving."

"I will bind it and pray to Gula," Mannu said.

"The goddess is busy answering many prayers. She will not have time for one small goat."

"I will pray loudly. She will hear me."

Zabītu's handmaiden is watching from the courtyard door. "Come, Mannu," the servant says. "Take the creature outside. I will bring rags for your purpose."

Mannu's father arrives home as the sun sets, its mellow light flattering the teeming city. He is in his prime. Anyone can see he is wealthy. His tunic is deep blue, finely woven, and dyed with expensive woad pigment, as befits a high administrator to the royal court. He has a prosperous belly. His beard is meticulously styled into cascading curls and smells of cedarwood oil.

"Where are my wife and son?" he asks the handmaiden.

"In the courtyard, Master."

Nabû-bēl-uṣur slips his sandals back on and goes outside. His name means Nabu, protect the lord. It is a prescient name, for the god Nabû has looked on him kindly. He has royal favor, an important job, a good wife, and a clever, obedient son. The courtyard is small but has everything a man could want. There is a clay bread oven and a grinding wheel to mill the grain. An olive tree, ripe with fruit, shades the patch of baked earth where his wife works her weaving frame. This evening, something else is under the tree—a small animal lying on a pile of river grass, its neck tethered to a stake by a length of hemp.

"*Bēlī*," his wife says nervously. She repeats *Bēlī*—the affectionate form of lord and master—as she prepares to defend her son's actions. "Our son found this kid wounded by a soldier's arrow. He bound its wound to staunch the bleeding. He feeds it warm goat's milk from the pouch I sewed."

In public, Mannu's father is imperious and demanding. At home, his demeanor softens. His wife plays him as well as she plucks the pantu.

As instructed by her mistress, the handmaiden appears with a cup of strong date wine for her husband. He is about to take a sip, looks at the sleeping animal, and says, "Yes, but—"

Mannu seizes the moment and addresses him formally but affectionately.

"*Abi*, I am determined to save the life of this poor creature so cruelly treated by two oafs who call themselves our King's men. I washed its wound with warm water. Do you remember when you cut your foot? Mother made a poultice of honey, crushed thyme, and flour and pressed it into the wound. I did the same. I will take care of it and keep the courtyard clean. May I have your permission? When she is grown, she can give us milk."

His father downs his wine quickly and holds out his cup for more.

"Yes, fine. Now, I want my supper. I have had a miserable day haggling with miserable merchants."

Later, Nabû-bēl-uṣur presses against his wife on their straw mattress. Mannu lies across from them in the bed chamber, soundly sleeping.

"He has the heart of a healer," she whispers. "He helps birds with broken wings. He tried to keep a litter of baby mice alive when a hawk took their mother and cried when he failed. His reverence for life is so strong he will not even let me step on a beetle."

Her husband knows where she is pushing the conversation.

"He will apprentice in my storerooms," he says, fluffing the feather pillow that only a prosperous man can afford.

"He will make an able grain overseer," she says, "but he will make a magnificent healer. A mother knows."

"A boy should follow his father's path."

She feels his stiffness against her buttock.

"Perhaps your next son will follow your path," she says. In the years since Mannu's birth, she has suffered miscarriages and a still-born. "It is my time of the month," she purrs. "I have been making offerings at the Temple of Ishtar, and I dreamed of a flower blooming the moment I gazed at it. The goddess will grant our wish —of that, I am sure. Let us make a grain overseer tonight and allow Mannu to follow his heart."

THE KID BECAME a healthy goat that hopped and scampered on four strong legs and rewarded its keepers with an abundance of milk and cheese. On an early summer morning, the air already heavy with heat, Nabû-bēl-uṣur wakes Mannu and says, "Rise, my son. Wash your feet and put on the clean tunic your mother has prepared. You are coming with me to the palace."

The boy is instantly alert, his eyes wide and thankful.

"Can Ninurta come too?"

"No."

"Will I see the gardens?"

"You cannot fail to see them."

At the door, his mother hugs her son and weeps.

"Why are you crying, Mother?"

He sees his parents looking at each other and notices his father's reproachful countenance.

"It is because you are growing into a fine young man," she says. She bows to her husband and rests her hands on the baby growing inside her swollen belly.

Mannu follows his father at a respectful two paces. A boy from the neighborhood runs toward him, wanting to play, but stops when he recognizes his father. Mannu waves him off and keeps at his father's heels. While he knows every fingerbreadth of the stone-slabbed roads, packed-earth alleyways, and all the market stalls and merchants along the way, his anticipation makes everything seem different. This is no longer the route an ordinary boy might take to the palace district but the petal-strewn path of one chosen to taste the forbidden fruit.

He has seen the massive bronze-plated gates of King Ashurbani-pal's palace countless times, always awestruck by their towering height and the colossal, winged bulls with human faces that flank them. As he passes through the outer ring of palace guards, he can see that the gleaming bronze panels are etched with scenes of royal hunts and processions. Soldiers acknowledge his father with bowed heads and the gates part.

He is inside!

He passes onto a grand courtyard of magnificent proportions where throngs of palace officials mill about and converse. From the outside, the palace walls are marvelous enough. From the inside, they steal the boy's breath. Colorful glazed tiles are adorned with massive carvings of lions, bulls, and supernatural beings, surely the gods themselves. King's guards are everywhere, standing erect in colorful tunics and bronze helmets, holding gleaming spears.

He looks to his left, and there they are, the gardens that spill over the palace walls. Terraces of greenery cascade from high plat-forms supported by massive stone columns. Fragrant herbs, date palms, and flowering vines flow over the edges, creating a lush green canopy with vibrant blossoms. Vine-covered archways and paths lead into the heart of the greenery. He hears the faint sound of water coursing through hidden viaducts, and he longs to wander among the plantings to see how the bucket screw works.

"Father. Can we enter into the gardens?"

13

"We cannot. We have business here."

"What business, Father?"

"You shall see."

They must pass through another set of heavily guarded doors to enter the palace's interior. The boy's sandals slip along polished floors and endless corridors filled with courtiers, scribes, servants, soldiers, and merchants. There are smaller courtyards here and there and shaded arcades. A grain merchant approaches his father, wishing to enter into a negotiation. His father dismisses him roughly, and the man cowers away, apologizing as he goes. Mannu knows his father is powerful—his mother has told him as much—but seeing him wield that power for the first time makes his mouth dry.

He feels the urge to say something but is afraid to ask about this man his father has wounded with his tongue.

He says this: "It is cool inside."

"The walls are thick," his father replies.

"Where does the King live?"

His father gestures. "The royal apartments are over there. I have never seen them. We are going this way."

Their route takes them through an inner courtyard, a serene space, its flagstones warming in the morning sunlight. A small, tiled fountain murmurs at its center, spewing clear water. Mannu's breathing stops. He is transfixed by the young girls practicing a graceful dance under the shade of a vine-covered pergola. They are clad in light linen dresses embroidered with delicate geometric patterns. They move to the rhythm of the steady clapping of their teacher, their anklets of tiny bronze bells jingling softly with each step. Their arms rise and fall like the wings of doves. Their feet trace fluid arcs across the stone.

One girl catches Mannu's eye. Her long, dark hair is braided with blue ribbons that shimmer in the sunlight. Her face is luminous, her expression focused on her movements, but this girl, unlike the others, has eyes that spark with joy. When their gaze meets, he feels a rush of wonder and curiosity. His perception of time slows, and what is the briefest of intervals seems deliciously long. The teacher calls out a correction, and the girl looks away, the moment over. Mannu lingers a heartbeat longer before his father's voice hurries him along.

They pass through administrative wings where scribes sit cross-legged at low tables, pressing styli into damp clay tablets. Finally, they reach the entrance to a complex of rooms. His father stops and looks down on him with an unsettling solemnity.

"Why are we here, Father?"

"You say you want to be a healer. This is where, with the grace of Ashur, one becomes a healer."

Mannu feels his heart beat out his joy.

"Truly, Father?"

"We must not keep the Rab Asû waiting."

When they enter the chamber, Mannu's nose wrinkles. Aromatic smells—earthy, bitter, pungent, and nutty—tickle his nostrils. Shelves with clay pots line the walls. The room has no windows; oil lamps set into wall niches and on tables illuminate it.

An attendant in a belted robe looks to his father to explain their presence.

"The Rab Asû expects me," his father says. "I am Nabû-bēl-uṣur."

The attendant tells them to wait and leaves.

Mannu takes a few hesitant steps to examine the long tables and is astonished at the array of glass vessels. He has seen glass objects for sale at the bazaar for huge prices, but they are not for ordinary people. Even his father does not possess any. Here were beakers and jars of all colors—green, blue, clear, and even yellow, like the sun. Most are filled with liquids. There are clay pots with dried leaves and clay tablets scattered about with writing his father understands.

The attendant reappears and takes them into a chamber with a window flooding a cluttered writing table with morning light. An old man sits on a high-backed chair and puckers his dry lips.

"I had forgotten this is the day I granted you an audience," he says.

The Rab Asû, the chief physician to whom the king exclusively entrusts his earthly body, has a commanding presence. When he peers at Mannu, the boy cowers like a mouse to a cat. He is far

15

older than his father. The ringlets of his hair and his oiled, braided beard are streaked with gray. His pale face is deeply lined, and his hooded eyes are murky and watery.

He rises to his full height, supporting himself on an ebony staff capped with the bronze head of an eagle. His finely woven robe is embroidered with plant motifs. A bulging leather pouch dangles from his waist sash. He wears a jeweled pendant around his neck bearing the likeness of Gula, the goddess of medicine and healing.

"This is the boy," he says. It is a statement, not a question.

"This is my son, Mannu-ki-Ashur."

"A lofty name." His name means who is like Ashur, the supreme god. "You

had high hopes for him."

"These hopes remain."

Mannu has not shifted his wide eyes from the old man. He feels his father's hand patting his head.

"You told me the boy is clever. Are you clever, Mannu-ki-Ashur?"

"I—" Words stuck in his mouth.

"I have that effect on children," the physician says humorlessly. "Come. Let us see if you are clever."

They return to the first chamber. The chief physician walks along the shelves, pointing his staff at the clay pots he wants the attendant to take down. Three pots are placed on one of the tables, and he orders Mannu to stand before them.

The physician extends a long, crooked finger. "I wish to make a medicine comprised of three parts of the contents of the first pot, two parts of the second pot, and one part of the third pot. Place the medicine into that empty pot. You may proceed."

Mannu has never been as frightened as this moment. He has dreamed of becoming a healer for as long as he can remember. Does the dream really depend on how he performs this enigmatic task?

He leans over the table and inspects the contents of the pots. Each contains dried leaves of a type he has never seen before. The leaves in the first pot are large, some the size of his palm. Those in the second pot are long and thin with serrated edges. The ones in the third pot are small and thick, like his pinky nails.

Three parts, two parts, one part.

He tries to calm himself and think.

What if I take three leaves from the first, two from the second, and one from the third?

The answer seems too easy, and then, he spots the flaw. No two leaves in any pot are the same. They vary in size considerably. How can one be precise with leaves so different from one another?

He closes his eyes to block out the fearsome sight of the Rab Asû. He wishes to put a cloth in his ears to dampen his father's loud nasal breathing. He searches the room for clues. On a table, he sees an implement similar to one in his own household, and mercifully, the answer comes to him.

"May I touch things?" he asks meekly.

"I do not see how you can make a medicine without using your hands," the old man says. "And you will refer to me as Master."

Mannu searches the tables and finds a bronze spoon smaller than a dining utensil. When he grabs the stone mortar and pestle, he searches the murky eyes of the old man for approval. Getting no reaction, he busies himself grinding leaves from the first pot the way he has seen his mother grind spices. When he has made a fine powder, he scoops up three spoonfuls, places them in an empty glass jar, and cleans the mortar with puffs of breath. He grinds the other leaves, placing two powdery spoonfuls of the second pot and one spoonful of the third into the jar. Finally, he gives the jar a good mix and presents it to the physician.

His father asks what he seems afraid to ask.

"Has he performed the task correctly?"

The Rab Asû does not answer. Instead, he poses a question.

"Why do you want to be an *asû*, boy?"

Mannu had never considered such a question. He's wanted to be a physician for as long as he can remember and blurts out, "It is something that comes from within."

The old man nods almost imperceptibly. "That is the correct answer. Do you know what you must do to become a physician?"

His voice cracks. Mannu says he does not know.

"You must spend at least five years as a junior apprentice, cleaning these rooms, doing chores, and observing—always observing. You must also attend palace school to learn to read and write. Following the apprenticeship, providing you survive the ordeal—yes, I can promise you, it will be an ordeal—you begin years of advanced work as a junior physician where you will study and memorize tablets on medicine, astrology, magic, and divination. You will prepare remedies and learn the organs of the body. Then, you might be assigned to the army, where you would travel on military campaigns and treat injuries and diseases at camp and the field of battle. Should you survive, you would return to Nineveh and, if judged worthy by me, or whoever might be rab asû in the future, then and only then would you become a physician to the royal court. Are you prepared to dedicate your life to becoming a healer, boy?"

Mannu nods eagerly. "When can I start, Master?"

"You have already begun. Bid your father farewell."

"Am I to stay here?"

"This is your new home. You will sleep on this very floor."

Mannu looks at his father through damp eyes.

"I will come to see you from time to time," his father says. "With permission of the Rab Asû."

"You are the rab karāni. It is allowed," the physician said, acknowledging his father's high rank. "But I beg you, sir. Within reason."

"When will I see my mother?" Mannu asks.

"Not before your apprenticeship ends," his new master says. "You have long since weaned off mother's milk."

Mannu reels from the news and fights to keep stoic.

He knows now why his mother cried so.

CHAPTER TWO

A WOOLLY MOUTH, A CATCH IN THE THROAT, THE HINT OF A CHILL.

Kate Mayne opens her eyes, escaping from a ridiculous dream, and coughs.

A voice under the covers mumbles, "What time is it?"

The light leaking through the gap in the curtains comes from the sodium-yellow streetlight. "It's still dark," she says. "What time did you get in?"

"Late," he says.

He's lanky and bony, and she feels a sharp knee as he shifts positions.

"Drinking?"

The words come thick. "Working at the library. Then the pub. Bit of both, s'ppose."

She feels a hand prowling her thigh.

"I don't feel well," she says. "I think I'm coming down with something."

The hand retreats without putting up a fight.

When she returns from the bathroom, she hears snoring and finishes dressing without turning on the radio.

She thinks, *I can't be getting sick. I've got too much on my plate.*

Standing at the kitchen countertop, she wonders if her coffee tastes a little off. There's a lot of flu about, and she'd be guilty as hell if she infected her seminar. Mug in hand, she wanders into the corner of the sitting room where Jeremy keeps his keyboard and music notebooks. She rationalizes spying on him this way: she's allowed him to suspend contributions to household expenses so he can write his opera full-time, and she has reason to believe he hasn't worked on it in ages. Composition books have been empty; bin bags full of lager cans. He writes his music longhand. She opens a notebook marked Act One and quickly closes it. He's on the same stanza as a month ago.

She pops a couple of Paracetamol and heads into the autumn chill, her shoulder bag heavy with everything needed for the day. It's still dark when she enters the Turnpike Lane Underground Station. Forty minutes later, the morning is bright when she emerges at Russell Square. Early on, the commute bothered her as she had enjoyed living in town, albeit with roommates, during her Ph.D. years. Her father, an immensely practical man, persuaded her to get on the property ladder. She had to look far afield to achieve her ambition of a proper house with a garden on a lecturer's salary. When she looked at the semi-detached house on Langham Road, it was her first time in Tottenham, a north-London town she knew only from its football club. It wasn't love at first sight, but bested the alternatives in her price bracket. A deal was struck after her father gave her enough of a downpayment to make the math work for the mortgage lender.

On most mornings, especially, when in the autumn, yellow sunshine fell on turning leaves, the short walk through the University College London Bloomsbury campus was a tonic for her soul. But today, she is steadily getting sicker and can't stop ruminating about Jeremy's sloth. The Institute of Archaeology is just off the UCL quad in a functional if uninspiring, building. She makes it into her cubby-hole office without bumping into any colleagues from the Assyriology Department and manages an hour of work before her morning seminar.

After tossing another tissue into the bin, she checks her

reddening nose in a makeup mirror and adds powder. There's just enough time to get a coffee before class, so she pops across the square to the Ginger Jules Café, where, waiting in line at the kiosk, the person she least wants to see approaches at ramming speed.

"Kate!" he says. "It's been ages. I was hoping I'd bump into you."

Wilson Banning had been in Kate's graduate class at the Institute. They dated a grand total of once during the first week of the first year, although at the time, she hadn't seen it as a date; she thought agreeing to get dinner was an act of polite camaraderie. He saw it differently and never stopped trying for another one, peppering her with emails and greeting cards, professing how gorgeous, sexy, and intelligent she was. Fortunately, after year one, fieldwork took them to different continents, and graduation solved the problem definitively, or so she thought.

"Wilson," she says, startled. "Yes, it has been a long while. What brings you to the IoA?" She knows why he's there; she's heard through the grapevine.

"I'm interviewing for a faculty position in the Mesoamerican Department."

She blows her nose and says, "Sorry. I've got a cold. My goodness, yes. Enid Parker's old slot. You're at Birmingham, right?"

"Right, you are," he says, checking her up and down the creepy way she remembers he used to. "Good department, but this is the mecca. Wouldn't it be fantastic to work with you again?"

"Wouldn't it," she says before hastily wishing him luck and telling him she has a class.

"I know," he says. "I checked the catalog—your seminar in advanced Akkadian. I'll shoot you an email to let you know how my interviews went. Put in a good word for me, why don't you?"

The seminar is tiny, with only two grad students. There's scant interest in learning dead languages, and Akkadian, the Mesopotamian language written and spoken from the third to the first millennium BCE, is not for the faint of heart. If you aren't planning on becoming a professional Assyriologist, there's little reason to put yourself through the years it takes to learn over its seven hundred cuneiform symbols and complex grammar. It's not as if interest in the language has faded in the modern era. The elderly professor who taught her Akkadian told her that when he was at Oxford, he was the only one in his group to learn cuneiform.

Kate knows the seminar students well and has become close with them. Both women have been at the IoA for several years, are well into their dissertation research, and are becoming proficient in Akkadian. To make the class challenging, Kate assigns them readings directly from the clay tablets in the British Museum's extensive collection. Her colleague, Irving Finkel, the bushy-bearded curator of the museum's one hundred thirty thousand cuneiform tablets, lets her students study the precious material in the Middle Eastern Lab.

"Mary, Bethany, don't get too close," she says, putting her books and coffee down and connecting her laptop to the projector. "I've got a bug. How'd you get along with K 2173+?"

"There's a lot missing," Bethany says of the broken, fragmented tablet.

"It's frustrating, isn't it?" Kate says. "If either of you wants to volunteer, Irving will happily let you sort through hundreds of his drawers looking for missing bits."

Both students roll their eyes, and Kate laughs in solidarity.

"Right. K2173+," Kate says. "Discovered by Sir Austen Henry Layard in 1849 during his excavations at Kuyunjik, Iraq, at the site of the destroyed Royal Nineveh Library of Ashurbanipal, it has fascinated scholars ever since. As you saw, it's a rather large tablet comprising fifteen re-joined fragments. It falls into the category of ghost tablets, or more specifically, anti-ghost tablets. Plagued by pesky ghosts who won't go away? Well, this tablet has the solutions you need." Kate projects a magnified photo of the tablet and points to a line. "Who wants to dive in?"

The students look at each other, and Mary, the more confident of the two, takes the bait.

"Ghost who keeps appearing—whether you be a strange ghost or a forgotten ghost or a roving ghost who has no one to care for him—"

Kate interrupts her. "Who is meant to utter this incantation?"

"The person who's seeing the ghost," Mary says.

"What's going on while the incantation is being said?" Kate asks. "Bethany?"

"The *āšipu*, the exorcist, has made a circle around the sufferer's bed with flour and placed two types of thorns inside it. During the incantation, the *āšipu* pours a potion of cedar oil, algae, bitumen, and sulfur onto the circle and the thorns."

"Correct," Kate says. "The barrier is intended to prevent the ghost from entering the bed and presumably the sufferer's dreams. The thorns provide some kind of symbolic defense. Okay, Mary, carry on."

Mary squints at her notes and says, "—whether you be a ghost who died as a result of a sin against a god or an offense against the king or a ghost who died when his fate was completed, do not approach, do not come close to my bed, may the wall hold you back, may the door turn back your breast. At the command of Ea, Shamash, and the exorcist of the gods, Assaluhi, you are abjured from Heaven, you are abjured from Earth. May it never release you as you are abjured. May Anzagar, who can loosen the bound, turn away your breast."

"That's very good, Mary," Kate says. "At this point, an incantation is recited three times. It's called the incantation against often seeing *mitū*, namely, dead people. But first, seven small loaves of bread are laid out, and an ox hoof filled with well water is offered as a libation. Bethany, can you translate the next bit?"

Bethany begins, "Ghost who has been set on me and pursues me day and night and abuses me, whether a strange ghost or a forgotten ghost or a ghost whose name is not invoked, or a ghost who has no one to pray for it, or a ghost who was killed by a weapon, or a ghost who died due to a sin against a god, or an offense against the king, may he accept this as his portion and leave me be."

Bethany, lacking confidence, looks to Kate for approval as she always does, and Kate delivers it.

Bethany beams and says, "They took their ghosts seriously, didn't they?"

Kate says, "When you read enough ghost tablets, you understand that the Assyrians, as the Sumerians and Babylonians before them, absolutely believed that ghosts were real and dwelled among them. I strongly doubt there were any Assyrians who believed otherwise. For them, it was an ironclad reality. Okay, who wants to do the next few lines?"

By the time the seminar is over, Kate is feeling sicker. A shudder of chills ripples her back, and her joints ache. She finds a piece of paper under her office door and plops down heavily to read it. It's from Wilson, who says he hopes to stop by and catch up after his interviews. She grunts, looks at her day planner, and decides nothing scheduled is sacred. *It's settled*, she thinks. *I'm going home.*

With paracetamol on board, she slinks out of the IoA, hoping to avoid bumping into Wilson, and retraces her steps to the Underground. On the train, she texts her nurse friend, Amrita, describing her symptoms and negative COVID test and asking if it could be the flu. Amrita, ever reliable, texts her right back. She says there's also a lot of influenza going around and that she'll call when her shift ends.

As she nears her front door, she tries to get herself in a positive frame of mind about Jeremy. She doesn't want to be triggered. Things have been on a downswing since he left his job to do music full-time, and she's not sure the relationship is still working. But if she finds him lying about, watching tele, and doing fuck all, she will have to let it roll off her back. She's too ill to deal with it today. And maybe she'll be pleasantly surprised and see him at the keyboard. She leaves her jacket and bag in the hall and tosses her keys in the ceramic bowl they bought on holiday in Marrakech. The lights in the sitting room are off, and it's quiet. No TV, no music.

Just as well he's out. Cup of tea. Straight to bed.

The sitting room hasn't been touched since she left. There's a cereal bowl in the sink. As she puts the kettle on, she hears a bump through the ceiling, and on the stairs, she hears Jeremy laughing like he's on the phone. The bathroom door is open on the landing, but the spare room door is closed. She pays it little mind.

"Jeremy?" she says, entering the bedroom.

The bed is unmade, and he's not there.

Her virus-addled mind points her to the spare room, which she realizes is above the kitchen.

She turns the knob and pushes the door. "Jeremy?"

She immediately feels stupid for not anticipating what she discovers.

Jeremy, in his panic, has hogged the duvet at the expense of his paramour, who is completely naked. Kate is impressed by her perfect figure and absence of embarrassment. Wordlessly, Kate closes the door and retreats to her bedroom, her blood, already hot from fever, on the boil. She kicks off her shoes, climbs into her side of the bed, and listens to the chaos on the landing.

"I didn't know she'd come home early."

"You're a proper wanker, you know?"

"Look, I—"

"Lose my fucking number, all right?"

The front door slams, and there is a long silence, giving Kate time to decide. She climbs out of bed long enough to do some housekeeping.

When Jeremy finally comes in, fully clothed, head, penitent, she doesn't give him the space to say whatever he was planning.

"I'm sick, and I'm going to bed," she says from under the bedclothes. A hand emerges to point at the mound of clothes, chargers, and miscellany on the floor. "Take your shit. When I wake up, I want you gone. Leave the keys. I never want to see you again."

"Kate, I—"

She shrieks at him, hurting her throat, but she's impressed by how primally effective it is. He meekly scoops his things and is gone.

~

AMRITA CALLS IN AFTER WORK. She lives in north London, in Walthamstow, so they see each other often. Prewarned about Jeremy, she comes prepared with practical and emotional support.

"First things first," she says, her small brown hands opening a box of test kits. "I've brought a flu swab."

Kate is on the sofa in her fluffiest robe and slippers. She nods.

The nurse swabs and dips and stares sagely at the plastic indicator. A red line quickly forms.

"There you have it," she says. "It's influenza. We'll get you sorted."

"What about my life?" Kate asks. "Can you sort that, too?"

"I'm not a miracle worker."

When Kate joins the laughter, Amrita tells her it's a good sign that she hasn't lost her sense of humor.

"Now that he's history, can I tell you what I thought about Jeremy?" Amrita asks. She doesn't wait for a reply. "Besides being cute, he was an opportunistic grifter; that's what I thought."

"Why didn't you tell me, Ammie?"

"Because you were happy."

"Until I wasn't."

"Once the shock of seeing what you saw fades, you'll be happy again. I bought some flu meds, in case that's what it was, and soup. I'll just heat it."

"At least they weren't in my bed," Kate says.

Amrita makes a face. "A real gentleman."

Kate slurps soup while Amrita drinks wine from a tumbler.

"He took everything, right?" the nurse asks.

"I think so."

"I wouldn't be shocked if he left something behind to give him an excuse to get a foot back in the door."

Amrita gazes around the sitting room, looking for telltale signs of the miscreant's life. It's a cozy front room decorated with hand-me-down furniture and a good rug from Kate's suburban parents.

"What's this?" Amrita says, springing from the armchair and bending under a side table. She waves the page of a music score, reads a line, and giggles. "Oh, my god! *My planet weeps for me.* What the hell is that?"

"It's from his opera," Kate says, "It's meant to be the first sci-fi opera."

"Can't wait," Amrita says dismissively. Something else catches her eye. "That's new," she says, plucking an irregular slab of baked clay from its display stand.

"It's a gift from me to me," Kate said.

"What is it?"

"A super-nice replica of a Neo-Assyrian cuneiform tablet from the British Museum. It's the *Epic of Gilgamesh*, the Babylonian great flood story that's similar to the Book of Genesis."

Amrita lightly ran her finger over the clay surface. "And you can read these little wedges."

"I can."

"I'm impressed."

"And I'm impressed by the things *you* can do that I can't," Kate says.

"We're just a couple of very impressive, blissfully unattached ladies," Amrita says, returning the tablet to its stand. "When you're better, let's go clubbing and see what sort of trouble we can get ourselves into."

CHAPTER THREE

MANNU AWAKES ABRUPTLY, MOMENTS BEFORE A WONDROUS DREAM reaches its climax. He has been watching a hawk circle the ziggurat of the Temple of Nabu, then swoop toward the ground. But instead of snaring prey in its talons and returning to the bright blue sky, it landed with a thud amongst the reeds of the riverbank. Mannu sprinted toward the downed bird, expecting to find it dead, but it was very much alive. It turned its head, staring at him with one penetrating eye, before lifting one wing only.

"Your left wing is broken," Mannu told it.

The majestic bird stayed still as he reached out, and the mere touch of his finger allowed it to spread its afflicted wing. It hopped onto Mannu's outstretched arm, dipped its head in thanks, and was about to take flight when Mannu's eyes opened to the new day.

An auspicious dream for an important day, Mannu thinks.

He is eighteen, a full-grown man, tall and handsome with a powerful, broad back, his black beard long enough to begin grooming and curling with oils and heated rods. After visiting the communal urinal, he returns to find his cellmate, Kisir, stirring.

When his junior apprenticeship began, he slept on the apothecary floor, close to his menial chores and responsibilities. Five years later, when he graduated as an apprentice, he moved to a dormitory for all the young apprentices training in the healing arts. There were three groups of lads—the *asû*, or physician apprentices like him: the *āšipu*, the exorcists, and the *bārû*, the diviners. They were grouped together because, in the future, they would have to work cooperatively to heal the sick.

They had different masters and different responsibilities, but they all attended the same classes in reading and writing. All was not always harmonious. Cliques formed, personalities clashed, and there were more than a few scuffles. The *bārû* would say: we will be the most important healers. We are learning the art of divination. Divine displeasure is at the heart of illness. By examining entrails and the position of the stars, we can interpret the omens and devise a treatment. The *āšipu* would say: No, we are the most important. Spiritual or supernatural forces cause illness and misfortune. We exorcists are learning the rituals and incantations to expel malevolent forces and placate the deities. The *asû* would say: No, you are both wrong. We are the most important, for we are the ones who will devise practical treatments based on our powers of observation and our knowledge of nature. We will learn how to perform surgeries, treat snake and scorpion bites, and extract treatments from plants and herbs. When their masters caught them fighting, they repeatedly reprimanded the boys and told them that their disciplines were equally important and that they must learn to cooperate.

Mannu was a genial sort who got along with most of the boys. Even the older ones respected his quick wit and physical prowess. If forced to fight, he would win. His one nemesis was Kisir-malik, an *āšipu* apprentice whose father was a very important figure at court, the *mašmaš bīt Ninua*—Nineveh's chief exorcist. The boy was haughty, and even his fellow āšipu loathed his superior attitude. While his high-born status made him off-limits, he often goaded others into fighting. Both Mannu and Kisir had excelled in their junior apprenticeships. Mannu was the top student in *lišānum ṭuppi*, the language of the tablets. Kisir was close behind but became frus-

GLENN COOPER

trated when Mannu's abilities with cuneiform writing and grammar surpassed his own. When their masters assigned them to live in the same cell for the last two years of their apprenticeships, both boys were unhappy. Shortly after the decision, Mannu complained to his father.

"Why Kisir?" he asked. "Surely they know we are not friends."

"That is why it was decided so," his father said. "You are destined to become important colleagues. They do not want you as antagonists. His father—"

"Yes, yes. Always his father—" Mannu said with a faint smile.

The enforced comity worked to a point, and the two boys grew to tolerate each other, although they never became friends.

"Is it time already?" Kisir groans.

The boy was not blessed with fine features. His eyes are too close, his nose is narrow and beaky, and his complexion is blotchy. When he contorts his face, as he does presently, his eyebrows touch, and he looks like an ogre.

"You had better hurry," Mannu says, donning his best tunic. "What would your father say if you were late for the ceremony?"

"He would say my son is so clever that his master excused him and let him sleep."

"I think not," Mannu says, sliding into his slippers.

Today, twelve young men will mark the passage from apprentice to junior practitioner. Mannu will become an *asû sehru*, a junior physician, and Kisir, a *mašmaššu sehru*, a junior exorcist. In recent years, they have learned their respective arts by diagnosing and treating sick animals. Soon, their masters will have them dealing with people. It will be years before they graduate as full practitioners of their disciplines, but they are eager to leave their apprenticeships behind.

The Temple of Gula, the goddess of healing and medicine, is in the temple district, in the shadow of the great ziggurat of the Temple of Nabu, the god of wisdom and learning and Gula's son. When the young disciples arrive, the temple's courtyard is already filled with family and well-wishers who garland them as they pass through the gates of the low, rectangular building. The main sanctuary is dominated by the alabaster statue of Gula, high on her throne, peering down with large, wise eyes, her left hand holding a staff, her right hand resting on her sacred companion, a large dog. They make their way toward the inner sanctum, where the graduation ceremony will take place, passing near the rooms where they had spent countless hours copying healing texts borrowed from the great library of King Ashurbanipal.

Their masters await them in the inner temple. They sit in three groups before them, the *asû* on one side, the *āšipu* in the middle, and the *bārû* on the other. Their family members enter, and there is a stir when Kisir's father, the city's Chief Exorcist, comes in last. Mannu steals a glance and grins happily at his father and mother, and his friend, Ninurta, a soldier now, proudly wearing the gleaming breastplate of the king's guards.

The masters of each discipline share ceremonial duties. They pray to Gula, seeking her blessing for the apprentice's future work, and chant incantations affirming the young men's roles in the divine healing order. Then, they lead the apprentices in oaths of service, exhorting them to use their knowledge to benefit the king and the people of Nineveh.

One by one, the young men are called forward by their master, and Mannu stands before the Rab Asû, the chief physician, who seems so much older than when he began his apprenticeship. The old man anoints his forehead with fragrant oil, whispers a personal blessing, and presents Mannu with a clay tablet inscribed with a medicinal text and a pouch containing a therapeutic herb, signifying his readiness to practice. Then, something truly amazing happens. The old master smiles at him for the very first time.

A feast follows. Graduates, their mentors, family, and friends gather in the temple courtyard, where servants bring trays of stewed and roasted meats, vegetables, bread, and beer. Mannu sits with his father, mother, and Ninurta on the cool, smooth stones. Kisir's entourage sits nearby at Gula's feet, the most auspicious place. Kisir's master has seen to it that Kisir's father has a chair.

"Dear Ninurta," Mannu's mother says. "Since you became a soldier, we do not see you. Look at how big you are!"

Mannu tries to pinch his friend's bulging biceps. "While I have been building my knowledge," Mannu says, "he has been building muscles."

"Have you seen battles?" Mannu's father asks.

"The defeat of the Elamites at Susa was before my time, sir, but there remain pockets of resistance of enemies who refuse to bend to our will. I have fought in those battles."

"Good man," his father says. "We pray that the last vestige of the Kingdom of Elam will be eliminated."

"The great god Ashur keeps the balance of the world," Ninurta says with a smile. "I kill, and Mannu saves."

"Mostly, I have been saving cattle and goats," Mannu says. "Now I am an *asû sehru*, I may begin saving people."

"We are proud of you, my son," his mother says.

Even his father, a man as hard as the alabaster goddess, professes his pride.

In the evening, Mannu and Ninurta roam the city as they had when they were boys. They are allowed to enter the plaza of the Palace of Ashurbanipal as they are well known to the palace guards —Ninurta is one of them, and Mannu studies there. They have been drinking for hours and must support each other to stay upright. The night air is cool and carries scents of date palms and almond tree blossoms from the hanging gardens.

"Tell me again why we are here?" Ninurta says, slurring his words.

"Because you have never seen the king's wonderous library," Mannu says, poking him in the chest.

"Well, you have never seen a column of five hundred of the king's soldiers on horseback," Ninurta says, poking him back.

"The library is here; the cavalry is not."

"Very well. Show me your precious tablets."

"I will read you some beautiful poetry," Mannu promised.

"Poetry! I do not want poetry. Read me stories of war and pillage."

"You are a bloodthirsty sod," Mannu laughs. "I shall find you a thrilling story."

The young men hear gentle laughter and turn to see a group of high-born young women crossing the plaza, their fine robes embroidered with gold swishing on the paving stones. Their heads are veiled, but Mannu recognizes one of them and stiffens. How many times has he spied on her since he was a boy? She turns her head for a second.

Was that a smile?

"What is it, man?" Ninurta says. "You look like you have seen a ghost."

"Not a ghost," Mannu whispers, "a goddess."

"The girl?" Ninurta whispers back. "Those are ladies-in-waiting. Is the girl you have been pining for your whole life among them? Which one is she?"

Mannu drags his friend away before he does or says something unforgivingly embarrassing, but Ninurta will not let it go.

"Do you mean to tell me you have never spoken?"

"Not a single word," Mannu sighs, "although I often see her from afar."

"Do you even know her name?"

"It is Bel-ibni," Mannu says.

Ninurta goes quiet and pulls away.

"What is the matter?" Mannu asks.

"I know people. I hear things," Ninurta says.

"Tell me. What have you heard?"

"I am sorry, my friend, but I have heard the King plans to add a girl named Bel to his concubine."

Mannu drops to his haunches, looking dazed.

"There are many fish in the river," Ninurta says, trying to be helpful.

"There is only one Bel. If only I could speak with her and tell her how I feel."

"What good would that do?"

"I have long dreamt of being with her," Mannu moaned. "Perhaps if she knew this, she could—"

"Could what?"

Mannu's voice trails off to a whisper. "I do not know."

Ninurta looks toward the night sky and says, "I should not do this, but—"

"What are you thinking?" Mannu says eagerly.

"I know the eunuch who keeps watch over these girls. I could ask him to let you have words with Bel."

Mannu throws his arms around Ninurta's huge chest.

"When? Tonight?"

"Yes, tonight. In a while. We must wait for them to return to their dormitory and give you a little time to recover from the drink. It would be wise not to present yourself as the drunken fool you are. We will have to see the library another time."

"You would not have liked it anyway."

The torchlit palace corridors are empty, save for the occasional guard keeping watch. Ninurta knows them and exchanges jokes as they pass. Two burly soldiers man the doors to the chambers of the ladies-in-waiting. Their stiff demeanor melts when they see their comrade.

"What in Ereshkigal's holy name are you doing here?" one of them asks. Soldiers are irreverent. Mannu would never invoke the name of Ereshkigal, the underworld goddess, in such a manner. "This is where they keep the girls, not the boys."

"I need to speak with their eunuch," Ninurta says. "My friend here, a physician, wants to see one of the girls."

"Bit young for a physician," the guard says.

"I am a junior physician," Mannu says proudly. "As of today," he adds to be fully truthful.

"Do this for me, and I will take your next shift," Ninurta says, playfully punching the guard's gut.

The guard leaves, and Mannu paces. He asks his friend about the guard's remark.

"I have always preferred boys to girls," Ninurta says with a wicked grin. "You did not know?"

"I never thought about it."

"Well, do not think about it now. Think of what you will tell the girl."

The eunuch appears at the door, his round belly swelling his fine white tunic. Ninurta draws him aside, and Mannu watches their heated, whispered exchange. His friend seems at an impasse until a reach into his purse turns the tide. The eunuch pinches the coin and ushers them through the doors.

"Wait in there," the eunuch says, pointing to a small antechamber. Inside is a bench and a fresco of an eight-pointed star, a lion, and doves—symbols of Ishtar, the goddess of women and fertility.

"You bribed him?" Mannu asks.

"Of course, I bribed him."

"But I cannot repay you. I have no money."

"It is my gift to you on your graduation."

Mannu hugs him and lets go quickly.

"Do not worry," Ninurta snorts. "I never fancied you. Too pale for my liking."

It seems like a dream.

There is a rustle of fine fabric and the smell of perfume, and she is standing there.

Ninurta slips into the hall, and they are alone. The eunuch's shadow is near the threshold.

Bel's veil is pulled back to her ears, and he can see her face more clearly than he has for years. Her fine, delicate features and flawless dark complexion turn his limbs liquid.

"I was wondering who would be bold enough to summon me from my bed chamber," Bel says. "Now that I see you, I am not surprised."

Her assertiveness spellbinds Mannu.

He manages to say, "You are not?"

"I have seen you looking at me on your way to the apothecary. You are one of the apprentices."

"I graduated today," he says shyly. "I am a junior physician."

"Congratulations," she says. "May Gula's blessings be upon you. Do you have a name?"

"Mannu-ki-Ashur."

"Greetings, Mannu-ki-Ashur. My name is—"

"I know your name," he says. "I have known it for a long time."

35

She does not dip her gaze in embarrassment as Mannu thought she might. She keeps looking into his eyes.

"I am flattered," she says. "What do you wish to say to me?"

His moment has arrived, and he does not know what will emanate from his mouth. He shocks himself with his directness.

"I have watched you from afar since I was a boy. I am a man now and—"

"And what?" she asks.

"And I love you."

He has cracked her façade. Her inquisitive smile fades. Her lower lip trembles.

"Can one love another when they have never spoken?"

"The answer must be yes," he says, "because that is how I feel."

Then, lightning strikes, setting his chest on fire.

"And I have watched you from afar," she says. "I did not know the word for how I feel about you. Perhaps it *is* love." And then, she looks toward the ground. "I am overjoyed to finally meet you, Mannu, but this is the last time we can speak. The King has chosen me for his concubine. It is a great honor. As for you and me—" She finally breathes the one word that explains their predicament. "It is šīmtu." Fate. Destiny.

They hear the eunuch clear his throat and say, "My lady!"

"I must go," Bel says.

They rush into each other's arms. He tilts her head back and kisses her. And then, she pulls away and is gone.

THE NEXT THREE years seem to pass as quickly as three months.

Mannu has made rapid progress as an *asû sehru*, and his master has just summoned him to the apothecary to inform him he will be allowed to treat a man of some importance. To date, the only people to whom he has plied his healing arts have been prisoners and the low-born. He is concerned about his master's frailty. The Rab Asû's tunic hangs loosely on his emaciated frame, and his joints swell and creak. It is not his place to speak to him about his health, but he dreads the day when death will come.

"Who is this man?" Mannu asks.

"He is Shulmu-beli-le'I, the royal baker, who has been unable to attend to his duties."

"What problem has this baker?"

"He has a pain in his temples so great he cannot knead his loaves or stoop to load the ovens. He lies in bed moaning."

Mannu's breast swells at the opportunity to treat a palace official.

"You must approach this matter with delicacy," Mannu is told.

"Yes, Master," Mannu says, leaning in.

"The baker's family first consulted the *Bārû Rabû* to determine if his illness is divine. The *Bārû Rabû* assigned one of his *bārû sehru*, your colleague, Urad-Ea-balatu, to see the man."

Mannu knows him well from their apprenticeship and likes the genial fellow.

"What did Urad find?" he asks.

"Through his examination of the entrails of a sacrificial sheep and the movement of celestial bodies, he determined that the baker has offended the goddess Ninlil. Recitations were made. Offerings of a sheep and sacks of flour were placed at the Temple of Marduk. But still, the pain persisted."

"Then, what occurred?" Mannu asks.

"The *Bārû Rabû* offered to see the patient himself, but the family offended him by summoning the Chief Exorcist, Kisir's father, instead. The father sent the son, and Kisir, who has been lauded for his expertise as a *mašmaššu sehru*, made an examination. He found that the man is possessed by evil spirits and prepared an exorcism. He purified the baker with water from the Temple of Ea, lit a fire of juniper wood to ward off malevolent spirits, and made incantations and recitations. Following this, he placed a clay statue of the baker under the man's pillow for two nights, then destroyed the statue to expel the spirit. Furthermore, an amulet with Gula's symbols was placed around the baker's neck, and beer and barley were placed before the statue of Nergal to appease the god of the underworld and ask for his help in calming any restless spirits."

Mannu nods while listening to the steps that have been taken.

"These are good remedies. Kisir is an excellent exorcist and magician," he says.

"However, despite these measures, the baker remains afflicted in his bed."

"I see," Mannu says with a wry smile. "And now the family wishes for the physicians to be called, and the Chief Exorcist, Kisir's father, is offended."

The old master chuckles. "More than a little. He burns with rage. So, my boy, it falls upon you to treat this baker and alleviate his suffering. But if you do, you might incur the wrath of the Chief Exorcist and his son."

"My duty is to the patient," Mannu says. "I will treat him to the best of my abilities."

"I have faith in you. Do what you think is necessary." A sigh whistles from his narrow chest. "I will deal with Kisir's father."

The baker lives within the palace to be near the royal kitchens. As Mannu winds his way through labyrinthine corridors to the baker's rooms, he is acutely aware he will pass near the quarters of the king's concubines. His heart bears the scars of every time he has seen Bel these three years since their solitary kiss. It has always been from a distance. Sometimes, he thinks she looks happy, sometimes sad, but always beautiful. He wonders if she thinks of him, because he cannot stop thinking of her. There is an open-air courtyard dotted with quince trees in which the concubines lounge. Today, as he lingers in its archway, it is empty.

The baker is a robust man with powerful forearms from a lifetime of kneading dough. His wife offers Mannu a cup of weak beer, which he declines. He kneels at the baker's bedside. The bed chamber has no windows, so Mannu asks the woman to bring the oil lamps closer. He examines his patient's head, pressing on the scalp, temples and gently over the eyes. He notices that the baker still wears the amulet of Gula that Kisir had given him. Mannu asks if he fell and struck his head, if he passed blood in his excreta, if his vision is failing, if he has fevers, if he has done anything to offend the gods. The answer to all is no. Mannu wants to know if the ministrations of the diviner or the exorcist had brought any relief to his headaches. The answer is no.

When he has finished his examination, he tells the baker he will return the following day with a remedy. When he leaves, he walks apace to a far-flung part of the palace complex. The king's library is a quiet place where he has spent countless hours copying medical texts onto wet clay for personal study. King Ashurbanipal believes it is his divine duty to assemble all the world's knowledge in one place, and he has instructed his military commanders to loot tablets from conquered lands and his ambassadors to buy and barter for texts. During his reign, the King, a scholar in his own right, has amassed a vast library of tens of thousands of clay tablets. The library is a series of interconnected rooms with orange tiled floors and shelves built into white plaster walls. Each room has a theme—literature, histories, poetry, hymns, divinity, medical, botanical, astronomical, mathematics, divination and omens, magical spells, law, administrative records of taxation and trade, royal correspondence and decrees. Royal librarians know where to find whatever an official needs among the stacks of kiln-baked or sun-dried tablets. The King himself comes to the library. The only time Mannu saw him close by was when the monarch passed with his entourage while Mannu was copying a botanical tablet. The young apprentice quickly averted his gaze, breathing in the heady scent of his splendidly perfumed and oiled beard.

Mannu does not need a librarian, for he knows which texts he requires for the baker. The chief librarian, so old that a snail could beat him in a foot race, looks up from his table and shows his gums.

"Ah, Mannu. You have a patient, I presume."

"The king's baker," Mannu says.

"An important man. Your master must have confidence in you."

"If hope to earn his confidence by making a cure. May I have some clay, master?"

"Help yourself."

In the room of medical texts, Mannu goes to the shelves that hold the several dozen *Sakikkū* tablets, an extensive compendium of physical symptoms, and recommended treatments for the diviner, exorcist, and physician. He finds the tablets he requires and takes an oil lamp to a table. Fire, the scourge of the city, is no threat in the library because there is no timber or cloth to burn other than a man's clothes. He scans rows of texts until he finds those pertaining to headaches.

If a man's head is constantly in pain…
If a man's temples throb like the beating of a drum…
If a man's head is heavy and his eyes darken…
If the pain moves from the neck to the forehead…

He finds the sections that match the baker's symptoms and copies the prescriptions onto a slab of fresh clay with a stylus. He believes the baker has all the symptoms of someone with an imbalance of bodily humors, and perhaps, too, an unseen spirit is gripping his head. He will prepare a poultice of willow bark, mint, and warm sesame oil to cool his temples and an infusion of barley water and licorice root to balance his humors. Kisir has surely prescribed the correct incantations to ward off a curse, but Mannu will repeat them at the patient's bedside when he administers his unguents and drinks and fumigates the room with cedar smoke and myrrh.

He copies the necessary recipes and incantations and walks past the concubine courtyard again on his way out. It is still empty.

MANNU IS WORKING in his cell. As an *asû sehru*, he has the luxury of his own quarters. One of the new apprentices, an eager lad missing a front tooth, breathlessly tells Mannu the Master wants to see him. Mannu finds the old physician hunched over his desk, working his stylus. His eyesight is failing, and his cuneiform lines are messy and slanted.

"Master?" Mannu says.

"The baker. How is he?"

"He is cured."

"He returned to his ovens?"

"Yes. He is happy."

The master's drooping mouth reveals he is not happy.

"Is something wrong?" Mannu asks.

"I was visited by Kisir's father. He was extremely angry. He says you claim credit for the baker's cure when it was Kisir's incantations that were responsible."

"I claim no credit. I administered medicines and repeated Kisir's incantations. If the baker gives me credit, so be it. What would you have me do?"

"Go to him and apologize for any offense taken."

"There was no offense given."

"Do not talk back to me, Mannu. You are the best junior physician I have ever trained. The gods bless your future. Kisir's father is an important man at court. You know this. The king favors him. It matters not if you have or have not given offense. Apologize and be done with it, and be sure to praise the man's son for his excellent incantations."

The Chief Exorcist has fine rooms near the royal residence.

Mannu accepts a tongue-lashing from the imperious master. He bows deeply in apology but will not go so far as to prostrate himself.

"Do you accept that it was Kisir who cured the baker?"

"Yes, Master," Mannu says, studying the floor.

"Then, you may go," the man hisses. "Know this, Mannu. Kisir will become Chief Exorcist one day. The king will favor him as he favors me. Your father has a good position, but it is not an important one. What will you become, I wonder?"

Mannu is seething as he heads toward his cell. He hardly pays attention to where he is until he hears the pleasant sounds of women laughing. He looks up and peers through the archway of the concubine's courtyard. The women are playing a throwing game with a ball woven from reeds and stuffed with plant fibers. One of the young women sees him and purposely throws the ball over the head of another so that it lands at Mannu's feet. He stoops to pick it up to toss it to the intended receiver.

"Here is your ball," he calls out.

The receiver is Bel. She looks at him with surprise turning to happiness.

"Mannu," she silently mouths.

"Bel."

The concubine's eunuch notices that one of his girls is up to no good and admonishes her sharply.

"I must go," Bel whispers, drawing close to take the ball from his hands. He can feel the warmth of her touch.

"Do you—?" he says.

She does not need him to finish. "I do," she says. "I think about you every day and every night."

CHAPTER FOUR

First term at the Institute of Archaeology is a month away, and London is baking in the late August heat. Kate stares gloomily at the thermostat on her office wall, wondering if it's connected to anything. She has shed as many clothes as decorum would allow and is still dying. Her laptop sits among an untidy collection of journals, notes, photographs, and a glass of iced water already too warm for her taste. She is about to refill it from the cooler when Wilson Banning darkens her door.

"There you are!" he beams.

"And there *you* are!" she parrots.

"Did you know they've given me an office just down the hall?"

"I did know that" she says. She had tried pulling a string or two to have the new faculty member put somewhere else, but she lacked the juice to pull it off. Wilson is dressed too smartly for the pre-term and the heat, and his white dress shirt has sweat stains under the armpits.

As if reading her mind, he says, "I'd forgotten how shit the air con was here."

She's not in the mood for chitchat, but she has no choice. "Getting yourself sorted?" she asks.

It's enough of an invite for him to take a chair.

"Getting there. Books on shelves, prints ready, but not sure where to hang them. Could use your eye. I recall you had an artistic flair."

In the old days, he would have said something like, "It could use a woman's touch," so his time on the Birmingham faculty hadn't gone to waste.

"Definitely," she mumbles.

"You look busy," he says.

"My grant's up for renewal. You know the drill."

"Indeed I do," he heartily nods. "I'm squared away for the next year, give or take. When's your well run dry?"

"Frighteningly soon. On a positive note, the foundation has given me positive renewal vibes. I'm hoping I'm reading the room correctly."

"Which foundation and do they do Mesoamerica?" he asks.

"Gosh, don't know. It's the Gerda Henkel Stiftung in Düsseldorf."

"Got a piece of paper." He jots down the name. "What's your project with them?"

"Don't want to bore you," she tries. She knows it will fail.

"Desperately interested," he grins.

"It's a cross-disciplinary study analyzing Assyrian administrative records, particularly grain and resource management texts, to try to understand how climate fluctuations affected the economy and royal policies. We're incorporating paleoclimate data and doing some economic modeling."

"We?"

"You didn't think I could do all that myself? I'm collaborating with a German climate scientist and an economist from UCL."

"I absolutely did think the brilliant Kate Mayne could do it all."

I've got to wrap this up before he asks me out, she thinks.

"What texts are you analyzing?" he asks, pinned to his chair.

"The BM collection and the one at the Vorderasiatisches in Berlin."

"That'll keep you busy." He goes quiet, presumably waiting for her to ask about his work, but she stands her ground and glances expectantly at her laptop.

"We must talk more," she says. "Need to crack on."

When he's gone, she gulps warmish water.

～

THE MUSIC IS BLARING from the Karaoke room at the Simmons Bar at Euston Square, and Kate has to touch heads with Amrita to hear her. It is Margarita Mondays—two for ten quid—and the place is packed out. When their schedules mesh, it's a perfect place to meet for an after-work drink, as it's roughly equidistant between the IoA and University College Hospital. They'd met there years ago when a group of nursing and archaeology students with a friend in common got to talking, and the two women immediately took to one another. These days, they try to meet at the bar every month or so and take the train home together.

They spy a few junior doctors on the prowl—Amrita recognizes them from the ortho ward—and they try to put up an invisible force field to ward them off. Force fields aren't real, and the doctors pounce.

"Damsels in distress," one of them says, showing teeth.

In these situations, Kate likes to leave it to her friend. Amrita is more of a pistol.

"Go on," she says.

"No, you," Amrita goads her. "Speak to them in Akkadian."

When they are both in the mood, watching hapless guys react to a dead Semitic language, heavy in consonants with guttural sounds emanating deep in the throat, is a hoot."

"I'm not feeling it Ammie," Kate says.

The nurse is left to work her magic.

"We're having a chinwag here," Amrita tells them sourly.

"We've got chins," one of the tipsy orthos says.

"Do you, now? I'm impressed by your knowledge of anatomy. Run along, and don't ruin our perfectly nice evening."

As the testosterone tide recedes, they hear one of them say, "Dykes."

"Pathetic," Amrita says. "Any woman who's not up for their macho shite is a lesbian."

"It's SOOO depressing," Kate says.

What follows is the inevitable discussion about men. Amrita's situation is different from Kate's. Her greatest threat to independence isn't men per se; it's her mother trying to set her up with a marriage broker. She sends Kate into stitches over her mother's latest antics, then asks if Jeremy is still bugging her.

"I thought I was free and clear of him."

"No!" Amrita says. "He didn't."

"He did. He called two weeks ago."

"I thought you blocked him."

"He called from a mate's phone."

"The sneaky bastard," Amrita exclaims. "What did he say?"

"Nothing original." She enumerates on her fingers. "He misses me. He screwed up. He was under pressure. He had writer's block. He was running out of money. He lost his way."

"Oh, my god. And you just listened to the rubbish merchant?"

"For a while. Until he said he still loved me."

"What'd you say?"

"Nothing. I hung up."

"Good on you, girl."

Their second round of cheap drinks arrives, and Kate wipes away an inch of salt from the rim.

"If only it ended," she says. "I'm thinking of becoming a nun and living in a monastery."

"You're not a Catholic, sweetheart. Is it the creep from work?"

"The creep from work," Kate says despondently. "Of all the places he could have gone, he had to bounce back to the IoA. I'm cursed."

"You're not cursed, luv," Amrita says. "You're a woman."

KATE ISN'T DREADING her mother's birthday party—it's not as bad as that. It bores her to tears. Twice a year—August for her mother and January for her father—there's a celebration at the house in Shepperton that the three Mayne children are expected to attend. The choreography never varies. Her father spins out cocktails while her mother serves the exact same menu: smoked salmon on toast with capers for starters, a roast with all the trimmings for mains, and a yellow angel-food birthday cake with white icing. Only the number of candles change. Kate travels down from London by train; her brother and his family drive from Farnham, and her sister drives from Richmond. The August party is preferable because the weather is usually nicer.

Her father is a precise man, constitutionally born to be the accountant he became. He is usually able to avoid parking by pulling into Shepperton station as the train arrives, and today is no exception. Kate knows he will greet her by asking how the journey was, and he does just that.

"Fine. No problems," she says, pecking his freshly shaven cheek.

"You're the first to arrive," he says, driving off. "Nice, dry day. There should be sun in the afternoon."

Kate looks out the window. The High Street is as dull as always.

"New Indian?" she asks.

"Yes and no," he says. "Patel sold it to his cousin, who renamed it. Same chef. We do their work, you know."

"I recall."

Her father owns a chartered accountancy firm in Shepperton. It handles individual and small company accounts but prospers due to steady work from Shepperton Studios, a mainstay in British film and TV production. Whenever one of the productions he has worked on is up for a BAFTA or Academy Award, he behaves like he was one of the creatives and throws a party for his golfing friends.

"Is mummy having the lunch outdoors?" Kate asks.

"Barring a meteorological anomaly, that is the plan," he says.

Kate already has a plan to claim a seat facing the river so she can lose herself watching boats pass. The family house is a nineteen seventies, four-bedroom detached home utterly devoid of character, save its hundred feet of frontage on the Thames. Growing up, her bedroom faced the river, and if not for that, she believes she would have gone mad.

She always wondered if the postman had impregnated her mother—assuming the postman had an adventurous streak—because she was the only marginally unconventional one in the family. Her mother grew up in Shepperton, left school early, and had been her father's first secretary. Her brother is a general practice doctor. Her sister is a property solicitor. Kate was a bright—some might say obsessive student who did exceptionally well on her A-levels and got a place at Oxford. When applying, her father advised her that business or law might suit her and provide for a comfortable future.

"If you became a lawyer, you could work with your sister one day," her mother said.

"I don't want to be a lawyer."

"Excellent medical school at Oxford, too," her father said, "though your brother thinks you'd hate medicine."

"I don't want to be a doctor."

"If you don't want to be one, you could marry one," her mother said. "That would be nice."

"What do you think you want to go for?" her father asked.

Kate had been reading the course catalog, trying to imagine different futures. Her favorite A-level had been Ancient History.

"I was thinking about Egyptology or Assyriology."

"No money in that," her father said, leaving for the den.

Her parents told themselves she would grow out of it and land on something more solid. She did not.

Kate's mother is in the kitchen, unbearably warm from the oven. She won't open the windows or door because she hates houseflies.

"Why haven't you put the screens in, mummy?" Kate asks.

"Ask your father," her mother replies.

"I'll do it, if you like," Kate says.

"We're having a party, dear. I'll be fine. You can set the table."

It's an excuse to go into the back garden and have a look at the river. There has been lots of rain, and the water is high and flowing mightily. She is hoping to see swans. The best part of growing up in Shepperton was the annual Swan Upping ceremony in mid-summer. Once she was old enough, she always volunteered to row up and down the river, counting and weighing swans.

She turns to the sound of screaming, and the twins come barreling toward her, competing to be the first to hug their auntie. That done, they keep going toward the bank.

"Stay behind the fence," their mother yells from the patio.

"Hello, Steph," Kate says with a wave.

Her sister-in-law is a practical woman who excels in domesticity, earning her high praise from Kate's mother. The two exchange a fleeting embrace and a few words about their journeys. It will be the last time they speak before they depart. Kate's brother, John, looks tired. He immediately starts complaining about the NHS and the state of medicine in Britain. Their father nods sagely and asks whether he'll finally come to his senses and vote Tory. Liz sets the table, freeing Kate to wander upstairs for a ritualistic visit to her old room. There isn't a speck of dust. Her mother is an excellent museum curator.

Kate can't understand why her mother seems so worked up about her sister's impending arrival until she breathlessly tells her that Margo is bringing a young man with her, a lawyer from her firm.

"What happened to the other one?" she asks. "Wasn't he a banker?"

"Oh, they're still very much an item," her mother says. "He's abroad, apparently."

"Then what's with the lawyer?"

"If you must know," her mother says conspiratorially, "she's bringing him for you."

Kate recoils. "Me?"

"Apparently, he's very nice. Margo thinks the two of you would hit it off."

"Gawd!" Kate cries. "Why didn't you tell me this was going to happen?"

"We were afraid you wouldn't come."

"You're right. I wouldn't have."

"Be a good girl and have a go," her mother says. "Your last young man—that Jeremy—was wholly unsuitable. We all knew it would end in tears, and we were right."

When Margo arrives with her colleague Aaron, Kate pulls her aside and tells her she will never forgive her.

"Mummy told you?" Margo says. "That woman can't keep a secret."

"How dare you set me up?"

Margo waits for a smile or a wink to see if Kate is joking but realizes she is not.

"He's really nice, Kate, and his parents are loaded. He'll show you photos of their pile in Hampshire."

Aaron isn't shy. He makes for Kate and declares he's heard good things about her. He's not bad looking but has pasty skin and a spare tire showing through his expensive polo shirt.

"You study Syria, I'm told," he says, clutching a gin and tonic for dear life.

"Assyria."

"Not the same thing?" he asks.

"Different area, different millennia," she says without a trace of humor.

He isn't deterred. "Tell you what. You teach me about what you do, and I'll teach you about what I do."

"And what is that?" Kate asks.

"Taxation law."

Kate sighs and searches the river for swans, but there don't seem to be any about.

CHAPTER FIVE

MANNU'S PROGRESSION AS A PHYSICIAN HAS BEEN REMARKABLE, MORE so because he is not a member of a family dynasty. His long-serving master, the Rab Asû, who took him on as a junior apprentice those many years ago, was himself the son of a Rab Asû. Mannu's father was an important administrator at the court, and if the boy, Mannu, had aspired to replace him as head of the royal grain storehouses, it would have been assured. But Mannu had other ideas.

His promotion from junior physician to physician happened in record time. At this juncture, most of his peers were assigned to the army. However, his master wanted him to stay in Nineveh.

"You are a wonder, my boy," he was told, "my most able pupil. It would be a waste if you were killed in battle or succumbed to a camp disease. No, you will stay here. I have spoken to the King's chief eunuch, the *Rab Sha Reshi*. He has agreed to make you a physician to the royal court."

Mannu's boyhood friend, Ninurta, had recently received a military promotion to *nabû ša rēši*, commander of a chariot unit, and Mannu had been hoping to join him in the field.

"Do I have a say in the matter, Master?"

"You do not," the chief physician had said. "You are head-strong, Mannu, but you must obey. We are all the King's servants. Remember this."

Now thirty-five years of age, Mannu is poised to receive another promotion, the greatest of all. It is a bittersweet time because his venerable master has died. By decree, there must always be a Rab Asû. Mannu's master made it known to the powers that be that he considered Mannu the only man qualified to be his successor. The chief eunuch, a man with full control of all administrative decision-making within the royal court, approved the promotion. There was a rumor that King Ashurbanipal had personally blessed the move, having been favorably impressed by Mannu's treatment of Queen Libbali-sharrat's stomach pains. Mannu's fellow physicians often gossiped that he would be the new chief physician, but Mannu refused to engage in this kind of idle chatter. He only learned the decision while attending to his master on his deathbed.

"It will be you," the old man whispered through cracked lips shortly before he took his final breath.

On the morning following his death, his master was buried in his family's tomb. That afternoon, Mannu was installed as the new Rab Asû. The ceremony took place deep within the royal palace in the innermost courtyard of the King's residence, a jewel of a garden full of fragrance, color, lush greenery, and an artificial waterfall that fed a graceful pool covered in water lilies. As Mannu watched through the window of an adjoining waiting room, the courtyard filled with his family, friends, colleagues, and court officials. Mannu's father was long dead, but his mother and brother who succeeded their father as keeper of the royal grain house, looked on from a front-row bench. His cousins and extended relations stood to the rear. His fellow healers, the physicians, and junior physicians of the court waited to escort him to the altar. Signaling that the ritual was about to commence, numerous palace officials entered and assumed their positions on benches and chairs based on elaborate court hierarchy. The Chief Exorcist sat next to the Chief Diviner. Both were young men, having assumed their positions in the recent past; both had been apprentices alongside Mannu. It was Kisir who inherited the role of *Mašmaš Bīt Ninua* upon the death of his father. Relations between Mannu and his old cellmate had remained chilly over the years, and there had been rumors that Kisir tried to intervene with the Chief Eunuch to block Mannu's ascension. On the day, Kisir's face looked pinched as if he had ingested a bitter herb, and he sat with his arms tightly folded.

After the Chief Eunuch, the Chief Scribe, the Vizier, and the High Priest of Nineveh took their places of prominence, Mannu felt a tap on his shoulder.

"Are you ready, friend?"

He turned to see the smiling face of the *Rab Kallâ*, the chief of the palace guard. Ninurta had distinguished himself as a great warrior in King Ashurbanipal's internecine war against his brother, the ruler of Babylon, and had been rewarded with command of the King's personal protectorate.

"Do not embarrass yourself," Ninurta whispered.

"How would I do that?"

"I was thinking you might fart."

Mannu laughed, then went quiet. "Do you think she will attend?" he asked.

Ninurta swore at him. "You are about to become the Rab Asû, yet you still behave like a boy. Forget about Bel! The King will not invite a concubine, even his favorite one, to a ceremony of this importance. The Queen will be here. Imagine what she would say. You and I should talk. I know of women who would make suitable wives for a man in your position."

As a royal physician, Mannu had seen Bel many times and once had even been called to treat her. She was twenty-five and pregnant with the king's child at the time. During the early stages of her confinement, she developed a vomiting sickness, could not keep food in her stomach, and was losing weight. The King had high hopes for the pregnancy. His queen was barren, and he relied on the fecundity of his concubines for royal heirs. His oldest son, Ashur-etil-ilani, the issue of one of his early concubines, was a weak, feckless man whom the king tolerated, at best. Other sons of other concubines

GLENN COOPER

were no more favored; he found them all lacking in intellect and physical strength. Visiting Bel in her rooms, the King raised a hand toward the heavens and declared that this one—this son—would be a worthy heir.

Mannu accompanied his Master, the Rab Asû, to Bel's quarters at the royal concubine. There she sat on her bed, looking pale yet lovely, her early stage concealed beneath her elegant robe. As the old master asked probing questions about her symptoms, Mannu stood behind him, watching her intently. Whenever their eyes met, he felt his chest flutter.

"I understand the exorcists have made incantations and offerings," the Master said. "Has there been any improvement in your condition?"

"Sadly, no."

"With your permission, my lady, this junior physician will perform an examination."

She blinked, showing her nervousness. "I give permission," she replied.

Mannu asked her to lie back and felt her belly through her robe.

"Does this cause you discomfort?" he asked, his voice quavering.

"None."

When he withdrew his hand, she brushed it with hers, a gesture unnoticed.

"You have an excess of bile, my lady," Mannu said, his skin tingling from her touch. "I will prepare an infusion of mint, cypress, and myrtle. It will surely lead to improvement."

Months later, the male baby she was carrying was miscarried, and over the years, she endured more miscarriages. However, the King never lost faith in her ability to bear him another heir, and much to the Queen's displeasure, she remained his favored concubine, Mannu could not imagine another woman taking Bel's place in his heart. Nor could he bear the thought of her with another man, even if that man is the King. He told Ninurta that he would be too busy as Rab Asû to worry about marriage, and before his friend could try to change his mind, the royal drummers heralded the king's arrival.

Ashurbanipal was powerfully built with a high forehead, dense eyebrows, and chiseled features. In public, he never let his countenance reveal anything short of ferocious confidence. His beard was more elaborately curled than any other man at court. A royal headdress obscured the curls of his thick mane. His robe, sashed at the waist, took the royal embroiderers months to sew. He was heavily adorned by gold jewelry on his ears, neck, and arms. The Queen entered three paces behind her husband and was no less resplendent. The majestic pair took to their jeweled thrones on a raised platform, and the ceremony began.

The Chief Eunuch of Nineveh, the Rab She Reshi, was a man in his fiftieth year named Sin-shumu-lishir. His power at court was nearly unrivaled, and he was the King's closest and most trusted advisor. Everything of any importance within the city passed under his generous nose. There is a certain sameness in the appearance of eunuchs. All had soft skin and a layer of doughy fat. Sin was different. If he had not been beardless, he might have been taken for a normal man. Because he was chosen at an older age than most children and was castrated by crushing rather than surgically removing his testicles, his maleness was greater. Although he had no facial hair, he was lean, with the appearance of a hungry hound. His face was often twisted into a sneer, and his raspy voice sounded like a beast's snarl. There were many eunuchs at court. The King trusted them because their sterility eliminated dynastic ambitions. From a young age, they were trained to take future positions in administration and military affairs, and the ranks of bureaucrats and generals were replete with them. Even the *turtanu*, the commander-in-chief of the king's army, was a eunuch. And, of course, the king's concubine was populated by them.

Sin had a placid expression as he took his position on the raised platform, bowed to the king and queen seated behind him on their thrones, and addressed the assembly.

"Your royal majesties, high priest and grand officials, citizens of Nineveh—today, with the blessings of the gods, we elevate Mannu-ki-Ashur to the high position of Rab Asû. The high priest will make us a purification ritual."

The High Priest, weighed down by the gold and bronze trappings of his office, took to the platform and began chanting to Ashur and Gula, invoking their protection and blessings. Lanterns were lit, and the courtyard filled with the spicy fragrance of incense.

When he was finished, the King rose for a short address. The Chief Eunuch had advised him of Mannu's accomplishments, and the monarch praised him for his dedication to the health of the royal court and his exemplary service, which merited him this exalted position. He added that the crown was saddened by the death of the previous Rab Asû but welcomed the new one with open arms.

Mannu listened to the speech, amazed the King was speaking about *him*. He looked at the audience and saw his proud mother wiping her face with a cloth. There were many smiling faces. And then, there was Kisir, who was glaring fiercely. Having a poor relationship with the city's Chief Exorcist was problematic, and Mannu resolved to smooth over their difficulties.

"Mannu-ki-Ashur, come forward and receive the symbols of your office," the King said.

Mannu stood beside the King and bowed deeply. He accepted the seal of the Chief Physician and placed it around his neck. He then received a finely crafted bronze dagger in a jeweled scabbard and a new robe embroidered with the image of Gula. He dropped to his knees, invoking the gods to witness his vows, and pledged his loyalty to King and Empire.

The Chief Scribe formally proclaimed Mannu's new status, vowing to swiftly record it on clay and add the tablet to the royal library's collection.

All rose for the monarchs' exit, and the celebratory feast began.

Mannu was the exalted Chief Physician of Nineveh.

TWO YEARS PASSED.

Mannu's days are filled with endless work and study. He lives in the rooms near the apothecary his old master used to occupy and sees a steady stream of important patients within the royal palace and temple complexes. Other physicians ask him to see patients throughout the city who have not responded to therapies. He is eager to summon the Chief Diviner and Kisir, the Chief Exorcist, whenever he suspects that gods, demons, or evil curses are involved in a patient's maladies. However, he is insulted that Kisir infrequently seeks his consultation. He trains apprentices and junior physicians. And he tirelessly experiments with plants and herbs, making new kinds of poultices, potions, and infusions, trying them on difficult-to-heal patients. Every time the royal library acquires new tablets on medicinal subjects from far-flung lands, Mannu scrutinizes them and takes notice of fresh ideas. His friend Ninurta often tries to introduce him to high-born women, but Mannu waves him off. He only desires one woman whom he knows is unobtainable.

Mannu hears from a palace courtier that Bel is pregnant again. Physicians do not involve themselves with matters of pregnancy and childbirth unless there is a complication. That is the work of midwives. It is said that she has passed the danger zone for miscarriages, and the King has been told to expect the baby in two months' time. One day, he is called to see one of the King's lesser concubines suffering from the flux and hopes to catch a glimpse of Bel, but the eunuch tells him she has been moved into special quarters closer to the King's residence.

"Do you know how the lady fares?" Mannu asks the eunuch. He realizes that his tone of voice is wistful.

"Why do you wish to know?" the eunuch asks suspiciously.

Mannu must be careful. Even the Chief Physician can lose his head.

"I treated her once while pregnant some years ago. I am hopeful she will give the king a son."

"May Ashur make it so," the eunuch says, sounding satisfied with his response.

~

THE CHIEF EUNUCH keeps a secret office in the temple district, away from prying eyes at the palace. Sin's rooms, deep within the Temple of Ishtar are well-appointed with the finest furnishings. His strongboxes contain silver, bronze, and copper coins and weighing scales for bribes.

Sin's chief deputy is a eunuch named Adad-ummi, a ruthless, multi-talented character. If Sin needs a man eliminated, Adad can accomplish the task with poison or blade. If he needs a letter sent to a foreign emissary, Adad can compose it and produce a clay tablet with perfectly straight lines of text of impeccable grammar and spelling. If Sin wants to hear music, Adad plays a passable lyre. He is in his fifth decade, heavyset, with a eunuch's smooth face and a thick padding of adiposity overlaying powerful muscles. He is Egyptian by birth, taken as a child slave during an Assyrian military campaign in Memphis, and castrated at age nine in the most extreme manner with surgical removal of testicles and penis. When he was a young man, another eunuch with a penis made fun of him for squatting to urinate like a woman. Adad slit his throat and squatted over his body to finish voiding.

Adad enters Sin's inner sanctum to announce the arrival of the envoy they have been expecting. The envoy removes his hood, bows, and he and Sin exchange blessings.

"How was your journey?" Sin asks. He has not yet given his visitor leave to sit.

"Long. Almost a full month. The roads have become rutted. The wheels of my chariot often broke. Should you not fix the trade roads now that Babylon is ours?"

Sin grunts as he does when he is not inclined to dignify a query with a response. There is silence until Adad loudly clears his throat.

"Ah," the envoy says. "I have brought you greetings and a gift from Prince Ashur."

He opens his cloak and removes a leather pouch bulging with silver.

"Give it to my man," Sin says, finally offering a bench. "How is the Prince?"

"He finds Babylon dull. He wishes to return to Nineveh."

"Return how?" Sin asks slyly.

"You know how."

The Chief Eunuch knows exactly how—as king.

Nineveh's senior courtiers know King Ashurbanipal will never make the same mistake his father did. King Esarhaddon had two sons, Ashurbanipal and his older brother, Shamash-shum-ukin. In an attempt to appease the dynastic ambition of both, as he lay dying, he appointed the more able Ashurbanipal as King of Assyria and Shamash as King of Babylon, a subordinate city in the empire. Over time, tension grew between the brothers. Shamash resented the inferior status of Babylon, as he was forced to pay tribute to Nineveh and recognize Ashurbanipal as the senior king. After years of increasing dissatisfaction, Shamash rebelled against Ashurbanipal, forming alliances with other regional powers, including Elam, Chaldea, and Aram.

Ashurbanipal responded with the full might of his army. The war between the two brothers dragged on for several years until the besieged Babylon fell, and Shamash committed suicide. Ashurbanipal, unhappy with his own son, sent him to Babylon as governor and puppet ruler of the conquered city. There he remained, stewing in his juices, awaiting his father's death.

"Prince Ashur was distressed to hear the news about the King's concubine, Bel-ibni," the envoy says. "This is the twenty-fourth year of the reign of the King, a very long time."

"The King is in excellent health," Sin says.

"He will not reign forever."

"On that, we can agree."

"The Prince is ready to be crowned whenever that sad day comes. He does not wish to be usurped by a bastard."

"Remind me," Sin says with a wicked smile. "Who was the mother of the Prince?"

The envoy is unperturbed. He knows the Prince is also a bastard, and he is but a messenger.

"Has there been any change in the condition of the concubine?"

"Her pregnancy is well-established. She will deliver a child in two months. The High Priest tells the King it will be a boy."

"The Prince will take that news badly. Is there no way to give him more favorable news?"

"I wonder what you mean?" the eunuch says, his eyes penetrating and unblinking.

"Do not make me say more," the messenger says.

"This concubine is dear to the King—very dear," Sin says, pouring himself and his guest spiced wine. "If the gods told him they would claim the life of either Bel-ibni or the Queen, he would choose the girl. She has been moved into rooms near the King's quarters and watched day and night by midwives and palace guards. The food she eats is the same served to the King. Even if a man could get close enough to smother her or snap her neck or run her through, the King would suspect your Prince Ashur and exact a terrible price. He is aware his son does not want to be displaced."

"Are you saying there is no way?" the envoy asks.

"I did not hear myself say that."

"Then, what must we do?"

"We?" Sin asks in a mocking tone. "Ask what *you* must do?"

The envoy raises his palms and shrugs.

"You must favor my strongbox with more than this small pouch."

The envoy smiles nervously and informs the chief eunuch that he has the means to meet this demand.

"Then return tomorrow with a sufficient bounty and leave the rest to me."

"Half tomorrow," the envoy says. "The rest, when she is dead."

THE FOLLOWING DAY, satisfied with the envoy's largesse, Sin meets his henchman, Adad. He shows him an iron gardener's trowel, its wooden handle broken from its tang.

"What would you have me do, Master?" Adad says.

"Find a putrid animal carcass and bring it to me in a sack."

If Adad has questions about his master's intentions, he does not voice them. He simply obeys.

∼

BEL WAKES to the scurrying of slippered feet. Her midwives inquired about her health. Her retainers dress and wash her. A tray with flatbreads, dates, figs, and fermented goat's milk is placed before her, and she eats alone, listening to the birdsong outside her window.

She dons a pair of soft slippers for her morning walk in the courtyard. She is followed closely by two midwives and the eunuch, who is never far. She rests her hands, as is her habit, on her bulging belly and takes in the sweet fragrances. This garden is among the larger ones inside the palace—more of a park than a courtyard, complete with grass walking paths that meander through fruit trees, palms, beds of exotic flowers, and a pond filled with frogs and silvery fish. She takes her favorite route three or four times daily. She and her entourage have trampled the winding path into a yellow ribbon.

Nearing the pond, Bel tells her ladies she can hear a bullfrog groaning and hopes it will show itself on a lily pad. She quickens her pace and suddenly cries out, collapsing in a heap. The eunuch barrels past the midwives and falls to his knees beside her.

"My lady! What has happened?"

"My foot!" she cries.

He gently lifts her leg and cannot contain his horror. Blood pours from the torn sole of her slipper. Instinctively, he feels around the grass, his fingers catching on something. He yells for the guards, and they come running. One of the men lifts Bel into his arms and carries her back to her bedchamber. The eunuch instructs another guard to dig out whatever he felt in the grass, then runs after Bel like a man possessed by demons.

∼

THE MIDWIVES tightly bind her foot to staunch her bleeding heel. Bel sits on her bed, protectively holding her belly and wincing in pain.

"Summon the Rab Asû!" the eunuch demands.

One of the guards knocks and enters the room. He hands the eunuch the piece of iron from the ground.

"This part with the blood was sticking out," the guard says.

"Bring all the gardeners who work in this courtyard to me," the eunuch says. "I must inform the King."

MANNU IS MAKING a potion in the apothecary when a breathless midwife rushes in and tells him what has happened. Alarmed, he grabs a leather satchel containing common supplies and medicines and runs through the palace. Bel's bed is surrounded by onlookers, and he has to push them aside to get at her. Her bandaged foot is red with fresh blood.

"My Lady," he says. "I am sorry you are injured."

She looks at him not as a star-crossed lover but as a scared patient.

"My baby," she mutters.

"An injury to the foot should not harm the baby," he says. "I need to unwrap it and inspect the wound."

Mannu asks for a basin of clean water and clean towels. He works quickly and efficiently, unwrapping, bathing, and gently exploring the deep wound with a copper probe.

"What caused this?" he asks her eunuch.

The eunuch shows him the piece of iron, a handleless trowel head. He is told the tang pointed upwards through the grass. Mannu inspects it, sniffing deeply. It smells putrid.

"Who would be so careless?" Mannu asks.

"We will find the answer," the eunuch says. "The gardeners have been assembled."

"I need to stitch the wound, or it will continue to bleed," Mannu says.

"The King must approve," the eunuch says, looking around frantically.

A senior palace guard informs them that the monarch is on his way, and Mannu keeps a towel firmly pressed against her heel.

When the King arrives, all the retainers save Mannu withdraw from Bel's bedside. Ashurbanipal looks troubled, his mouth in a knot. He bends his tall frame over the bed.

"My Bel, light of my life, what evil has befallen you?" he cries.

"My King. I stepped on something," she says. "The Rab Asû tells me I should not fear for the baby."

"Is this true, Chief Physician?" the King asks.

"Yes, my King, but I would like to close the wound with stitches with your permission."

"Do what you must," the King says. "Eunuch, come with me. Show me what she stepped on."

Mannu threads a bone needle with sutures of sheep guts. He apologizes for the pain he is about to cause. She holds hands with one of her ladies as he closes the deep wound with a continuous stitch. He is impressed by her bravery; she neither cries out nor whimpers.

"You did well, My Lady," he says. "I am almost done."

With the blood flow staunched, he applies a thick paste of honey and myrrh resin to keep the wound clean. Suddenly, they hear curdling screams coming from the courtyard as King Ashurbanipal personally slays every one of the courtyard gardeners.

"Those poor wretches," Bel whispers. "I am sure what happened was an accident."

THAT NIGHT, Mannu gets little sleep. He worries about Bel's wound. Despite his reliable treatments, the injury was deep, and the iron that pierced her foot had a foul smell, a feature that augurs poorly. He prays to Gula for her blessings. If, by the grace of the goddess, the wound remains clean, he is sure she will make a full recovery. At first light, he rushes to her room, finds her asleep, and asks the women how she is.

"She slept soundly," he is told. "Shall we wake her?"

He tells them to let her sleep but has them lift the covers so he can gently touch her foot above the bandage. Her skin is cool.

Relieved, he takes to a bedside chair and waits. From the court-yard, he hears the sounds of new gardeners replacing the blood-stained grass where their fellows died with fresh sod.

His face is the first thing she sees when her eyes flutter open, and her smile gladdens his heart.

"How do you feel, My Lady?"

She lifts her head, and one of her ladies rushes over to slide another pillow underneath it.

"I feel good, Rab Asû."

"Do you feel pain?"

"A little."

"May I examine your foot?"

"Yes."

He detects no odor when he unwraps her bandage, but he is displeased at the ooze of sticky yellow fluid along the reddened line of sutures.

Perhaps she has been studying his face because she asks, "Is something the matter?"

"There is an imbalance. I will rub a new medicine into the wound."

He mixes a frankincense resin into the honey and slathers it on before redressing the foot.

"I will return midday to check on you," he says.

No one is close enough to hear her say, "I will count the hours."

Mannu finds the concubine's head eunuch, whispers instruc-tions, and hurries to the royal library to consult the *Sakikkū* tablets of medical symptoms. He has seen Bel's problem many times before. A patient's body is pierced, and the wound becomes red and hot. Yellow pus begins to flow. A swelling develops under the skin. The patient develops high fever. If the swelling is not drained by a needle or knife and the correct medicines applied, the patient will die. He will do everything in his power to prevent a bad outcome, but he will need help.

The old librarian greets Mannu warmly and asks if he needs assistance.

THE PHYSICIAN OF NINEVEH

"I will be reading the *Sakikkū*," he says. "Please bring me clay so I can make a copy."

In the alcove where the *Sakikkū* tablets are kept, Mannu finds the ones dealing with *sam ānu*—red, hot, and swollen areas of the skin. He finds the texts he needs and begins copying the prescriptions.

If the skin contains liquid, when you press with your thumb, you open up and make an incision in the skin. You dry up the liquid. You wash a linen cloth. You sprinkle it with oil and put it on the wound. You grind powdered kiškanû and potter's clay. You put it on the wound. You bandage the skin for two days. You remove the bandage. You mix roasted kasû with roasted barley flour and daub it on the wound. You bandage the wound for one day. You crush burāšu and mix it with isqūqu flour, and make it into a dough with kasû juice. You bandage the skin with it. If the skin contains liquid on the eighth day, you make three incisions. You continually bandage the wound.

Mannu puts the copied tablet into his satchel and rushes off to see the Chief Diviner, but he is not in. When he reaches the rooms of the Chief Exorcist, he sweating from his rapid pace. A junior *āšipu* is in the front room, memorizing an incantation.

"I must see the Chief Exorcist," Mannu says.

"Very well, Rab Asû," the young man says deferentially.

Kisir stands at his desk, packing a satchel with clay tablets. The two men greet each other with obligatory kissed cheeks.

"Ah, Mannu. I was just about to leave. The aide to the Vizier suffers from headaches. I would normally have one of my *āšipus* handle this, but the Vizier insisted on me."

"I think you should send one of your *āšipus*," Mannu says.

"And why is that?"

"Do you know who Bel-ibni is?"

"The king's pregnant concubine?"

"Yes. She has become sick after stepping on a spike in her garden."

"I heard that the King ran his sword through six of his gardeners. Is this why?"

Mannu recounts the story, and Kisir agrees to come at once.

"Does the king know I am summoned?"

"The concubine's eunuch is informing him."

"We must include Enlil-nadin."

"I have just been to see the Chief Diviner. He is at a temple ceremony, but one of his lads will bring him to meet us."

Mannu and Kisir arrive at Bel's room to find her sitting in bed, her leg on a pillow, as Mannu had instructed. She seems alarmed by the presence of the Chief Exorcist.

"I thought I was improving," she says.

"It is a precaution, My Lady," Mannu says. "The Chief Exorcist, Chief Diviner, and I will work together to heal you as quickly as possible."

"It is for your sake and the sake of your baby," Kisir adds. "I must see the wound."

The Chief Diviner arrives after the wound is exposed and sticks his nose in.

Enlil is a rotund, pompous fellow who has a habit of grunting at his own sage thoughts.

He says, "On my way here, I saw six crows perched to the left of the palace gate and none on the right. And here we have a *sam ānu* of the left foot."

"Is that bad?" Bel asks.

"It is not good," Enlil says. "Sickness on the left side of the body is always bad."

Bel's face drops, and Mannu fumes. He believes that causing fear is anathema to the healer's ethos.

"Worry not, My Lady," Mannu says. "There are many factors to consider. That is but one."

Kisir announces that he believes demonic forces are at play. *Sam ānu* is a sure sign that the demon goddess Lamashtu is targeting a person. He will soon begin a series of bedside purification rituals. Lamashtu surely has consorted with one of the gardeners to harm her. The king was correct to execute them all to make sure he got the culprit.

Enlil promises to return in the afternoon. He will sacrifice a sheep and examine its entrails. Depending on what he finds, he will conduct prayer and purification ceremonies.

He leaves, muttering, "*Sam ānu* is very bad. Very bad, indeed."

Mannu stays behind to re-bandage the wound and reassure Bel that it is good that they have been able to treat the wound quickly.

"I am not often called to see the patient this early," he says.

"Still, I am frightened," she says.

"Will it calm you if I make a bed in the next room? Then I could tend to you night and day."

She nods and is about to reach for him when she sees one of her ladies watching.

"Good. It is settled," he says.

FOR MANNU, the next week was a blur.

Despite Kisir and Enlil's incantations and rituals and his medicines, Bel became sicker. Her wound got redder, the pus thicker and more copious. Then, as expected, fluid accumulated under the tough skin of the heel, and Mannu had to lance it repeatedly to drain pus. She would wince stoically, but he knew he was causing her great pain, and doing so hurt his heart. Red streaks appeared on her ankle and lower leg and lengthened daily. Her skin became warm, then fiery hot. Mannu had linen cloths soaked in cold water and juniper applied to her chest and gave her a potion of willow bark, but the fever kept coming. When it peaked, she would develop a faraway look in her eyes and speak to herself.

One night, as Mannu sat beside her bed, mopping her wet brow, he heard her say, "Do you love me?"

Bel's eunuch was nearby and said incredulously, "Did she just ask you if you loved her?"

Of course, she asked that! Mannu wanted to yell. *And I want to tell her that I do! I love her more than life itself.*

But, he said, "It is the fever. She was speaking to the King."

CHAPTER SIX

As THE DAYS PASSED, BEL WORSENED.

Despite Kisir and Enlil's chants, incantations, rituals, and animal sacrifices, and Mannu's medicines, her stitches opened, and pus oozed from deep within her heel. Angry red streaks crept up her leg to the knee. Her body was almost always hot. She grew listless and had to be prodded to take food and water.

King Ashurbanipal's grief turned to anger. He accused his exorcist, diviner, and physician of inadequacies and refused to listen to their protestations.

Kisir said that the goddess Lamashtu was a powerful adversary and that she was likely employing ghosts to torment his concubine. He hoped his magic spells and incantations might still break the hold of the evil spirits. Enlil said that the omens were bad, particularly the spots he observed on the liver of a sacrificial sheep. Nevertheless, he would press on with prayers, offerings, and sacrifices and place protective wax figurines around her bed and amulets and charms on her body. Mannu told the king he was using the most powerful medicines in his apothecary.

Ashurbanipal dismissed his healers with a backhanded wave and bellowed, "She must not die! My son must not die!"

In the second week of her illness, Bel got worse.

Mannu was sleeping in the room nearby when one of her midwives, a kind-hearted woman named Tashmetum, awoke him and told him to come quickly. By the light of an oil lamp, he found Bel moaning and breathing heavily. Her eyes were shut.

"My Lady," he said, shaking her. "Bel!"

The next morning, with daylight streaming through the window, Mannu examined her more closely. Her wound was unchanged, but there were new, mysterious markings on other parts of her body. Tiny red spots on her chest and back. Small red lines under her fingernails resembling splinters. Purple bumps on her fingertips. Mannu rushed to the library to see if the *Sakikkū* described such findings, but he found nothing.

As the week progressed, her situation became graver. Her breathing became raspy, and her ankles swelled.

ON THE FIFTEENTH day of her illness, Mannu awakes in his vigil quarters and hastens to her bedside.

"How was she during the night?" he asks Tashmetum. "You did not call me."

"There was no reason. Alas, she is unchanged."

He feels her skin. It is blazingly hot.

"Cool her with wet linens soaked in thyme," he orders. "How is the baby?"

"She does not bleed. The baby lives. Please, Rab Asû, I beg you to save her. Never was there a more precious woman."

Mannu seeks out Kisir and finds him in his rooms, studying a tablet.

"Is there nothing more you can do?" he asks the exorcist.

Kisir strokes his beard and says, "This concubine has greatly angered Lamashtu; this is beyond doubt. None of our magic is working. Alas, we cannot heal every sufferer. You know this to be true."

Mannu raises his voice. "This woman is the King's favorite. She carries a royal heir. She is no ordinary sufferer. You know how the King rages."

Kisir has always possessed a disquieting smile, like a giant lizard. "I have told the King that my magic is powerful. Enlil has told him that his spells are powerful. Have you convinced him that your medicines are powerful?"

Mannu understands the message. If Bel dies, Kisir and Enlil will conspire to make the King believe he is to blame. He stalks off to the hanging gardens to clear his mind. He wishes his old master were still alive. Whenever Mannu had a difficult patient, the old physician always had excellent suggestions. Now, with life ebbing from the woman he loved, he desperately needed the wisdom and experience of a healer who had lived a long life. Seated by a tranquil pond, he decides to visit a wise old physician who left the King's service because of infirmity.

Shulgi-eresh lives in the neighborhood where Mannu's mother and brother still reside. Passing by his childhood house, old neighbors recognize him and bow in respect, and he resolves to stop to see his mother on his way back to the palace. At Shulgi's house, his daughter welcomes Mannu and takes him to the courtyard, where her father is dozing in the sun.

The wizened old fellow blinks in confusion, and Mannu reminds him who he is.

"Ah, Mannu," he says. "Are you still working for the Rab Asû?"

"I am the Rab Asû," Mannu says.

"Are you?"

"Our master died. Do you not remember?"

"Oh, yes. Yes, indeed, he says, although Mannu is not convinced he does.

"I have a difficult patient. I am wondering if you might assist me in her care."

Shulgi straightens himself on the sack of grain he was reclining against. His chest swells proudly.

"Yes, of course, my dear Mannu. I should like that very much."

When he was finished describing the situation, Shulgi stifles a yawn, clearly fatigued by paying attention to the long recitation.

"Well," Mannu says. "What do you think? Are there any medicines I have not thought of? Is there some magic that the chief exorcist and the chief diviner have not employed?"

"You are correct. This is a difficult patient. I am not surprised the usual measures fail to heal her." He pauses to think, then says, "When I was a junior physician, there was a magician named Tukulti who worked for the chief exorcist. Tukulti was a strange man. A difficult man, some might say. He had his own ideas. Very peculiar ones. He thought that the best way to act against evil spirits was to use the black magic banned since the time before the great flood. The chief exorcist looked the other way—even though the use of black magic was punishable by death—because there was a time or two when Tukulti achieved remarkable results for desperately ill patients, but he went too far. He conjured up a spell and made a patient disappear."

Mannu raised his eyebrows. "Disappear? What do you mean, disappear?"

"He was there, and then he was not. And he never returned. His family never saw him again. They were angry. They went to the chief exorcist and said, Listen, your magician came to our house to heal our son, and he did not heal him. He made him disappear. They demanded compensation."

"What did Kisir's father do?"

"What could he do? He paid. And then he dismissed Tukulti."

"What became of him?"

"As far as I can remember, he went to live outside the city walls. I once saw him at his house—if you can call it a house—many years ago."

"Where?"

"You must go through the southern gate, the Mushéhuššu Gate, and follow the road toward Babylon. Do you know the trade outpost near the king's hunting grounds?"

"I know it."

"There was a camp there where laborers and farm workers lived. That is where Tukulti lived. I do not know if the camp remains or if Tukulti is still alive."

"Thank you, Shulgi. I will try to find him."

"If you do," Shulgi says, "Ask him where he sent the man who disappeared. I have always wanted to know."

MANNU FOREGOES the visit to his mother and stops by the palace stables to get his favorite horse. The Mushéhuššu Gate, adorned with a scaly creature with a long tail and neck, was named for the mushussu, a dragon favored by the god Marduk for its protective powers. The portion of the Babylon road nearest the city was crowded with merchants who offered travelers anything they desired —from beer to flesh. Mannu kicks his horse to a gallop and passes through the fertile agricultural land that feeds the great city.

Soon, he is riding through the groomed parkland the king calls a paradise, where he hunts boars, deer, aurochs, and the most prized quarry of all—lions. Maintaining the vast parkland requires many workers, and Mannu sees their settlement in the distance. Arriving, he runs his eyes along the simple mud-brick houses on either side of the rutted road, searching for someone to ask about an old magician in their midst. A woman emerges from one of the houses, dumping a piss pot into the road.

Mannu pulls up and calls to her. "Do you know where Tukulti-Ninurta lives?"

"Who?" the woman says.

"Tukulti, the magician."

"I do not know him."

He gets the same lack of recognition until he tries a boy leading a spiny-tailed lizard by a rope around its neck.

"The old magician? I know where he lives. Would you like me to show you?"

"I would indeed."

"It will cost you a quarter of a shekel."

Mannu laughs. "That is what your father is paid for a day of labor."

"My father is dead," the boy replies matter-of-factly.

"Very well. A quarter of a shekel, but only if he is there."

The house where Mannu is taken is behind the row of street-facing ones in a sewage-strewn alleyway. The walls have deep cracks, and the thatch is ancient, with bald spots that surely let in the rain during the wet season. There is no door to knock on, just a sheet of dirty linen covering the portal.

"Hello?" Mannu shouts through it. "I am looking for Tukulti-Ninurta, former magician and exorcist to the royal court."

Hearing nothing, he calls out again. The boy fidgets.

A thin, reedy voice responds. "Who seeks Tukulti-Ninurta?"

"I am Mannu-ki-Ashur, Rab Asû of Nineveh."

"Is that so? Why does the rab asû wish to meet an old magician who can barely see?"

"I need your help with a patient I cannot heal."

"Who sent you?"

"The old physician Shulgi-eresh."

"Ha! Shulgi! I liked him. I am glad he is alive. You may enter."

The boy extends his hand, and Mannu crosses it with a coin.

Inside, the house is ramshackle, with broken and crudely repaired furniture. In the center of the room is a fire pit, an iron pot overhanging it on a frame. A swirl of smoke escapes through the gaps in the thatch. Tukulti shows himself from the rear, pushing himself from his bedframe. He grabs his walking stick and hobbles forward. He is emaciated, the thinnest man Mannu has ever seen this side of a skeleton. His hair is white and patchy, his beard wispy and unkempt, his eyes white and hazed.

"You say you are the rab asû?"

"I am."

"Come closer. I told you I cannot see."

Mannu steps forward.

"Young for it, are you not?"

"I suppose I am."

"The last one is dead?"

"Regrettably, my master died a few years ago."

"And who is the chief exorcist now?"

"His son, Kisir."

73

"Is he as much of a fool as his father?"

Mannu decides it might be helpful to appear as an ally. "As the father goes, so goes the son."

Tukulti shows his few teeth and says, "Very good. Come and sit. Take the chair. I will take the floor."

Mannu protests, but the old man insists, and Mannu lowers himself gingerly, hoping the chair does not give out.

"Why did that rascal Shulgi send you to me? It is a miracle he is still alive, but no more so than me, I suppose."

"I have an important patient who, I fear, is dying. I have been working with the chief exorcist and chief diviner for two weeks, and none of our therapies heal her."

"How important?"

"The king's favorite concubine, heavily pregnant with his child. The king is anxious for another heir."

Tukulti plays with his beard, rolling a wisp around a finger.

"You had better tell me more."

Mannu describes Bel's course and the treatments rendered. The old man listens with his eyes closed. To make sure he has not fallen asleep, Mannu pauses here and there, precipitating an irritated, "Come on, come on!"

When he is finished, Tukulti opens his eyes and says, "Your magic and medicines are weak. This woman is afflicted by the strongest demons and most vicious ghosts."

"What should we do?" Mannu asks.

The old man cackles. "What are you prepared to do?"

"Anything under the sun," Mannu says earnestly.

"The sun has nothing to do with what she needs. She needs the magic of the blackest night. I was dismissed for using black magic. It is a dangerous weapon, banned in the empire, and ignorant men fear it. You do not strike me as an ignorant man."

"Shulgi told me you made a patient disappear."

Another cackle. "Yes, yes, it is true. I made a foolish mistake. I would not have made it again had I not been dismissed. The patient had no means of reappearing. I should have sent myself, procured the treatment, and used my powers to return."

"Tell me—where did you send him?"

"I cannot say because I was not there!" Tikulti says as if the question was ridiculous. "Tell me, Mannu-ki-Ashur, what do you know about time?"

"Today is today. Yesterday was yesterday. Tomorrow is tomorrow. That is what I know," Mannu says.

Tukulti makes a rude gesture. "You studied what they wanted you to study. I studied the truly ancient texts of wisdom—the ones written before the great flood. The old ones had strong black magic, more powerful than the pale magic used today. And you physicians! You are pathetic. You think only of dried roots and herbs and stinky oils."

Mannu brushes off the insult and asks the shriveled old man to enlighten him.

Tukulti hums in pleasure at his visitor's humility and says, "Do you know the Mul Apin?"

Mannu says he has heard of the Plough Star texts but admits he had never read them.

"The royal library has several excellent copies," Tukulti says. "Our forebearers were keen observers of the heavens. By studying the moon, the sun, the stars, and the constellations, they came to profound conclusions about time as a circle. The stars move through the heavens and back again from whence they came. The seasons follow. Summer goes, then comes again the following year. Do you believe we can change the flow of time?"

"I do not know," Mannu admits.

"Yet, you have heard the Prayers to the Gods of Night, have you not? We pray: May the gods of the night, which I have approached, heed my prayer and accept my supplication. May the judgment pronounced against me be voided; may my sins be remitted! May my spell be broken; my ban be dissolved! May the bonds of my hands be loosed; may the fetters of my feet be released! May the god who is angry with me be pacified! May the goddess who is furious with me be soothed!"

"I know these prayers," Mannu says.

"All exorcists employ this incantation," Tukulti says. "We pray to the gods to change a person's fate, so by reason, we believe they can alter the circle of time in their favor. But my fellow exorcists were scared to use magic to change time. I was told this is the realm of the gods, not men. I argued to the chief exorcist, a stubborn and inflexible brute, thusly: I said we conduct our Akitu festival at the end of each year, do we not? During the festival, we reenact the creation of the world to reset time for the new year. So, just as the gods can alter the flow of time, so too can man. He berated me and sent me away to the countryside for penance and reflection."

"Yes, but—"

The old man does not tolerate interruption. "Listen to me, Mannu-ki-Ashur. My fellow exorcists were like timid lambs, but I was bold and fearless. I searched the King's library for texts describing the magic I sought but found none. Then, in my exile, I passed through the city of Kalhu. The chief exorcist of that place did not know that I was out of favor and offered me lodgings at the Temple of Nabu. There, I met an old librarian, even older than I am today, who kept the temple archive. He respected me, and I respected him. One day, after imbibing too much beer, he told me something astonishing. He said he had a forbidden text, an ancient tablet written by a powerful magician at the dawn of time. It contained incantations and potions of the blackest of magic he discovered hidden in a temple wall that had tumbled down when the earth trembled. When he showed it to the chief exorcist of the city, he was horrified and demanded the librarian destroy it. But the librarian disobeyed and kept it hidden within his archive."

"What kind of magic was it?" Mannu asks.

Tukulti pauses long enough for Mannu to beg him to continue.

"It was a guide for moving through time—the incantations that must be invoked, the potions that must be consumed."

"What did you do with it?"

"I made a copy and returned to Nineveh, where I said nothing about it to the Chief Exorcist or my fellow magicians. And I did nothing for years until I came to treat a patient wasting away from a cough. I knew him since I was a boy. He was not of my blood, but he was like a brother. None of the medicines given by your old master helped him. None of my magic helped him. He lay dying, and I decided to invoke the ancient magic."

"To what end?" Mannu asks.

"I desired to invoke Nabu and Gula to open the path through time and send my patient to a time and place where he might find a cure for his illness."

Mannu is leaning so far forward that his chair is in danger of tipping over.

"Say more—"

"Here is what I reasoned. Knowledge increases with time. Future healers might know more than we do, so the boy could be cured by sending him into the future. I made the potion the text prescribed. I changed the incantations to fit my purpose. I conducted the ritual. And lo and behold, the patient vanished. He was there, before me, and then, when I opened my eyes, he was gone."

"And you never learned what happened to him?"

"I did not. Perhaps he was saved. Perhaps he was not. As I told you, I was foolish. I made no provisions for his return. Perhaps, deep in my heart, I did not believe the spells would work."

Mannu rises and holds his hands to his head in an excited state.

"Can you teach me these spells?"

"You heard what happened to my patient."

"I would go myself, just as you said you would."

"I do not have to teach you. I have the text I copied from the tablet of Kalhu with the changes I made if I ever were to make the journey myself. However, I strongly advise against its use. You are a young man with an esteemed future. This is dangerous magic, difficult to control. There is a chance you will be lost forever on the great circle of time."

"Show it to me," Mannu says defiantly.

❧

THE CHIEF EUNUCH, Sin-shumu-lishir, tells his man, Adad-ummi, to shut the door. His office at the palace is close to the King's quarters, and the corridor is teeming with courtiers.

"What news?" he asks.

Adad knows the subject of the question, for it is the same one Sin has been asking every day since Bel stepped on an iron spike.

"The concubine eunuch tells me she is fading. The healers are powerless."

"How long must we wait?"

Adad shrugs his heavy shoulders. "It is difficult to say."

Sin shakes his head. "I am not paid until she breathes her last."

"I can make it happen tonight if you wish."

"And risk being found out? No! We must wait for Nergal to drag the creature to the underworld."

MANNU SITS by Bel's bed, watching her face, which is peaceful now. But only minutes ago, it was contorted, as if the demon controlling her fate was tormenting her. He touches her neck, and the heat of her body passes to his fingers. She has become thinner. It has been days since she has taken food. For sustenance, Mannu has her attendants sit her up and drop honeyed water and beer into her mouth, which sometimes she swallows, sometimes she gags.

He waits by her bed until he sees darkness from her window, and before leaving, lowers his mouth to her ear and whispers, "Tonight is the night, dear Bel. With the grace and protection of the gods and goddesses, I will have a cure when I see you next. I beg of you, stay alive. Please, my love. Stay alive."

He looks around, sees he is still alone with her, and kisses her forehead before heading into the night.

MANNU GOES to his apothecary to finish preparing the potion he needs for the magic to work. He has trimmed the stems and boiled the leaves in water. All that remains is to filter the brew through

78

cheesecloth. When he arrives, he is surprised to see his friend Ninurta sitting on the floor, his back against the wall. He is not wearing his uniform, and more surprisingly, he is intoxicated, with a skin of wine in his lap.

"My friend!" Ninurta shouts. "How I have missed you."

"We saw each other only days ago," Mannu says.

"I meant tonight. Tonight, I have missed you."

"Why are you out of uniform?" Mannu asks.

"Why, indeed? Ah, there is a tale to tell. Would you like me to tell you?" He holds up the skin. "Oh, I am a poor friend for not offering—will you drink with me? I have here the strongest date wine in the city."

"I cannot drink tonight. Please, tell me what has happened."

"Your friend, who sits before you, has been relieved of command of the palace guards until my military tribunal. Here am I, a disgraced soldier. Did you not hear me, Mannu? Disgraced."

"Yes, I hear you, but I do not understand. What have you done?"

"Only what comes naturally," Ninurta says. "Only what I have done my entire life."

"You mean your proclivity for men?"

"Spoken like a physician!" Ninurta exclaims. "Yes, my love of men."

"Your preferences are not against the law," Mannu says. "How are you disgraced?"

"Ah, the story. You know the taverns along the River Ḥussur? Of course you do."

Mannu admits he takes pleasure there from time to time.

"A tavern I favor has a prostitute I greatly favor, a beautiful lad —oh, you do not need to hear about his beauty. Last night, I went there and I lay with him. And with accursed luck, the door opens, and who should see me? Only my deputy commander of the guard, a pompous turd with legs, who has longed for my position. He was looking for his whore, a cheap-looking hag, and walked through the wrong door."

Mannu says, "Embarrassing? Perhaps? Grounds for a tribunal?

No! You are certainly not the highest ranking member of the army to lie with a man."

Ninurta draws deeply from the skin. "Ah, but how do they lie? On top or below? How many of them were branded as *šinuhtu?*"

Mannu understands the problem. Lying with a man was tolerated, but being effeminate and passive, especially in the army, was not.

"Listen, my friend," Mannu says. "We will make sure that the best advocate in the city speaks for you in your tribunal. I am sure honor and position can be restored."

"No, I am doomed," Ninurta says mournfully. "They have even ordered me to leave barracks. Where will I live? I cannot bear the disgrace of returning to my mother's house."

"You will stay here in my quarters," Mannu says.

"You have but one bed, and I do not wish to sleep with my friend."

"It is not a problem," Mannu says. "I have to leave the city. I go tonight."

"Why?" Ninurta cries. "When will you return?"

"I seek a cure for Bel. I do not know how long I will be gone, but for her sake, I must hurry."

"Poor, poor, Bel" Ninurta says. "I know how you love her. Can I go with you? I will protect you on your journey."

"I must go alone. Here, let me help you up. You should go to sleep now. You have had enough wine."

Mannu leads him into his bedchamber and lowers him onto his mattress.

"Farewell, my oldest and dearest friend," Ninurta says. "May the gods help you find your cure."

MANNU WAITS until the middle of the night. He has carefully studied Tukulti's tablet and has learned the incantations by heart. He has hiked beyond the city walls and has collected the plants prescribed

—*ḫanbū, ēṭū,* and *šināti-ṣalmu*—and prepared the potion as the text prescribed.

At this hour, the palace guards rarely, if ever, patrol this part of the hanging gardens. It is a lovely spot reminiscent of a forest glade, its grassy center ringed by swaying palms and flowering trees. It would not be so bad if it were the last place he sees before disappearing forever into some unimaginable void.

He marks out a circle that symbolizes the boundaries of time by trampling the grass and wonders if he should have bidden farewell to his dear mother, his best friend, Ninurta, and his physician colleagues, but to do so would have risked the enterprise. All he can do is pray they will forgive him.

He places three objects around the circle—a blank tablet of clay for the god of wisdom, Nabu, a sprig of medicinal thyme for the goddess of healing, Gula, and a jar of water, a symbol of purity and clarity. If found, no one will know their meaning.

He looks to the black, clear sky, filled with innumerable points of light.

It is time. There is no reason to delay. He begins his incantation between a shout and a whisper—soft enough not to reach the ears of palace guards, loud enough for the gods to take notice.

O Nabu, scribe of the heavens, keeper of the tablets of destiny,
You who know the fate of all things, present and future,
Open the gates of time for your humble servant.
Lend me the wisdom of what is yet to be written,
The knowledge inscribed in future stars.
Inscribe upon my mind the words of healers not yet born,
And guide my hands to save those who suffer.
By your hand, let the circle of time flow backward and forward.
And in this sacred circle, let the past and future converge.

O Gula, mistress of life and breath,
Healer of body and soul, mother of physicians,
I beseech you to grant me the cure I do not know.
Lead me through the veil of time to the land of distant healers.

To the gardens where unknown herbs grow,
And into the halls where learned healers practice.
By your hand, may the threads of fate be woven anew,
And may your servant return with the knowledge to heal,
With the wisdom to cure what cannot yet be cured.

Now, he stands in the center of the circle, eyes closed, hands lifted to the stars, and recites.

By the stars above and the earth below,
By the breath of life and the ink of destiny,
Let me pass through the rivers of time.
Nabu, Gula, open the path!
Take my mind to the distant day,
To a time where knowledge shines like the moon,
And wisdom flows like the River Idigna.
Take me to a master to guide me,
And teach me to heal Bel, who is afflicted.
As I stand upon this sacred ground,
May my spirit travel beyond the reach of this age.

Seven are the stars that guard the heavens,
Seven are the gates that guard the unknown,
Seven are the learned healers.
By their hands and mine, may time bend,
And may I return with the cure.
I will pass through the seventh gate and return to Nineveh with the light
of knowledge.

Mannu ends the ritual by drinking his bitter potion and turning his body in place, pouring water from a jug onto the ground in a continuous circle, symbolizing the flow of time. When no more water is left, he lets the jug slip from his hand and dizzily stands, waiting for something to happen.

At first, there is nothing, and he begins to doubt Tukulti.

Crazy old magician, he thinks. *Why did I—*

As a boy, he tried to swim across the great river when the water was high and the current was strong. He made it halfway across when his arms and legs grew tired and cramped, and he succumbed to its might. He was powerless to fight, and he was carried downstream. He could only gulp air whenever his head bobbed above the water. If it had not been for a fisherman casting his net at a fortunate moment, snaring him and dragging him to safety, he would have perished.

Suddenly, Mannu is in that river, although he is not wet. He hears the roar in his ears. He feels his body hurtling downstream. He is powerless against the mighty forces, but he is strangely calm. His eyes are closed—he cannot and does not want to open them. His speed increases impossibly, and still, he does not panic. Everything seems as it should be. He thinks of the woman he loves—not in her sickbed, but healthy and gracefully dancing. He sees her so clearly.

And then, there is nothing.

CHAPTER SEVEN

POLICE CONSTABLES OZZIE RIVERS AND JOAN HERON'S RUSH-HOUR patrols of Piccadilly Circus are usually fairly dull affairs. Despite the density of people and vehicles, particularly during the peak tourist seasons, their shifts are dominated by mundane tasks and giving directions to confused out-of-towners. That's not to say there aren't moments of excitement, usually involving pickpockets, mobile phone snatchers, drunk and disorderly types, and drivers fender-bending trying to navigate the roundabout. A year ago, the pair caught someone who robbed a jeweler on St. James Street, which earned them a commendation.

On this fine autumn evening, when the sun is getting low and the traffic is beginning to thin, they shuffle their feet under the statue of Eros, pretty much lost in their thoughts. They have been partners for two years, and once they have recounted their off-duty activities since the last shift, they do not have much to say to each other. So far, this afternoon's most compelling event has been a dog-walker whose Cocker Spaniel ran off down Regent's Street when its lead snapped. Dog and man were subsequently reunited.

Suddenly, people are shouting and pointing down Coventry Street.

PC Heron sees it first and says to her partner, "Gawd, what do we have here?"

~

MANNU HAS GONE from darkness to light, from being swept along in incredible motion to suddenly being stationary, from the sounds of rushing water to jarring, unfamiliar noises. He is too scared to open his eyes fully because the few things he has glimpsed make no earthly sense.

Much of what he hears is so alien and incongruous he cannot square them with anything in nature. He knows the sound of thunder, wind, mighty rain, and floods as a river spills its banks. He knows the sound of heraldic trumpets and drums, of soldiers marching in a column. He hears none of these but a screeching, rumbling cacophony punctuated by sharp, loud, ungodly noises.

Then, there are voices—human voices, not animal cries, of that he is certain. But they are in a tongue he cannot understand. Some of them are loud and boisterous. Finally, there is something he can recognize. Laughter—for laughter is the same in all tongues.

He opens his eyes a little wider. People—if he can call them that—are pointing at him, shouting, and laughing. They are dressed in the strangest costumes he has ever seen. None has a proper tunic or robe. Women display their bodies most shamefully. Men are beardless with short hair. They clutch weird rectangular objects that reflect the sun into his eyes.

There are other truly unbelievable sights. Gargantuan buildings that dwarf Nineveh's tallest ziggurats and temples. Gleaming beasts, larger than aurochs or horses, racing by at enormous speeds.

It is then that Mannu looks down and sees he is naked. The shame and degradation are overwhelming. He tries to cover himself with his hands, but it is useless.

The magic has not worked, he thinks. *I have been cast into the underworld. I am dead.*

A curdling scream escapes his throat, and he begins to run.

≈

"HEY, YOU! STOP!"

PCs Rivers and Heron take off after the naked man.

"Where the hell did he come from?" Rivers asks.

"He must've bailed from a car," Heron says.

"Here's me thinking nothing much was going on," Rivers says.

The officers barrel through the crowd around the fountain. Someone shouts at them to let the guy have his fun. A young woman yells, "Hey, Mister, come back! You're not half bad!"

The streaker runs down Coventry Street past the Hard Rock Cafe and turns right onto Haymarket, the police in hot pursuit.

"Can't believe someone can run that fast barefoot," Heron says, sucking air.

"I'm calling it in, in case we lose him," her partner says, reaching for the push-to-talk button on his vest.

≈

MANNU'S PANIC knows no bounds. He has never felt such fear. The ground is hard and rough, not like the smooth paving stones of the Temple District. His maleness flops around like a fish pulled from the river, and he is humiliated. He almost welcomes the horrific gallu demons which will certainly appear at any moment, dragging him further into the depths of the damned.

He keeps his eyes on the ground, occasionally looking up as not to collide with the throngs of half-people, half-demons who crowd the path. One steps in his way, pointing a shiny rectangle at him.

≈

"YOU GETTING THIS, BRUH?" a pedestrian asks.

"You know I am," his ginger-headed companion answers. "I'm going out live on my channel. Hey, yo! All my followers—it's Atomic

Ginge here for me lads and lasses. Check out this dude legging it starkers at Piccadilly. Just another day in the London loony bin. Catch it quick before the pixel gods make me pixelate the fuck out of it."

~

MANNU LEADS with his shoulder and slams into the red-headed monster, knocking him to the ground with surprising ease. *What kind of demon is so easily defeated?* he thinks. He keeps running.

~

ATOMIC GINGE IS on his knees, picking up his shattered phone. As the police officers run past him, he shouts, "Oi, see that? This poser's knocked me over. Whatcha going to do about it?"

"Catch him for starters, mate," Rivers replies, pumping his legs.

"We don't want him reaching Pall Mall," Heron tells her partner.

"Too right," Rivers says. He gets on his radio and asks a mobile unit to assist with the intercept.

~

MANNU KEEPS RUNNING until he can go no further. He has come to a by-way with two continuous columns of otherworldly creatures rolling along in opposite directions on thick black cartwheels. One of these creatures moves faster than the others, weaving in and out, flashing lapis-blue torches, and emitting ear-piercing screams. The creature comes to a halt, and two demons jump out, yelling in tongues.

Mannu stops. He pivots to run in the direction he has just come.

But two more demons are approaching fast. There is nothing left for him. He will die as warriors do.

He screams, "Away with you demons!" and charges.

RIVERS AND HERON skid to a stop when they see the naked man turning on them.

"Stay back!" Heron shouts, but the man doesn't obey.

He keeps coming, screaming his head off unintelligibly.

Rivers unholsters his Taser and yells, "Stop, or I will Taser you!"

The man barrels forward, waving his arms.

They have seconds until contact.

"Taser! Taser! Taser!" Rivers shouts, deploying the weapon.

MANNU SPOTS the yellow object in the demon's hand. When the insect that flies from it bites him in the chest, he feels the most intense pain he has ever experienced. Worse, seized by some malevolent spell, his body ceases to function. He crashes to the hard ground, and the demons are upon him.

"TASER DEPLOYED," Rivers radios.

"He's out of control, this one," Heron says, struggling on her knees. "We'd best cuff him behind." She reaches for her bracelets. "Come on now, Sir. Let's have you roll over onto your stomach, all right? Don't you worry. We're going to get you the help you need."

The duty sergeant's car speeds from Pall Mall up Haymarket in the wrong direction and pulls alongside.

"Where's his clothes?" the sergeant asks.

"Good question, Guv," Heron says. "Got a blanket in the boot?"

The sergeant retrieves one, much to the dismay of the sidewalk brigade, who start booing.

The naked man squirms hard against his cuffs.

"Think he's on drugs?" the sergeant asks.

"Most def," Rivers says.

The sergeant gets on his radio and says, "Control, can we have an ambulance dispatched to the Pall Mall end of Haymarket?"

Heron presses down on the man's shoulder to keep him from moving.

"Sir, can you tell me your name?" she says.

"I don't suppose he's got his ID secreted on his person," the sergeant says, chuckling. "Where'd you first make contact?"

"Bang in the middle of Piccadilly," Rivers says. "He wasn't there, and then he was. Must've been a passenger in a vehicle."

The sergeant says, "All right. Hang tight till the medics arrive. We'll get this sorted. Use your mobile ID to check his fingerprints. That'll speed things up."

"Right, Sarge," Heron says, fishing through her vest for her scanner.

"Ozzie, can you clear the sidewalks?" the sergeant asks.

"Okay, folks," Rivers announces to the gathering crowd. "Show's over. Save your phone's batteries. Be on your way."

"Encore!" a lusty woman shouts out.

Mannu has been lifted onto a narrow bed, his hands bound in irons. To his horror, he is carted inside the belly of one of the rolling beasts, where two demons in green garb with blue rectangles on their shoulders stand over him, manipulating his person in unspeakable ways. His arm is strapped to a plank, and he feels a sharp pain, then sees his lifeblood flowing into a beaker. The huge beast begins to move, and he screams in terror.

The EMT is irritated. "Settle yourself, Sir. You're in good hands. No cause for shouting, all right? Have you taken anything? Any drugs?"

The patient answers in grunts and snarls.

"Why aren't you wearing clothes?" the EMT asks to no response.

The Assistant Ambulance Practitioner, a woman in a headscarf, says, "What's your name, luv?"

Their patient screams again and begins to thrash at his stays.

"Can we give him something?" the AAP asks, staring wide-eyed at the monitor. His heart rate is one-seventy."

"I don't think that's wise before we know what he's on. It's sinus tach. He's young. He can handle it." The EMT calls to the driver, "What's our ETA?"

"Ten minutes in this bloody traffic," the driver says.

The EMT uses his best version of a compassionate tone. "Sir, we're taking you to hospital now. They'll take good care of you."

AT THE UCL LONDON HOSPITAL EMERGENCY DEPARTMENT, the ambulance crew wheels their patient to the triage desk.

The EMT tells the nurse, "Agitated male, found running around Piccadilly Circus in his birthday suit. Tasered by police. No ID of any sort. Police did a field fingerprint scan. He wasn't in the database. He's alert but unresponsive to questions, so drug or medical-psychiatric history is unknown. BP one-forty over ninety, sinus tachycardia settling down, normal temperature. That's it. He's all yours. Oh yeah—the police want their blanket back."

"What's not to like?" the nurse says and has him wheeled to an observation bay, where he is transferred to a bed and secured in four-point restraints.

By the time a doctor sees him, he is sleeping.

"Hello, Sir," the doctor says. Can you tell me your name?"

The patient opens his eyes, blinks at her, and begins tugging at his restraints again.

"Do you speak English? If not, we have translators here."

More thrashing.

The doctor calls a nurse over.

"He looks Middle Eastern, don't you think? Can you get them to send an Arabic translator?"

"Could be Iranian," the nurse says.

"Could be. Get a Farsi one too. Let me do a quick neuro exam, and we'll draw bloods. If his toxic screen is negative, he'll probably need a head CT."

"They're backed up in radiology," the nurse says.

"Of course they are," the doctor says. "Today's a day that ends in a Y."

MANNU HAS BEEN MOVED to another strange chamber within a building that dwarfs the royal palace. Demons dressed him in a thin robe and wheeled him inside a box with shiny doors that began to move once he was inside. When the doors opened, they wheeled him through corridors filled with strange objects and beings.

He remains bound to a bed by his hands and feet. Something sharp is stuck in his arm, connected to a fluid-filled, translucent bag suspended on a rod. There is another being in a bed beside him, a very old creature, moaning in pain.

Mannu thinks, *Is this my fate? To be tortured and kept in the bit kišarri, the underworld's House of Dust, where the dead dwell for eternity? I have failed to save Bel-ibni, and I am condemned.*

His bladder is aching terribly, but he is too proud to let his urine flow where he lies. The discomfort mounts and becomes so painful that he cries out. In time, a female being dressed in blue answers his cries and speaks in tongues. She points to his groin, and he instinctively nods. She unties one of his hands and gives him a vessel made of a substance he has never seen. He understands. He is to let his urine flow thusly. The female pulls a curtain around the bed and leaves him to relieve himself. He is grateful that at least this torture was short-lived.

DURING MORNING ROUNDS in the hospital's adult medicine ward, the internal medicine consultant leads a group of registrars, house officers, and medical students into the room of a newly admitted, noncommunicative patient.

"Tell me about this fellow," the consultant says.

The Foundation Year 2 house officer, a female physician who has been up all night, snaps to weary attention. As she speaks, the patient is watching them like a trapped animal.

"This is an unknown male, aged approximately thirty, I'd say, who was brought in yesterday by the police with an episode of delirium of some type. More specifically, he was observed screaming and running around Picadilly Circus without clothes and had to be apprehended by Tasing. He had no form of identification on his person—obviously—and he wasn't in the police fingerprints databases."

The consultant guffawed. "Yes, I did see the pictures in the morning papers, never suspecting he would appear on my ward!"

The FY2 is less gleeful. "The patient was awake and seemingly alert but has not been able to communicate with us due to a language barrier. Since he appears to be of Middle Eastern extraction, appropriate translators were brought in, but apparently, he doesn't speak or understand Arabic of Farsi."

"Some local dialect, perhaps?" the consultant asks.

"They say not."

"He does have a rather distinctive beard," the consultant says. "I've never seen curls like that. Perhaps that might offer some clue to his identity. Carry on."

"On admission, the patient had normal vital signs, appeared well-nourished, and had normal general physical and neurological exams. His lab values were remarkable only for borderline anemia and eosinophilia. We'll want to do a workup for parasites, but I don't think it's relevant to this episode. His toxic screen was negative, so we've excluded drug or toxin exposures."

"Sooo—" the consultant says theatrically, "neurological or psychiatric?"

"We're still waiting for his head CT," she says. "Typical delays. I can't tell you when it's going to happen. I've requested a psych consult, but it's pointless, really. They won't be able to talk with him, and they're going to say exclude brain pathology anyway."

The consultant folds his arms and peers at the patient. "Well, get the social work department involved. Once he's cleared medically, we'll want this gentleman off our ward and sent somewhere more appropriate to his needs. Hopefully, someone will recognize him from his photos in the news and will come and claim him. You can work up the eosinophilia in outpatient clinic. Probably has hookworm if he's from the Middle East. And, please, untether him. He looks placid enough."

"What if he takes off?" the house officer asks.

The consultant smiles like a wicked boy. "Then—voilà—we've freed up a bed."

Mannu sighs in relief when the demons circling his bed disappears. And he is overjoyed when a female in blue enters a short time later and unties his restraints. Perhaps the goddess Ereshkigal has heard that Mannu-ki-Ashur was a good man who lived a good life and did not deserve harsh punishment.

A corpulent, black-skinned male enters, wheeling a cart—surely a Nubian demon. Smiling, he presents Mannu with a platter containing foodstuffs and does the same with the old man. Mannu realizes he is hungry and surveys the assortment of strange offerings. None are recognizable, so he samples them. The white squares are bread-like but tasteless. The yellow mound is like chicken eggs. A small box contains some kind of dried grain. Another contains milk. He tries the brown drink in a cup and spits it out but hungrily consumes everything else with his fingers. He looks over and sees the old man eating with silvery metal tools. Mannu takes the knife and puts it under his leg.

How careless of them to give me a weapon.

CHAPTER EIGHT

King Ashurbanipal is furious.

When he checks on Bel-ibni's well-being that morning, he is informed that the Rab Asû is nowhere to be found.

"Where is Mannu-ki-Ashur?" he bellows. "Find him."

Palace courtiers scramble to search for the physician. They go to his apothecary, his official palace quarters, even the house of his mother, but there is no sign of him. Reports are tendered to Sin-shumu-lishir the Chief Eunuch, whom the King has tasked with solving the disappearance.

Sin is secretly delighted the Rab Asû is gone, as it furthers his hopes the King's concubine will soon perish. The representative of Ashurbanipal's son, Prince Ashur, remains in hiding within the city, ready to ride to Babylon with the news of the concubine's death. Sin is anxious to collect Ashur's bounty on her head, and that is all he thinks about as he listens to his minion's reports. One of them asks if they should question Mannu's colleagues, the Chief Exorcist and Chief Diviner. Another suggests talking to Mannu's known close friend, Ninurta-sharru, the dismissed commander of the palace guards.

"The *šinuhtu?*" Sin scoffs.

"He is the childhood friend of the Rab Asû," is the reply.

"Mannu-ki-Ashur never took a wife. Perhaps they are more than close friends," Sin muses. "Find Ninurta and question him."

Later, Sin hears a disturbing story, prompting him to summon Kisir-malik.

Kisir is an important man accustomed to others treating him with utmost respect, but the Chief Eunuch is the King's hand and wields terrifying power. Sin shows no deference.

"I have heard that you possess information about the Rab Asû," Sin says.

Kisir stands uncomfortably before the seated chief eunuch. He is aware of Sin's man, Adad, lurking in the shadows.

"I do not know where Mannu has gone," Kisir says. "The last I saw him was in Bel-ibni's bedchamber four days ago."

"Yes, but you know who has spoken with him."

"That is so," Kisir says uneasily. "Through the ranks of the ašipūtu, I heard that Mannu met with Shulgi-eresh, an old physician who is no longer in the King's service."

"When did this meeting take place?"

"Three days ago, I was told."

"What else were you told?"

"Mannu sought the old fellow's counsel to find a way to heal Bel-ibni."

"Would you say it is unusual for the Rab Asû, the most senior physician in Nineveh, to ask an old man for help?"

"It is not uncommon for elders to possess useful knowledge," Kisir says diplomatically.

"And did this elder give Mannu useful knowledge?"

"I do not know. I have not seen Mannu. I have not spoken to Shulgi-eresh."

Sin tents his fingers. "Tell me, Chief Exorcist—can Bel-ibni be healed?"

Kisir shifts nervously and answers carefully. "With the blessings of the gods—yes. However, powerful demons and ghosts are trying to kill her, and I cannot say they will not succeed. Our strongest magic has not helped. The Chief Diviner sees troubling signs."

"I wonder," Sin says. "Who will the King blame if Bel dies?"

Kisir is quick with an answer. "Beyond the demons and ghosts who plague her, he should blame the Rab Asû who has disappeared. Perhaps Mannu knew his medicines were weak. Perhaps he fled, fearing he would be blamed."

Sin seems to like what he hears, and his thin lips crack into a smile. Relieved, Kisir bows and backs toward the door.

SIN SENDS his man to Shulgi-eresh's house to interrogate the old physician. Shulgi's daughter tells him he is napping, but Adad pushes past, marches to his bed, and pulls him to his feet by his tunic.

"The Rab Asû visited you," he says. "What did you tell him?"

In his confusion, Shulgi seems to remember the previous rab asû.

"He has never blessed my humble house with his presence," he insists.

"That is a lie," Adad says.

"A lie? I never lie," Shulgi says indignantly.

His daughter has been listening, and she endeavors to help.

"Father, you remember, do you not? Mannu-ki-Ashur is the new rab asû. He visited a few days ago."

"That young man was the rab asû?" Shulgi says, puzzled.

"Yes, Father. Do you recall telling me how young he is?" She implores Adad, "Please forgive him. He is forgetful sometimes."

Adad repeats his question. "What did you tell him?"

Shulgi brightens. "Oh, yes! The new one. He wanted to know how I would treat a sick woman, heavy with child, in the grips of malevolent spirits."

"What was your answer?" Adad demands.

"Tukulti."

Adad says, "What is Tukulti?"

"Not what. Who!" Shulgi says. "I told him about an old magician named Tukulti, who once used black magic to heal a very ill man. He made him disappear! He never came back! The young fellow was very interested in what I had to say. I told him where he might find Tukulti. Where is the Rab Asû?"

Adad says, "He has disappeared."

Shulgi laughs so hard he loses his balance and falls onto his bed.

SIN HABITUALLY ASSERTS his dominance by having visitors stand while he reclines on cushions. This maneuver does not work with the emaciated old magician, Tukulti-Ninurta, whom Adad has dragged from his hovel outside the city walls. After a short while, Tukulti's hand slips from his walking stick, and he tumbles to the tiles, groaning.

"Get him a bench," Sin tells Adad, putting a perfumed cloth to his nostrils to mask the old man's stench.

"Ah, that is better. Might I have a cup of beer?" Tukulti asks, showing the few teeth in his mouth. "And a piece of bread?"

Sin waits impatiently for the magician to eat and drink, then demands he tell him about his visit with Mannu.

"I liked him," Tukulti says. "He was polite, unlike so many in Nineveh."

Sin looks at him venomously and says, "I am waiting."

"Yes, polite, as I said. He was failing to heal a sick woman, an important person, I was led to believe. Shulgi, the physician, told him I was a good magician—which I was—and he was interested in learning black magic."

"It is said you made a sick man disappear," Sin says.

"Oh! You heard about that. It is true. The magic is strong."

"How would it benefit a sick man to disappear?"

"That is the question Mannu-ki-Ashur put to me. My answer was a lesson."

"A lesson? On what subject?"

"Time! I taught him about time!" Tukulti cackled.

By the time the old magician finished his discourse, Sin was in a state of high agitation. He began giving orders to his minions. He sent people to find Kisir and immediately bring the exorcist back to him. He dispatched Adad to Mannu's work and living areas to retrieve every clay tablet he could find. And he had an attendant take Tukulti to be bathed because he could no longer bear his foul odors.

Kisir arrives, hiding his displeasure of being dragged from a woman's bedside in the middle of a healing incantation.

"How can I be of service?" he asks, setting his jaw.

"Are you aware that your *āšipu*, Tukulti-Ninurta, practiced black magic?"

"My *āšipu*?" Kisir says. "I do not even know who he is. He was certainly never in my service."

"He worked for the previous chief exorcist," Sin says.

"I am not my father," Kisir says testily. "Perhaps you should tell me what you know—or should I say, what you think you know, Chief Eunuch."

"Careful," Sin says. "Do not take that tone with me. It will not profit you. Black magic is being practiced in Nineveh. This old magician, Tikulti, has taught it to Mannu."

"Mannu! Practicing black magic? I refuse to believe this."

"Bring me Tikulti-Ninurta!" Sin yells, and the old man is led in, dressed in a clean tunic and new sandals, his wispy hair and beard neatly combed.

Kisir eyes him up and down and says, "I do not know this man. You there. You say you are a magician?"

Tukulti grins, a fortunate wretch with a full belly and clean skin, approaches Kisir so that he might better see him and says, "Good Sir. You wear the robe of the chief exorcist. I was in your father's service. He was a difficult man—I am certain you know this."

"We are not here to discuss my father. Tell me, what do you know of black magic?"

Tukulti cackles. "I know what I have learned."

"Where did you learn it? Who taught you?"

"Do you know the city of Kalhu?"

"I know it."

"The old librarian of Kalhu found a tablet hidden in a wall at the Temple of Nabu. Upon it, there was written an ancient prescription for a powerful magic unlike any I had seen. There were incantations to speak and a potion to brew."

Kisir sneers in disbelief. "What was the nature of this black magic?"

"Time and how to harness it."

Kisir cannot control himself any longer. "Chief Eunuch!" he cries. "Why must we concern ourselves with the rantings of an old fool?"

Sin stares Kisir down. "The King has commanded us to find Mannu-ki-Ashur, who abandoned his duties and left Bel-ibni without a physician. This old fool is the last person to see him before he disappeared. That is why we must take his rantings seriously."

"Very well," Kisir says, backing down from a confrontation with the all-powerful administrator. "Tell me, Tukulti-Ninurta, where is this ancient tablet?"

"It should be in Kalhu, where I left it. I made a copy and took it with me on my return to Nineveh. Later, I made a further copy with changes to the incantations to suit my needs. That is the tablet I gave the Rab Asû—or rather, he took it."

Kisir throws his hands in the air and asks Sin, "What more can I do? What more can I say? I ask your leave so that I might return to my duties."

Sin seethes at him. "Your duty is to stay here until I say I am finished with you."

An hour passes before Adad returns with a sack slung over his shoulder.

"Have you found Mannu's tablets?" Sin asks.

Adad replies that he has retrieved every tablet he could find in his work and living areas, and sets them on the table. Tukulti has been sleeping upright on a bench, his hands and head resting on his walking stick. Sin harshly wakes him, dragging the old man across the room and asking if any of the tablets are his.

Tukulti lowers his head and scrutinizes the assortment of some twenty texts.

"This smooth, dark one! That is my copy of the Kalhu tablet. And this one is a copy of the Kalhu tablet in Mannu's hand."

"How do you know that?" Sin asks.

"See there? It has his name upon it at the bottom. And the clay I still soft."

"And behold the cleverness of Mannu-ki-Ashur," Tukulti says. "The tablet written by him includes the incantation to return to Nineveh. He has written it as I would have done."

Sin asks Adad where he found these two tablets.

"They were in the Rab Asû's temporary quarters near the concubine, Bel-ibni," Adad says. "They were under his pillow."

Sin says, "Kisir-malik, this is why I kept you here. Read the texts without delay."

The Kalhu tablet is a generous size, with small, neat writing. He takes it to the window and begins to study it.

After a while, he mutters, "It is ancient, indeed. The writing harkens back to the Kingdom of Ur.'

"But can you read it?" Sin asks nervily.

"We scholars can read the old texts. I need only your patience."

Sin has little of that, and he paces, stares, and grunts.

As Kisir reads silently, his lips move to the rhythm of the text, and his eyes widen in amazement. When he is done, he approaches Tukulti, who has fallen asleep again.

"Wake up!" he barks.

Tukulti blinks in confusion, a dream interrupted.

"Have you used this magic?" Kisir demands to know.

"I used it one time. It was not entirely satisfactory," he says, chuckling.

"What do you mean?" Kisir asks.

"I was desperate to heal a man, someone dear to me. My friend was dying, and none of our treatments worked. I used black magic to send him on the great circle of time to a healer who might cure him."

"Did you cure him?" Kisir asks.

"I cannot say. I made the potion exactly as the tablet instructed. I conducted the ceremony exactly as the tablet instructed. And then —my friend disappeared, never to return."

"Wait!" Kisir exclaims with excitement. "I remember. I was just a boy. I overheard a conversation. One day, my father came home very angry. He told my mother that one of his *ašipūtu* had made a sick man disappear, and the man's family was demanding compensation. That was you?"

"That was me," Tukulti says with a shy smile. "I realized the error of my ways. How was my friend to make the return journey on the circle of time? I made the necessary changes to the spell. The next time, I would send myself, learn the cure from a wise healer from the future, and use the magic to return. Alas, there was no next time. Your father dismissed me, and I was exiled."

Kisir is dumbstruck. "You believe the Rab Asû practiced this magic?"

"I do not know," Tukulti says with a shrug. "I sit in my miserable house. I hear nothing. I see no one. If you say that Mannu-ki-Ashur has disappeared, who am I to dispute you?"

One of Sin's men enters and whispers in the chief eunuch's ear.

"Send him in," Sin says.

A palace guard enters, his hands full.

"Show me," Sin says. "Where did you find these?"

"On one of the garden terraces," the soldier replies. "They formed a triangle."

Tukulti begins to cackle in delight.

Kisir rushes forward and says, "Behold! A blank tablet, a sprig of thyme, and a water jar."

Sin pulls Kisir into an alcove for a private conversation. "What do they mean?" he asks.

"Tukulti's tablet speaks of these talismans," Kisir says. "The thyme is for the blessing of Gula; the tablet for the blessing of Nabu. Water purifies the spell. There can be no doubt. Mannu-ki-Ashur has practiced black magic. He has journeyed on the circle of time to save Bel-ibni."

CHAPTER NINE

THE DEMONS IN BLUE ENTER HIS ROOM, ROLLING A CHAIR WITH wheels like a chariot basket, but one you sit upon rather than stand. They gesture for him to leave his bed and take the seat. He cautiously complies and is wheeled into the chaotic corridor, which is filled with demons moving about determinedly. The corridor is bright, but there are no windows or torches. Surely, this is accomplished by magic. Once again, he enters the box through silver doors that miraculously slide. He perceives he is falling, although he remains stationary.

The doors open again, and he is pushed along a cool, dark corridor into an even darker place: a cave with infernal metal objects and blinking lights—perhaps tiny torches. His chair comes to a halt. His demon attendant speaks in its strange tongue and motions for him to climb onto a metallic bed. He stands, hiding his stolen knife in his palm.

∽

THE CT TECH checks the patient's wristband against the radiology requisition. He is supposed to ask the patient for his date of birth to validate his identity, but he has been briefed about this one. The diagnosis on the scan requisition is acute confusional state—exclude space-occupying lesion.

He tells the other tech, "Oh yeah. This is the guy who's a complete unknown."

"Like a rolling stone?" she asks.

"Funny. No point asking him questions."

"If we can't ask him about implants, we'd better wand him."

As he waves the magnetometer over the patient, it begins to beep loudly. They collectively groan and investigate, soon prying the piece of hospital cutlery from his hand.

"Christ!" he says. "I'm calling security."

"C'mon," she says. "The poor guy's scared witless. You couldn't cut a piece of steak with this. Let's get him done and send him back up."

MANNU'S KNIFE has been discovered using some type of magic.

He decides it would be pointless to battle these demons in their lair, and he gives up the weapon without a fight, climbs onto the metal bed, and rests his head on a small pillow. The male demon places something soft into each ear. He tenses his muscles as the bed begins to move, and he finds himself inside a tunnel, like the narrow passageway between two areas of a cave. The demon male's voice echoes in his ears, and he blinks in non-comprehension.

Suddenly, he is assaulted by the loudest, infernal thumping he has ever heard. It sounds like Ereshkigal, is trying to signal her consort by striking the ground with her staff, and Nergal is responding with his terrible staff.

He begins to scream and thrash.

"SIR! YOU NEED TO LIE STILL!" the tech shouts.

Screams fill the CT room.

"We've got to abort," his partner says. "Poor guy is freaked the fuck out."

As he slides from the tube, the patient calms down.

"I'll call transport," she says. "Mark him down as uncooperative."

"At least we didn't get stabbed," he replies.

～

AT AFTERNOON MEDICAL ROUNDS, the FY2 asks an FY1, for an update on their mystery patient. He is a very young-looking physician with abundant chest hair sprouting from his scrubs' V-neck.

"A joyless day," he begins. "First, he tried to smuggle a knife into the CT scanner, and then, he freaked out during the scan. They couldn't complete it."

"Bad boy," the FY2 says to the patient, who looks up at her with cold eyes.

"The psych consultant stopped by, and without being able to communicate, wrote the world's most useless note."

"We had to check the box," the FY2 says. "What about the social workers?"

"Also non-productive. They said that without identification, they couldn't offer any placement suggestions. They said that the police have to keep trying to figure out who he is."

"You talked with them?"

"Yeah."

"What did you say?"

"That it was their job to liaise with the police."

"And?"

"And—I hope they do it."

"For fuck's sake," the FY2 says. "Williams will ream us out in the morning if we don't have a discharge plan."

"I've got nothing, boss," the FY1 says. "That's why they pay *you* the big money."

She laughs and asks if there's anything else.

"Oh yeah," he says. "The nurses told me they had to teach him how to use the bathroom today. He acted like he'd never seen a toilet before."

The FY2 rolls her eyes and says, "This just keeps getting better and better."

THE OLD ONE in the bed beside Mannu receives visitors in pale blue tunics who assist him from his bed onto a chair. Then, they begin to move one of his arms up in the air, to the side, in circles. All the while, he moans. The female demon places something in his hand and makes a fist.

They are going to strike the poor wretch, Mannu thinks.

The male demon notices he is staring and pulls a curtain.

The moaning continues, but he cannot see what tortures are being inflicted.

Mannu feels sorry for him. If he were in Nineveh, he would try to heal him with medicines and have the exorcists perform a ritual. But he is not in Nineveh and is no closer to helping Bel.

He closes his eyes and prays silently.

I am far from home, trapped in the underworld with cruel demons. May the gods protect Bel-ibni while I am gone. May they help me find a healer to teach me how to save her life.

THE NIGHT-SHIFT NURSES on the adult medicine ward gather around the nurses' station to take report from their late-shift colleagues.

"Good day off, Sarah?" the ward coordinator asks her colleague.

Sarah is a cheerful woman of Jamaican descent who replies, "Too good. When it's too good, it makes it tough to come back. Know what I mean?"

"I know exactly what you mean."

"Lots of new ones?" Sarah asks.

"Six," one of the staff nurses says.

"Mercy," Sarah says. "You'd better crack on if you ladies are going to get out of here."

The ward coordinator starts running the list, reviewing salient patient details. Then, she says, "Saved the best for last."

"Oh, yeah?" Sarah says.

"Room 612. Unknown male."

"Unknown, handsome, naked male," another nurse laughs.

"Do tell," Sarah says. "I'm all ears."

THE DEMONS HAVE LEFT the old man and have pulled the curtain open. He is back in his bed, sleeping.

Thank the gods, his ordeal is over, Mannu thinks.

Then, he notices something on the man's bedside table that makes his heart race. The only way he can know for sure is to get closer, so he climbs from his bed and creeps toward him.

When he is close enough to touch it, he exults, *Nabu, god of wisdom, you have heard my prayer! I know now what I must do!*

He snatches it from the old man's table and returns to the safety of his bed.

It is a lump of beautiful clay, as brown as the river clay in Nineveh, smooth and without grit. With practiced hands, he begins shaping it.

Surely, this is the answer. The demons do not understand my tongue, and I do not understand theirs. But all civilized beings understand writing. These may be demons, but unlike wild beasts or ignorant laborers, they possess strange and powerful abilities. They are nūru—cultured—and therefore, ṭupšarrūtu— literate.

When he has fashioned the clay into a smooth slab the size of his hand, he casts his gaze toward finding a stylus. He knows he will find no river reeds here, but there must be something else of use. Hiding the clay under his pillow, he cautiously prowls the room. Finding nothing suitable near the old man or his own side, he turns to the tiny chamber where his waste products are miraculously carried away in a whirlpool. There, on the white rectangle with silver spigots from which water flows on command, and under the silver tray affixed to the wall that reflects his image like a still pond, he sees something he had not noticed. It is a pouch that allows one to see inside without opening it. There is some kind of tool with a thin white handle and bristles, like the bristles of the *šahû*—the wild boar of the forest. Pulling at the pouch until it opens, he snaps off the bristle head and inspects the handle. It is neither wood nor metal, but it will do. He is happy. With some smoothing, it will work! He falls to his knees and begins polishing the handle against the hard floor tiles.

Before returning to his bed, he closes the door to the little room so he can work undetected, and with clay in one hand and stylus in the other, he begins to write.

SARAH BEGINS her vital signs rounds at eleven. A half-hour later, she enters Room 612, curious about the mystery patient. He is upright in bed, wide awake, and when he notices her, slips something under the covers.

"Well, hello there," she says exuberantly, flashing a wide smile. "My name is Nurse Sarah. I'm told you don't speak English. If that's right, you won't have any idea what I'm saying, isn't that so?"

The patient stares at her curiously.

"All right. We'll find other ways to communicate, won't we? Let me check your vitals," she says, wheeling the blood pressure machine.

He has been trained to stick his arm out, and Sarah rewards him with a nod and another bright smile.

"Good lad," she says, sliding the cuff over his arm. "The girls were right about you. You are a very fine specimen. You look as healthy as a horse, if you must know. They need to find out who you are and get you back to your loved ones. They must be frantic."

She finishes, and he withdraws his arm, staring mutely.

Sarah starts toward the stroke patient but pivots and says, "Look, I'm just going to ask. What were you hiding just now? We're only giving you plastic utensils after the nasty business in the CT scanner. You haven't gotten your hands on something dangerous again, have you?"

She snatches at his covers with feline swiftness and discovers the clay slab.

"What do we have here?" she asks. "Give us a look."

She is surprised when he willingly shows her what he was hiding. The clay's smooth surface is indented with neat rows of small symbols.

"Lord almighty. I have no idea what I'm looking at," she says. "Did you make that out of Mr. Murphy's physio clay?"

She hands it back but is again surprised when he gestures for her to keep it.

"All right, dearie," she says. "I'm sure it means something to you, but it's meaningless to me."

MANNU CLOSES his eyes in the dimmed light and reflects on his decision. Something about this last Nubian demon was reassuring. Perhaps it was her genuine smile or her gentle touch when she slid the strange armband over his elbow.

I pray to the gods that this one will convey my message to the healer I seek.

"I'M TAKING MY BREAK NOW," Sarah informs her colleagues.

She usually coordinates her breaks with her friend when they're both on duty, and she takes the lift to the pediatric ward, where all the nurses know her.

"She's already in the break room," one of them says.

Amrita is tucking into a Tupperware container of leftovers.

"Sorry. I was famished," she says.

"You needn't wait for me, luv," Sarah says, opening her container.

"What's yours?" Amrita asks.

"Shepard's pie. It's from Tesco. Don't laugh. Theirs is better than mine."

"I've had it," Amrita says. "It's good. Easy shift?"

"Yeah. No drama. Everyone's behaving, more or less. Oh, there's one strange bird, a bloke who was admitted day before yesterday, running around Piccadilly Circus buck naked. Doesn't speak a word of English, and the interpreters can't find a language he knows. No ID, of course, and the police don't have him in their fingerprints database. Strange, eh?"

"I'll say. What's the matter with him?"

"Nothing serious. Most everything's come back negative. Problem is, the social workers can't place him without knowing who he is."

"So, you're stuck with him?"

"Seems so."

"What's he like?"

"Super handsome. Swarthy complexion, Middle Eastern, by the looks of him. Ever see the old Omar Sharif films, like Lawrence of Arabia?"

"Nope."

Sarah Googles the movie and shows Amrita the picture.

"Oh yeah," Amrita says. "That's a good looker."

"He made something out of physio clay and gave it to me."

"Aww. He likes you," Amrita says.

"Want to see it?" Sarah asks, reaching into her smock.

Amrita's eyes light up.

"What?" Sarah asks. "You know what this is?"

"I've seen something like this before. At my friend's house. Can I take a picture?"

"Course you can."

KATE CURSES herself for not muting her phone before she turned in because she is awakened in the middle of the night by a WhatsApp ping and an illuminated screen. Getting a 2 a.m. text is unusual, so she feels compelled to grab the phone off its charger.

When she sees it's from Amrita, she immediately worries something is wrong, but it's nothing like that. It's a photo of a brown slab with the message, *What do you make of this?*

She clicks on the photo to enlarge it.

"What the fuck?" she yells at the top of her voice.

She shares a common wall with a neighbor and worries they will call the police.

CHAPTER TEN

Sin dismisses everyone from his chamber, save Kisir and Adad.

"The King must not hear of this," he says to Kisir.

"Surely, there is a danger in hiding something as consequential as this," the exorcist says.

"I have my reasons. Your realm is magic and demons and ghosts. My realm is protecting the throne and the empire." He spits out the next sentence like a viper spitting venom. "You must, and you *will* take my word on the importance of keeping this *sīru*." He pounds his table as he says secret.

Kisir maintains an outward composure, but his wavering voice belies something else.

"What will you tell the King about Mannu?"

"I will tell him that he knew his medicines were weak and his skills were small. He realized he could not save Bel-ibni, and fearing the wrath of the Great King, he fled the city. This, I will tell him."

Kisir began to bob his head. "Yes, yes—I see the merit."

"Of course you do," Sin says with unmasked contempt. "When the concubine dies, perhaps the King will not turn on the Chief Exorcist if his ire toward the Chief Physician burns as hot as a smelter."

"Yes, I see," Kisir says. "Yes."

"And here is a promise to you, Kisir-malik. If the King discovers the truth about Mannu's disappearance, I will inform him that you allowed one of your exorcists, Tukulti-Ninurta, to practice black magic, an act punishable by death or exile."

"He will not hear about Mannu from me," Kisir assures him. "I understand the delicate nature of the situation.

"Good. Now, take the tablet of Kalhu and the tablet written by Mannu. Make a faithful copies and give them to my man, Adad, but show no one else. Study them well. Make the potion they prescribe. Bring me the tablets and the potion by the morning."

"Do you intend to use this magic?" Kisir asks with frightened eyes.

"Do as I say, and do not question me further."

When Kisir has left, Sin pours two glasses of wine and beckons Adad to sit with him.

"Adad-ummi, you have been my obedient servant these many years."

Adad drinks his wine impassively.

"You have risked your life for me more than once," Sin continues. "Are you prepared to do so again?"

Adad utters the only acceptable word.

"This mission will require all your considerable skills. You may find yourself in an unknown land. You must not fail."

"I understand, Master."

"When Kisir brings you a copy of the tablets, commit the incantations to memory. If you fail to do so, you will not be able to return."

"My memory is perfect," Adad says. "How will I make the potion for the return journey?"

"Mannu will know. You will have to take it from him."

Adad says he understands and adds, "If I find Mannu-ki-Ashur—"

"Not if," Sin says. "When."

"When I find him, what so you want me to do?"

"He must not find a cure for Bel-ibni. I have promised the

Prince the concubine will not bear his father another heir. When you find Mannu, kill him."

Adad nods. "Will I go alone?"

"You will not be alone. It might be difficult to locate Mannu. You must travel with someone who knows him well—who knows his mind and doings and someone who knows how to fight."

"I was a soldier in my youth," Adad says.

"Yes, your youth. I want a younger man to accompany you. Bring Mannu's friend Ninurta-sharru to me."

"Very well, Master," Adad says, putting his alabaster goblet down.

"And this, too. Before you depart on your journey, kill the magician Tukulti-Ninurta and the physician Shulgi-eresh and throw their bodies into the river."

Ninurta knows Adad by sight; he has seen him at the side of the Chief Eunuch often. When the muscular Egyptian searches the apothecary and finds him in Mannu's room, Ninurta notices his sandals are stained with fresh blood.

"The Rab She Reshi wishes to see you," Adad says.

"Why?"

"It is not for me to say. He wishes to see you immediately."

Although he dislikes this harsh summons, he accompanies the hulking eunuch. As he waits in Sin's empty reception room, he feels undressed without the customary uniform of the palace guard commander.

Finally, Sin enters with Adad.

"There you are, Ninurta-sharru," Sin says. "How good of you to come."

"You summoned me," Ninurta says.

"Indeed I did," Sin says, taking his elaborate cushioned chair and leaving his visitor to stand. "Give him wine, Adad."

Ninurta takes the heavy goblet, considering whether it might be poisoned, an easy way to end his career permanently. He is still suffering the effects of his drunken binge. If pressed, he has an excuse not to drink it.

"Am I here to discuss my dismissal?" Ninurta asks.

"No," Sin says. "You are here because of Mannu-ki-Ashur. Your friend has disappeared. You are staying in his rooms. What do you know of his disappearance?"

Ninurta stiffens, but Mannu did not tell him details about his mission, so there are no confidences to betray.

"I only know he was going on a journey to look for a cure for the King's concubine, Bel-ibni. He did not tell me where he was going. I offered to accompany him, but he refused."

Sin seems delighted to hear this. "You and Mannu are good friends, are you not?"

"We were friends as children; we are friends still."

"We are concerned about him," Sin says soothingly. "We fear Mannu has gone somewhere dangerous. We are anxious for him to return with a cure for the good lady. We want you to find him and help him return safely."

"I would gladly accompany Mannu on his journey, but alas, he did not tell me his destination."

"We know where he is," Sin says.

"Tell me," Ninurta blurts, "and I will ready my horse."

"You must wait until morning," Sin says. "You will stay the night in my quarters, readying yourself with good food and good rest. You will speak to no one but Adad, who will go on this journey with you."

"As you wish. Will you not tell me where Mannu is?"

"All will be revealed in the morning," Sin says, rising and telling Adad to show Ninurta to his room. "And know this, Ninurta. If you succeed in this mission, I will reinstate you as the commander of the palace guard and strike any disgraces from your otherwise fine record of service to the King. Adad, see me when the former commander is settled."

In time, Adad returns, informing Sin that Ninurta has sustenance and a bed and that his door will be guarded.

"Very good," Sin says. "I have one more instruction."

"I am listening, Master."

"When you find Mannu and kill him, kill Ninurta too. Nineveh will be a better place without that *šinuhtu*."

THE DAWN CAME GENTLY, but soon, the city baked in harsh sunlight.

Kisir slept little that night. It took him until dusk to find the plants he needed and many hours more to brew the leaves into a potion. Routine tasks for a physician were difficult for an exorcist unaccustomed to such work. As he makes his way to the chief eunuch this morning, he prays he has undertaken all the steps stipulated in the Kalhu tablet in the correct sequence and manner.

Adad also had a sleepless night. He spent all available hours chanting the incantations in a low singsong, checking his memory against the text.

Even while performing his morning ablutions, his lips are moving. Before leaving his room, he sharpens his sheath knife.

Ninurta slept soundly and wakes with a ravenous appetite. A servant delivers a tray of food and empties his chamber pot. He only learns his door has been guarded when he tries to leave to feed and bridle his horse.

"You may not leave until Adad-ummi comes for you," the eunuch guard says.

"I need my horse readied," Ninurta says.

The eunuch repeats himself and pushes the door shut.

ONLY LATER, in Sin's private courtyard, does Ninurta learn the truth of his journey. He sees Adad standing under a tree, eyes closed, moving his lips. He watches as the chief exorcist lays three objects onto the grass in the shape of a triangle—a blank clay tablet, a sprig of an herb, and a jug of what seems to be no more than water.

When Kisir places two stoppered glass vials at the center of the triangle, Ninurta says, "I do not understand what is happening.

Where are our horses? Where are our provisions? It seems you are preparing a ritual, not a journey."

"A ritual that becomes a journey," Sin says. "You will follow the same path that Mannu undertook. He did not travel by horseback or chariot. He traveled by means of magic. Black magic. Do the words frighten you, Ninurta-sharru?"

"Nothing frightens me," Ninurta says defensively, hardening his lips.

"Good, because you will need the bravery of a great warrior. Mannu has traveled on the circle of time to find a healer to teach him how to cure Bel-ibni. He did this without my knowledge or that of the Chief Exorcist. We do not know where he has gone. It was foolhardy for him to go alone, so we must send help. Only by repeating the ritual precisely as Mannu did can you hope to find him. Adad knows the incantations. The talismans on the grass are offerings. The vials at the center contain the potion you must drink at the final moment. Beyond that, we can provide no instructions. You and Adad must use all your cunning and strengths to find Mannu and help him succeed. Do you understand?"

"I understand, Chief Eunuch," Ninurta says, snapping to military attention.

Kisir says, "All is ready. Adad-ummi and Ninurta-sharru proceed to the center of the triangle. Adad, you may begin."

The two travelers stand beside one another, and Adad begins to chant in a sweet voice that seems to surprise Kisir and Ninurta, but Sin has heard him sing while plucking the lute.

O Nabu, scribe of the heavens, keeper of the tablets of destiny,
You who know the fate of all things, present and future,
Open the gates of time for your humble servant.
Lend me the wisdom of what is yet to be written,
The knowledge inscribed in future stars.
Inscribe upon my mind the words of healers not yet born,
And guide my hands to save those who suffer.
By your hand, let the circle of time flow backward and forward.
And in this sacred circle, let the past and future converge.

Kisir follows along, reading the Kalhu tablet as Adad chants. He hears him make a mistake. Instead of saying, *By your hand, may the threads of fate be woven anew,* he says, *By your hand, may the threads of fate be woven together.* Kisir is about to intervene when Adad twists his face in disgust and makes the correction himself.

He comes to the final verse.

Seven are the stars that guard the heavens,
Seven are the gates that guard the unknown,
Seven are the learned healers.
By their hands and mine, may time bend,
And may I return with the cure.
I will pass through the seventh gate and return with the light of knowledge.

Adad sighs in relief that he has reached the end and nudges Ninurta to pick up one of the vials.

The two men put vials to their lips and drain the green liquid, and in the blink of an eye, they are gone.

Giddy with excitement, Sin charges into the triangle, waving his arms about.

"Did your eyes see what mine have seen, Chief Exorcist? They have disappeared! The magic worked!"

Kisir is on his knees, tears streaming into his beard.

"I have never witnessed a spell so powerful," he cries. "I have devoted my whole life to the magical arts, and only now do I realize how weak my powers have been."

"Yes, but this is black magic, Chief Exorcist," Sin says. "Lest you be tempted to employ it, I would have no choice but to sentence you to death."

Adad and Ninurta are hard men who would never scream, but their terror rises in their throats. They turn in a tight circle, trying to comprehend what their senses are feeding their brains. It is night, but a strange round object atop a high pole illuminates this deserted alleyway. It is brighter than any torch they have ever seen, but no flame is visible. There are many alleys in Nineveh—but none look like this, for the buildings on both sides are made of small rectangular red stones rising to great heights. And all have large windows—too numerous to fathom—made of clear glass, a precious material in Nineveh. They freeze at an unearthly sound and turn to see something that makes their blood run cold. An enormous beast on thick black wheels rumbles past on a road perpendicular to the alley. It stops, and two demons in unfamiliar garb emerge. They wheel large black and blue boxes that the beast lifts high, ingesting their contents before putting them down.

"We must hide," Adad says.

When they have partially concealed themselves in a shallow doorway, Ninurta says, "We have no clothes."

"I see this," Adad hisses. "My knife, too, is gone."

"What is this infernal place?" Ninurta says. "Did your spell miss its mark? Have we arrived in the underworld?"

"I recited the spell as it was written," Adad says.

"Quiet!" Ninurta whispers. "Footsteps."

Two YOUNG MEN in jeans and hoodies strut down Wardour Street and turn left onto Peter Street. At three in the morning, this part of Soho is dead, and they like it that way.

Speaking in Albanian, the one called Arber says to Besian, "Where's he supposed to be?"

"Just down here. Berwick Street Market."

"He'd better have the shit."

"He's good. You'll see."

Suddenly, they stop and tense their muscles. Two men are lurking in the narrow entrance to a closed burger restaurant.

"What the fuck?" Arber, the jittery one says.

They feel for the flick knives in their jeans, on high alert because of the cylinders of rolled fifty-pound notes in their pockets.

A few more steps, and they see the crouching men are naked.

"Fucking pervs," Besian says loudly in English. "Go fuck off somewhere else."

The men stand. One is heavyset, with big slabs of muscle, and the other is wiry, with an athlete's body.

"Get a fucking room, mate," Arber says in English.

The men serve up cold stares.

"I don't like this," Besian says in Albanian, pulling his knife. "They look like Turks. I think the Turks are trying to fuck us."

Arber draws his knife, too. "Weird fucking beard on that one," he says.

"You got five seconds to clear the fuck off," Besian threatens in English, waving his knife in a wristy circle.

"WHAT ARE THEY?" Ninurta asks. "Their skin is pale and bloodless. And what of these uniforms?"

"I do not know what they are, but they brandish knives," Adad says. "We must take their clothes and weapons."

"Will they fight like men or demons?" Ninurta says.

"There is only one way to know," Adad says, folding his hands into claws.

The larger of the two demons babbles at them in a strange tongue and moves aggressively toward them.

Soldiers in the Assyrian army train extensively in wrestling and grappling should they lose their weapons in combat. Ninurta is younger, and his skills fresher, but Adad is also formidable. Although Ninurta sustains a forearm slash, disarming the two demons proves surprisingly easy. With precise, swift maneuvers, he and Adad have their opponents in chokeholds and feel the fight drain from their bodies.

"Should we end their lives?" Ninurta pants.

Adad grunts, signaling he is unsure. He says, "These are weak demons. Perhaps we should not anger the stronger ones by slaying their brethren. Let us leave them close to death."

Hearing this, Ninurta releases his hold and lets his being slip to the hard ground.

"Take the smaller one's clothes," Adad says. "Hurry."

It takes trial and error to figure out how to don the strange apparel and undergarments. Instead of putting them on, Ninurta wraps his demon's undergarment around his bleeding arm and slides his legs awkwardly into the stiff blue leggings. When dressed, they retrieve the knives, finding in amazement that they fold into handles made of a substance other than wood or metal. Then, they explore the bulging pouches in the leggings.

Ninurta holds out a thick cylinder of some unknown material. "What is this?"

Adad shakes his head and shows Ninurta a similar cylinder. They also find shiny, thin rectangles of smooth metal and glass that frighten them because they glow when touched and thin, red and blue objects of an unknown material.

"What magic is this?" Ninurta murmurs, throwing his glowing rectangle down.

"Come," Adad says. "We must find Mannu-ki-Ashur. The gods willing, he is not far away."

They have only gone a short distance when a solitary figure steps from the shadows of a portico into the magical light.

In an instant, Ninurta is transfixed, for this is the most beautiful being he has ever seen. It is male, tall, and slender, with the blackest of black skin—surely a Nubian of some sort. Its face seems chiseled of flawless black alabaster, with fine, pleasing features, especially a full mouth and wide, welcoming eyes. It suddenly taps a long, graceful finger against its left arm.

Ninurta understands! The being is communicating with him, for his left arm is bleeding, soaking through the white fabric of his hooded outer garment. When Adad withdraws his knife, Ninurta begs him to put it back.

"I think it means us no harm," he says.

～

IT IS a slow night with few punters about, and Chinedu Okoro hasn't turned a trick since midnight. He is close to giving up and heading home when he witnesses the strangest street fight ever. Usually, he would keep himself hidden and out of trouble, but his inner voice tells him he is not in danger.

Stepping from the alcove of a comic book store, he says, "You are bleeding."

The handsome young man grasps his arm and nods his head.

"I saw what you did, and I am cool with it. I will not call the police. I hate these Albanians and their drugs. Why were you naked? You don't have to say. I thought I had seen everything in Soho, but now, I truly have."

The two men stare at him mutely.

Chinedu asks, "Do you speak English?" When they don't reply, he says, "Okay, I understand. Do not worry."

He knows illegal immigrants when he sees them. He had been a refugee from Nigeria who had to learn the ropes on his own. At least he knew English when he came. These men seem lost in every way.

"You're from Syria, I'll wager," he says. "Or Afghanistan. I think maybe mules took your money and left you stranded with nothing, not even the clothes on your backs."

He beckons them with a crooked finger.

"Come with me," he says. "I will fix your arm." He pantomimes the bandaging of the bleeding appendage. "You do not want to stay here. Those fuckers are still breathing. You must go before they wake up and call their friends. They are dangerous men."

"HE WANTS US TO FOLLOW HIM," Ninurta says.

"Do you think he knows where Mannu is?" Adad asks.

Ninurta cannot take his eyes off this beautiful black face. "I do not know, but in my heart, I feel he is good."

CHAPTER ELEVEN

AMRITA'S TWELVE-HOUR SHIFT HAS BEEN OVER FOR AN HOUR, BUT she has agreed to wait for Kate to help her get onto the wards before the official visiting time. Kate called her twice between two and six, so she knows her friend hasn't slept much.

They meet just past eight at the hospital cafeteria, where Kate buys a tea and leans over the table.

"This is crazy," Kate says breathlessly. "Can I see it?"

Kate buries her face in the clay tablet. She has given countless cuneiform demonstrations to students of every age and has a series of YouTube videos on the subject. She has never seen modern cuneiform rendered so well.

"Did anyone see him do this?" she asks.

"I don't think so. He just gave it to one of his nurses."

"Where did he get the clay?"

"His roommate's a stroke patient. It's physio clay for hand strength. He must've taken it."

"What did he use for a stylus?"

"No clue. I said I'd try, but I never made it to his floor. I got busy with my patients."

Kate isn't hiding her excitement. "Look at it," she exudes. "The

122

characters are flawless. The grammar and syntax are perfect. The lines are perfectly parallel. It's—"

"Perfect?" Amrita says.

Kate giggles. "I didn't sleep. Sorry. I get this way. I can't wait to meet him."

"Wait no longer. Drink up. And keep the clay."

At the lift, Kate asks, "You say they tried different interpreters?"

"That's what I was told. We don't have his name or any identifying info."

"I know his name," Kate said.

"How?"

"He wrote it on the tablet. He says it's Mannu-ki-Ashur."

The lift arrives, and they start up.

"What else does it say?"

The lift is full, and Kate has to whisper. "That he's a physician from Nineveh seeking a cure for his patient."

"Where's Nineveh?"

"In Iraq."

"Well, that's progress," Amrita says brightly.

"Not really," Kate says. "Nineveh hasn't existed for over two and a half thousand years."

Amrita stops at the ward coordinator's workstation and tells her she wants to see the mystery patient.

"May I ask why?"

"My friend, Kate, thinks she might be able to communicate with him."

The no-nonsense coordinator says, "Have at it, then. We'd love to shift him. His bed is needed."

The door to Room 612 is partially open, and as Kate follows Amrita inside, she is lightheaded from anticipation. It's a double room and the unknown patient is in the bed closest to the door. She sees a figure, motionless and reclining under the sheets. She hopes he is asleep, so she might have a moment to study him unselfconsciously.

His beard, she thinks. *His beard! And his hair!*

His squared-off beard, glistening with an oily product, rests full and black on his muscular chest. It looks like it had once been tightly curled in neat horizontal rows, but the curls have relaxed messily. His shoulder-length, ink-black hair also has cascading rows of sagging curls.

She knows this kind of archaic styling. She has seen it on count-less Assyrian statues, but never—outside of films—in real life. She dreams of men who look like him. She blinks in confusion, and at that moment, he opens his eyes and turns his head.

She is startled by his swarthy, good looks and his piercing eyes, so dark they are almost black. They bore into her. She intensity of the gaze scares and attracts her at the same time.

She composes herself, steps closer, and says, "Hello. My name is Kate Mayne. I'm a professor at the Institute of Archaeology. I am pleased to meet you."

The man stares back, saying nothing.

"You are Mannu-ki-Ashur?"

Those dark eyes open wider, seemingly in recognition of his name.

Kate holds up the clay tablet, and he responds by straightening his back and nodding vigorously. Then, he begins speaking in the guttural language that has befuddled the translators.

"*Ia Mannu-ki-Ashur, rab asû ša Ninua. Mātāka lā taparras? Ūmu līmur-rāk. Epēšu anta utukku amēlu?*"

Kate feels her knees buckle. The floor comes up fast.

"Kate!" Amrita shouts. "Are you okay?"

MANNU SWINGS his legs over the bed. For a moment, he forgets he is wearing a short, wholly unsuitable garment. The female being who spoke his name has collapsed onto the floor, and as a healer, his instinct is to come to her aid. He kneels and reaches for her hand.

It is warm, a good sign.

The other female, who wears the familiar blue uniform of this building's inhabitants, holds the stricken woman's head and speaks to her in their native tongue. He watches her eyes flutter open. What eyes they are! The deepest blue, like the finest lapis lazuli gemstones. And what a rare face—as pale as the full moon, with small, delicate features like a child's. The females of this land do not cover their bodies or heads in public places, and though he is a physician who has seen much, he has been shocked by the spectacle. Because she has no scarf or veil, he can see her long hair flowing onto the floor —hair that surely is the work of magic because it is an impossibility, as bright and yellow as the midday sun. She moans. Her blue eyes search the room and find him. She is surely a demon—the most beautiful demon he has ever seen in this strange, horrible land, but strangely, for the first time since his arrival, he is not afraid.

～

"WHAT HAPPENED?" Kate mumbles.

Amrita tells her she fainted and asks if she's eaten today.

"I don't think so."

Kate realizes her hand is enveloped by his. She doesn't immediately pull away but has to when Amrita helps her to her feet. The patient seems embarrassed by his skimpy hospital gown and climbs back into his bed to cover himself.

"If you want to stay, I'll get you a chair and a glass of juice," Amrita says.

Kate thinks that's a good idea and follows Amrita into the corridor to compose herself.

"Did you understand what he said?" Amrita asks.

"It was in Akkadian."

"Your dead language?"

"Apparently not as dead as I thought. He said, My name is Mannu-ki-Ashur, chief physician of Nineveh. Can you speak my language? Please tell me if you are a demon or a person."

Amrita's expression says it all, but she says it anyway. "Okay. This guy is seriously off his nut."

"Yeah," Kate says, "but how many nuts speak Akkadian?"

"There's always a first for everything," Amrita says. "I'll be right back."

She returns with a chair from the nursing station and a juice box, which Kate thirstily sucks down, trying to process what she has seen and heard.

"So, how many people speak Akkadian nowadays?" Amrita asks.

"Fluently? Conversationally? Maybe half a dozen of us in the world. There used to be a few more, but they died off. Our lot—Assyriologists—learn the language to read cuneiform texts. The few of us obsessive enough to teach ourselves how to speak it are kind of nutty. We amuse ourselves by having conversations at the bar during conferences. The more wine, the better it goes. We know who we are—it's a small group. This gentleman isn't in it."

Amrita shakes her head and says, "Ready to go back?"

The patient is back in bed, staring as she enters. Amrita pulls the chair up and says she'll wait outside. Kate sits, folding her hands over her lap. She can't help notice the furtive glances at her bare legs; she wishes she hadn't worn a dress.

She speaks to him in Akkadian.

"I speak Akkadian," she says, using the ancient name for the language, *Akkadû*. "My name is Kate Mayne. I am a person. I am not a demon. Please tell me about yourself. Where are you from? How did you learn to speak *Akkadû*?"

The patient runs his fingers through his thick hair, further disrupting the curls. He delivers his answer in a tone of unconcealed exasperation.

"I have spoken my name. I am Mannu-ki-Ashur. I am a physician. I am from Nineveh. All people in my kingdom speak *Akkadû*. I beg of you; prove you are not a demon."

Kate furrows her brow. The two of them stare at one another, both incredulous, both fearful, both riveted by an elemental attraction. Her underarms are moist. She tries to concentrate on the task at hand. It's hard work finding the words and grammatical constructs to fuel a genuine conversation. The term he used for *prove* was a legalistic one—*tērtu*, generally referring to giving evidence in a court.

"How can I prove this?" she asks.

Mannu considers the question and responds, "Demons do not bleed."

Kate feels she is getting tangled in this man's psychosis, but she decides to go along with it for now. She removes a notebook from her bag, opens it, and, wincing, drags a page over a finger. She holds it up to show the paper cut.

Mannu's reaction is immediate and profound. He begins to weep. Kate is stunned and watches his face, waiting for what will happen next.

"I believed I was in the underworld," he says when he gains composure. "Is everyone here a person?"

"We are all—" She struggles to remember the right word. It comes to her: *awīlūtu*, another legalistic term. "Human beings."

Words tumble from his mouth. The language is harsh and guttural, but Kate recognizes the plaintiveness.

"I am overjoyed to hear this. However, please tell me where I am. What is this place?"

He seems so genuine in his bewilderment that Kate answers nonjudgmentally. "This is London, England."

He repeats the name awkwardly and phonetically. "Lon-don. Ing Lan. I do not know this place."

"You have never heard of London?"

He shakes his head. "How far is it from my home of Nineveh? How many leagues?"

She is taken aback by his use of *parsāti*—leagues—the ancient measurement of the distance a person could travel in an hour— about four to five miles.

Rather than playing that game, she replies, "Nineveh does not exist. It was destroyed over twenty-five hundred years ago."

Mannu lets his head fall back to the pillow. She can make out his mumbling.

"Mighty Ashur, please help me. I do not understand what is happening to me."

Kate tires of his charade and demands to know the truth.

"Please tell me how you traveled to London. We must know who you are and how to contact your family."

Mannu turns to her and says, "Tukulti-Ninurta taught me the forbidden magic of the ancients. I uttered the spells and drank the potion. I beseeched the gods to send me on the circle of time to a place where I could learn how to heal Bel-ibni, concubine to the King, who carries his heir. The magic took me here. Shamefully, I arrived without clothing."

It's against her better judgment to keep fueling his fantasy, but she asks anyway. "Which king?"

"King Ashurbanipal," he answers.

She knows how to put an end to his farce. Assyrians tracked years by a few methods. One was the length of time a monarch reigned. Another was by the *limmu*, or the kingdom's high official for whom the year was named.

"You say you are from Nineveh in the time of King Ashurbanipal," she says. "Tell me the year you come from by length of the King's rule, and by its *limmu*."

The man answers. "*Šattu ušu illimu ša Ashurbanipal šarru rabû. Šattu ša Bēl-šakin-ṭēmi limmu.*"

Kate is wrong-footed by his instant response. She can't work out the internal consistency between the two methods in her head. She feels his eyes on her as she pulls out her phone to looks up the data.

I am from the twenty-ninth year of Ashurbanipal, the great king.

She does the math: 640 BCE.

She finds a table of *limmus* on her phone. *I am from the year of Bēl-šakin-ṭēmi—the lord who establishes justice.*

Her memory is jogged. The *limmus* for the latter years of Ashurbanipal's rule haven't survived. He could have thrown out any name without fear of being exposed as a fraud.

Kate abruptly stands, angry at herself for humoring his twisted tale.

"I do not like the game you are playing," she scolds. "You are a scholar. Only scholars know Akkadian. I believe you are from Iraq or perhaps Syria. If that is true, you studied with either Professor Ammar Al-Dulaimi or Professor Ziad Al-Assad. I am surprised I do not recognize you because I know all the Assyrian scholars in the world. I want to hear the truth!"

He buries his face in his palms and says, "I do not know these people or places. I am Mannu-ki-Ashur, physician of Nineveh. The gods know this is the truth."

She fishes in her bag for a business card. He inspects it blankly.

"If you decide to speak the truth, call me," she says.

"I do not know what this is," he says, waving the card. "I always speak the truth—" He ends by calling her *mārtu ṣahri qanê*, woman with bright hair.

"My name is Professor Kate Mayne," she says curtly. Then she repeats herself in Arabic, *If you decide to speak the truth, call me*, for surely he also speaks Arabic.

"I do not understand this tongue," he says.

"Fine," she snaps in English. "I'm done here."

The moment she exits his room, she feels a pang of absence, bewitched by the way he looked and the secret language he spoke. But she has her pride. She won't let him play her for a fool.

CHAPTER TWELVE

CHINEDU IS A BIG TALKER. EVEN THOUGH HE KNOWS HIS TWO NEW friends don't understand him, he keeps up a constant stream of one-sided conversation.

"The Underground doesn't run at this hour," he says, pulling out his phone. "I'll book an Uber. Sometimes, they can be scarce on a weeknight—okay, very nice. Here's one, three minutes away. We'll get you sorted, mate. Keep the pressure on that cut."

The Uber pulls up to them on Brewer Street. The driver seems cautious about picking up rides in Soho in the middle of the night and peers at them through an open window.

"Aw, mate. You're bleeding, aren't you? I can't have you bleeding in my car."

"My friend was involved in a minor scuffle," Chinedu says. "He will not get any blood in your car. I will add twenty in cash over the tip for the trouble, all right?"

"Yeah, sod it. Get in."

Chinedu opens the rear door, but the refugees—as he thinks of them—are motionless and bug-eyed, nattering to each other in their language.

"Come on. In you go," Chinedu says.

Ninurta and Adad freeze in terror.

"He wants us to enter inside the beast!" Adad says. "What if it eats us?"

"I think the Nubian means us no harm," Ninurta says.

"If only we can make him understand us, he can help us find Mannu," Adad says.

"We will find a way," Ninurta says.

Ninurta decides to enter first. He holds his breath, ready for the worst, and climbs onto a padded bench.

"I am not harmed," he calls out to Adad.

The Egyptian follows him and looks around in bewilderment.

"Can we be sure we are not dead?" he asks.

"I am bleeding," Ninurta says. "Dead men do not bleed."

Chinedu gets in next to the driver who checks in his mirror and says, "You got to put your belts on, mates."

"They do not speak English," Chinedu says. "I will help them."

He opens the door next to the handsome one and, talking away, buckles the belt around him.

"Don't look so scared! You do not have seatbelts in your country? I will do your friend's, too." He lifts the man's right hand and squeezes it around his bloody arm. "Keep the pressure," he says.

He can see the larger man's petrified face when he opens the other door.

"Shhh. Shhh. You will be fine. It is just a seatbelt. There is nothing to be scared of big man."

The driver leans over the seat, "You fellows are giving off bad vibes, to be honest. You're not illegals, are you? I can't stomach 'em. Can't be aiding and abetting, if you know what I mean?"

"No illegals here," Chinedu says cheerfully. "Just some gents on a late-night pub crawl who ran out of pubs."

~

"WE ARE MOVING!" Adad whispers. "I cannot look."

But Ninurta keeps his eyes open, spellbound by the unfathomable sights. Scattered demons roam the dark streets, beasts on wheels, like their own, move along at frightening speeds, buildings soar toward the heavens, and magical lights of every color pierce the blackness of night.

He thinks, *If we find my brilliant friend, Mannu, he will explain these miracles, for they are beyond the comprehension of a poor soldier.*

~

THE UBER PULLS UP to a row of Victorian terraced houses on Crowndale Road, and Chinedu says, "Welcome to Camden!"

He slips the driver a twenty and tells him he's getting five stars, but the fellow is moody and wants to check the seat for blood.

Chinedu has to unbuckle the passengers, who exit, looking shell-shocked.

"See? No blood," Chinedu says. "We are good?"

The driver swears under his breath and takes off.

"Come and see my castle," Chinedu says.

His studio flat on the second floor is comically basic. The main room has a bed that takes up most of the space with a ratty sofa pressed against it. The rug is a bath mat and a small TV stands on an old suitcase. The kitchen is not much larger than the bed, but the bathroom has an incongruously generous tub. Since there is no closet, all of Chinedu's clothes are on a coat tree or in cardboard boxes.

The visitors stand on the bathmat, hollow-eyed.

"I know, I know," Chinedu says, peeling off his leather jacket. "It is small, and the rent is crazy for what it is, but Camden is quite central. Once you get to know the city, you will see how expensive London is. Before we do another thing, let me tend to your arm. Remove your sweatshirt." When nothing happens, he says, "I will help you."

The man lets Chinedu remove the outergarment and the bloody underpants tied around his upper arm.

"It is not as bad as I thought," Chinedu says. "Let me get my first aid box."

He returns with disinfectant and a bandage roll and washes and wraps the wound.

"That disinfectant had to sting!" he says. "You did not even flinch. You are a tough fellow. Put this back on." He pats the mattress. "You can sit on the bed. Now, let us move on to a very important subject. I think you have the Albanian's cash. Sharing is caring, you know. Let us have a look."

He points to his pockets; when that doesn't register, he taps on theirs.

Ninurta understands and hands over the contents of his pockets. He says something to his companion, who does the same.

Chinedu sits on his sofa and whistles a long, low note.

"Those boys were open for business. God almighty!"

Removing the rubber band from one of the cash rolls, he peels off bills, one at a time, counting out loud. It takes a long, sweet time to finish making a messy pile.

"Thirty grand!" he exclaims. "And the other one is the same size. Sixty thousand pounds! You boys hit the jackpot tonight. We do not have to worry about the Albanians going to the police. What would they say? Bad men robbed us of the money we were going to use for drugs? Here is what I propose. You can stay here for now. I will teach you how to go about things. You keep one roll. I will keep the other one. Okay? Deal? Let us shake on it."

He extends his hand, and when they do not respond, he grasps theirs and gives them a shake.

"There. We have settled it. What else do you have? Ah, cash cards. Not good for us. We will cut them up. And this phone is very bad. They can track it. I will remove the SIM card, and we will be safe. Now, who is hungry?"

~

133

Adad and Ninurta are cross-legged on the floor, contemplating the food the Nubian has produced. They have many questions and no answers.

Ninurta puts a finger onto the heaping bowl of Nigerian Joloff Rice, which the Nubian prepared in his cooking room.

"It is hot! I looked in there. There was no cooking fire."

"More magic," Adad says. "I do not see familiar foods. What is this white food? What food is red?"

Ninurta pokes the mound and says, "I do not know, but look at this. It could be the meat of a chicken. I will try it."

He picks up a small portion of peppery stew with his fingers, prompting the Nubian to laugh at him and wave a silver implement. He shows them how he uses it to shovel food into his mouth.

"They do not eat with their hands?" Adad asks.

Ninurta samples the exotic fare and chews it, and his mouth and tongue begin to burn. All he can do is open wide and breathe rapidly to cool it down.

His distress triggers more laughter from the Nubian, who races to his cooking room and returns with water vessels.

Ninurta gulps it and breathes easier.

"Were you poisoned?" Adad asks angrily.

"I do not believe so," Ninurta says. "Look how the Nubian consumes large quantities. It made my mouth burn, but it was not from the heat of the food. There is another reason I do not understand."

Ninurta reaches for the stew, this time with one of the silver implements that resemble small bowls with handles.

"You are having more?" Adad asks.

Ninurta smiles. "Despite the pain, I enjoy the way it tastes."

Chinedu is having a fine time of it. God has blessed him with a fortune, and his mind is spinning with ideas. Some of the money will go to his family back home. Maybe he will throw out the furniture the last tenant left behind and buy new things. A Scooter would

THE PHYSICIAN OF NINEVEH

make his life better. Maybe he will take a break from street hustling and take a cookery course. Hustling is dangerous work—if it's not the robberies and beatings, it's the diseases. He dreams of becoming a chef—clean and respectful work.

He finds the naïve refugees amusing. The big fellow with hard eyes worries him, but the young, handsome one with twinkling eyes is a charmer. It's always the eyes—windows into the soul, his grandmother always said. You can know a person from their eyes.

He springs up and returns with three bottles of beer.

"I was waiting for them to get cold," he says, continuing his running monologue. "This is Harp Lager. It is very popular in Nigeria. It is more expensive than some beers, but it is the taste of home. See what you think. Also, it will help with the spice."

Both refugees seem startled by the cold bottles and don't know what to do with them.

"The Brits like their beer in a glass, but we drink it from the bottle back home. See?"

Chinedu glugs from the amber bottle and finishes with a loud *Ahhh.*

The men look to each other for support, do likewise, and then chatter in recognition, clearly relishing the taste. Chinedu is certain of this because both men quickly drain their bottles.

"I have thirty-thousand reasons to get you gentlemen another beer."

After a while, little stew remains, and all the beer is gone. Even the big man filled his belly, grimacing at every swallow.

Chinedu takes to the sofa and points to his chest emphatically. "Chinedu," he says. "My name is Chinedu. Chin-e-du." Pointing to the younger man, he asks, "What is your name?"

He deals with the utter lack of comprehension by standing over him and repeating the exercise, saying "Chinedu" with each chest tap of his own chest and asking for the man's name with each tap of his.

The dam breaks. The young man opens his eyes wide in recognition and says, "Ninurta! *Šumī-ia Ninurta!*"

Chinedu does a little dance, shouting Ninurta with each stomp.

135

Pointing, he says, "Okay, big fellow. What is your name?"

Ninurta smiles and obliges. "Adad. *Šum-šu Adad.*"

Ninurta and Adad confer, and Adad says, "*Šumī-ia Adad.*"

Chinedu continues his romp around the tiny studio. "Ninurta! Adad! Adad! Ninurta!" then delights them by saying, "*Šumī-ia Chinedu!* My friends, this is our first conversation!"

~

AFTER A GIDDY SESSION of naming things (beer—*šikaru*, bowl—*mīšānu*, bed—*ēru*), Chinedu collapses in fatigue.

"It is time for bed," he says. "I will take the sofa. You may share the bed."

He pantomimes the action by pointing and using their names, and they seem to understand.

"Who wants to use the toilet first?" he asks, dragging them to see the facilities. Reacting to their looks of confusion, he says, "You cannot tell me you do not have toilets and baths where you come from. All right, here are the basics. This is the sink. Sink."

When he turns the tap, Ninurta and Adad flee the room and must be persuaded to return.

Ninurta puts his hand under the stream and says, "*Mû?*"

"Yes, *mû!*" Chinedu says. "Water! See? You can wash your face. You can drink from it."

Ninurta drinks first, then encourages Adad to try. Both are amazed.

Chinedu climbs into the empty bathtub and says, "And here is where you wash yourself," pantomiming scrubbing. Hopping out, he inserts the drain stopper, turns on the tap, and says, "*Mû!*"

This demonstration precipitates an animated discussion in their language.

"And this is the most important of all—the toilet."

He opens the lid, and they peer inside.

"*Annû mû?*" Ninurta asks.

Chinedu makes exaggerated nods, attempting to teach the word yes, and says, "Yes. It is *mû*—water."

There is more chattering.

"Now, how in God's name can I explain to you how to use a toilet? It is beyond belief that you have never seen one. Okay, we are all men here. I will demonstrate."

With that, he unzips his fly, pulls his penis out, and urinates into the bowl. When done, he pulls the flush lever.

The whirlpool sends them fleeing again, chattering in alarm.

Herding them back, Chinedu lowers the seat and says, "And this is how you defecate." He sits, clothed, and simulates the act by grunting, smiling, pulling at the toilet paper roll, and flushing again. "You see?"

Ninurta understands and urgently fumbles at his stiff leggings. When he donned the jeans in the alley, he secured them, trial and error, by tugging at the zipper, but he didn't understand the button. Now, when he unzips, the jeans slip to his ankles, exposing his buttocks. Unembarrassed, he urinates into the bowl and pulls the lever, laughing as his urine disappears.

"My goodness! You are very athletic," Chinedu says admiringly.

Adad decides to go next and, with Ninurta's help working the zipper, drops his jeans.

Chinedu recoils in horror. "Oh my God! You poor man! They chopped off your cock and balls! I can see why you are fleeing from those beasts."

Ninurta understands his reaction and says, "*Ša rēši*," while making a cutting gesture.

"Eunuch?" Chinedu says. "They turned that poor man into a eunuch? I thought conditions were harsh in my country. You had it much worse. Here, Adad, let me put the seat down and give you some privacy."

~

Later, lying side-by-side on this soft bed, Adad and Ninurta listen to Chinedu's soft snoring.

"This is a strange and terrifying land," Adad whispers. "I cannot bear to look through these windows. Who lies on a bed in the sky like birds in a nest?"

"Yes, it is beyond belief," Ninurta says. "Yet, we are fortunate this Nubian happened upon us. I am certain Chinedu is a man. He cannot be a demon. Demons do not eat and drink and perform bodily functions."

Adad grunts in agreement.

"More than that, Chinedu is a good man," Ninurta says. "He is helping us."

"We need his help finding Mannu," Adad says. "We have learned a number of his words, and he has learned a number of ours, but they are insufficient to communicate our needs."

"We will find a way to make him understand," Ninurta says. "I pray to the gods Mannu has found a good man like Chinedu to help him."

CHAPTER THIRTEEN

KATE LAYS HER HEAD ON HER DESK, HOPING FOR AN HOUR'S SLEEP before a scheduled dissertation meeting with one of her grad students. It's the only thing on her calendar, and afterward, she plans to slink back to Tottenham and crawl into bed.

But she can't get the handsome fraudster out of her thoughts. *What's the purpose of his elaborate ruse?*

Or maybe it's something else. Somewhere, someone might be searching for a missing Assyriologist suffering from a mental breakdown or some sort of amnesia. Should she put out a group email to her academic contact list?

She feels herself drifting off when there is rapping on her door.

She groans and says, "Come in."

Wilson Banning's head appears, followed by the rest of him. She is never in the mood for Wilson, but today it's especially irritating. She cringes at the sight of his too-tight jeans, cowboy boots, and rakish scarf loosely draped around his neck.

She thinks, *What have I done to deserve this walking affectation?*

"Hello, Mayne," he says.

For some reason, he has started, rather preciously, calling her by her last name. Kate believes reciprocating would send the wrong signal.

"Hello, Wilson."

"Busy calendar today?" he asks hopefully. "I was wondering if lunch might be in the stars."

"Oh, gosh, today?" she says, faux glancing at her phone. "I'm flat out, I'm afraid."

"Too bad." He delivers the creepy stare she dreads. "I know a man isn't supposed to say this to a woman, but you look a bit like crap today, Mayne. Coming down with something?"

"You're right, Wilson. A man should not say that to a woman. But if you must know, I'm sleep-deprived."

"Burning the old two-sided candle?" he asks. "It does catch up. Deciphering those endless lines of tiny cuneiforms has to take a toll. Now, Mayan hieroglyphs—"

"I really need to keep plugging away before my next meeting," she says, coming off a little harsher than she intended. Then she lightens the brush-off with a lilting, "Off you go, now."

But the last thing Wilson said jogs her memory, and she begins searching through old emails for a chain from a year or so ago.

She finds what she's looking for. It's from a friend of hers, Roger Partridge, a curator at the British Museum's Middle East Department, addressed to her, copying Roger's boss, Irving Finkel.

Subj: New text, BM 2024,0476,1

Kate,
While it's unrelated to your principal subject of interest, I wanted you to know that we've recently pieced together an exciting medicinal tablet from the Nineveh collection. We have a marvelous volunteer, a Mrs. Beddington, a retired security services employee (!), who is a wizard at piecing together tablet fragments, of which we have tens of thousands. She's been at it for several years, and recently, she's assembled a good bit of a physician's prescription for a patient with stomach pains. Do stop by if you'd like to see it.

Mrs. B is still hot on the trail, and we won't publish it or put it online in NinMed or Oracc until we know if more of it can be found.

Roger

Kate reads her reply which congratulated him on the discovery and said she looked forward to stopping by and having a look. Roger replied with a comment about an upcoming symposium in Berlin, and the chain went off in another direction.

Kate is certain she never went to see his tablet, but it gives her an irresistible idea. She texts Roger, asking if he ever publicly posted 2024,0476,1, and the curator responds quickly.

No, why?

She asks if she can swing by to see it this afternoon, and he replies that he may not be in, but he'll have it out for her.

OK if I take a photo?

Of course you can, as long as it's only for personal use. Plan to publish it soon.

~

WHEN KATE FINISHES with her grad student, she heads on foot through a fine autumn drizzle to the British Museum. Roger has left Kate's name with the security department, and after showing her UCL credentials, she passes through one of the staff entrances with direct access to the museum sub-levels.

The Middle East Department laboratories are adjacent to the old basement galleries, a group of underground rooms closed to the public more than two decades ago because they lacked access for the disabled. Two galleries had been devoted to Assyrian reliefs from Nineveh dating to the seventh century BCE, recounting the story of King Ashurbanipal's wars with the kingdom of Elam. The museum eventually redisplayed some pieces in public galleries; others remain on wooden pallets on the floor.

Roger's lab is bright and climate-controlled, and Kate finds

Claire, an assistant curator and several students at work. Claire greets Kate and relays Roger's apologies, but she has the tablet ready on one of the tables.

"It's only a wee one," Claire says in a Glaswegian accent, "but it's quite lovely."

Kate agrees with her. It's roughly rectangular, about five square inches, with a honey-colored patina and a smooth surface. Her practiced eye detects about two dozen fragments expertly glued, leaving only some tiny gaps in the text. The cuneiform writing is precise and diminutive, and Kate swings over the magnifier to read it more easily.

She finds the text interesting, but it doesn't make her heart pound. Assyrian medicine isn't her thing. Her academic bread and butter administrative records of grain storage.

The curator says, "The wonderful thing about this tablet is that it details several cures never before described in texts of the period. Some are quite wild, especially the enemas!"

"Yes, I saw that. Roger said I could take a picture."

"Yeah. Fine. No worries."

Kate rarely leaves the museum without going to the public exhibits on the ground floor to see her favorite Assyrian sculpture in Gallery 10a.

The Banquet Scene of Ashurbanipal, a large gypsum wall panel dating to around 645–635 BCE, was excavated in the nineteenth century in Kuyunjik, modern-day Mosul, Iraq, by Austen Henry Layard, from the ruins of Nineveh's North Palace. There are many stronger tourist magnets elsewhere in the museum, and Kate spends a few minutes with it totally alone.

The relief shows King Ashurbanipal reclining on a couch, enjoying a royal banquet in a lush garden of trees, vines, and hanging ornaments. His queen sits on a throne under a palm, drinking with him. Servants fan the royal couple, offering drinks and playing music.

But there is another macabre element in the tableau that belies the bucolic tranquility of the moment. In the background, the severed head of Teumman, the defeated Elamite king, hangs rotting from a tree, a reminder to Kate that her favorite ancient civilization, with its soaring achievements in culture and the world's first writing, was also savage and brutal.

~

VISITING hours are in full swing, so Kate can see the mysterious Akkadian speaker without Amrita's assistance. The door to Room 612 is open, and she can feel her body revving with anticipation as she crosses the threshold.

He is in bed, lying on his side, facing away from the door. Despite her silent entry, he quickly turns and sits upright, wholly unsurprised.

"I was waiting for you," he says, "I do not like this place, but I knew the woman with bright hair would return."

It requires the utmost concentration to slip back into the dead language. "You can call me by my name. It is Kate."

He tries it out. "Kat-e"

"No, Kate."

He gets it right.

"How did you know I would return?" she asks.

"I knew this because of the magic. I asked Nabu and Gula to take me to a place where I might learn how to heal Bel-ibni. Amidst a host of terrifying sights and sounds, you appeared, the only one to speak my tongue. The gods have sent me to you."

"I am not a healer," she says. "I cannot teach you how to heal this person."

He seems disappointed. "Can you take me to a healer who will teach me?"

Kate remembers when her brother was in medical school and taking a psychiatry course. He used to delight in telling her about peculiar psychiatric disorders. His favorite—and hers—was folie à deux, a rare syndrome where two people share the same delusions.

She did not want to be the deux to his un.

"I do want to talk to you about healing," she says, preparing to expose his delusion—or lies.

He is, without doubt, a highly educated Assyriologist who might have studied all the published Assyrian medical texts, perhaps even unpublished ones from whatever institutions he had attended. But he cannot know about the cures in Roger's tablet.

"You say you are the chief physician of Nineveh."

"Yes, I am the rab asû."

"Then, you will know how to treat a person with a piercing pain in the stomach."

He nods vigorously and says. "There are different remedies. How long has there been pain? What age is the person? Is the person a man or a woman? What is the season? Have ghosts plagued the person?"

His deflections are clever, she thinks. *My gambit's going to fail.*

She opens the picture of Roger's tablet on her phone and says, "I will read you the beginning of a cure for a person with a piercing pain in the stomach. The chief physician of Nineveh will know the complete cure."

He nods and opens his palms to the ceiling, which she interprets as a sign to proceed.

"You pound nuhurtu asafetida tīyatu and he drinks them in beer," she reads. "You boil down *šammu peṣû* in oil and you pour it into his anus. You heat up leaves from *šarmadu*, leaves from *ašāgu* and leaves from *baltu* in water and you wash him with it."

She stops there. It takes a few moments, but the man transforms before her eyes, his face blossoming with excitement and curiosity.

"How is this possible?" he says. "What magic is this?"

She stares at him, unsure where he is going.

And then, he closes his eyes and says, "You pour juice from *šunû* and juice from *kasû* into his anus. You boil down *burāšu* and *kukru* using a small copper pot. You smear the mixture on a piece of fabric and you bandage him with it."

Kate stares at the photo on her phone as he speaks, mouthing the same words.

She fights her spinning head, determined not to faint again, and grabs the railing of his bed. He places a large hand on hers.

"Will you fall again?" he asks.

The hand is warm and reassuring, but she pulls back and says, "I will not fall. Tell me, how do you know this cure?"

"I know it because I used these medicines to treat an old man with pain in his stomach. I cured him."

"Can I show you something?" Kate asks, trembling.

She hands him her phone. He takes it from her tentatively and looks at the photo, his face contorting in confusion.

He turns the phone around and around, saying, "I do not understand how my tablet fits into this flat box?"

Her voice is no more than a whisper now. "You called it *my* tablet. Why do you call it that?"

"I call it my tablet because I was the one who wrote the text to teach junior physicians how to cure others with such a sickness," he says, furrowing his dark brow. "I wrote it not two years ago. Tell me how you came to possess it, and why is it broken?"

She doesn't know what to do. She doesn't know what to say.

There has to be a rational explanation, but she feels herself sliding down an impossibly slick slope into a pit where his delusion will merge with hers.

Hallelujah! Hallelujah, Hallelujah.

Her ringtone is Handel's *Messiah*, and he drops the phone in horror.

Kate snatches it from the bedspread, sees the caller is Roger Partridge, and retreats to the hall.

Roger can clear this up, she thinks. *The only explanation is that this man has been to Roger's lab or someone has shown him a photo.*

"Hiya, Kate," he says. "Claire told me you were in. What did you think?"

"Roger, have you shared the tablet's text with anyone outside the museum—by writing or image?"

"I haven't, no. You're the first quote-unquote outsider to see it."

"Are you sure?"

"Completely sure, but I'm itching to publish it now that we've found the last bit."

She speeds along, not processing what he's just said.

"And you haven't had a visitor, an Assyriologist—a fellow in his thirties or forties, Middle Eastern, squared-off, curly beard, who speaks Akkadian?"

"Have you been drinking?" he laughs.

"No, I'm serious."

"No visitors matching this description, I assure you. I was calling because Claire tells me she neglected to mention the very recent discovery by Mrs. Beddington, the retired woman who's been diligently combing through our drawers of fragments. She's just found the colophon. It fits perfectly. We haven't glued it in place yet, but once we have, I'm having publication-quality photos done and writing it up."

Colophons are the standardized inscriptions at the end of cuneiform tablets, giving information about their content, place of origin, date, and authorship, and Kate holds her breath in a kind of dread anticipation.

She thinks, *Do I want to hear this? If I do, will I ever be the same?*

"Still there?" Roger says. "Did I lose you?"

Her mouth is parched, her tongue, sandpaper. "No, I'm here. Can you read it to me?"

"Here goes—in translation," he says eagerly. "*Tablet number one of a cure for stomach pain. Written in the house of the chief physician in the city of Nineveh in the thirty-eighth year of Ashurbanipal. Whoever removes this tablet without permission will not live long. Whoever sees this tablet, let him return it to Mannu-ki-Ashur, chief physician of Nineveh.* That's it. Pretty great, don't you think? Kate? Kate? Are you still there?"

CHAPTER FOURTEEN

AMRITA IS SCHEDULED FOR ANOTHER NIGHT SHIFT, BUT SHE acquiesced to Kate's pleadings and agreed to come into town a few hours early.

Outside the John Lewis on Oxford Street, Amrita asks, "You're being awfully mysterious. Want to tell me why you dragged me here?"

"Because you're the most wonderful friend in the whole wide world," Kate says, hugging her.

"Oh, my God," the nurse said. "What are you getting me into?"

"Shopping," Kate says with a forced lightness. "Just a bit of shopping."

"Are you feeling well?"

"Never better. Let's go."

The department store is bustling this time of day, and Kate is mumbling about a directory. "Where is—?" She spins. "Oh, there!"

Amrita follows her through the ground floor, and when Kate stops in a department to get her bearings, Amrita says, "Menswear? You want to shop for menswear?"

"That's why I need your help," Kate says. "And your moral support."

It's a lightbulb moment for the nurse. "You're not! Tell me you're not."

"I think I am," Kate admits. "I need your help with this."

"To buy clothes. For the mystery man," Amrita says.

"His name is Mannu-ki-Ashur. Mannu for short."

"And once you've dressed him like a doll?"

Kate remains silent for too long for her friend's comfort.

"No, no, and no! You're not. You can't."

"He needs me," Kate says. "He has no place to go."

Amrita folds her arms across her chest like a parent preparing to lecture a child.

"We're not doing anything until we talk. We'll get some tea, and we will talk."

The café is on the second floor. They find a table in a quiet corner, and when Kate takes her first sip, Amrita pounces.

"Have you completely lost your mind? You're not seriously considering taking responsibility for a stranger with a highly uncertain background."

"I know his background—at least, I think I do," Kate says, her eyes burning with intensity. "It's mad—completely bonkers, but I believe he's being truthful about who he is."

"Kate Mayne," her friend says with deadly seriousness. "You are one of the most sane and level-headed people I know, which is why I'm worried about your mental state. The Kate I know would laugh her head off if someone else claimed that a man from a dead civilization popped up naked in Piccadilly Circus."

"Would you please just consider the facts—one by one?" Kate pleads.

Amrita sighs.

"All right—point one: he speaks fluent Akkadian. Only a handful of us in the world can pull this off. I know them all. They are dear friends. Mannu's Akkadian is far superior, surpassing anyone I've ever known, including my mentor at Oxford."

"But it's still possible for someone alive today to get this good at a language, even a dead language, isn't it?"

"Yes, it's possible," Kate concedes, but highly, highly unlikely.

"Point two: he has no modern identity. You told me the police couldn't find his fingerprints."

"That just means he wasn't known to them," Amrita says. "He could be a wanted man wherever he's from."

"Okay," Kate says, "maybe not the strongest point. Point three: I gave him a test that's impossible to get right unless he's being truthful, and he aced it."

"When?"

"I went back to the hospital a few hours ago."

"You didn't."

"I did. I went during visiting hours. Now listen to this, Amrita," she says, leaning over the bistro table. "There's a cuneiform tablet at the British Museum that's only been pieced together recently. They're always trying to assemble the jigsaw pieces of the thousands of cuneiform tablet fragments that have been sitting in their trays for over a hundred years. No one outside the museum saw this new tablet until they showed it to me this morning. Never. No one else has seen it."

"So?"

"It's a medical tablet from the museum's Nineveh collection that dates to the seventh century BCE. It describes a cure for someone with a stomach ache. It's elaborate—you do this with this herb; you do that with that plant, et cetera. It's a cure no one has seen before in Assyrian medicinal texts."

"So?" Amrita repeats.

"Mannu claims to be a physician. Not only a physician but the chief physician of Nineveh. A man with his training and expertise would know about this kind of cure, wouldn't you think?"

"I have no idea," Amrita says.

"Fine, but wouldn't you agree that an imposter, or someone with a psychiatric condition, or an amnesia victim who happens to be fluent in Akkadian, couldn't possibly know about an unpublished cure from twenty-five hundred years ago?"

"Yeah, maybe," Amrita says, munching a biscuit.

"I read the first line of the tablet to Mannu. Guess what happened?"

"I can't, but you're going to tell me."

"He knew the rest of it by heart. Every. Single. Word. I asked him how he knew it."

Amrita is suddenly interested. "What did he say?"

"He said *he* wrote it."

"Oh, God, this is getting so weird," Amrita says.

"There's more," Kate says. "Point four. A museum volunteer just found another piece of the tablet that fits onto the bottom. It's a colophon—like the signature line of a letter or a memo. It states that it was written in 642 BCE by the chief physician of Nineveh. *Mannu-ki-Ashur.*"

Amrita stares at Kate for a few moments before saying, "Okay. Now you're freaking me out. There's got to be an explanation."

"I've been agonizing over this," Kate says, "but only one fits the facts. Mannu-ki-Ashur came here from the past."

"Time travel, Kate? Now, you've lost the plot. How do you suppose he did that?"

"He said he used magic. He was desperate to find a cure for one of his patients. He prayed to the god Nabu and the goddess Gula and invoked powerful magic to transport himself into the future in search of a cure."

"You kind of had me going," Amrita says sternly, "but now you've gone off to cloud-cuckoo land."

"Listen to me," Kate says, taking Amrita's hand. "The Assyrians were deeply religious. They believed their gods controlled every-thing in the world and the heavens. They believed absolutely in the power of magic to influence the gods to ward off evil spirits, heal the sick, and even affect the weather and their harvests. Mannu told me he used a forbidden, ancient magic—think black magic—asking the gods to send him to a place where he could gain the knowledge he needed. The magic worked."

"If you could hear yourself," Amrita says.

Undeterred, Kate asks, "How were Assyrian beliefs in religion, magic, and miracles different from our modern beliefs? I'm not very religious, but I've got a vague belief in a magic Jesus somewhere out there in something we call Heaven. Others, far more devout than me, believe that Bible miracles—water into wine, the loaves and fishes, walking on water—happened exactly as described. You're a practicing Hindu, are you not?"

Amrita nods.

"Then you believe that Vishnu has four arms, Shiva has a third eye, Ganesha has an elephant's head, and our souls can be reborn. Most Hindus probably think that Christian beliefs are rubbish. And most Christians probably think that Hindu beliefs are rubbish. And we all think that Assyrian beliefs were rubbish. But what if they weren't rubbish? What if they were real?"

Amrita puts her cup down and looks for a tissue to dab her welling eyes.

"I'm not a deep thinker like you, Kate. I love my family, I love my job on some days, I love my friends—especially you—and I love to have a good time. I don't know if what you're saying is true or bollocks. All I know is I'm scared you're talking about inviting a strange man into your house. I'm scared I'm going to wake up one day to hear that my best friend's been assaulted or murdered."

"I'm scared, too," Kate says. "That's why I need your help buying him clothes and getting him released from hospital. I'd also like to ask you, most humbly, to take off work and stay with me at my house tonight."

Amrita scrunches her face. "So I can get assaulted and murdered, too?"

Kate laughs. "Definitely, not that."

KATE ISN'T sure where to start. Amrita suggests underwear is as good a place as any. The salesman in the department notices them and sidles over.

"Boyfriend? Husband?" he asks.

Kate is flummoxed. "Uh—"

"Well, we're going to need to know size and preference, won't we?" he says.

"What do you think about size?" Kate asks Amrita.

"He's a good-sized lad. Large, I'd say."

"Duly noted," the salesman says. "Now, preference. Boxers? Briefs? Boxer briefs?" He pauses and says, "We even have thongs if that interests the gentleman."

Kate surveys the mannikins.

"Boxer briefs seem a safe enough bet," Amrita says.

"Noted. Lastly, color."

"Red is pretty," Kate says.

"Stay away from bright colors," Amrita advises, and they settle for black.

"Trousers," Kate mumbles.

The salesman offers to help them with all of the gentleman's requirements and leads them to racks of trousers.

"Jeans are simple enough," Amrita says.

"I can't see him in jeans," Kate says. "Do you have dark everyday trousers?"

"These?" he asks, holding up something that matches her description.

"Yeah, those are good," Kate says.

"Waist size and length?"

"Amrita, help!" Kate says.

"What's your size?" she asks the salesman.

"Thirty-two waist, thirty inseam," he replies. "If I had my wish, I'd be taller."

Amrita says. "He's fairly muscular and tallish, isn't he? Let's go with thirty-six, thirty-four."

They leave the store half an hour later with bags bulging with underwear, socks, trousers, casual shirts, t-shirts, a windbreaker, and, taking a stab at his foot size, a pair of black trainers.

Ordinarily, they would have walked—it's a perfect autumn day —but Kate is anxious to get to the hospital.

As the taxi heads down Great Portland Street, Amrita says, "What would your well-dressed Assyrian wear?"

"Tunic, cloak, belt, sandals," Kate says. "Shit, I forgot a belt."

"You forgot more than that," Amrit says.

"What?" Kate asks.

"Your common sense."

~

KATE AND AMRITA split up at the hospital, with Kate heading to Room 612 and Amrita going to the discharge office.

Mannu brightens at the sight of her. "I have been waiting for you, Kat-e." He corrects himself. "No. Kate."

She raises the John Lewis carrier bags and says, "I have clothes for you. You will find them strange, but they are clothes that men in London wear."

"Will I leave this place now?"

Her lack of perfect fluency and the limitations of the language make it grindingly difficult to express herself fully, but the conversation is making her giddy. It's the first time they've talked since she's come to grips with his truthfulness.

"I hope you can leave. My friend is talking to the administrators of this place."

Mannu nods his understanding. "I know many *šāpirū*—administrators," he says. "My father was one. He was the chief of the King's grain houses. They can be stubborn men."

Mannu has uttered the magic word—*grain*—for Kate is the leading Assyriologist in the world on the subject of grain management and economics.

"Your father was the rab karāni?" she sputters.

"Yes, he was the rab karāni."

"Tell me his name."

"My father was Nabû-bēl-uṣur."

If she had any doubts about Mannu's story, hearing his father's name has obliterated them. How many dozens of tablets has she studied containing the colophon of Nabû-bēl-uṣur? How many times has she cited him in journal articles and lectures? She even named her dearly departed cat Nabu in his honor.

"Your father was an important man," she says.

"How do you know of him?"

"Many of his *tuppu*—clay tablets—survive."

"In Lon-don?"

"Yes, in London."

"Why are they not in Nineveh?"

"It is a long story I will tell when we have time. Now, I would like you to clothe yourself."

"You will help me cure Bel-ibni?" he asked.

"I will try to help you."

She glimpses his stoicism as he fights off tears. He tightly closes his eyes and whispers his thanks to the gods.

"The magic brought me to you, Kate," he says, his eyes piercing her like x-rays. "*Attī nazartāni*—you have saved me."

It's the first time in her life she has felt this special. Her battle against tears is less successful than his.

She fumbles and sniffles through her carrier bags, and says, "Let me show you the clothes. These go first—underneath. These go over. You pull this thing we call a zipper and secure them with this thing called a button. Here is how buttons work. These go on your chest. Here are more buttons. These go on your feet. First these, then these. You tie these in a bow. Do you understand?"

He nods. She isn't sure.

"I will wait outside. Call me when you are ready."

In the hall, Kate is consumed by conflicts. One Kate is excited and energized—feeling more alive than ever before. The other Kate is a jiggling mass of worries and uncertainties—more scared than ever before.

Thank God for Amrita, she thinks. *I couldn't do this alone.*

Her ping-ponging thoughts halt when she hears her name. In his accent, it sounds more like Cat than Kate, but she likes it fine that way.

He's standing by the bed, proudly displaying his new costume.

"Do I look like a man from Lon-don?" he asks.

It's the first time she's seen him upright. He's tall—maybe five feet ten or eleven. In his time, he would have towered over most men. His shoulders are wide, his hips narrow. His beard and hair have lost much of their curl. She can tell he's self-conscious because he's constantly fingering them.

154

To put him at ease, she says, "Yes, you look like a London man. Also, your beard looks like the beard of a London man."

"I do not have my curling irons," he says apologetically.

"It is better for London," she says. "There is one small problem."

His buttons are off by one, and she approaches him to fix them, like a mother about to help a small boy with his shirt.

"I can touch?" she asks.

"Yes, you can touch."

She has to start over. When his shirt opens, she glances at his powerful chest, carpeted in black. Her fingers brush his chest as she does the buttons. She feels the flush of embarrassment. Perhaps he's noticed, because he smiles.

"There. That is proper," she says when done. "Let me fix your bows, If I may."

She kneels to improve his shoelaces, and when she rises, he thanks her.

"The goddess, Ishtar, protects men who travel on dangerous journeys. Ishtar has delivered you to me."

Amrita arrives, looks Mannu up and down, and brings Kate down to earth.

"Oh, my God, we did an amazing job. Everything fits. Did he like the pants?"

"I didn't watch him put on underwear," Kate says, "and I couldn't possibly find the words to ask the question. More importantly, how did you get on?"

Amrita waves a few papers.

"Unknown male is officially discharged. He was medically cleared. He's got no pending charges with the police. The social workers didn't have a plan for dealing with him and everyone's delighted you've taken responsibility."

"Me?"

"As much as I love you, it wasn't going to be me. Before we leave, you've got to go downstairs and sign some papers."

"Fine. Not a problem."

"He's a good-looking fellow, isn't he?" Amrita says, suddenly panicking. "Tell me he can't understand me."

"Not a word." Kate breaks into Akkadian and says, "This is my friend, Amrita. She will also help you."

Mannu bows to her.

"How do I say hello?" Kate tells her that the Akkadian word for hello is peace, and Amrita parrots it back. "*Šulmu,* Mannu."

Delighted, he bows again and says, "*Šulmu,* Amrita," pronouncing her name perfectly.

Amrita melts. "He's quite the gentleman, isn't he? Think he's ready for Tottenham?"

Kate says gamely, "There's only one way to find out."

CHAPTER FIFTEEN

CHINEDU AWAKES TO FIND THE REFUGEES SITTING ON THE EDGE OF his bed, staring at him.

"Good morning to you!" he says, recalling his bountiful night.

Before going to bed, he hid his roll of cash in a cereal box, and the first thing he does is dash to the kitchen to ensure his new friends haven't looted it. Relieved, he returns with a carton of orange juice, takes a swig, and offers it around.

"It is good!" he says.

Ninurta and Adad have been awake for hours. No longer frozen by fear, they are frozen by uncertainty. They urgently need Chinedu's help but have had the courtesy not to disturb a sleeping man. Ninurta sniffs at the orange liquid, lets a small amount reach his tongue, and smiles.

Chinedu laughs and says, "Ahhh. It is good! Say it. Good."

Ninurta has a bigger swallow and says the word.

Chinedu is delighted. "Yes! Good!"

"What is it?" Adad asks.

"It is a sweet drink unlike anything I have tasted," Ninurta says. "I like it."

Adad tentatively samples it, then gulps more down.

Chinedu looks at his watch and says, "My goodness! Half the day is already gone. It is Saturday, my friends. I am going to take you to Camden Markets. It will blow your mind. We can have breakfast, lunch—whatever our hearts desire. What have you done with your cash?"

He pantomimes counting the bills like he did last night. Ninurta immediately understands, pulling the roll from his jeans.

"You should not take that out with you, my friend. Too many light fingers about. Give it here." Pulling off the rubber band, he says, "I will just take a few for our expenses. We will leave the rest under the mattress."

IT IS WARM FOR SEPTEMBER, with blue skies and picture-perfect clouds drifting in gentle winds.

Chinedu keeps prattling down the High Street, pretending Ninurta and Adad understand him. To casual observers, there is nothing unusual about the group—just three mates in jeans and hoodies on a weekend lark.

"Will you look these crowds! It is as busy as a festival day. The sun is shining—a perfect day for being out and about. With our newly found prosperity, we can be like the rich tourists who eat and drink whatever they like and buy anything they desire. Well, I am hungry, and I desire a hamburger. What do you say? Hearing no objections, we shall have hamburgers."

WALKING THROUGH THIS CROWD, Ninurta feels remarkably at ease. It is as if a magician has made him invisible to his enemies. Clinging outer garments and awkward footwear cover his body. A hood hides his face. No one seems to look at him. No one seems to notice how different he is.

This is what it feels like to be a ghost, he thinks.

He strides shoulder to shoulder with the hooded Adad. They

have concluded that if Chinedu is a person, those who walk these streets must also be people. The entities that roll on wheels? Perhaps they are demons. Adad grunts at every shocking sight, and, in a low voice, he serves up a stream of observations and questions Ninurta cannot possibly answer.

"These women who show their flesh surely must be harlots selling their bodies openly."

"Are the men without beards eunuchs like me?"

"They keep dogs on tethers. I see no hunting grounds. Do these barbarians slaughter them for food?"

"Many possess glowing rectangles and often look at them. We must discover their purpose."

"Look at this small river. The current is pitiful. How can fish thrive in these brown waters?"

"Do they live in these buildings? Where are their temples?" Where is the palace of their king?

"Keep searching for Mannu. He could be walking among them. Remember why we are here."

Ninurta is more interested in the wonders of this world—the bright colors and magical lights, the piercing sounds, the exotic smells, the miraculous unfathomable sights he can hardly describe. And he is enchanted by the Nubian, Chinedu, with his chiseled face and sweet, happy demeanor. He wishes they shared a common tongue to better know each other.

Chinedu waits for him to catch up, then begins speaking, making exaggerated gestures with his hands.

He is trying to teach me a new word!

"Are you hungry?" Chinedu says, pantomiming, patting his stomach, then taking a bite of air and saying *Mmm.* "Hungry."

Ninurta says, "Hun-gree."

He mixes words with his pantomime. "Now say: I want food. I am hungry."

"Iwa foo. I mm hun-gree."

"Yes! Very good! We will eat food because we are hungry."

Ninurta earnestly tries to mimic him. "Yes. Good. Wee. Hun-gree."

"Good enough," Chinedu says, entering the Waterside Halls. "We are here."

The Flip & Sear Burgers is packed solid. Chinedu looks around and pounces when a group vacates a table.

He pats two stools, and when Ninurta and Adad fail to get the hint, he forces them to sit by their shoulders.

"You stay here. I'll order," he says. "Wagyu beef," he says. "The best of the best."

When he returns with a tray, his two hooded friends are cemented in place, lost and petrified amidst the chattering diners.

Chinedu slides a juicy double cheeseburger, a pile of French fries, and a can of Coke before each man and says, "You will never be the same. There is life before a Wagyu burger, and there is life after a Wagyu burger. Enjoy."

They stare at the masses of food, unsure what they are or what to do with them, until Chinedu lifts his burger to his mouth and starts chomping. Emboldened, they pick up the hot buns, sniff at them, and then take small bites.

Ninurta breaks into a smile and takes a second, bigger bite. Adad raises his eyebrows and does the same.

"What did I tell you?" Chinedu laughs. "Try the potatoes!"

The Assyrians exchange a few excited words between bites but are more interested in eating than talking. Adad takes French fries by the handful, stuffing them into his mouth.

"Slow down, big man," Chinedu laughs. "No one will steal them."

When Chinedu pops his soda, they stare at the hissing can and watch in fascination as he drinks from it.

Chinedu pops their tabs for them. Both men take sips; both men spit them out.

Chinedu almost falls off his stool, laughing. "Who does not like Coke-Cola? Where in the world are you from, my friends?"

Pulling out his phone, he opens a world map, puts it on the table, and says, "Show me. Where is your home?" He's frustrated by their blank stares and zooms in on the Middle East. "It must be one of these countries. Afghanistan? Turkey? Syria? One of these? I do not even know what these ones are called. Okay, this is Uzbekistan. This one? None of them?"

He gives up and finishes his meal.

"Everyone comes from somewhere," he says to himself. "All right, my friends, I have introduced you to Wagyu burgers. Now I will introduce you to a proper English pub called The World's End. Do not worry. No more Coke for you. They have a beer I greatly enjoy."

ON THE CROWDED STREET, Adad asks, "What kind of food did we eat?"

"I do not know, but it was delicious," Ninurta says. "Food here is plentiful."

"Where does he take us now?" Adad asks.

Ninurta spins. "Did we not pass this way?"

"Yes! There is the building with vegetation growing from its walls," Adad says, pointing at an ivy-covered façade. "I am disheartened. We follow this Nubian like donkeys, but how will this lead us to Mannu?"

"We must learn their tongue," Ninurta says. "If we cannot speak to them, we cannot ask if they have seen Mannu. Chinedu has taught me several of his words. I will try to learn more so I can ask about Mannu."

Adad steps off the sidewalk onto the road, and a mighty blast emanates from one of the wheeled monsters. The eunuch yelps and jumps aside.

"We must learn about these demons," Adad says, "and how to defeat them."

The Nubian leads them inside a building, a cool, dark space where throngs of people stand and sit drinking amber beverages from large glass vessels. Although there are no musicians, a loud sort of music emanates from the thin air.

Both travelers grin and utter the same word: *kāru*—tavern.

Chinedu leads them to an empty table littered with beer mats, empty glasses, and a discarded newspaper, and then weaves to the bar.

"The tavern is more like home than any place we have seen," Ninurta says, vaguely curious about the newsprint with its symbols, especially its pictures. "Smell the air. Look at the vessels. People are drinking—" Instead of *šikaru*, he uses the foreign word they learned. "—beer."

The humorless Adad chuckles.

"See?" Ninurta says. "I speak their tongue."

Chinedu impresses them with his ability to carry three large vessels of beer.

"Try this *šikaru*," Chinedu says, further impressing, as they had not realized he was learning their words, too. "It is called Camden Hells. The English like their beer warm. In my home, we like it cold. This beer is nice and cool."

Ninurta picks up his pint glass and says, "I do not know what you said, but I will say something before we drink. I hail the ancient goddess Ninkasi, who brings beer to our world and even this world."

Chinedu admires how they chug their pints to the bottom of their glasses.

"I like what I am seeing!" he exclaims. "It is good we have plenty of cash. Do not go anywhere. I will be right back with two more pints."

"I think he goes for more good beer," Adad says.

"The god Girra, bestower of good fortune, delivered us to Chinedu," Ninurta says. "We bless you, Girra."

"And we bless you, Ninkasi," Adad says, eyeing Chinedu's untouched vessel of beer.

They drink their next pints more leisurely. Chinedu sips his first languidly, studying Ninurta's strong jaw and powerful hands. Ninurta gets his attention by pointing to an image in the newspaper, slamming his finger onto an image of a man kicking a round object with his foot.

"You want to know who this is?" Chinedu asks. "Some footballer."

Ninurta points again.

"You want to know what this is? Photo. It is a photo."

"Pho-to," Ninurta says.

"Yes! Very good. I will show you another photo."

He takes his phone out and quickly snaps a shot across the table.

"It is a good one," Chinedu says. "It captures your essence."

He holds it out to show Ninurta his picture and says, "Photo. Ninurta."

At first, Ninurta does not understand what he is looking at, but when it dawns on him, he puts his hands over his eyes and starts shaking.

"It is okay, my friend," Chinedu says. "If you do not like the photo, we can take more until you find a better one."

A barmaid interrupts with a tray and says, "Want me to clear this away?"

"That would be lovely," Chinedu says.

She takes the empties and says, "Paper yours?"

"It is not."

Ninurta is still shaking but has recovered sufficiently to open his eyes again.

As the barmaid lifts the copy of *The Clarion* and goes to fold it, the front page is briefly visible. Ninurta cannot read the headline, **Caught Bare-Handed: Rush Hour Shock as Piccadilly Streaker Gets the Zap**, but he sees the image of a naked man surrounded by the police.

"Pho-to!" Ninurta cries. "Mannu-ki-Ashur!"

CHAPTER SIXTEEN

Seated in the back seat of the Uber with Kate, Mannu finally has someone to help him understand this strange world. With every heartfelt question, Kate becomes more certain that Mannu must be genuine.

Listening from the front, the Pakistani driver asks Amrita what they're speaking. "I can usually tell where someone's from. Can't make that one out."

"It's a dead language," Amrita says. "They like to show off how clever they are."

"Oh, yeah? Cool."

"Please tell me," Mannu says, waving his hand. "What is this thing that moves us so swiftly along the ground?"

"It is called an automobile."

He tries the new word, but it gets caught on his tongue.

"How does it move? I see no horses or oxen. Is it magic?"

"We call it a machine. It is not magic. It has a motor fed by a substance like oil."

"Does this *ma-cheen* come from the gods?"

"No, it comes from men. Since your time, men have learned to make many marvelous things."

He considers her answer and says, "You said something that troubled me greatly. You said Nineveh no longer exists. You said it was destroyed. Were you speaking the truth?"

Kate looks out the window at the bustling city, feeling like someone tasked with telling a child that his parents were killed in an accident—that the world, as he knew it, is no more.

"I am sorry, Mannu. I spoke harsh words when I did not believe you were from Nineveh. I should have spoken more gently. However, I did speak the truth. I know it is terrible, and I am sorry."

Mannu blinks at her, his eyes glistening. "What becomes of Nineveh? What becomes of *māt Aššur*—the land of Ashur? What becomes of my people?"

She chooses her words carefully. "Your empire grew large—too large to govern and protect itself from your enemies. Your enemies joined arms and attacked Nineveh with one army. The city fell."

"When?" he asks, his face becoming rigid. "When does this happen?"

"Some thirty years from your time. I am sorry, Mannu. It is hard for me to say and, I am certain, harder for you to hear."

He vigorously shakes his head. "The gods would not allow this. We are the people of Ashur who blesses and favors us. He will help us smite our enemies."

Kate can only say, "I will always be truthful."

"Did I die in this battle? Did my brother? Did Bel-ibni die? Did the King die?"

"I only know the fate of King Ashurbanipal. He dies twenty years before Nineveh falls."

"How? How does the King die?"

"There are no writings about his death."

"You spoke of my father and his tablets. You say you have seen them. How is this possible?"

"When Nineveh fell to your enemies, many buildings were destroyed. Over countless years, sand and earth buried the remains, and the city was lost. Long before I was born, men dug through the earth and discovered the lost city. They discovered the ruins of your buildings. They discovered the tablets kept in the great library of

165

King Ashurbanipal. When these men returned to London, they brought the tablets with them. Most were broken. Many are now repaired. Do you know this library—the library of Nineveh?"

The emotions welling inside of him erupt in anger. "Do I know of it?" he shouts. "It is where I study! It is a sacred place of learning! It is a temple to knowledge!"

Amrita leans over the seat, startled by the outburst, and says, "All right back there?"

"We're fine," Kate says. "We're on a delicate subject."

The driver searches his rearview mirror suspiciously, and Amrita reassures him, "These uni professors do get worked up sometimes."

Kate starts to reach for Mannu's arm but pulls back.

"I know you are troubled," she says. "These truths are hard. I have learned about the land of Ashur by reading tablets from your great library. This is how I know of your father. This is how I know of your cure for stomach pains. Meeting you is a gift of enormous value. There is much I can learn from you."

Mannu is visibly overwhelmed. All he can do is bury his head in his hands to blot out this city that lives while his city has died.

"I did not come here to teach you," he says bitterly. "I came to learn how to cure Bel-ibni. When I have learned the cure, I will return to my time and my place. If what you say is true, in the years that come, I will lift a sword and defend my city."

THE SUN IS LOWER than the rooflines when Kate, Amrita, and Mannu arrive in Tottenham.

"We are here," Kate says quietly.

Mannu opens his reddened eyes.

"The buildings are not as tall."

"We have traveled away from the center of the city. Buildings are smaller here. This is my house."

Standing on the sidewalk, he surveys the structure and says, "But this is a house of great size. How many people live here?"

Kate laughs and says, "I am the only one."

"Then, you must be wealthy."

"What's he saying?" Amrita asks.

"He thinks I'm rich to live in a big house like this."

"You need to take him on a tour of Buckingham Palace," Amrita says. "See what he thinks, then."

INSIDE, Mannu immediately bends to remove his shoes. Kate and Amrita do likewise to make him feel comfortable. His eyes flit from one unfamiliar object to another in the sitting room.

"Please, sit," Kate says. "I would like to offer you food and drink."

He presses the soft sofa cushions before lowering himself.

"I do not require food," he says, "but I am thirsty."

"If you were home, what would you drink?" she asks.

"I would drink beer."

"Oh, my," Kate says to Amrita. "He wants a beer. I don't have any. There's a mini-mart at the end of Langham Road. Would you mind?"

"Yes, I would mind," Amrita says. "If you think I'm leaving you with him, you need your head examined. What am I saying? You already need your head examined. If he's desperate for a beer, we all go."

Kate sighs. "I can't put him through a trip to the mini-mart right now." Switching languages, she tells him, "I do not have beer. I can offer you water. I also have wine."

"I will take water for my thirst and wine to rest my mind."

When Kate provides the literal translation, Amrita says, "I'll get the wine. I seriously need to rest my mind, too."

He praises Kate's cheap French table wine as fine and exotic and says, "You told me you would always tell me the truth."

"Have I not?"

"You say you are not wealthy. Yet, behold your myriad possessions. Not even the wealthiest person in Nineveh has such fineries."

Kate examines her lounge with fresh eyes. Her sofa is from John

Lewis, the rug is second-hand, and most of the furniture, bric-a-brac, and paintings are pass-me-downs from grandparents.

"This world—my world—is far wealthier than yours," she says. "I am not poor; neither am I wealthy."

Amrita is rattling around the kitchen, looking to pull together a supper. When she surfaces to refill her wine glass, she tells Kate she'll do her best with what there is.

"You've got chicken," she says. "I can do a curry with the spuds and peas. Do you think he'll like it spicy?"

"Better go with mild," Kate says. "Christ! I only have a shitty white loaf. They ate a lot of bread."

"I'm not making naan from scratch," Amrita says. "Too much work. I'll do up lots of rice."

"They didn't have rice."

"Who doesn't like rice?" she says, retreating to the kitchen.

Well into Mannu's second glass of wine, Kate can see its effects. His face is softer, his posture, more relaxed. He has stopped inspecting the mysterious objects in the room and has his eyes lowered in quiet contemplation or meditation. But Kate is anything but calm. The past eighteen hours have taken their toll, and reality has taken hold. She's exhausted the denials and skepticism. The man calling himself Manu-ki-Ashur has cleared the hurdles. Over the years, she's fantasized about what she would ask if she could have a conversation with someone from the past, and here he is in her sitting room—a living, breathing, virile Assyrian.

Mannu raises his head.

"You are trembling," he says.

"Am I?"

"See? Your hands. Are you afraid of me?"

"I am not afraid of you," she says. "I am afraid of your magic. You have made a great journey on what you call the circle of time. You have traveled many years into the future to this time and this place. I did not believe such a journey was possible, but here you are."

"The magic taught to me by Tukulti, the magician, is fearsome, is it not?" he says. "There is good reason why it is forbidden in the kingdom. I used it in desperation. But you should not be afraid. The magic will not harm you."

She forces a laugh. "Maybe I need more wine."

He takes her seriously. "Yes, wine is good medicine for fear." Then, out of the blue, he asks something unexpected. "Where is your husband?"

"I do not have a husband."

"Did he die of disease or from battle?"

"I never married."

He appears shocked. "But you are—"

"Not young?" she says with a smile.

"True. You are not young."

She finds his lack of inhibition refreshing—it's something a child might say.

"In my time—in this time—some women marry later in life. Some choose not to marry."

"The woman with dark skin, like mine. Does she have a husband?"

"Amrita is not married."

Bewilderment wrinkles his face.

"Why does she stay in another room?"

"She is cooking supper for us."

"That is her job?"

"No, she is a—" There is no Akkadian word for nurse. "—a type of healer."

He leans forward, hopefully. "Can she teach me how to heal Bel-ibni?"

"I do not know. We can ask her."

Voices drift in from the kitchen television and Mannu startles.

"Men have come. Do you hear them speak?"

She assures him no one is there, but when he remains agitated, she leads him into the kitchen, where the news is on. The images on the small screen don't have the soothing effect Kate imagined. Mannu steps closer, calling the gods to stop this perverse display of magic, free the beings from this hideous box, and restore them to their natural size.

"What's he going on about?" Amrita asks.

"He thinks people are trapped inside the tele."

"Oh, is that all?" Amrita says, stirring the curry.

Kate tries to explain television, but given the paucity of Akkadian vocabulary relevant to modern technology, it's a tall order.

"In our time, men have made many marvels you could not imagine in your time. This is not magic. These are pictures that move. There are no people inside this box. I beg you to believe me. In this world, you will see many things that are difficult to believe. Remember what I said. I will always tell you the truth."

He looks unconvinced but nods. "I remember," then sniffs the air and looks over Amrita's shoulder. "How does she cook? Where is the fire?"

"This is another marvel of our time. There is no cooking fire. It is difficult to explain."

He grunts, dissatisfied.

Amrita turns to offer him a taste, but he doesn't know what to do with the spoon in his face.

There is certainly no word for curry, not even a word for stew, so Kate opts for *tabītu*, which means a cooked dish. "It is a cooked dish made with spices from her country called India."

He repeats the foreign word. "In-di-a. Where is In-di-a? Why has she come to the land of white faces?"

Amrita laughs at Kate's translation and says, "You'd have to ask my grandparents."

Kate has an idea and hurries into the sitting room.

Returning, she opens an atlas and shows him a map of the world. "Look. Here is London. Here is India. And here, "pointing to Mosul, Iraq, "is where you are from."

Mannu doesn't seem to understand anything about Kate's show-and-tell. He runs his hand over the page and asks, "What is this? What are these pictures and these symbols?"

Employing a couple of English words, she says, "This is a *book*. We do not write on clay tablets. We write on something we call *paper*. We do not use clay tablets. These symbols are our writing.

These pictures show how the world appears. You can see that Nineveh is far from London."

He pauses in deep thought. "The magic sent me on the circle of time, not only to a faraway time but a faraway place."

"Why do you believe this happened?" Kate asks.

His chest heaves. "The magic delivered me to you. You are—" He uses an unfamiliar word—*mammanūtu*."

She has to use her phone to find the meaning in her English-to-Akkadian dictionary.

"I am not *unique*," she says. "I do not know how to help you. I told you. I am not a healer."

He shakes his head. "You say you do not write on clay, yet you can read and speak my tongue. How many people in your time read and speak my tongue as you do?"

Kate holds up her fingers. "Perhaps six. No more."

"You see?" he says excitedly. "There is a reason I have been delivered to your time and your place. It is you. I beg you. Ask this woman from In-di-a if she can teach me how to heal Bel-ibni."

"He wants to know if you can teach him how to treat his patient," Kate says.

Amrita laughs. "Don't look at me! I don't want that kind of responsibility on my head. I'm just a simple ward nurse. Now, if he wants to know how to hang an IV bag or check vital signs, I'm his woman. P.S. Supper's ready."

"She says she cannot help you," Kate says.

MANNU THANKED the gods for his food, then voraciously consumed the curry and rice. Amrita guessed that he probably hadn't eaten the hospital food. They ate mostly in silence.

When he had his fill, Kate clears the table.

"Don't suppose he does the washing up," Amrita says

When Kate returns to the sitting room, Mannu is up from the dining table, exploring her possessions. He pulls books from shelves, inspects them curiously, then replaces them in their spots.

"This is my small library," Kate says.

"You read these?" he asks.

"Yes. Do you see this one?" she says, pulling a slim volume. "I wrote this text."

He raises his eyebrows. "A woman wrote a text? What is its subject?"

"It is about buying and selling grain in the land of Ashur. Let me show you your father's name written in your tongue and my tongue."

He stares in amazement at a photo of a tablet with his father's colophon and murmurs, "You are indeed unique, Ka-te—no, Kate."

His gaze suddenly fixes on a side table, and he lights up excitedly.

"You possess the most important text!" he exclaims. "Here is Ša naqba īmuru—He who saw everything! I know this very tablet! I have read it many times in the King's library."

He cradles Kate's replica of the tablet of the *Epic of Gilgamesh* in his hands. The original was found in pieces during the excavation of Ashurbanipal's palace. The Assyrians knew the ancient Sumerian text by its opening words—He who saw everything.

"It is one more sign that you are unique, Kate."

Amrita emerges from the kitchen, drying her hands. "It's been a long enough day. I'm going to get ready for bed. Where are we putting him?"

"I thought the spare room," Kate says. "He's too big for the sofa."

"That's fine. I'll kip with you, then. His nurses told me he didn't know how to use the toilet and sink at first."

"Can he now?"

"He got the hang of it. He needs to learn how to operate the shower—he's a bit ripe—I don't have the strength to tackle it till the morning. Do you have a cricket bat?"

"Why?"

"Protection! We're sleeping with a strange man down the hall."

"Do I look like someone with a cricket bat?" Kate asks. "No one in my family—not even my brother, played."

"Every Indian household has one," Amrita says. "I assume you've got a hammer."

Kate shakes her head disapprovingly but steers her friend to the closet under the stairs.

"Come, Mannu," Kate says. "I will take you to your sleeping chamber. It is up these stairs."

Kate takes the shopping bag with the rest of his new clothes, and Amrita leads him upstairs to see if he can manage the bathroom fixtures. Kate turns down his bed. The last time the spare room was occupied was during her ex-boyfriend's tryst, and she feels a ripple of queasiness recalling the nakedness. Jeremy left a few of his clothes behind as a pretext for contacting her, but she's ignored him. She's got them stuffed in a trash bag at the back of the closet.

Amrita drops Mannu off, saying, "Your flush lever's different from the hospital's, but I've got him sorted. He's a bright lad. Fast learner. I'll be in your room with Maxwell's Silver Hammer."

Kate laughed. "I'm sure we won't need it. I'll be in soon."

As Mannu stands awkwardly beside the bed, Kate understands the impropriety of a man and woman alone in a bedroom.

She quickly empties the bag of clothes onto the top of the dresser and tells him he can use one of the t-shirts for sleeping.

"I give thanks for the generous gifts," he says.

She is about to bid him the traditional Assyrian bidding of a peaceful night when she stops herself and, instead, says, "I have so many questions I wish to ask."

"You may ask them," he says.

"I will ask only one tonight. It is the most important one," she says. "Who is Bel-ibni, and why have you risked your life to help her?"

When he takes a deep, stuttering breath, she encourages him to sit. He lowers himself onto the side of the bed, and she takes the side chair.

"Bel-ibni is concubine to the King," he begins. Despite the guttural, staccato cadence of the language, she can hear profound sadness in his voice. "She is his favorite concubine, and she carries his child. The fortune tellers say it will be a son. It is no secret that the King desires a new heir. His son, Prince Ashur, is no longer in favor."

"You say that Bel-ibni is sick," Kate says.

"Yes, she is very sick. None of my medicines cure her. The spells and rituals of the exorcists and diviners do not cure her. Every day, her death draws nearer."

"What kind of sickness does she have?"

"Her body is hot," he says mournfully. "Her breathing is fast. She sleeps night and all day and wakes only to moan. She will not eat. A powerful and savage ghost afflicts her."

"I can hear the emotion in your voice," she says. "I think Bel-ibni is important to you."

Finally, tears.

She doesn't know how to console him.

His sobs garble what he says, but she thinks she hears "*Ēribassi.*"

Kate is angry at herself for her kneejerk twinge of jealousy. "You love her?"

"I have always loved her. I have loved her since she was a girl. But she belongs to the King. She bears his child. I have never been with her. I can never be with her. That does not mean I have ever stopped loving her."

His grief melts her heart. "Do you have a wife?" she asks softly.

"How could I marry?" he says. "My love for her was too powerful. That is why I must save her." Frustration crowds out his tears, and he pounds a fist into his palm. "Too much time passes. I do not know if she still lives. I must find a cure!"

Kate knows she shouldn't touch him, but her urge to do something comforting is too powerful and she stands to lay hands on his shoulders.

"I know someone who can help," she says. "We will talk to him in the morning."

CHAPTER SEVENTEEN

CHINEDU RETRIEVES THE COPY OF *THE CLARION* FROM THE BARMAID, seeking to understand Ninurta's outburst.

"This man?" he asks. "You know this man?"

Adad sees the photo, too, and he and Ninurta engage in frantic discussion.

Ninurta repeatedly stabs the photo with his finger and says, "Mannu. Mannu-ki-Ashur."

"Is he your friend?" Chinedu asks. "Friend?"

They stare at him.

Chinedu decides to act it out with Ninurta. "Me," he says, tapping his chest. "You," he says, tapping Ninurta's. "Friend," he says, putting his hand over his heart. "Chinedu and Ninurta are *friends*."

The demonstration sails over Adad's head, but Ninurta understands.

"Mannu. Ninurta. Friend."

"I see!" Chinedu says. "His beard is like yours. Like you, he was dumped on the street without clothes. The same mules must have betrayed you. You are refugees from the same country. You want to find your friend, Mannu!"

175

Ninurta grasps only a few of Chinedu's words but nods rapidly and repeats, "Mannu! Friend!"

"Give me a minute," Chinedu says. "Let me read the article."

~

"I DO NOT UNDERSTAND what is happening," Adad says.

"Do you not see?" Ninurta says. "This is Mannu. They call this a *pho-to*. They must use magic to make them. You see how Chinedu captured my likeness with a glowing rectangle. They captured a likeness of Mannu. He must be here, close to us. And behold, he arrived, as we did, without clothing."

"Then, we can find him!" Adad exults. "You are learning their tongue. Ask the Nubian how to find him!"

"I do not know the right words."

"You must!"

"I will try."

Ninurta mulls over his limited vocabulary—*beer, bed, water, friend, photo*—and wonders how to make Chinedu understand.

~

CHINEDU DEVOURS THE NEWSPAPER STORY, increasingly aware that his friends are talking loudly and drawing attention.

BY DEREK CHAPMAN, Staff Writer.

Metropolitan Police responded to reports of a bearded and naked man running through a crowded Piccadilly Circus late last night. When officers attempted to make contact with him, he took off running down Haymarket toward Pall Mall. Rather than complying with their instructions, the man turned and charged at police in a threatening manner, and officers were forced to deploy their Tasers. He was handcuffed and detained without further incident, and no officers were injured.

A social media influencer, Leonard Prouty, who goes by the

online name Atomic Ginge, was live-streaming the foot chase when the man barreled into him, smashing his mobile phone. *The Clarion* has exclusively obtained footage of the incident from Mr. Prouty, and interviewed him about the incident.

"I'm always on the ready," Prouty said. "Mayhem and merriment are never far away, especially around Piccadilly. And—boom —there he was—a right nutter flying about in his birthday suit. I'm streaming it live to my channel when the bloke comes at me like I'm at the running of the bulls in Spain, and I go flying. I'm fine, but my phone isn't. Good news is, I've gotten over a million views so far."

The naked man, who appeared to be of Middle Eastern extraction, has not been identified as of the deadline for this story. The Ambulance Service transported him for observation.

CHINEDU SLIDES the paper under his arm, puts a finger over his lips, and says, "Shhhh! You boys are making a scene. Come with me."

On the street, Ninurta presses his case to the best of his ability.

"Pho-to! Mannu! Friend!"

"I understand," Chinedu says, tapping his skull. "I will help you find your friend, but I must think. We will return to my flat and see what we can do."

They do not understand Chinedu's intention and continue to press their case.

"Pho-to! Mannu! Friend!"

Chinedu simplifies his response, producing an exaggerated head nod with every utterance. "Yes! Yes! Yes! Mannu. Friend."

Ninurta receives the message and, in English, replies, "Yes! Yes!"

He informs Adad that the Nubian will help them, and they have a quiet walk home.

At the flat, Chinedu sits them on his sofa while he makes stovetop coffee. They sniff the beverage, wrinkle their noses, and decline. While Chinedu sips his bitter brew, he verbalizes the idea percolating in his head.

"I know you will not understand what I say, but I do like to talk

177

out loud. Here is what I am thinking. There is no point in contacting the police. They will not help us find Mannu, and if I say his friends are looking for him, they will be suspicious about your immigration status. I do not know about this so-called influencer, Angry Ginge. What would he know anyway? I must speak with the person who wrote the article, Derek Chapman. I will persuade him to help us. There you have it. That is my plan."

Satisfied with his solution, Chinedu finishes his coffee and takes to his phone. His Internet search pays immediate dividends when he discovers that *The Clarion* lists a contact email and phone number for members of the public to submit stories. And his eyes widen, when he reads on their website that, *We're always after good stories and we pay big money for them every day.*

"He tells the refugees, "I will call the newspaper. Now, shhh. Be quiet while I speak."

Chinedu calls the contact number and stands to walk and talk. The bed and sofa don't leave much real estate to pace around, so he circles the room in a tight pattern. He is shunted to different extensions and asked to hold several times, but eventually, he reaches the reporter, who speaks in the clipped voice of someone who, simultaneously, is bored and short of time.

"Derek Chapman, here. How can I help you?"

"Mr. Chapman," Chinedu says, reading from the folded newspaper. "I am calling you concerning your article in your newspaper entitled, Caught Bare-Handed: Rush Hour Shock as Piccadilly Streaker Gets the Zap."

"Yeah? What about it?"

"The man in Piccadilly has two friends who arrived in London in similar circumstances. They wish to reunite with him."

"Similar circumstances? Whaddya mean?"

"Naked, in a state of confusion, and speaking no English."

"Oh, really? Where are they from?"

"I do not know their country of origin."

"And how do you know these men—what did you say your name was?"

"My name is Chinedu Okoro. I have made their acquaintance."

Chinedu can hear the reporter typing while talking. "And where are they now, Mr. Okoro?"

"They are staying with me."

"And where is that?"

"I would rather not say. However, I am willing to meet you and provide more information, provided you can help locate their friend."

"I might be able to do a meet. Where do you propose?"

"There is a café in Camden."

"Camden? Really? Mr. Okoro, let me take your number and call you back—alright?"

"Yes, that would be fine. And Mr. Chapman, your website talks about paying for stories."

"Yeah, yeah, we'll see about that, won't we?"

DEREK CHAPMAN'S looks have always been his strongest suit. Despite coming from a lower middle-class family, he has the erect posture, strong jaw, casually tussled mane, and on-demand good diction, that allow him to pass for someone from money. He parlayed his 2:1 degree in politics from a minor university to a job writing for a regional online newspaper, and from there, landed an entry-level position at *The Clarion*. As one of many staff writers, he spends his time snorting for truffles with the rest of the dogs. It was pure happenstance that he was the dog in the newsroom when a police report came in about a naked streaker.

Fresh from the call, Derek looks for his boss, the senior news reporter, but discovers he's out sick. That gives him the golden opportunity to go up a rung and speak to the Deputy Editor, a man Derek brown-noses as often as he can. He hovers over Martin Pinter's desk in the open-plan newsroom and waits to be noticed.

Pinter finally looks up from his keyboard and says, "What?"

"Martin, you know that story I did the other day about the Piccadilly streaker who got Tased?"

"AKA, Derek's first front page? Kudos, I'm sure, but you'd better not be asking me for a raise."

"Not at all, Martin. I've had a call from someone, an African chap by name and accent, who says he's with two men who arrived in London under the same circumstances as my streaker."

"How do you mean?"

"Naked, confused, no English. Sounds like traffickers ripped them off and abandoned them in central London. Anyway, the two blokes are looking for their mate, and the caller wants my help in exchange for the story and cash."

"How much does he want?"

"He didn't say. He wants to meet me in a café in Camden."

"Why Camden?"

"Dunno. Lives there, maybe?"

The editor grows irritable. "If he gave you his name, surely you can look him up and see if he's got a Camden address."

The barb stings and Chapman deflates. "Yeah, will do. Straight away."

"Okay, trundle off to Camden, then. Naked men dumped in London by human traffickers isn't half bad. But don't talk figures, for fuck's sake. Get the story, brief me, and I'll decide how wide the purse strings open—if at all."

CHINEDU ARRIVES at the café with Ninurta and Adad, sits them at a window table, and then orders another coffee for himself and orange juice for them. It's obvious they can't understand why they've returned to the High Street. Chinedu tries to prep them as simply as he can with gestures and the few words Ninurta has picked up. He doesn't try with Adad, whom he's decided is a hopeless case.

"Yes. Mannu. Yes." Chinedu points to the door, uses two moving fingers to describe a walking man, and says, finger across lips, "Shhh."

Ninurta nods, says, "Yes," in English, then tells Adad in Akkadian, "A man is coming here. He will help us find Mannu. The Nubian does not want us to speak when this man arrives."

Glass Coffee on the High Street takes its name from the huge storefront windows that picture-frame the patrons, and Derek Chapman easily spots the people he's meeting from across the street. Chinedu has been scrutinizing everyone who enters, but Chapman makes it easy by coming straight over.

"You must be Mr. Okoro," he says, eyeballing the other two.

"Yes, hello!" Chinedu says with his usual sparkling smile. "I will get you a coffee or any drink you like."

"No, I'm good," Chapman says, grabbing a seat. He nods at the two swarthy men in ill-fitting hoodies and jeans across from him and pulls a mini-recorder from his suit jacket. "Mind if I record this?"

Chinedu asks why.

"I don't want to get anything wrong, do I?"

In Chinedu's line of street work, he knows to always settle on the price beforehand.

"It is okay, but we should discuss the money before you record."

"So, here's the way this works," Chapman starts, with the put-on swagger of someone who's never negotiated this kind of thing. "You need to give me a general idea of the nature of this information, I will relay that to the powers that be at the newspaper, and they will decide on its monetary value."

Chinedu nods gravely. "Yes, but I already told you the nature of the information."

"Indeed you did. It was very general." Chapman openly clicks on the recorder. "A few more specifics would go a long way. For example, where are these gentlemen from? How did they get to London? Did they cross the channel in a boat? Come across in the back of a lorry? Why were they dumped on the street, naked? Who were the traffickers? Were they from the same country as them? How did you enter the picture? You know, those sorts of things."

"They do not speak a word of English, Mr. Chapman. I do not know their language. I showed them a map, but they did not acknowledge any country. You can ask them your questions, but they will not understand you."

Chapman glances at the two sullen men. "So, what am I paying for?"

"You are a reporter for a London newspaper," Chinedu says. "I believe your readers would be interested in learning how these men endured harsh treatment in their new country. I will give you access to them. With your resources, you can find an interpreter who knows their language and can ask them all your questions. But, as an immigrant myself, I do not want their identities or location made known. They have suffered greatly, and I do not want to see them deported to an uncertain fate."

"And what's your immigrant story, Mr. Okoro, if I may ask?"

"That, I am happy to divulge. I am from Nigeria. I came here and lived for a time with my mother, who sadly passed away."

"What kind of work do you do?"

"I would rather not say."

"You sound educated."

Chinedu laughs. "That was my plan. I was a good student in Nigeria. My mother wanted me to go to university. But after she passed, I found myself homeless and have lived the life of a Charles Dickens character."

"Ha! You've read Dickens. That's a good angle. Give me something to take back to my people, and we can talk money. Where did you find them?"

Chinedu has no intention of describing how the refugees ripped off a couple of street dealers. "I cannot say."

Chapman insists, "Come on, something juicy!"

"All right," Chinedu says. "This man, the big fellow. When he was a boy, he endured castration."

"Castration!" Chapman says a little too loudly. "How do you know that?"

"I have seen him. No cock. No balls. See how the younger one has a thick beard? This man's face is hairless."

Chapman's face brightens. "A eunuch. The headline writers will have a field day with that one. I will take a coffee now, if you don't mind."

When Chinedu goes to the counter, Chapman whips out his phone and takes a couple of quick photos.

When he delivers the coffee, Chapman has a sip and says, "I'll be right back. I've got to make a call."

Chinedu watches the tall, fair-haired reporter walk up and down the sidewalk outside the café, having an animated conversation, during which his editor authorizes him to offer a thousand but go no higher than five. When he returns, Chapman declares he has good news.

"My people are interested in the story. You give us access to these gentlemen, allow us to find the appropriate interpreters, and let us confirm he's a eunuch, and we will pay you one thousand pounds sterling. Happy?"

Chinedu crosses his arms, energized by the opening salvo in a negotiation.

"I am not happy," he says. "First, you must find out what happened to their friend. His name is Mannu. Is he in the custody of the police? The immigration authorities? Is he in hospital? Bring me this information and pay me five thousand pounds. If we come to an agreement, I will even allow you to see the eunuch in the flesh. He is not shy."

Chapman extends an arm across the table. "Mr. Okoro, we have a deal."

CHAPTER EIGHTEEN

AMRITA IS UP FIRST, TRYING NOT TO DISTURB HER BEDMATE, BUT Kate is a light sleeper. Sunrise is a ways off.

"Sorry," Amrita says. "Hope I didn't bother you. My sisters always said I spin like a top in bed."

Kate rubs her face to get the blood flowing. "If you did, I didn't notice."

"Good news is, we weren't murdered," Amrita said.

"I don't think we had anything to worry about. He's a gentle man with a kind soul," Kate says.

"So you say. I've got to do a day shift to make up for yesterday. Can I use the shower first?"

"Go ahead."

"I'll put the kettle on," the nurse says, choosing one of Kate's bathrobes from the closet. "I could call in sick again. I don't love leaving you alone with him."

Kate checks her phone and says, "I feel perfectly safe. No one makes the journey he made without good intentions and a pure heart."

"After a night's sleep, you're still convinced about his loony story?"

Kate swings her legs over the side of the bed. "You know me better than anyone, Ammie. When have you ever seen me chasing after fringe ideas?"

"With one exception, you are the most practical, level-headed, and sober person I know."

"One exception?"

"Jeremy."

Kate forces a laugh. "He started out all right. You even approved. I remember you did."

"Only at first. Once he got comfortable, his inner jerk came out. You were too slow to react."

"All right, all right. One blot on my record," Kate says, finding her slippers. "But I don't think my judgment is off on Mannu. If you'd asked me two days ago if I believed in time travel, I'd have laughed my face off, but today—well. The fact is, there's no one alive who speaks like he speaks and knows what he knows. The new tablet from the museum sealed it for me. Not only did he know it by heart, it had his bloody name attached."

"Yes, so you've said," Amrita yawns.

"I'll just sneak into the loo. Then it's all yours," Kate says.

"So, what's your plan?"

"I'm going to try to help him. My brother's just texted me. He'll see us today."

"Us? You're taking him to see John? If you tell him who you think Mannu is, he'll have you committed."

At the door, Kate says, "Gawd, I won't be doing that. I'll need to be creative."

After Kate swaps the bathroom with Amrita, she notices the door to the spare room is ajar. She gently pushes it open just enough to poke her head in and is startled by the sight of Mannu sitting rigidly on the side chair, fully dressed in his new gear. The only thing awry is untied shoelaces.

She makes her brain switch to Akkadian and says, "Good morning. Did you have a restful night?"

"Yes. Thank you, Kate." He says her name with one syllable on the first try.

She realizes her robe is open a bit far, but his stare goes to her feet.

Bunny slippers, she thinks. *How do I explain bunny slippers?*

"*Kīsu*—shoes," she says. "Shoes that look like animals to make a person laugh."

He nods seriously at her explanation.

"Would you allow me to fix *your* shoes?" she asks.

"Yes."

She kneels and ties the laces. On her way up, she feels his hand brush a strand of her hair. She wonders if it was it accidental or on purpose?

"Would you like a morning meal?"

"I would like water," he says.

She kicks off her slippers and returns with a glass of cold water.

"Where are your animal shoes?"

"They ran away."

The joke breaches his defenses, and he cracks a smile.

"I will get dressed," she says, smiling, too. "I will have a morning meal. You can join me."

BEFORE AMRITA LEAVES, she goes into nurse mode and teaches Mannu how to use the shower and brush his teeth. Kate—ever-prepared—has a supply of new toothbrushes and bars of soap. He declines hot drinks at breakfast but enjoys cereal with milk, which he slurps directly from the bowl endearingly, like a child.

Kate worries about subjecting Mannu to a journey on the crowded underground line and a train, so Amrita offers her car, which she only uses for weekend shopping and holiday trips.

As Amrita leaves, he deeply bows, placing his hand over his heart.

"He does act like a gentleman," Amrita says to Kate, "but the moment he doesn't, get away and call me."

"Stop worrying."

"No, I won't. Call me after your brother."

Before leaving for Farnham, Kate has to take care of a few time-sensitive academic chores. Before tackling them, she looks for a video to teach Mannu a few things about the modern world. She finds one on YouTube about the thirty most beautiful cities and reminds him that what he sees on the television are merely pictures that move.

As she works from the dining table, she keeps glancing at his shifting expressions that remind her of a child's wonder and awe at Christmas seeing presents piled high under the tree.

"Did you like what you saw?" she asks when the video ends.

"This is your world?" he asks.

"It is the same world as yours, only a different time."

"I do not understand your time," he says. "I wish to return to mine. When will we see the man who can help me?"

She sees her Uber pull up. "We will leave now," she says.

After a short ride to Amrita's house, Kate puts Mannu into the passenger seat of the red Ford Puma and starts it up.

"You can make this move?" Mannu asks.

"Yes," she says, putting it into gear. "See?"

The route to Farnham loops around London on the M25, then south on the M3. Rush hour is over, but the traffic is still thick. The harsh mid-morning sun forces Mannu to squint at the motorway scenery, and when Kate dons sunglasses, Mannu becomes alarmed and asks what has happened to her eyes.

After an hour, he asks, "I think we travel a great distance to see this man."

"It would take a long time by horse," she says, "but in this world, we travel swiftly with these automobile machines."

"I prefer a horse."

"When I was a girl, I enjoyed riding horses."

"Why did you stop what you enjoyed?"

"I became an adult, and my life became too busy."

He pauses, and she can see him silently nodding when she glances over.

"Is it the same for you?" she asks.

"The chief physician is busy from sunrise to moonrise every day.

Many people need healers. I must make medicines and train the junior physicians."

"When you were a boy, what did you enjoy doing?"

His words soften and become less guttural. "The days never seemed to end. I was always moving, and I never grew tired. I ran through the tall grass along the riverbank. I cast my net for fish and frogs. I ran through the marketplace where merchants would give me olives and dates. I ran around the ziggurats, the temples, and the royal palaces and learned the names of flowers and trees in their gardens. I raced my friend, Ninurta, and competed with him to see who could throw a wooden spear farther. But all of this ended when I became an apprentice healer."

"How old were you?"

"I was eight."

"So young," she says.

"Who is this man we will see?" he asks in a sudden shift.

"He is my brother."

"How can he help me?"

"He is a physician."

He leans into his shoulder belt and says, "I am happy to hear this. I am excited to see his apothecary and the wonderous plants, herbs, and oils physicians in your world use to heal the sick."

"Ah, yes," she mutters in English. "You might be rather disappointed. I've seen his medicines closet."

The Glade Medical Practice is located in a wooded office park near the center of Farnham. Kate's brother is in a group of general practitioners caring for over ten thousand NHS patients. The car park and waiting room are packed on arrival, and Kate worries about her brother's schedule. She tells Mannu that she will not reveal his true identity. He asks why, and she tells him to trust her—that it will be better that way.

"Hello," Kate says to the receptionist. "I'm here to see Dr. Mayne. I'm his sister, Kate."

"Oh, hi!" the young woman says. "I see the resemblance. Is he expecting you?"

"He is, actually. Gosh, it looks awfully busy today."

"To be honest, we're always backed up. I'll tell him you're here. Hopefully, he won't be too long."

Hopes were dashed. It was a long wait. Kate fidgets and plays with her phone. Mannu sits erect, hands on his legs. After an hour, he asks who these people are.

"These are sick people waiting to be seen by a physician."

He frowns at the concept. "In my time, physicians go to the homes of the sick."

Kate's parents used to talk about GPs making house calls. "That used to happen here," she says, "but no longer."

"Are the exorcists and diviners in this building, or must the sick people travel elsewhere?"

"We no longer have exorcists and diviners," she says. "Only physicians. And nurses like Amrita who help the physicians do the healing."

"No exorcists? No diviners?" he says before lapsing into deep thought.

Eventually, a nurse appears and takes them to her brother's office.

John Mayne looks harried, like someone holding onto a schedule by his fingertips. He is lanky, his sleeves rolled up, tie tucked into his shirt, stethoscope slung around his neck.

"John, hi," Kate says, giving him a small hug. "How's everyone? How are the twins?"

"Everyone is fine. Boys are hellishly hyperactive. If I had the money, I'd ship them off to a boarding school."

"I'm sure they'll outgrow it," Kate says, unsure of that. "Thank you so much for making the time. It's chock-a-block out there.

"One of our partners is on hols," he says. "Chaos ensues. I apologize for having to make this short, and having my lunch while we talk. So, this is your visitor from Iraq."

"His name is Mannu Ashur. As I said, he doesn't speak a word of English."

John extends a hand, and Mannu looks at it curiously.

"Should I be bowing? Doing a namaste?" John says, slightly irritated.

In Akkadian, Kate instructs Mannu to grasp and release her brother's hand.

"Right," John says, retreating to his paper-strewn desk. "Formalities over. Don't they speak Arabic over there? I've got some Arabic-speaking patients. Didn't sound like Arabic to me."

"He comes from a very remote village with their own dialect," Kate says, rolling out her invented explanation. "The ruins of an Assyrian temple were discovered there, and the IoA is trying to get the rights to excavate. Mannu has come to London to complete the negotiation."

Ever blunt, her brother says, "What can this possibly have to do with me?"

"While he's in the UK, he was hoping to get a medical opinion about a woman in his village. Apparently, the care she's receiving is falling short, and there's a fear she might die."

"Don't like doing these sight unseen consults, but go ahead. Tell me about her."

Kate tells Mannu to describe Bel's illness and provides a running translation, smoothing out the antiquities.

"She is a woman near to his age who is heavily pregnant. About two weeks ago, she stepped on a piece of iron and badly cut her foot. It sounds like the foot became infected because it oozed pus."

"Ask him what antibiotics she's been given?"

In response to Kate's question, Mannu gives her a list of herbal and plant extracts, and various exorcisms.

She cuts him short and tells John, "It's not clear to me that she received antibiotics. It really is very remote. They don't have a doctor there. A local woman, an herbalist, has been treating her."

"Good God!" John exclaims. "This isn't third-world care. It's in another league." He takes a bite of his sandwich and says, "Go on—"

"Now, some two weeks later, she has high fevers, and her

breathing is fast. She constantly moans, and they're having trouble waking her up."

"Over two weeks, you say," John blurts out. "If she's still alive after two weeks, it's definitely not tetanus and probably not acute bacterial sepsis. What about her skin? Ask about rashes and whatnot on her skin."

Mannu starts telling her about Bel's skin.

"He says she has little red spots on her chest and back and purple spots on her fingertips. And under her fingernails, he's seen small red lines resembling splinters."

"Does he have photos?"

"Unfortunately not."

"Too bad. Sounds like petechiae on her chest, splinter hemorrhages under her nails, and Janeway lesions on her fingers. It's a classic presentation."

"Of what?" Kate asks.

"Subacute bacterial endocarditis," he says, chomping another bite of his tuna sandwich.

"In non-doctor-speak, please—"

"I think the wound infection of her foot became bloodborne, and she now has a bacterial infection of one or more of her heart valves. The skin manifestations are from showers of emboli breaking off and lodging in the skin's capillaries."

"What's the treatment?" Kate asks.

"Antibiotics, of course."

"Which one?"

"Come on, Kate! I can't answer that. She needs blood cultures. Once they've isolated the bug and tested its sensitivities, they'll know which antibiotics to use."

Kate isn't translating any of this for Mannu, and she can see his frustration mounting.

"John, this village has no medical facilities, and the family won't transport her to a town or city. I think Mannu is looking for your best guess on what to use."

"Christ! You're putting your dear brother in a very ethically

x

challenged position. Make sure my name is never mentioned, okay?"

"Of course. Never."

"If this place is so remote and backward that they don't have access to doctors or antibiotics or anything that smacks of modernity, the bacteria involved—probably strep or enterococcus—have likely never developed resistance. Simple penicillin ought to work as well or better than anything."

Kate breathes easier and tells Mannu that her brother is recommending a treatment.

"Ask him which plants I need to make this treatment."

"He wants to know how to make the penicillin from plants," Kate says.

Her brother finishes chewing the last bite of lunch and says, "Now this is getting farcical. Penicillin is dirt cheap and is available widely. Even in remotest Iraq, for Christ's sake. And it doesn't come from plants. It comes from mold."

Kate thinks fast. "I think what he's asking is broader than this one patient. I believe he wants to be able to produce penicillin and make it available for the people in his village."

"Well, that's beyond me. He'd need to speak to a bioengineer or pharmaceutical manufacturer. I've got to press on, Kate. It's been nice seeing you, though more than a little strange."

"Wait," she pipes up. "Don't you know anyone who can give him a simple recipe for making it? A back-of-the-envelope method?"

John shakes his head and says, "You're too much. This better not come back to bite me on the ass, but I went to medical school with a bloke who's a microbiology professor at King's College London. He's a big cheese. I suppose I could put you in touch."

She springs up and hugs him around the neck.

"You're my favorite brother," she says, a family joke.

"Well, I can't say at the moment you're my favorite sister," he says.

"It has to be tomorrow at the latest, John. Mannu is leaving the country soon."

"You're definitely my second-favorite sister," he says. "I'll make a call."

On the way back to Tottenham, Kate tries her best to explain a subject she's fuzzy about. Compounding her problem, her meager knowledge of human anatomy is light-years ahead of Mannu's.

The best she can do is this: "My brother says that Bel-ibni has a sickness of the heart that started in her foot."

"That is very bad," Mannu says mournfully. "The life force comes from the heart. Emotions come from the heart."

"Do you know that hearts have spaces inside like small chambers?"

"I have seen the hearts of sheep and other animals, but not what lies inside them. I do not know what you speak of," he says.

She decides there's no point in trying to explain valves. Or bacteria.

"My brother knows a medicine he hopes will cure her, but it does not come from plants or herbs. We will try to see another physician tomorrow. He might know how to make the medicine you need."

"I pray to the gods this is so," he says. "Thank you, Kate."

He briefly touches her closest hand on the steering wheel. It's the most heartfelt touch she's ever had. She wishes it had lasted longer.

Before returning Amrita's car, Kate stops to buy beer and some decent bread and fixings for dinner. Back in Tottenham, she makes tea, which he tastes and declines. While she has a cup, he gulps a glass of pale ale.

"Oh gosh, you poor man," she says in English. "You must be dying of thirst."

She pours him another, and calls Amrita to let her know how the day went.

"Do you think John's going to come through?"

"I hope so, but who knows? He thinks the whole thing is strange."

"He's not wrong, is he? So, what's the plan?"

"Fingers crossed, it's London tomorrow for his friend."

"I'm going to stay the night again."

"There is absolutely no need, Ammie. Resume your life. Please."

"I'm not happy about that, but I'm only ten minutes away once I'm home. I'll be checking the sky for the bat symbol."

MANNU FALLS asleep on the sofa while Kate makes a pressure-cooker beef stew. When it's ready, she grazes his shoulder, and he wakes in a state of confusion.

Embarrassed, he says, "I did not know where I was. I thought I was in Nineveh."

"I have prepared food. Are you hungry?"

"I am hungry."

"It is another dish from my world. I hope you will enjoy it."

He has learned to eat with utensils and attacks the stew with his spoon. At the sound of a text, she pounces on her phone.

It's from John: Gordon Cross thinks it's the nuttiest thing he's ever heard, but he'll see you at the Dept. of Infectious Diseases at Kings 2:15 tomorrow. You owe me.

There is no Akkadian word for news. "I have a good announcement," Kate tells Mannu. "Tomorrow, we will see an important physician to learn about a cure."

AFTER DINNER, Kate turns off most of the lamps in the sitting room, lights candles, and, long into the night, indulges her fantasy of questioning someone from her favorite era. He happily provides fulsome answers to every question. She gives fleeting thought to taking notes and making a recording, but that's the academic in her, not the person. This is a conversation between two people bridging the millennia, and turning it into a piece of scholarship doesn't seem right.

He talks about the everyday life of Assyrians and his childhood as the son of a prominent man, running free through the sprawling city. He tells her about the magnificent art and architecture of Nineveh, ornate religious festivals, the fragrant hanging gardens, and life at the court for royals, courtiers, and servants. He describes the dignity and intellect of King Ashurbanipal, the wondrous palace library crammed with tablets he knows as whole, she as broken and fragmentary, court politics, army life, and the empire's enemies. He talks about his training as a physician and how his belief in magic, ghosts, and the deities intertwines with his medicinal treatments.

She is mesmerized by his deep, sonorous voice and, at times, closes her eyes and imagines herself not in her flat but in a house in Nineveh, smelling bread baking in the courtyard, hearing urchins outside playing street games. When she opens her eyes, she sees his flashing, coal-black eyes staring at her.

She realizes the time and says, "Can I ask you one more question?"

"You may."

"Tell me more about Bel-ibni."

"From the first day I saw her when she was but a girl and I was but a boy, I cherished her. I cherished her beauty and grace and her good heart. As the years passed and we grew older, the gods played a cruel game and kept us apart. Though we rarely saw each other and spoke few words, I believed she cherished me, too. When the King chose her for his concubine, I knew I had lost her forever. However, I did not stop loving her. There is a poem about the courtship of the goddess Ishtar and her consort, Tammuz. Tammuz is separated from his love and says, My heart is as troubled as the heart of a dove, I weep bitterly, tears flowing down my face—"

Kate recites the next line, "Since suffering has come, I am no longer suited for the king's presence."

"You know it!" Mannu exclaims.

"I know it well," she says. "It is very beautiful. Surely, there must have been many beautiful and desirable women at court. You never once thought about marriage?"

"Never once. The matchmakers tried to change my mind, but I held firm, for I never met a woman to compare with Bel." He turns away and gazes into the flame of the nearest candle. "I confess I sometimes visit the houses of pleasure by the river, but there is no love in such places." Turning back to her, he says, "Why do you not marry?"

She gives him a shy smile. "I never met a man I cherished as much as you cherish Bel-ibni."

"May the gods lead you to such a man," he says.

At his bedroom door, she bids him a good night's sleep. He returns the wishes, running his hand over his beard.

"Tomorrow, when we see the important physician, I will be ashamed of the state of my beard. The curls are gone. Are barbers in your time skilled with curling irons?"

She laughs lightly and says, "Do not worry. You look perfect just the way you are."

He lowers his head, and she senses a kiss is coming, but she will never know because there's a knock at the door.

CHAPTER NINETEEN

Derek Chapman struts like a peacock into the newsroom of *The Clarion* with a copy of the morning edition tucked under his arm. He makes sure to pass the desks of fellow staff reporters, flashing the V for victory sign to anyone unfortunate enough to make eye contact. Except he means it as a double entendre and says "Number two" to whoever cares to engage with him.

One of his colleagues, who always gives as good as she gets, shoots a sour stare and says, "Whatever do you mean, Derek?"

"You know exactly what I mean," he says, waving the paper. "Second front page, baby."

"Oh, that. I thought you were touting a recent lavatory triumph."

"Funny," Derek says. "Maybe you should do comedy instead of journalism."

He opens the paper at his desk and proudly absorbs the front page. The larger of the two photos is his shot of Ninurta and Adad in the Camden coffee shop, showing men's hollow expressions. The smaller photo is the strategically pixelated shot of a naked Mannu barreling toward Atomic Ginge. Once again, the headline writers have come up with a corker: **Undressed Quest in the Capital: Eunuch and Friend in Nude Pursuit for Lost Mate**.

He'd argued with his editor over calling the large man a eunuch.

"Derek, did you or did you not see his undercarriage?" the editor said.

"Did I pull his trousers down in the middle of a bloody diner? No, I did not. Did the Nigerian fellow attest that he'd seen said undercarriage? Yes, he did."

After an extended back and forth, the editor agreed to the designation as long as the copy clearly stated it was solely based on Mr. Okoro's assertion.

He's read his article four times this morning, but a fifth time won't do any harm.

By Derek Chapman, Staff Writer.

In a surprise twist to our exclusive story about a bearded and naked man running amok through Picadilly Circus and central London before being Tased and apprehended by the police, *The Clarion* has learned of two other men who arrived in London under identical circumstances. In the early hours of 25 September, Mr. Chinedu Okoro was on Peter Street in Soho, where he observed the two men seen in this exclusive *Clarion* photo, naked and disorientated on the sidewalk. Although they spoke no English, Mr. Okoro, out of concern for their well-being, took them to his home in Camden, where he fed and clothed them and tried to learn their identity.

It was at that time that he made the chilling discovery that one of the men had been subjected to the removal of his genital organs as a boy and was, therefore, a eunuch. *The Clarion* has not independently verified this claim.

Mr. Okoro, who emigrated to London from Nigeria some years ago, believed that the men, who appeared Middle Eastern, might have been trafficked by an unscrupulous gang who dumped them naked on the streets of London.

After the men saw our previous front-page story, they told Mr. Okoro that the Piccadilly streaker was a missing friend. Mr. Okoro subsequently contacted this reporter for help reuniting the men.

When asked why he undertook this remarkable humanitarian gesture, Mr. Okoro said, "As someone who came to London myself in less than ideal circumstances, I know how frightening the experience can be. I also know that refugees who lack documentation can have a difficult time with the authorities. I plan to contact a refugee assistance agency when these men feel more safe and secure. The younger gentleman is picking up some English, and I hope to learn where they are from and what they went through."

The Clarion would be interested in hearing from any member of the public who has further information about these naked and afraid refugees.

DEREK LEANS BACK, fingers interlaced behind his head, smiling at the ceiling tiles. His reverie is interrupted by another staff reporter who once had lorded over him about nabbing his first front page.

"Congratulations, Chapman," he said. "How's it feel to join the club?"

"I joined it a few days back, didn't you see?" Derek says in a taunting mood. "This is my second. That makes the score two to one. Full time. Game over. Thank you very much."

Undeterred, the other reporter says, "I read you didn't verify the fellow was missing his bollocks. There's also an unverified report making the rounds that you're a complete wanker."

Derek keeps on the lookout for Martin Pinter, the Deputy Editor, who hasn't shown his face this morning. There's never been a better time to ask for a raise. He's been stuck on twenty-eight thousand pounds since joining the paper, which, in his mind, is a ridiculous wage for someone living in London. He's tired of his cheap lodgings and slovenly roommates and is determined to strike now, as his iron has never been hotter.

His phone rings with what he hopes is the first of many congratulatory calls. Instead, it's an angry voice.

"I did not give you permission to take a photo, Mr. Chapman!" Chinedu rages. "You have put me and these men in danger."

Derek is not about to apologize. "Mr. Okoro, I did not need permission to photograph in a public place. And what is the basis for your saying that you are in danger? Why is publishing their photo a threat to you?"

Derek notes the length of time it takes for a reply.

"The traffickers who left him in such a state might come after them—and me," Chinedu says.

"Now, why would they do that?" Derek says.

"I do not know, but I never would have consented to the interview if I knew there would be a photo."

"Right. I'm sure you'll be fine. Now, listen, I've got some good news for you."

"You found their friend?"

"No, not that. I've got an envelope for you with a check for five thousand pounds. Would you like to come and collect it?"

"Yes, I will come," Chinedu says, "but tell me, what have you done to find their friend, Mannu?"

"Mr. Okoro, I just arrived at my desk. If you let me off the phone, I will start calling my contacts."

Derek wasn't lying. He has contacts at several London hospitals and the Ambulance Service and dives into the project. His motivation isn't an obligation to Chinedu Okoro. It's the prospect of another exclusive story, maybe another front page. During his time with the paper, Derek has cultivated a group of relatively low-level healthcare employees whom he pays for juicy tidbits on celebrity patients and politicians. The information rarely goes beyond so-and-so was admitted to hospital last night, but this might be enough to launch a broader query. Here, he is hamstrung by not having the patient's name, but nothing ventured, nothing gained.

He spends a couple of hours working the phone, calling hospital security guards, admissions clerks, janitors, ambulance drivers, and dispatchers, asking if they had any knowledge of a naked patient picked up in the early hours of the twenty-fifth near the junction of Haymarket and Pall Mall.

Helping himself to a cup of pod coffee, he spies Martin Pinter sauntering in and rushes over before the editor can open his shoulder bag.

Pinter looks up and says, "Derek. If you're here for praise, then I will dispense it. Well done. With that, I've got work to do."

"Yeah, thanks for that. I'm working on finding who the first bloke is and where he's at."

"Good. Keep me in the loop."

"I wonder if this is a good time to discuss my salary? I haven't had a bump since I joined, and—"

"Let me stop you there," Pinter says. "Times are tough for traditional journos like us. Ad revenues are down, there's a hiring freeze, and I've heard rumblings about redundancies. I can assure you that with your recent coups, you're position is safe, but can I give you a raise? I'm afraid that's not in the cards until the climate improves. All right?"

Derek holds his ground as the editor buries his head in his bag, pulling out a laptop and searching for his fountain pen.

When Pinter looks up, he says, "Derek, why are you still here?"

~

ON THE WAY to his workstation, Derek silently curses, and he swears out loud after listening to the voicemail from a source at the Ambulance Service. The dispatcher claimed he had the information Derek wanted, but it would cost five hundred quid.

Derek has the authorization to pay sources up to a hundred pounds without higher-level sign-off. To meet the dispatcher's demand, he needs approval from the one person he doesn't want to see again today.

The Deputy Editor looks up and says, "Don't tell me you're taking another run at me."

"It's something else," Derek says. "I need authorization to pay an Ambulance Service source five hundred. He knows which hospital admitted my streaker."

"Can you get him lower?"

"Said he was firm."

"Okay, do it. Now, run along and bring me a story."

Derek makes the call, agrees to the price tag, and learns that the streaker was admitted to University College Hospital in the early morning of the twenty-fifth. It's good news and bad news. He has a source at the hospital, but it will take a personal visit and yeoman's service to extract the nugget of gold.

An hour later, Derek strolls into the discharge office at the hospital and waves at one of the women behind the partitioned counter.

Close enough for her ears only, he says, "Hello, beautiful."

No one but Derek ever calls the discharge clerk beautiful, and she beams back, "Hey, handsome."

"Due for a coffee break?" he asks.

"It's slow enough. I can go now."

At the cafeteria, Derek leans across the table and says, "Haven't seen you for ages."

She swallows a mouthful of sugary bun and says, "You haven't needed anything from me in ages. I think you only come by when you want something."

"You're right," he says. "I want you, and I want a tidbit."

"What kind of tidbit?"

"I did an article about a nutter running around Piccadilly Circus starkers."

"Oh, I saw that!"

"Yeah. Seems he was taken here on the twenty-fifth and was admitted as an Unknown Male. I need to find him. Could still be in hospital. Could have been discharged."

She bats her eyelashes dramatically. "Oooh. Going to cost you."

"Yeah? What's the tariff, then?" he asks. In the past, he's had to cough up a meal here and there but has never had to take her home.

"I'm thinking a swanky Italian restaurant," she says.

"Could do," he says. "That's definitely on. See what you can find out, and we'll compare calendars."

He waits in the lobby until she returns with a slip of paper, which he unfolds for a peek.

Unknown Male, discharged on 28 Sept care/of Dr. Kate Mayne, Langham Rd, Tottenham

"How about Tuesday night?" she says.

"It's a date, beautiful."

On the way back to the office, Derek's mind seethes with the animosity of an underappreciated and exploited employee, hardly noticing the postcard weather. He's delivered the goods. Two front-page stories in a week, and they won't even toss him a bone. He passes through Fitzroy Square and begins to circle Fitzroy Square Garden a few times to think through a germ of an idea. By his third circuit around Georgian landmarks, he'd played the angles, worked through the risks, and settled on the plan. Taking to a park bench, he verifies that a Kate Mayne owns a flat on Langham Road and that, curiously, she's a lecturer at UCL's Institute of Archaeology, not a medical doctor as he'd assumed. The question of why she would take on the responsibility of signing out his streaker piques his interest.

He uses his personal mobile for the call. He doesn't want the paper to have a record of it.

"Hello, Mr. Okoro. Derek Chapman here. How are you, Sir?"

Chinedu is at his flat, where he's been teaching Ninurta a few more useful English words and phrases like the names of utensils, and the real triumph—hello, my name is Ninurta.

"Yes, I am fine, thank you."

"Excellent. I have some good news."

"Yes?"

"I've located your Mannu fellow. Why don't we meet and I can pass you the information."

"Perhaps you can tell me over the phone," Chinedu says.

"Yeah, here's the thing, Mr. Okoro. I need to know how important the information is to you."

"I do not understand."

"Here's what I'm willing to do," Derek says. "I will give you the information and your check for five thousand pounds. In exchange, you will give me five thousand pounds in cash."

"I am sorry," Chinedu says, "but I do not understand."

"It's simple, really. I would like to be paid five thousand for the work I've done on your behalf, which has nothing to do with my job as a reporter. You will fund my fee with your check. Now, do you understand?"

"Yes, I understand. You want to be paid, but it is too much."

"My price is fixed. It is non-negotiable."

Chinedu looks at handsome Ninurta, eager for more words, and Adad, always sullen and silent, with those suspicious eyes of his. Since Mannu is their friend, he reasons, the payment should come from their roll of drug cash.

"Very well," Chinedu says. "I will pay."

Buoyant, Derek says, "If you need to cash the check for the cash, I can go to the bank with you."

"I have the cash."

"You do? Well, that makes it easy, doesn't it?"

"However, I have one condition. I demand proof of Mannu's location. I will not hand over a payment of this size merely for an address or a telephone number."

"What kind of proof did you have in mind?"

"You are a good photographer, Mr. Chapman. Show me a photo of Mannu."

~

AN ADVANTAGE of having roommates is that one has a car, and another has a dog. That night, Derek borrows both and drives to Tottenham for a bit of two-pronged intelligence gathering. Proof of the streaker's location will earn him a nice chunk of cash—the bonus the paper should have meted out. And there's the potential for another big story if he can figure out why this UCL lecturer is involved.

He finds Kate Mayne's flat, parks across the street and takes a walk in the dark with his roommate's little mutt. He's learned that dog walkers blend in well in many situations where single young men do not. He slowly passes by her front room, and spies a man and a woman through parted curtains. On his second pass, he makes out a head of blond hair, matching the UCL photo of Kate Mayne and the long hair and dark beard of his streaker. He has a camera with a telephoto lens, but to use it without suspicion, he needs to reposition the car for a better angle.

"Come on. Good boy, or is it girl? Walkies are over."

Once he's moved the car to a better spot, he trains his long lens on the window and adjusts focus and zoom.

When the face of his streaker fills the frame, he clicks the shutter multiple times.

"Got you."

After Derek emails the photos to himself, he looks through the viewfinder again, and catches the two of them walking up the stairs through the front door's clear transom.

Tossing a chew toy onto the back seat, he says, "Play with this, and for the love of God, don't bark."

He looks for a bell, but there isn't one, so he knocks several times until there's an answer.

Kate opens the door a crack and looks hard at the tall, well-dressed young man.

"Dr. Mayne," Derek says. "I'm very sorry to disturb you at this hour. My name is Derek Chapman. I'm a reporter with *The Clarion*. I wonder if I could ask you some questions about why you signed out of hospital the naked man who was seen running through central London on the night of the twenty-fifth?"

She slams the door on him.

He knocks again to no avail, then pushes his card through the mail slot, and says, "Call me, Dr. Mayne. I'm like a dog with a bone. I will find out why you took a naked refugee home with you."

CHAPTER TWENTY

IN THE MORNING, KATE WRESTLES WITH THE GERM OF AN IDEA, unsure if it would be cruel.

She puts it to him. "Before we see the physician, would you like to see what remains of the land of Ashur?"

"Yes, I would like to see this," he answers immediately.

She thinks he is probably ready to endure a trip on the Underground, and they take her usual route into town. He sits beside her, wincing at the clattering and swaying of the carriage. She pats his hand for reassurance and whispers they are in no danger.

It is cooler today, and a whippy wind scatters an early crop of autumn leaves along Great Russell Street. Arriving after a brisk walk from Holborn Station, Mannu stares slack-jawed at the museum's massive colonnaded façade and asks Kate, "Is this a temple? A palace?"

"It is like a temple. A temple to the past. We call it a museum. It is where we display the art and objects produced by people who lived before our time."

"Here lies the land of Ashur?" he asks.

"Some of it, yes."

Mannu stumbles like a drunk through the disorientating glass-roofed Great Court, and Kate takes him by the arm into the galleries.

"Are you ready to see these things?" she asks. "They might upset you."

"I will see what has become of my land," he says.

She leads him through one of the Egyptian rooms, barely giving him time to register a reaction because they quickly enter the first Assyrian room, Gallery 6, where two colossal, winged human-headed lions stand before an archway.

When he doesn't seem to react, she says, "These are—"

He doesn't require a prompt. "They are the guardians of the old palace of King Ashurnasirpal at Kalhu. This is not possible."

"You know them?" she asks.

"My father took me when I was young—" His voice trails off when he sees a giant lion carved of pink limestone. His voice cracks with emotion. "This lion stands beside the Temple of Ishtar in Kalhu."

"Come," she says. "I will show you things from Nineveh."

They enter Gallery 9, a narrow corridor with stone reliefs on opposing walls, and seeing these, Mannu collapses to his knees, and Kate thinks he will wail. A guard sees him and rushes over, inquiring if the gentleman needs medical assistance. Kate tells him it's only because her friend hasn't eaten and helps Mannu to his feet.

"These are from the old palace of King Sennacherib," he says. "I was last there only a month ago. And here they are in your time and your place."

Some stone reliefs show Sennacherib's monumental construction projects—quarrying, transporting limestone, and installing enormous, winged bulls at the palace's main entrances. Others depict the King's military campaigns.

Mannu moves to run his hand along the stones, perhaps to convince himself they are real, but she tells him they are precious and he must not touch them.

He nods in understanding and follows her lead.

"Here is my favorite place," she says in Gallery 10, standing before The Banquet Scene of Ashurbanipal from the King's palace at Nineveh. "I come here often."

Mannu can no longer staunch his tears, and choking on his words, he says, "I pass this carving every day when I walk from my apothecary to Bel-ibni's sick room. It makes me feel close to her, but I am very far away."

"I am sorry," Kate says. "I should not have put you through this ordeal."

"No, it is good you brought me here. It is important I know what becomes of my land. If there is more, I will see it, but I would like to ask a question."

"You may."

"Why do you come here often?"

Kate has never asked herself why. She's always put down the gravitational pull to her academic interests, scholarship, that obvious sort of appeal.

"When I gaze at this carving, I feel closer to people like you."

He nods solemnly and says, "I understand."

He touches her arm. Again, his light touch is exciting.

"I have one more place to show you," she says.

Gallery 55 is on the upper floor. She takes him up the west stairs, through the rooms of ancient Levant, to the exhibit she knows will be impactful, a stylized bookshelf behind glass containing cuneiform tablets from the great library of Nineveh.

As Mannu's eyes dart from tablet to tablet, Kate recites in Akkadian, "I, Ashurbanipal, learned the wisdom of Nabu, laid hold of scribal practices of all the experts, as many as there are, and I examined their instructions."

"He is a great and wise king," Manny says, "Here are but a few of the tablets from the great library that holds all the wisdom of the world."

"You know these texts?"

"I know them all. I love them all. Oh, I wish to return to my time, where none of the tablets are broken, and I can dwell in the library in study and contemplation from the first to the last light of day."

"It must be a wonderful library," she says wistfully.

"Oh, it is so very wonderful."

WITH TIME REMAINING before their appointment with Professor Cross, Kate takes Mannu to a Middle Eastern restaurant for food he might recognize. Her idea hits the mark, and she watches with pleasure as he gobbles down plates of hummus, falafel, and flatbread.

After lunch, as they amble down Drury Lane to Kings College, Kate can tell he is getting more accustomed to the sights and sounds of London. Fewer experiences cause him to startle and flinch.

PROFESSOR GORDON CROSS has the habitus of an oversized cherub with a matching personality. Kate had worried that any friend of her brother's would be as dour and unapproachable as him, but Gordon is friendly and breezy. It tickles her that his trouser legs are inches too short and that one of his stays is missing, giving his collar the appearance of a bird with a broken wing.

He takes them to his rather spacious office down the hall from the research microbiology labs and offers coffee, which she declines for both of them.

"It's terribly good of you to see us," Kate says.

"I was delighted to hear from your brother. I can't think of the last time I saw John. Must've been one of our reunions, but who remembers the details of those boozy affairs? Well, John might, actually. Never much of an imbiber, your brother."

"Yes, the sober one of the family," Kate says.

"Indeed. Now, then. He gave me a brief introduction to your quest. Was he pulling my leg? Is this your non-English-speaking Iraqi who wishes to learn how to make penicillin in a rural village?"

"This is Mr. Ashur, and no, John wasn't pulling your leg."

"Why doesn't he just buy it from a pharmacy in the nearest town? Penicillin is one of the cheapest pharmaceuticals in the world.

They could even apply for a grant to any number of charitable organizations."

Kate is prepared for this question and others. Whether Gordon Cross believes her remains to be seen.

"His village is deeply insular and conservative. In a way, they live a pre-industrialized way of life. They are completely self-sufficient. They eat what they raise and cultivate. They rarely marry outside their village. They avoid products from the outside world. They dig wells for their water and burn oil in their lamps. Their medicines are traditional herbal remedies. I'm told these are effective for many ailments. However, they have no good treatment for bacterial infections. Minor cuts and scrapes can get infected, and they can do nothing to prevent infected wounds from becoming serious problems. A woman in the village became very ill from a foot wound. John said it sounded like endocarditis."

"Yes, he told me about her clinical findings," Gordon says. "A textbook example of subacute bacterial endocarditis."

"Mr. Ashur hopes to learn how to produce a basic antibiotic to help this villager and others. Can you help him?"

Gordon's smile rounds his cheeks into rosy crab apples. "It's completely daft, but yes, I can provide a basic methodology. It will produce penicillin. The question is, will it produce a final product potent enough to treat the infection? Endocarditis typically requires high doses to be effective. On the other hand, if the villagers have never used antibiotics for people or livestock, the bacteria should be exquisitely sensitive. No resistance pressure, you see. So, the only way to know if the home-brew method works is to try it."

"Can you give us a recipe?" Kate asks.

"Indeed, I can. But you'd better take notes."

She pulls a notebook from her bag and waves it.

"Excellent. I assume you can communicate with the gentleman and translate your notes into Arabic or whatever."

"It's whatever," Kate says. "They speak a rare local dialect."

"All very exotic," Gordon says, closing his eyes momentarily as if retrieving a file from his memory bank. "Right. The first step is to grow the mold-producing penicillin, specifically *penicillium notatum* or *chrysogenum*. Don't worry about the scientific names. The nice thing about these molds is that they grow like the clappers on spoiled food, especially bread and fruit. So, I'd start with a good hunk of stale bread and a bunch of dates, figs, melons, or some such, put them in a large clay pot, and put them in a warm, damp place—in the shade, I'd say. You don't want it to be too hot. Keep it moist by sprinkling water when needed. Within a day, the mold will start growing. Then, you must feed the little dears. What they need is a source of sugar. The best thing to use is a handful of crushed wheat or barley suspended in a liter or so of clean water. That will create a nice nutrient broth for them to pour into the clay vessel. A day or two later, the liquid in the pot will contain penicillin. Got it so far?"

"Yes," Kate says. "Word for word." She glances at Mannu, who has been staring inquisitively at her notebook. In Akkadian, she says, "He is giving us the recipe."

Mannu nods and simply says, "Good."

Gordon continues, "Now, the next step is to separate the liquid, which contains the penicillin, from the solid mass of mold. To do this, they'll need to filter the moldy liquid through the finest cloth they have—linen, wool—whatever is finer. Then, they will have to extract the penicillin from the filtered liquid. The way to do this is by using a mild acid. Acetic acid, AKA vinegar, will do nicely."

"How much vinegar?" Kate asks.

"Hmmm. This is an inexact science, as specified. Let's say two or three tablespoons of vinegar for every liter of fluid. In relatively short order, they'll see two layers. They must pour off the clearer upper layer, leaving the cloudy lower layer. That's where the penicillin is. Ready for more?"

"There's more?" Kate asks, looking up from her writing.

"Oh, yes! Now, they must concentrate the penicillin to make it more potent. This is simple to do, but it must be done carefully. They need to heat the vessel of liquid over a gentle fire to evaporate water and leave concentrated penicillin behind. Do not boil it! That will destroy the antibiotic. Aim to reduce the water content by—say, half. You could accomplish the same by leaving it in the sun, but it would take donkey years." The microbiologist looks at Kate's exasperated face and says, "Don't worry! Almost there."

"Glad to hear it," she says, shaking her hand.

"To make the broth into a clinically useful product, they must repeat this concentration step another time or two. Gently heat the liquid until half of it evaporates. Do this twice, and you should have a nice dose of oral penicillin in a volume of roughly one hundred milliliters. Will it be a precise dose? No, it will not. Will it be an effective dose for a serious infection? Try it, and see. Best I can say. Of course, there's no way to make a sterile intravenous preparation in primitive environs, so it's oral or topical dosing only."

"All this for one dose?" Kate asks.

Gordon shrugs his round shoulders. "Maybe two. Who knows? For a case of subacute bacterial endocarditis, I'd recommend throwing the kitchen sink at it—so one dose three times a day. Of course, this patient would need a couple of weeks of therapy, so the whole process would need to be done in a production line, putting up multiple pots of fermenting bread and fruit daily. Now, I could give you my best guess of the amount of penicillin produced by this method in units per milliliter, but it's of academic interest only. Your friend will simply have to see if the patient is cured. It could work. I believe it should work."

"How long should the patient be treated?" she asks.

"Endocarditis requires extended therapy. I'd recommend a good month."

Kate slaps the notebook shut, thanks Gordon profusely, and when she stands, Mannu stands. He has learned the practice, and when Kate shakes the professor's hand, he follows suit.

"Tell your Mr. Ashur I wish him the best of luck," Gordon says.

Kate tells Mannu, "The physician has taught us how to make the medicine for Bel-ibni. I will explain later what he has said."

Mannu wipes his moist eyes and says, "Please tell the great physician that I pray that the gods Ashur and Nabu bless him with peace and happiness."

Kate tells Gordon, "Mr. Ashur says, God bless you."

CHAPTER TWENTY-ONE

SIN-SHUMU-LISHIR, THE CHIEF EUNUCH OF NINEVEH, CATCHES HIS breath whenever a shadow darkens his door, hoping the next who enters will be Adad, returning from the great unknown, bearing tidings of the deaths of Mannu-ki-Ashur and Ninurta-sharru.

It would be unseemly for Sin to visit the concubine personally, so he summons Kisir, who is keeping a close watch on Bel-ibni.

Sin has demanded an audience with Kisir nearly every day. At this point, the exorcist expects arrogant treatment, and he is accustomed to standing like an underling before the reclining eunuch.

"What is her condition?" Sin demands.

"Her life slips from her," Kisir says.

"How much longer? Hours? Days? Weeks?"

"I do not know," Kisir answers.

Dripping with sarcasm, Sin says, "You are a learned man. A great healer. Answer my question."

"Not hours, not weeks."

"Then, days. How many days?"

Kisir sighs. "It is difficult to say. Perhaps four or five. She is young and strong, but her affliction is serious. Despite our spells and rituals to drive away the demons, the ghosts who torments her will not loosen their grip. We can but pray to the gods that Adad and Ninurta find Mannu and help him return with a cure. Otherwise, Bel-ibni will die, and with her, the King's child."

"Yes, we all pray for a favorable outcome," Sin says. "Return tomorrow with another report. If her condition changes, inform me immediately, any time of the day or night."

~

KING ASHURBANIPAL TREATS his Chief Eunuch as harshly as Sin treats those below his station. He makes Sin stand and wait for an hour before he enters the throne room with his entourage. And he leaves him standing while he sits on his cushioned throne.

"Why have you not found Mannu-ki-Ashur?" the King bellows.

"Great King, the palace guard has scoured the city," Sin says, bowing deeply. "My spies and informers have cast their nets wide. I have offered a reward in gold from my personal coffers for his delivery unto me. I believe he has fled Nineveh, fearing your wrath for his failures as a healer."

Ashurbanipal is red-faced and furious. "My new commander of the guards informs me that my previous commander, Ninurta-sharru, has also disappeared. What do you know of this, Chief Eunuch?"

"We are also looking for Ninurta-sharru," Sin says. "O King, as you may know, Mannu and Ninurta have been friends since childhood. Their disappearances could be unrelated, but I believe otherwise. I suspect they have fled together, both in disgrace."

The King shifts uncomfortably on his throne as he prepares to utter a distasteful word. "It has come to my attention that Ninurta, the man entrusted with my protection, is—*šinuhtu!*" he roars.

"It is true, Your Majesty. He was caught in the act."

"Yet, you, Chief Eunuch, the man who holds more power than anyone but me, approved Ninurta for his position."

Now, it is Sin who is uncomfortable. He has never seen the King so furious, and he senses danger circling him like a bird of prey.

"Ninurta had distinguished himself as a warrior soldier. I knew

215

nothing of his base desires and practices. He hid his secrets well. Perhaps his friend, Mannu, has his own secrets." Then, thinking better of his excuses, he says, "However, I have failed my lord and master. Your harshest punishment will be too light."

Ashurbanipal rises and smashes his staff onto the floor hard enough to crack a tile.

"My courtiers are incompetent! My healers are incompetent! My concubine and my unborn child are dying! I condemn Mannu-ki-Ashur and Ninurta-sharru to death. Other condemnations will follow. If you do not wish to be among them, Chief Eunuch, bring me Mannu and Ninurta."

LATE AT NIGHT, Sin's men smuggle Prince Ashur's envoy into his quarters for another of their clandestine meetings.

The envoy uncloaks himself and accepts a glass of honeyed wine.

"I tire of living in hiding at a filthy inn by the river," he said.

Sin sighs apologetically. "Although the concubine still lives, the Chief Exorcist tells me her end will come within days."

"Have you found the Chief Physician?"

"We have not."

"It is well he fled," the envoy says. "The King would have his head on the day his unborn child dies, as he will take the heads of the exorcists and diviners."

"And mine, too, if I am not careful," Sin says. "I wish to live so that I may serve your lord, Prince Ashur when he ascends to the throne."

"You are a cunning man," the envoy says. "I wager that, like the scorpion, you are hard to kill."

Sin laughs heartily. "If I survive, I will add the scorpion to my cylinder seal."

"I have received a message from my prince," the envoy says.

"The messenger receives a message," Sin jests.

"He grows impatient. It takes five days for news to travel

between Nineveh and Babylon. I can see him now, standing on the walls of Babylon, bellowing at the skies, waiting for a rider to appear."

"Beyond expressing his frustration, what was his message?" Sin asks.

"Today is the first day of the week," the envoy says. "If Bel-ibni is dead by the sixth day, the day of Ishtar, the Prince will double your reward. I do not know how wealthy you are, Chief Eunuch, but satisfy my lord, and he will make you wealthier still."

Sin raises his cup in appreciation and says, "One requires a head to spend silver and gold."

CHAPTER TWENTY-TWO

Outside King's College, Mannu is anxious to hear what "the great physician with round cheeks" told her.

Kate raises her voice over the noisy traffic on The Strand. "He told me important information about making the medicine we call penicillin. He gave me instructions on making this medicine from substances that will be easy to find in Nineveh."

Kate has never seen Mannu smile so broadly. "Tell me. What are these substances?"

"Bread, dates, water—" She interjects an English "damn" when she blocks on what else Gordon said. "Oh, yes, crushed barley. And vinegar. And you will need clay pots and finely woven cloth."

"That is all?" Mannu says incredulously. "Can you teach me the *niširtu?*"

Kate doesn't recognize the word and has to look it up on her phone.

"Yes! I can teach you the formula—I will tell you what you must do each day. However, I worry because there are many things to remember."

"I remember formulas when I write them."

"I am the same way," she says over the din of a passing double-decker.

"You will tell me, and I will write the formula on a tablet," he says.

"You mean on clay?"

"Yes. I need clay, like the clay I used in the building of the sick."

Kate frowns and thinks, *Where am I going to get clay?*

It comes to her, and she blurts in English, "Art supply. Craft stores."

She searches her phone and finds a Cass Art store on Charing Cross Road, only half a mile away.

"I know where to find clay," she says. "We will go there now. It is close." It occurs to her that she left out one important detail about the penicillin manufacture. "I forgot that you will need one more thing," Kate says. "You will need time. It takes two or three days to make the medicine."

His smile evaporates. "Then, we must hurry and continue the quest."

"But you have learned how to make the medicine?" she asks.

"I cannot return to my time without the plants for my potion."

Kate is blindsided. "What plants?"

"I will tell you their names. Then, you can show me where to find them."

Plants? Kate thinks. *I hate gardening.*

"MODELING CLAY," Kate asks the clerk at Cass Art. "Do you sell modeling clay?"

"On the back wall, you'll see a sign for casting and modeling."

Kate leaves the selection to Mannu, who is puzzled by the selection on the shelves. When he requires clay, he sends an apprentice to the river to scoop some from the bank. Here, the clay is cut into rectangular slabs and covered in strange clear wrapping.

Kate realizes he is stymied and says, "There are two colors—red and white. And there are different sizes. You must choose the color and the size."

He nods and uses his thumb to indent a block of Gedeo air-drying natural red clay.

"This is good clay," he says. "Tell me the length of the formula, and I will tell you how much clay I must have."

Kate has seen his neat, small cuneiform writing. She chooses the one-and-a-half kilogram size, enough for a few tablets.

"Now we need to find a stylus," she says, searching the racks. "There!" she says, grabbing a packet of wooden pottery tools. "Can you make this stick into a stylus?"

He inspects it and says, "I can shape it with a knife. It will be good."

As Kate pays for the items, Mannu looks baffled.

She tells him, "This card is how we buy from shops. It is like your coins or barter. It is too hard for me to explain more."

"You do not have to explain all that confuses me," he says. "I am confused by most things in your world."

It's early afternoon, and Charing Cross Road is already jammed with rush-hour traffic. Kate watches Mannu, worried he might veer off the sidewalk and be clipped by a cyclist.

She pulls him away from the curb and says, "You must tell me more about these plants."

THE MEETUP with Derek Chapman isn't until the afternoon, so Chinedu spends the morning at his flat teaching Ninurta more English. He tries to explain that they will find their friend soon by showing him and Adad the photo of Mannu that Chapman emailed. The two Assyrians murmur questions to each other: Is this house near to us? Who is this woman with bright hair? Does she know how to cure Bel-ibni?

"Mannu, friend!" Ninurta says, adding the question, *ēnu*, the word for where.

"We will see your friend, Mannu, today," Chinedu says. He

repeats today multiple times, pointing at the ground for emphasis. "Say today."

Ninurta has learned that "say" means repeating what Chinedu said.

"To-day," he says.

"Very good!" Chinedu points forward and says, "Tomorrow." After Ninurta wraps his tongue around that, he points to the rear and says, "Yesterday."

He tries to convey the meaning after his pupil can say the words fluidly.

He points at the ground each time with exaggerated head nodding and says, "Today we see Mannu. Today, Mannu. Today, Mannu."

"Today, Mannu," Ninurta says.

Chinedu points forward and shakes his head. "Not tomorrow." He points behind, still shaking. "Not yesterday."

After a few rounds of this, Ninurta radiates with understanding and says, "Today, Mannu!"

Adad looks at him from the sofa and asks what he is saying.

"Chinedu is telling me that we will find Mannu today."

"Are you certain?"

"I believe it to be so."

"When will we see him? In the light of day or the dark of night?"

Ninurta says to Chinedu, "Today, Mannu?" as he goes to the door and pretends to open it.

"Yes, soon," Chinedu says. "We will go soon."

Ninurta knows what yes means. He tells Adad that he thinks they will see Mannu soon. Adad grunts and closes his eyes.

Chinedu tries his hand at teaching colors. Finding a color chart on his phone, he and Ninurta call out names until they've worked through the spectrum. Then, with Adad's head drooping, the Nigerian playfully moves onto parts of the body from the top down.

At lips he touches his lips then tenderly touches Ninurta's.

"Lips," he says, smiling.

"Lips," Ninurta repeats.

"Mouth," Chinedu says, opening his.

"Mouth," Ninurta says, his eyes dancing.

Chinedu edges closer until their thighs are touching. "I see how you are looking at me," he whispers. "You are a beautiful man. I think maybe you like me as much as I like you. You do not know what I am saying, but I think you still understand."

Ninurta smiles at the whispering.

"Kiss," Chinedu says, planting a kiss on his own hand. "Kiss."

Ninurta copies him.

Chinedu leans in, says the word again, then ever so lightly, kisses Ninurta's lips.

Ninurta pulls away. Chinedu starts to say he is sorry if he misjudged him. Ninurta looks to the snoring Adad, smiles, then kisses Chinedu back.

"That was nice," Chinedu purrs. "Perhaps—"

His phone rings. Adad wakes, and the moment is gone.

The call is brief, and Chinedu tells them, "Come. We will go find your friend, Mannu."

Before they leave, Chinedu writes down his name and address and folds the paper around a wad of banknotes from Ninurta and Adad's cash roll. He attempts to explain to Ninurta, as best he can, that if they are separated, he will have money and know-how to return.

Ninurta looks mystified as Chinedu slides into his jeans pocket and continues his pantomime explanation.

While Chinedu talks, Adad slips into the kitchen, steals a paring knife, and hides it in his hoodie.

There's a taxi rank on the High Street, and Chinedu opens the door for the Assyrians. He points to a black cab and has Ninurta say, taxi a few times. To complete his lesson, he pats the wad of bills and paper in Ninurta's pocket and says, "Taxi. Chinedu."

Climbing in the first taxi, he tells the cabbie, "We are going to the London Eye."

∼

It's the first time Ninurta and Adad have seen central London in the daytime, and they stare in amazement as the buildings get taller and the crowds thicker. On the Waterloo Bridge, their muscles tense. They yelp at the realization they are suspended over a river.

"Your mates all right?" the driver says.

"It is their first time in London," Chinedu says. "They are not used to big cities."

The taxi stops at Jubilee Gardens, and Chinedu makes sure Ninurta watches as he pays the driver. But he and Adad are transfixed by the giant Ferris wheel rising beside the mighty river.

"It is hard to explain," Chinedu says. "Come."

He spots Derek in the park, basking in sunlight near the children's playground.

"Have a seat," Derek says, patting the bench. "I see you brought your unusual friends."

"What do you have for me, Mr. Chapman?"

"I have your check and an address. What do you have for me?"

"Five thousand pounds in cash."

"Shall we trade?" Derek asks.

Adad says to Ninurta, "Behold! The giant wheel is turning. There are people inside. What is the purpose of this wheel?"

"Perhaps it is a means of execution, where they throw prisoners to the ground from a great height," Ninurta says.

Derek thumbs the stack of fifties. When he counts to a hundred, he says, "It's a pleasure doing business with you. Let me know what these refugees get up to, all right? If there's another story in it, you could earn your cash back. *The Clarion's* got plenty of dosh for stories because they pay their reporters like shit."

When Derek strolls away, Chinedu points to the Eye and says, "I would take you on the ride to see the sights, but I think you want to find your friend. We will find another taxi and go see Mannu."

At a coffee shop on the Charing Cross Road, Kate buys a latte for herself and a juice for Mannu. She has him taste the coffee and laughs as he recoils.

"I thought you would not enjoy this beverage," she says. "Please tell me more about the plants you require. What are they? What is their purpose?"

"They are for the magic ceremony. I stood in the circle of sacred objects, made the incantations, and drank the potion. That is how I came here."

"What are the sacred objects?" she asks.

"A sprig of *ṣēru* for Nabu, a clay tablet for Nabu, and a jar of water for purity and clarity."

Kate looks up *ṣēru* and says in English, "Yes, thyme. Easy enough." Then she says in his language, "Do you read the incantations?"

"No, I learned them."

"And the plants. What are they?"

"One is *šināti-ṣalmu*. Another is *ḫanbū*. The third is *ēṭū*. Do you know where I can find them?"

Kate shakes her head weakly. "I do not know them. I do not know what they are called in my time. Do they have any other uses?"

"They are useful medicines. I use *šināti-ṣalmu* for coughs and wounds. I use *ḫanbū* for fluid in the chest. I use *ēṭū* for fluid in the legs and diarrhea. This was the first time I prepared them in a single potion."

"Where do *you* find them?"

"By the river. At the edge of fields. The *ēṭū* grows in the palace gardens."

She looks up the plant names in her Akkadian dictionary but finds nothing identifying their genus and species.

This is hopeless, she thinks, wanting to cry.

"I think you do not know these plants," Mannu says gravely.

"You are correct," she says with a wan smile. "I wish I possessed the knowledge."

He reaches across the table and touches her hands. "When I seek knowledge, I go to the great library."

Kate looks at his powerful hands and uses his prompt.

"If I can show you pictures of the leaves and flowers of these plants, would you recognize them?"

"Yes, I would recognize them."

"Then, come. I know where to go."

～

THE TAXI LEAVES CHINEDU, Ninurta, and Adad at Kate Mayne's address in Tottenham. Chinedu compares Derek Chapman's photo with her house, satisfied the front window and the curtains match.

"Is Mannu here?" Adad asks Ninurta.

"I think so," Ninurta says.

Adad grips the handle of the knife. It is not wood or bone, but feels good in his hand.

"Come, let us surprise your friend," Chinedu says. "He will be joyous to see you."

He knocks on Kate's door, waits, and knocks again. Stepping to the bowed front window, he peers inside and raps on the glass.

"No lights," he says. "Let us check the back."

The flat is at the end of a row of attached houses, so there's easy access through the small garden. He knocks on the rear door a few times. The glass is frosted; it's dark inside.

"I am sorry," Chinedu says. "We will have to come back later."

"Mannu, no?" Ninurta says, dejected.

"No Mannu. Mannu is not here." Chinedu pantomimes walking away and returning with his fingers. "We will come back for Mannu."

Ninurta nods and translates for Adad, who angrily spits on the ground.

～

MANNU IS speechless as he absorbs the low-slung, sprawling brick edifice of the British Library from its broad, sun-splashed plaza.

"This is our great library," Kate says proudly.

She has taught him the word book, and he says, "Here, you keep the *books* of your empire?"

"And all the empires in the world," she says.

"How many books does your king possess?"

She doesn't know how to convey a number like two hundred million. "Almost as many as the stars in the sky" will have to do.

"Will we find my plants here?"

"I hope we will find pictures of your plants in books and instructions where to find them."

Kate shows the attendant her member's pass and gives Mannu a minute to stand agape in the main reading room.

"I have seen many wondrous things," he says, "but none compares with this chamber."

"I think I would feel the same if I saw Nineveh," she says.

She takes him to the Humanities Reading Room and its reference desk, where she recognizes one of the librarians who has helped her over the years.

"Hello, Marilyn!"

"Dr. Mayne! So nice to see you."

"I have a colleague from Iraq with me today. I'm afraid he doesn't speak English."

The librarian waves, and Mannu bows to her."

"How gallant! Can I help you with something today?"

"We're looking for books on the plants of Iraq, particularly those with medicinal properties. They need to have good photographs or drawings of the specimens."

The librarian clucks approvingly. "That's why I love this job. There's always something new. I'm interested to see what we find. Do you want to look at the catalog or leave it to me?"

"I feel quite safe in your hands," Kate says.

Kate takes Mannu to an empty table and mostly, they silently wait.

After a while, he does ask, "There are many people here. What do they read?"

"Many different things," she says. "Books on history, poetry, religion, the natural world, mathematics."

"Are they high officials? Are they healers?"

"They are ordinary people," she says.

"Why do they read?"

"To learn."

He purses his lips and nods. "This is good."

When the librarian returns, she is wheeling a small cart.

"I've got you a nice assortment, Kate," she says. "Some of them have beautiful color plates. If you don't find what you need, I'll make another run into the stacks."

Kate gives them the once-over, translating titles for Mannu as best she can. Most are from the nineteenth or early twentieth century, with line drawings or water-color plates of specimens. A couple are modern.

"This one is on medicinal plants of Iraq—our name for Assyria. This is on the wild plants of Iraq. This one is about the herbs of Iraq. Oh! This one on Iraq's medicinal herbs and plants is only a few years old, and it has beautiful pictures." Even better, she sees that one of the authors is an Oxford University academic. "Mannu, the man who made this book, the plant scholar, is from the school I studied."

"Then, it must be a good book," he says.

"Let us see," she says, opening it. The spine cracks with its first opening.

It's virginal, she thinks.

The book is lavishly illustrated with bright photos. She turns the pages one at a time, asking Mannu if he recognizes any.

Halfway through, he excitedly points and says, "This is *ḫanbū!*" too loudly.

She hushes him and says, "Excellent! Let me read about it."

Marrubium vulgare. White horehound. It features upright square stems with a white felted texture. Its opposite leaves have a wrinkled surface, a white woolly underside, and blunt-toothed edges. The small, white flowers are arranged in whorls encircling the stem. Distributed widely throughout Iraq and the Middle East, has a long history of use in traditional medicine, particularly for treating respiratory conditions and digestive disorders. White horehound is known for its expectorant properties, making it helpful in relieving coughs and clearing mucus from the lungs.

She snaps a photo of the page with her phone and turns more pages.

With few pages left, Mannu pounces again.

"This one?" Kate asks. "Are you certain?"

"*Šināti-ṣalmu!*" he says. "I am certain."

Althea ludwigii is a species within the Malvaceae family, commonly associated with the broader group of plants that includes hibiscus and marshmallow plants. The leaves of Althea ludwigii are usually alternate, with a simple, broadly ovate with a softly hairy surface.

The flowers are notable for their delicate beauty, typically ranging from pale pink to a deeper rose, often with a darker center. This species, common throughout Iraq, the Middle East, and parts of Europe, is noted for its medicinal qualities. Its soothing and anti-inflammatory properties have been useful in easing breathing and respiratory ailments.

She takes more pictures and says, "We are doing well, Mannu. We must find the last one."

With only a sliver of pages left, Kate is discouraged, but before she gets to the back cover, Mannu grabs her arm and says, "Here is *ēṭū*."

Tamarix ramosissima. The tamarisk, scientifically known as Tamarix, is a genus comprising numerous species of large shrubs or small trees known for their distinctive appearance and adaptation to arid environments in Iraq, the broader Middle East, and Africa. Tamarisk plants typically grow as dense, bushy shrubs or small trees. The leaves are small, scale-like, and arranged alternately along the branches. Tamarisk flowers are small and delicate, usually pink or white. Tamarisk has been used in traditional medicine for its antiseptic properties, making it useful for treating wounds and preventing infections. It also acts as a diuretic, helping manage fluids in the body. Traditionally, tamarisk also has been used to treat digestive issues such as diarrhea and other gastrointestinal disturbances.

"Now we know the names of your plants," she says triumphantly.

"Then let us go and collect them for the potion," he says.

Her victorious feeling quickly dissipates. "We might find these plants in Iraq, but Iraq is far away, and you cannot go there."

"Why can I not?"

She doesn't even try to explain concepts of identity papers, passports, and visas.

"It will take a great deal of time," she says.

"Bel-ibni does not have a great deal of time," he says.

Kate turns to the biographies of the authors and says, "I will call the man who wrote this book and ask for help."

Outside, on the plaza, Kate rings the number of the Oxford Botanic Garden and Harcourt Arboretum, where Tristram Coffin is a professor of botany and director. Grimacing at the voicemail prompt, she leaves a detailed message.

"The plant scholar did not answer. We will go to my house and wait for his reply."

"There is little time, Kate," he says with a catch in his throat.

She gives him a small, soothing touch. "I know. I know."

ON THEIR RETURN, they begin the work of transcribing Gordon Cross's penicillin recipe from English to Akkadian. Kate sits opposite Mannu at her dining table as he shapes a hunk of modeling clay into a flat slab the size of his large hand, whittles a pottery tool into a stylus, and produces the first straight line of cuneiform with lightning speed.

How often had she imagined a scribe doing what she is seeing? How often had she held an ancient tablet in her palm and felt a deep connection to the maker? Her breathing slows. She experiences a pleasurable, heady rush.

He looks up. "I am ready for the next step."

She snaps back to action and finds her place in her notes.

"Put the clay pot in a warm, damp place, in the shade. Keep it moist by adding some water when needed."

Another perfect line of small cuneiform characters appears in the clay.

"I am ready for more," he says.

"Add one handful of crushed barley to a jug of clean water. Pour it into the clay vessel."

And on it goes until cuneiform symbols mark the clay from top to bottom.

"Will you add your *ša muhhi*?" Assyrians call the colophon *that which is at the end*.

"This is not an official text," he says. "It is for learning."

"I would like to have your name."

"Tell me why?"

"So I can look at it when you are gone."

THAT EVENING, Kate and Mannu settle into an odd domesticity. Kate makes dinner in the kitchen while Mannu studies his tablet, memorizing it by repeating each line aloud.

"Will you take a meal?" she says, laying the table.

"I will take a meal," he says, joining her.

Over a hodgepodge of stew, she asks if he can remember the recipe. He replies by closing his eyes and reciting it word-for-word.

"I am impressed," she says.

"One must have a strong memory to become a rab asû," he says. "I will keep studying until I know I will not forget."

Kate hears her phone from the hall and runs to dig it out of her bag in time.

The caller is formal. "Oh, yes, am I speaking with Dr. Mayne?"

"Yes."

"This is Tristram Coffin, returning your interesting call. Is this a good time?

"It's perfect, thank you!"

"You say you were at Oxford? An Assyriologist? Now, at the IoA?"

"Martin Silverdale was my tutor at St. John's."

"Oh, bless me! Marty was a chum of mine. Gone too soon."

"I was so happy to find your book this afternoon. It's beautifully done."

"Thank you. Praise is always welcome. Tell me which species interest you?"

She refers to her notes. "*Marrubium vulgare, Althea ludwigii,* and *Tamarix ramosissima.*"

"Intriguing assortment. May I ask why these?"

On the journey home, Kate concocted a vaguely plausible story for this very question.

"I have a student who was studying a cuneiform tablet that described a medicine made from these three plants, as best as we can tell. They're called by their Akkadian names, of course. We want to follow the recipe and send the potion to UCL chemists and biologists to see if it has medicinal properties. The problem is these are plants from Iraq. We don't have the wherewithal to send her on an expedition."

"I see," the botanist says. "You want to know if you can find them closer to home."

"We were hoping against hope that we wouldn't have to leave London," she says, then holds her breath.

"How would one-stop shopping be?" he asks jovially.

"That would be amazing."

"How much of each specimen do you require? And is it leaves only? Stems? Flowers?"

"Oh, gosh. Can you hold a moment while I check?"

She hits mute and asks Mannu hurriedly, the sharp-edged Akkadian words sticking in her throat.

"Hi, sorry to keep you waiting," she says to the botanist. "Leaves only. A large handful of each species would be enough."

"Well, here's what I shall do for a fellow Oxfordian, not to mention Marty's student. I shall write a letter to the director of the Royal Botanical Gardens at Kew asking him to provide what you need. They have plentiful specimens of all three species. A small haircut won't do any harm."

She has to take care not to shout. "Kew Gardens has them all?"

"Indeed they do, all within the Temperate House. You may ask why they are kept in the environment of a temperate glass house, when modern Iraq has an arid climate. The answer is that in your time period of interest, Assyria was wetter—more like our modern Mediterranean climate."

"How long would it take to get the specimens?" she asks.

"Oh, I don't know. There's a protocol. You'll need to supply a statement of interest. There's an approval process involving a research committee. But with my endorsement, I'm fairly certain you'll have your specimens within a month or two."

There's a bench in Kate's hallway. She slumps onto it.

"A month or two?"

"Hopefully, yes."

Kate's head is spinning. "If we wanted to see the plants first— just see them—how would we find them?"

"The fastest way is to buy a ticket like any visitor, go to the main Victorian glass house—the Temperate House, as it's called, and ask any docent. Send me your particulars via email, and I shall grease the skids."

She stumbles back to the sitting room, where Mannu is ladling more stew into his bowl.

"What is wrong, Kate? Have you become sick?"

"I am not sick."

"Have you found my plants?"

She nods and gulps. "I know where they are. But we will have to steal them."

THEIR DOMESTICITY CONTINUES into the evening. Kate sits beside him on the sofa, listening as he hammers the cuneiform text into his memory. She is researching Kew Gardens and tending to urgent work emails. Her department chairman, Saul Mazur, wants to meet her in the morning about a first-year grad student accused of plagiarism, and Kate won't be able to postpone it. She'll have plenty of time to return from work, collect Mannu, and get to Kew while it's still open.

She catches him glancing at her, and he catches her doing the same. Her sagging sofa cushion inches them closer until their legs touch. She inhales through her nose. Mannu doesn't smell like other men. He hasn't used scented products. His body odor is natural—a spicy earthiness.

"Mannu, tomorrow, I must leave you. You will wait here for my return."

He puts his tablet down.

"My soul will wander like a restless ghost until I see you again."

A rough surf surges in her ears.

"As will mine."

He shifts until he faces her full-on.

"My heart must be heard," he says urgently. "In all the land of Ashur, I have never seen a woman like you. You have great beauty. You have great strength. You have great intellect. My feelings grow by the hour. I fight them because I have long loved Bel-ibni and vowed to be faithful. But I will never be with Bel. She belongs to the King."

"I belong to no man," she says. The moment seems simultaneously real and unreal.

He opens his arms. "Would you belong to me if only for one night?"

She doesn't hesitate. "Yes. I would belong to you."

She feels his arms around her and hears him say, "Then, let us go to your bedchamber."

CHAPTER TWENTY-THREE

ARBER AND BESIAN HAVE BEEN TRYING TO GET THEIR FINANCIAL house back in order after the devastating loss of sixty thousand pounds to a pair of naked muggers. They are in a deep hole with their gang's boss, an unforgiving brute who boasts of chopping off the heads of people who cross him. They've returned to the scene of the crime every night, hoping to find the men who ripped them off, and tonight, before heading to Soho again, they catch a bite at an Albanian cafe in Barking. Over plates of Korçë meatballs and beer, they are discussing how to make up their shortfall, when an old fellow at the next table grabs his cane and tosses his spent newspaper onto the table.

Besian notices something on the front page and grabs for it.

"Yeah, don't bother to ask. Just take it," the old man spits out in Albanian.

"Go fuck yourself," Besian says.

Besian slaps the paper down in front of Arber, jabs a thick finger at the photo of Adad and Ninurta, and says, "What the fuck!"

He and Arber almost knock heads reading the article, and when they see a name—Chinedu Okoro, and a location—Camden, Besian says, "We got the motherfuckers."

~

THE THREE SIT on Chinedu's floor, surrounded by the detritus of a Nando's chicken dinner.

Adad belches and says, "Night has fallen. When will we see Mannu?"

Ninurta makes a walking sign with his fingers and asks Chinedu, "Mannu?"

Chinedu says, "We will go soon. I will get an Uber."

They startle at the sound of a fist against the door.

Chinedu stands and says, "Who is there?"

The banging continues.

"I think you have the wrong flat."

A voice calls out. "Chinedu Okoro?"

"That is me. What do you want?"

The person at the door has a heavy accent. "We want to talk to you."

There's no peephole, so Chinedu hesitantly opens the door a crack and instantly regrets it.

Besian puts his shoulder to it, and Chinedu is thrown back, landing on chicken bones.

The Albanians are armed. Besian brandishes a comically large Zombie knife with coarse serrations, and Arber wields a tire iron. Before anyone reacts, Besian hauls Chinedu to his feet by a fistful of shirt, curls an arm around his neck, and presses the knife to his throat.

"It's them," Arber says. "They're wearing our fucking clothes."

"Where's our fucking money?" Besian says.

Adad and Ninurta talk to each other in low, urgent tones.

"What the fuck are you two saying?" Besian says. "Give us the sixty grand, or I open his neck."

"We have the money," Chinedu croaks.

"Where?" Besian asks.

"I will show you."

"He'll get it. Tell him where."

Chinedu is describing a hiding place in the kitchen, when Ninurta acts.

He and Adad have coolly assessed the threat and divided the responsibilities. Ninurta will take on the man with a knife and Adad, the one with a rod.

Ninurta's speed and agility are dazzling. He goes from cross-legged on the floor to hurtling forward as if shot from a cannon. There's no subtlety to his tactics. He simply rams into Chinedu, sending him and Besian to the floor. When Besian tries to push the Nigerian off him, Ninurta takes his wrist in a bone-crushing grip.

Adad is older, heavier, and long past his soldiering days, but it's not his adversary who gets the better of him. It's a Nando's serving tray. He slips on the plastic and flies backward, landing half on half off the sofa. That gives Arber enough time to move forward and smash the tire iron into the back of Adad's head.

The eunuch utters a loud "Ughh" and goes still.

Besian looks shocked at Ninurta's strength. He yells in pain as his wrist bones are mangled, and drops the knife.

"Hit him!" Besian screams. "Get him off me!"

Arber raises the iron bar, ready to smash Ninurta's skull when he looks down with a look of abject surprise.

Besian's twelve-inch knife is lodged inside his abdomen up to the hilt.

"Bes—?" he starts to say before collapsing.

Chinedu has crawled toward the kitchen, allowing Besian to pick himself off the floor. He's partway to his feet when Ninurta turns on him, brandishing the knife dripping Arber's blood.

He manages to say, "No, don't" in Albanian before Ninurta thrusts it into his chest. There is no better swordsman in Ashurbanipal's army, and Ninurta needs but a single blow to dispatch this feeble enemy.

Adad is seriously injured, but Ninurta's concern is for Chinedu. He helps him up, checks the shallow cut on his neck, and gets a towel from the bathroom.

"You saved me," Chinedu says. "They would have taken the

money and killed us. But you were magnificent. I did not know you were a warrior."

When Adad groans, they go to him.

Chinedu uses his towel to staunch the gash on Adad's scalp. They lift him to the sofa and lie him on his back with his head on a pillow. His eyes open and search the room and he babbles something in Akkadian.

Ninurta kneels, saying, "You are injured, but your head is like a rock that no man can split."

Adad only says, "Mannu."

"You must rest tonight," Ninurta says. "We will find Mannu in the morning."

Chinedu brings Ninurta a beer, and both men drain their glasses on the edge of the bed, taking in the gory scene.

"What in the name of God are we going to do with them?" Chinedu says.

THE ANSWER COMES an hour later when one of Chinedu's Nigerian acquaintances returns his call.

"My brother," Chinedu says. "You are the only one I know who can help me in my hour of need."

"If you need bailing out of the nick, call your pimp."

"I am not in jail, and I no longer have a pimp."

"Out on your own, are you? Good for you. What's your mess?"

"It involves the removal and disposal of two bodies from my flat. Do you still have your van?"

Chinedu grits his teeth at his friend's laughter.

"I assure you. My situation is not amusing."

"You really got a couple of stiffs in that shithole of yours, Chinny? How the fuck that happen?"

"Can you help me, Abi?"

"I can, but it will cost more than you have."

"How much?"

"Five grand per stiff."

"Abi! Come now!"

"Price is firm, Chinny. Serious risks involved. Take it or leave it, brother."

"Okay, Abi, but come now."

"That's ten grand in cash. Not five hundred now, rest when I'm an old man. You got cash?"

"I have cash."

"Then, we're in business."

THREE HOURS LATER, Chinedu's flat is corpse-free, with only a few remaining blood smears.

Abi and a pal of his arrived with a couple of tarps and whistled at the carnage.

"Well and truly deceased," Abi says. "Who were they?"

"Just assholes," Chinedu said succinctly.

"What's with the guy on the sofa and the one with a beard who ain't saying nothing."

"Friends of mine," Chinedu said.

"Well, I know your skinny ass didn't put these mothers down. Which one's Rambo?"

Chinedu gestured toward Ninurta.

"Mad props to you, my brother," Abi said to a scowling Ninurta.

Chinedu paid with money from the Assyrians' dwindling bankroll, and Abi commented favorably about Chinny's solvency.

"Checked their pockets?" Abi asked. "Need them clean."

Abi's friend is assigned the task and digs up a driver's license and a few hundred pounds in cash, which he happily pocketed. Besian had a car key for a BMW.

"Let's see if they drove here," Abi said, going to the window and pressing the lock button.

A black 3 Series saloon flashed its lights from a spot across the street.

He tossed the key to Chinedu and said, "You better move the motor, Chinny. Points straight to your skinny ass."

Chinedu asked where they were dumping them, and Abi said it would be somewhere deep and wet.

Money counted, bodies were rolled into tarps, tarps were carried to the van, a mop was deployed, and it was done.

Adad has been vomiting into the mop bucket, and now, Ninurta sits him up to take sips of water.

"Mannu," Adad mumbles stubbornly.

"You must sleep," Ninurta says. "We will find him in the morning."

Ninurta covers him with a blanket and soon, Adad is snoring.

Chinedu turns the lights low, pours more beers, and runs a bath.

"You have blood on you," he says to Ninurta. "I will wash my warrior and make you clean."

He leads Ninurta to the tub, strips him naked, and has him climb in. Ninurta closes his eyes in pleasure as Chinedu sponges him, then dries him with a bath towel.

"This has been a terrible night," Chinedu says, taking him by the hand to his bed. Ninurta does not know what he is saying but understands its meaning. "There is only one way I know to heal the wounds of violence, and that is love. Lie with me, Ninurta. I pray that morning will not come fast."

CHAPTER TWENTY-FOUR

IT'S STILL DARK WHEN KATE STIRS. SHE SWEEPS HER ARM, BUT THE bed is empty.

"Mannu?"

There's a light coming from the hallway. She smiles at her nakedness because she always sleeps in a night dress. The one she keeps under her pillow is wedged between the headboard and the mattress.

She hears footsteps on the stairs, and Mannu appears at the doorway holding a tray. He is splendidly naked, as if chiseled in marble.

"You are awake," he says. "You told me you had to rise before the sun. I did not know how to prepare the hot, bitter drink you favor, but I have the cold juice of the orange fruit. I also have a bowl of dry grain with the milk of a cow. Is this acceptable?"

Kate beams and laughs. "Yes, it is acceptable. We call this breakfast in bed." She uses the English word for breakfast, as she doesn't think there's an Akkadian one.

He repeats the word awkwardly and places the tray beside her.

She pats the bed and says. "We will have breakfast together."

They share a glass and a spoon.

"In Nineveh, do lovers take food in bed?" she asks.

"Perhaps dates," he says. "And almond nuts." He frowns and says, "Kate. I wish to tell you a truth. I sometimes lie with women for pleasure. But last night was the first time I laid with a woman for love."

Kate bursts into tears. It's the most beautiful thing anyone has ever told her. But Mannu is alarmed, and he reaches for her, toppling the empty glass of juice.

"Did I offend you?" he asks. "If I hurt you, may the gods curse me."

"No," she sobs. "You did not offend or hurt me. I have been with men. But no man ever said he loved me like you have done. These are tears of joy. And sadness."

He nods in understanding.

"Must you leave?" she says.

His chest heaves. "I must save Bel-ibni. I love her, too, but it is a different love—I know this now. My longing for Bel has been the horse pulling my chariot. It has kept me moving forward since I was a boy. Yet, in truth, I do not know her. She has been in my mind but never in my arms. That cannot change. But you—you are different. The gods brought us together, and though our time has been short, I have come to know your heart and soul. You have shown me the face of true love, and for this, I am thankful."

"Then stay," she gasps. "I can teach you about this world. You can learn our language, our ways. We can be happy together."

"This is not my place nor time," he says. "Your world frightens me. It will always frighten me. And if I stay, Bel will die. I cannot live knowing this. I must find the plants, make the potion, and return to Nineveh."

Kate dries her face with her bunched-up night dress, tosses it onto the floor, and opens her arms.

"Then, we must live each minute as if they were years."

∾

KATE LEAVES her house at first light, then turns to her front window where Mannu is standing at the parted curtains, his long black hair flowing over the collar of his modern shirt, his beard hopelessly uncurled. They gaze at each other for a few long seconds before she walks on.

On the Underground, Kate can't remember arriving at the Turnpike Lane Station or boarding a Piccadilly Line train. She is lost in her thoughts, her emotions raging.

What if none of this is happening? What if I've gone mad—a lunatic lost in psychosis?

The hell with this stupid meeting. Why don't I get off at the next stop and go back to him?

What's the poem? It's better to have loved and lost than never to have loved at all? Was Tennyson full of crap?

What if I don't help him find the fucking plants? He'd be stuck here. With me. Could I live with that?

The familiar sight of Russel Square Station snaps her to attention, and she trudges through a soupy, gray drizzle to her office.

KATE'S departmental chair is a good academic and a nice enough man, but he has a penchant for indulging in painstaking details. His meetings habitually run needlessly long, and this one is no different. Kate knows the plagiarizing student from her Introduction to Akkadian class. He's an unremarkable young man who might not have gained admission to the program if there had been a stronger crop of Assyriology applicants his year. He hasn't run afoul of Kate's class but a foundation course called Archaeological Methodologies taught by someone outside her department, none other than her irritating admirer, Wilson Banning.

Wilson can't hide his delight at seeing her and takes a strategic chair before anyone else can claim it.

"Where have you been?" he whispers. "I've been looking for you this week."

"Have you?"

"I'm thinking of having a Halloween party at my new flat. I thought maybe you could help with the planning and execution. You know more of the people at the IoA than me."

"It's only just gone October," she says.

"I wanted to get it on your calendar."

The meeting starts and quickly fades into the background as thoughts of Mannu crowd out everything else.

Random snippets waft in and waft out.

Saul Mazur welcomes Wilson and jokes about the Mayan civilization being a new kid on the block.

Wilson passes out copies of the student's essay.

Wilson is saying, "The paragraph that caught my attention was—"

The chairman is saying, "Do you have the output from Turnitin to share with us? I find—"

Another professor is saying, "I tend to use Ouriginal instead of Turnitin for plagiarism detection. In my hands, the side-by-side results—"

Mazur is asking, "Kate, what's been your experience with this student? Kate?"

She's forced to return to the banality.

"We don't have essays in my class, so I have nothing to add. He's a middling student. Cuneiform's not really his thing."

After nearly two hours, they vote to give him a written warning, and she's free—at least she hopes so.

Wilson follows her to her office and makes a run at lunch. She wants to explode. A scene flashes through her mind of her teeing off on him at the top of her lungs, telling him to fuck off forever, that she's in the midst of a situation, that she's madly in love. But none of this happens.

"I'm sorry, but I can't make it today."

"Too bad. I've found a new café that does a mean chili con carne."

She gathers her things and runs toward the tube station.

≈

MANNU IS PACING Kate's sitting room, reciting the formula for Bel's medicine, making sure he remembers every step and every detail. Kate told him she would return as soon as possible, but he does not know how long this will be. He has been deeply immersed in his work. The only interruption he experienced was a green object in the hall that made a repeating, loud noise twice.

He hears a metallic sound at the front door and goes to the hall, ready to take her into his arms.

The door opens, and he tenses his muscles.

The man coming through the door has keys in his hand and a startled face.

"Oh yeah, hi there. I rang a couple of times to see if Kate was in. I'm Jeremy, her ex. She's probably mentioned me. I'm just here to pick up some of my gear she's had stashed away. Don't suppose you know where she's got it."

Mannu glowers at him and his meaningless babble.

"Yeah, look, mate, I didn't know she's got a new fellow and all," Jeremy says uneasily. "If it's not too much of a bother for you, I'll just see if I can find my kit, and I'll be off. All right?"

Mannu holds his ground and his tongue.

"Listen, I come in peace," Jeremy jokes, extending a hand.

Mannu has learned that the correct response. When he shakes, Jeremy relaxes and sprouts a grin.

"So, where're you from, mate?" When there's no response, he says, "Okay, I get it. Not from around here. One of Kate's Middle Eastern colleagues—or maybe more than a colleague, as you're barefooted and lounging about. I don't speak Arabic, I'm afraid, so we'll have to make do with sign language. I'll just have a rummage through the closets. Won't be a minute."

Mannu watches him climb the stairs, thoroughly bewildered, but the pale stranger does not seem to be a threat.

Jeremy returns with a bin bag of his clothes.

"Found it straight away. Spare bedroom. Scene of my denouement. Final crime. You know, mate, I think I recognize you from somewhere. Probably can't enlighten me, but I'm thinking we've met before. Maybe one of her work dos? Whatever. All's well in love and war. Have a nice time with her, all right? I've moved on. Never happier. Glad to see the back of this place." He drops his keys onto the plate where Kate keeps hers. "Don't need these anymore."

Mannu is prompted to clasp hands again, and when he has done so, the stranger departs.

~

ADAD SLEEPS fitfully throughout the night and stumbles to the bathroom in the early hours. His movements wake Ninurta, who disentangles from Chinedu's long limbs and sits up, concerned the eunuch will vomit again. When Adad returns to the sofa, Ninurta settles back and starts to drift off, but he becomes alert when Adad starts mumbling in his sleep. He strains to listen.

"Yes, Sin. Yes, my master. I will kill Mannu. Kill."

A dream, Ninurta thinks. *There is a tormenting demon inside his head.*

~

THEY SLEEP UNTIL MIDDAY. Although Chinedu is a psychological mess following the night's violence, he finds solace in adoringly tending to Ninurta.

He's made it clear he wants his new lover to remain in bed while he fusses in the kitchen, and before long, he brings Ninurta a sizzling plate of food.

"My warrior," Chinedu says with a smile. "I have made you an English breakfast. Eat up. When your friend wakes, I will feed him, too. I do not like that man. He has cold eyes. But he is your friend. Do you like the meal?"

Ninurta is starving, and although he doesn't recognize some of the foods on the plate, he gobbles everything, sopping the runny yolks and baked beans with his toast.

Chinedu has breakfast beside him, and Ninurta takes his hand when they are both done. He says something Chinedu can't understand, but the Nigerian fathoms its meaning.

"Yes, it was a wonderful night for me, too," Chinedu replies.

"You are very special. A fierce warrior one minute and a tender lover the next. I never met a man like you. I will teach you a new sentence. I am happy." Chinedu points to his chest and repeats, "I," then to his smiling mouth and says, "am happy."

After a few tries, Ninurta is saying it too.

Adad stirs again, sits up, and Ninurta jumps out of bed before he is seen with the Nubian.

"How do you feel," Ninurta asks him.

Adad groans and touches the blood-caked gauze that Chinedu used to dress his wound.

"My head was split like a melon," he says.

"Can you stand?"

Adad rises and sways unsteadily.

"Can you remember the dreams you had?" Ninurta asks.

"I do not. Why?"

"You were speaking in your sleep."

"What did I say?"

"You spoke of killing Mannu."

Adad instantly angers and cries, "You are mistaken. I never said such a thing." The outburst makes Adad hold his head in pain.

Ninurta lets the matter pass and says, "Chinedu has made good food. It will make you stronger."

"When did the morning light come?" Adad says, squinting uncomfortably at the bright window.

"The sun is high now," Ninurta says.

"I will eat, then we must find Mannu," Adad says, weaving his way to the bathroom.

KATE STOPS at Amrita's house to borrow her car again. The nurse is at work but has left the keys. She returns home in the early afternoon, and literally runs into Mannu's chest.

"Now, I am happy," she says.

He kisses her and then says. "I, too, am happy."

"What did you do when I was gone?"

"I learned the formula. I can remember every word. Also, a man came."

She blinks at him. "What, man?"

"A thin man with bloodless skin."

"Did you open the door for him?"

"He entered without my assistance."

"What did he do when he was inside?"

"He climbed the stairs and left with a bag."

"Jeremy," Kate spits out.

She bounds upstairs. The closet door in the spare room is open, and Jeremy's clothes are gone.

The bastard kept a key, she thinks.

Mannu is waiting at the foot of the stairs and kisses her again.

"He was my friend," Kate says. "Now, he is not my friend."

"I did not like him," Mannu says.

She kisses him again.

"I would like to lie with you again," he says, "but we must gather the plants."

"I know we must," she says with a heavy sigh.

CHINEDU IS SHOCKED by the mess the Albanians left in their car. The floorboards are littered with crumbled cartons of cigarettes, fast-food wrappers, and spent lottery scratchcards. A copy of *The Clarion* with its picture of Ninurta and Adad and mention of Chinedu answers his question of how they were found.

He has Ninurta sit beside him and gives Adad the back seat.

"If I owned a beautiful car like this," Chinedu says, "I would not use it as a trash bin."

He quickly figures out how to use the sat-nav, gets the best route to Tottenham, and delights in the BMW's acceleration.

Ninurta shows off his English to Chinedu. "We go Mannu?"

"Very good," Chinedu exclaims. "Yes! We go Mannu in the car. Did I teach you car? Say car." He slaps the console. "This is a car."

"Car," Ninurta says, eliciting great praise.

Ninurta can hardly contain his excitement at the prospect of seeing his friend. He tells Adad, "I believe we will find Mannu today. I believe the gods are with us."

"I pray it is so," Adad says. "The Nubian moves us swiftly. When we find Mannu, we must learn if he has the cure for the concubine and the plants for the potion so we may return to Nineveh. If not, we must join him in his quest. May the gods help us leave this dreadful world soon."

Ninurta grunts and says nothing.

CHINEDU TURNS onto Kate's street and looks for a parking space. He swears in Nigerian at the solid row of cars lining both sides, then rejoices at his luck when a red Ford Puma leaves the curb on the opposite side.

"I will turn around and come back for it before someone else takes it."

Ninurta glances at the red car as it passes them. His spine straightens, and his eyes open wide.

"Mannu! It is Mannu!" he shouts in Akkadian.

Chinedu understands him well enough.

"Where?" he says. "Where is Mannu."

Ninurta knows both words. "Red car."

"What? That one?" Chinedu says.

"Mannu. Red car."

Chinedu uses the open space for a three-point turn and follows Kate's car toward the North Circular.

When Ninurta tells Adad what is happening, the eunuch nods his aching head and feels for the kitchen knife in his hoodie.

CHAPTER TWENTY-FIVE

It's a particularly gloomy London afternoon, the wind swirling, the slate-colored sky spitting. Kate arrives at the Kew Royal Botanic Gardens and pulls into a car park at the edge of the three-hundred-acre site. The last time she visited was a school trip. Her memories of the day are hazy, as she had been embroiled in some kind of school-girl drama that eclipsed horticulture. Kate has a word with the ticket seller about the time, and they enter the grounds with a little over an hour until closing.

"Is this where we will find my plants?" Mannu asks.

"I hope so," she says, secretly hoping they wouldn't.

It's a wet walk down the Princess Walk to the Temperate House. Along the way, remaining visitors in the open gardens head toward the comfort of the enclosure. As they approach the massive Victorian glass house, Mannu looks shocked.

"What can this be?" he asks.

"For part of the year, London is cold," Kate says, trying for a simple explanation. The Assyrians did not have names for the seasons and would not have known frost or snow. "Some plants cannot survive the cold. A house made of glass is warm all the time. The scholar told me your plants grow inside this glass house."

Entering the North Wing, they inhale the rich earthiness of the soil and fragrance of hothouse blooms and hear chirps and calls of wild birds that have flown inside. Kate loves seeing the wonder on Mannu's face as he grasps the scale and volume of a space the size of two football pitches on end.

"I do not have the words to express my feelings," he says.

She laughs. "But you know the hanging gardens of Nineveh."

"The royal gardens are not inside a palace made of glass," he answers, turning in a circle.

"Let us walk," she says. "Tell me if you see your plants."

PULLING INTO THE CAR PARK, Chinedu says, "Why in God's name is your friend coming here?"

Adad and Ninurta speak excitedly as they watch Mannu exiting the red car with a woman.

"Go to him," Chinedu says. "What are you waiting for?"

Ninurta has the same idea. "Let us go, Adad! He is walking through the gate."

Adad frowns at the crowd, an impediment to a quiet assassination, and says, "Not yet. We must learn why he comes here. We do not want to interfere with his plans. Let us follow him unseen. Tell the Nubian what we will do."

Ninurta touches Chinedu's shoulder, vigorously shakes his head, and says one of the words he knows. "No." He pats the dashboard and points toward the floor.

"You want to stay here?" Chinedu asks, pointing in the same direction.

"Yes."

They wait until Mannu is out of sight, and Adad tells Ninurta. "We can go now."

Ninurta opens the car door, surprising Chinedu, who says, "First you do not want to go, now you want to. You are acting strangely."

At the ticket counter, the attendant tells Chinedu, "We close at five, you know."

"It is fine," Chinedu says, purchasing three tickets. "My friends have come a long way. A short visit will satisfy them."

Adad keeps an eagle eye on Mannu, who is well ahead of them, walking down a straight path toward a miraculous building that looks to be made of light. The rain is steadily falling, and others converge on the same path.

"What is this place?" he says to Ninurta, waving his arm expansively at the parkland.

Ninurta shrugs. "Mannu is the Rab Asû, the most learned man in all of Nineveh," he says. "He will have a reason to be here."

It finally dawns on Chinedu what is happening from how his companions are furtively slow-walking.

"I understand!" he says. "We are following secretly. You are trying to see what he is up to. I think there might be more to this story than a simple friendship. I have never followed someone before. It is a new experience."

Kate and Mannu walk along the paving stones of the central walkway of the glasshouse, searching the specimens lining the path. Mannu examines the leaves and blossoms, and she reads the signage. Taiwan incense cedar. Camellias. Nepal Yams. Hundreds of different ones. Maybe thousands. She goes onto her phone to refresh her recollection of her photos of the plates from Tristram Coffin's book.

I'm so not a botanist, she thinks.

The path diverges while she's trying to memorize them, and before she realizes it, he's gone left while she's gone right. She's not bothered. Two people can cover more ground than one.

Adad, Ninurta, and Chinedu wait to enter the hothouse until Mannu has gone a fair ways. Inside, Adad and Ninurta are awestruck; Chinedu is impressed, too.

"I have heard about this place. We have nothing like this in Nigeria. Nothing at all."

Ninurta tells Adad, "It is full of bushes and flowers, even trees. And look! The sides and the roof are made of precious glass! What is the purpose of this palace? Does it belong to their king?"

Adad smiles. "Do you not see? Mannu comes here for his potion. This is where he will find his plants."

"Then let us go to him," Ninurta says.

"No! Let him be. If we go to him, he will stop his work. We will show our faces when he finds what he needs."

Ninurta begrudges the logic, and they keep their distance.

Kate spots a woman with a smock and a nametag.

"Excuse me. I wonder if you could help me find some specimens?"

"If I can. What are you looking for."

Kate rattles off the Latin names.

The docent pushes out her lower lip and says, "Actually, I'm standing in for the gentleman who does educational work in the Temperate House. I'm a bit of a palm tree expert. I usually work in the Palm House, you see."

"Oh, dear," Kate says politely. "Tristram Coffin told me they'd be in here."

"Gosh, you know Tristram? He's a wonderful man. He treats all of us extremely well."

"He seems nice," Kate says.

"I'd point you generally toward the far end of the house," the docent says. "Your varieties seem more Mediterranean than anything else or at least southern European or north African. Best of luck and good hunting."

Chinedu notices spiral stairs to a gallery at the center of the glasshouse.

He tugs on Ninurta's hoodie sleeve, points upward, and says, "We should go upstairs. You can watch Mannu from up there."

After a round of pointing, Ninurta understands and tells Adad they should ascend to spy on Mannu from above. Adad agrees and the three climb to the verdant gallery level, taking care not to hang over the railings conspicuously.

Kate is suddenly uneasy at letting Mannu out of sight and retraces her steps. She finds him kneeling, inspecting a plant largely obscured by another's exuberant fronds. It's a delicate-looking thing close to the ground with spidery stems, small hairy leaves, and delicate rose-colored blossoms.

"*Šināti-ṣalmu*," he says calmly.

Kate looks for the signage. *Althea ludwigii*. Family *Malvaceae*.

She lays a hand on his shoulder.

He looks at her but doesn't seem happy.

"The plants are small, and the leaves are sparse. I will need all of them."

She swallows and thinks *If this ever gets back to Tristram Coffin, I'm in serious trouble.*

From the gallery, Adad points to a crouching Mannu and says, "He has found something."

"What are you doing?" Kate says. "No!"

Mannu is reaching to pull one of the *Althea* plants but stops abruptly. "Why should I not? This is the one I need."

"We cannot take them now. We must wait until all the people have gone."

His eyes ask why again.

She comes up with a reason he'll understand. "The king owns these plants. We are not permitted to take them."

"We must steal them?" he asks.

She nods solemnly, revealing her plan. "We will steal them when everyone is gone. Until then, we must find the others." She points toward the end of the glasshouse. "This way."

"I believe he found one of the plants," Adad says, "but why did he not collect it?"

Ninurta says, "Are you certain we should not reveal ourselves and help him?"

Adad is adamant. "We must let him search without interruption."

Chinedu checks his watch and tugs at Ninurta's sleeve. "There is not much time!" He shows Ninurta the watch face, but his reply is a vacant stare.

In the South Wing, the foliage is denser, forming a thicket where the bushes and trees merge into a mass of greenery. Kate and Mannu move in slow motion, inching forward. She has ceased looking at the morphology of leaves and flowers because her brain is blending all the shapes and colors. In frustration, she relies on the labels. While she is gazing down, Mannu is gazing up at a shrub his height with feathery plumes of pink flowers growing on slender branchlets.

Kate notices him reaching to touch some feathery plumage. She locates the shrub's sign. *Tamarix ramosissima.*

"*Ēṭū,*" he says.

The glasshouse loudspeaker crackles to life with an announcement.

"Ladies and gentlemen, the Botanic Gardens closes in ten minutes. As it will take several minutes to reach the exits, you must leave the Temperate House at this time. We thank you for your visit and hope to see you again."

"What did he say?" Mannu asks.

"He said we must leave," Kate says, looking around. Visitors are starting to head for the gates.

"Will we leave?" he asks.

"We will not."

She thinks *I can't believe I'm doing this*, then takes his hand and pulls him into the foliage at its densest point. Six feet deep, it feels like the middle of the jungle. She can no longer see the walkway or the glass walls. They crouch on the moist soil and inhale its essence. A bright green ring-necked parakeet flies overhead and squawks shrilly.

"Are we hiding?" Mannu whispers.

"Until the night," she whispers back, "and we are alone."

At this, she opens her tote bag wide and shows him the fruits of her planning: bottles of water, packets of food, an empty Tesco bag for the specimens, kitchen shears for collecting them, and a flashlight.

He smiles at her and says, "I see your plan. I would like to kiss you."

They kiss in their jungle hideaway, and she says, "This feels magical."

"Yes," he says. "Magic."

At the announcement, Chinedu grabs Ninurta and says, "We must go. The man says we must go. How can I explain this to you?"

He does his finger-walking sign and urgently points toward the exit.

Ninurta nods and tells Adad, "Chinedu says we must go. See how people leave the glass palace?"

Adad leans over the railings, looking toward the far end of the building.

"Mannu has disappeared into the forest," he says. "Did you not see him reaching for the pink flowers? He found the second plant. He is not leaving. He needs the third plant. He is hiding, and we must do the same."

"Where?" Ninurta asks.

Adad points to a thicket of spiky fronds in a gallery bed.

"There. The bushes will hide us," Adad says.

Ninurta pulls at Chinedu, who sees Adad disappearing into the foliage.

"Chinedu. Ninurta. Go," Ninurta says, pointing toward Adad.

"What are you doing?" Chinedu says. "It is closing time. We must leave now!"

Ninurta uses ersatz sign language to convey his intentions, but Chinedu is having none of it.

The loudspeaker blares again.

"Final call, ladies and gentlemen. The Botanic Gardens closes in five minutes. We will be locking the doors to the Temperate House shortly."

Chinedu is frantic now. He pulls away from Ninurta and says, "I am not staying! It is against the law. I cannot be arrested for trespass, not with what happened last night. I have their car! I must get rid of it. Please, come with me."

But Ninurta only understands that Chinedu is upset and demanding to leave. He says he is sorry in Akkadian and must stay with Mannu.

Chinedu gets the gist of his declaration, squeezes the pocket, where Ninurta has the wad of money and Chinedu's address, checks to be sure Adad isn't watching, and tenderly kisses him.

Ninurta has the look of a man who will never see his lover again, but duty calls, and he reluctantly joins Adad in the bushes.

～

IN THE HOUR and a half between closing time and sunset, there is intermittent activity inside the Temperate House. Docents say goodbye to each other and leave for the night. Cleaners enter to pick up stray litter and empty the bins. Kate and Mannu get very low and quiet during the security sweep by the Kew Constabulary, the small force of security officers responsible for policing the Botanic Gardens. Two officers walk the lower paths and the gallery, talking and joking.

When the locks finally clunk shut, Kate and Mannu have some water and tuck into snacks. Kate has date bars which he munches gratefully.

As the daylight fades, he asks if they can resume their search.

"We must wait until it is dark so no one will see us from the outside."

"We will go when we have the plants?" he asks.

"The gates are locked," she says. "We will have to wait until morning and leave when others arrive."

He pulls her close. "Then, we will wait."

A soldier knows how to wait, and Ninurta can sit on his haunches for a day if need be. Adad is cross-legged. He is older, his joints are stiffer, and his head throbs terribly from his injury, so he shifts his weight on his buttocks, massages his calves and thighs, and rubs his temples.

"When will we show ourselves?" Ninurta whispers.

"Soon," Adad whispers back. "When he has completed his quest, we will reveal ourselves."

"I wonder—who is the woman with bright hair?" Ninurta asks.

"A whore, no doubt," Adad says. "My spies inform me that your friend oft visits the brothels by the river."

"We all have our secrets," Ninurta says.

"You, especially," Adad smirks.

Ninurta lashes back, "I wonder what yours are?"

∼

NIGHT FALLS—A cloud-shrouded, black night. It is dark inside the Temperate House, save the red glow from the exit signs and low-voltage incidental fixtures along the central pathway.

Ninurta remains on his haunches while Adad naps against a palm tree. Then, the soldier hears rustling and silently creeps to the railing, where he sees a small light moving near Mannu's hiding place. He smiles, knowing that his friend has resumed his quest.

Suddenly, he hears a low gurgling noise. Returning to Adad's side, he is alarmed to see frothy spittle running down the eunuch's cheek. The fellow also reeks of urine. Ninurta shakes him. At first, he says nothing, then his eyes flutter open, and one hand goes from his wet face to his soaked crotch to his aching head.

"What has happened?" Adad asks.

"A demon possesses you," Ninurta whispers. "It made you spill your bodily fluids."

"It must have entered my head when I was struck," Adad whispers. He tries lifting his dominant right arm, but it is weak. "Still, it torments me. My eyes are dimmed as if covered by coarse cloth. Where is Mannu?"

"He is searching again," Ninurta says.

Adad nods and keeps working his right hand, reaching inside his pocket for the handle of his knife and squeezing it as hard as he can, which is far from as hard as he needs.

Kate uses her flashlight discretely in case there are patrols.

"Another miracle of your world," he says. "You can hold light in your hand without a flame."

He searches near the South Entrance, looking everywhere for the distinctive wrinkled leaves and delicate white flowers he knows so well. After half an hour of exploring, they arrive at the last plantings before the exit. He spots their leaves and Kate reads the label at the same time.

"*Marrubium vulgare*. White horehound," she says.

"My *ḫanbū*," Mannu says, dropping to his knees. "The potion is complete."

He looks through the glass roof to the sky for the moon or a familiar pattern of stars, but the clouds obscure the heavens. Undeterred, he chants a prayer of thanks to Gula for her bounty, and his low and melodious tones reach the gallery.

When he is done, Kate wipes away tears, shows him how to use the scissors, and holds her plastic carrier bag open wide.

Ninurta moves to the railing and watches Mannu stuff cuttings into a bag. Adad approaches him slowly with an anguished look, his right arm dangling at his side.

"He has the plants," Ninurta whispers. "We can reveal ourselves now. What is the matter? Is it the demon in your head?"

"Ninurta-sharru," Adad whispers back. "You are a soldier. Long have you served your king. Is it not so?"

"It is so," Ninurta says, puzzled.

"Soldiers must obey the commands of their masters. Is this not so?"

"It is so."

"Then, I must tell you the truth of our mission. My arm is too weak, and my seeing too dim to fulfill the commands of my master, Sin-shumu-lishir, Chief Eunuch to our mighty ruler, Ashurbanipal." Adad holds Chinedu's kitchen knife in his left hand. "I cannot thrust this knife straight and true."

Ninurta remembers Adad's words uttered in his sleep, and fear streaks his face.

"Why would you wish to thrust a knife?"

"Because I have been commanded to kill Mannu-ki-Ashur. He must not be allowed to return to Nineveh with a cure for the concubine."

"Tell me why?" Ninurta asks, his throat constricted in horror.

"Prince Ashur, eldest son to the King and heir to his kingdom, fears Bel-ibni, for the child she carries threatens his succession. Sin ordered me to wound Bel with a putrid iron. Mannu invoked forbidden magic to travel in time to save her. Sin sent me to follow Mannu and kill him so he could not return with a cure. He sent you to help me, and now, Ninurta-sharru, you must wield the knife. I know the incantations and how to brew the magic potion. You and I will return to Nineveh as heroes. Sin will restore you as commander of the palace guard. One day, you may become commander of all the King's armies. No one will know how you disgraced yourself. Here, Ninurta-sharru, take the knife and fulfill your destiny."

Ninurta's body shakes. He takes the knife and begins down the spiral stairs. Adad struggles with his eyesight, and Ninurta has to wait for him at the bottom. Ninurta peers down the dark pathway and makes out the shapes of Mannu and the woman harvesting the last plant.

He pierces the silence of the glasshouse.

"Mannu-ki-Ashur! My friend Mannu! It is I, Ninurta-sharru. Let me see your face. Let me embrace you."

Adad whispers, "During the embrace, plunge the knife into his neck."

Kate is dumbstruck hearing another man calling in Akkadian. She looks to Mannu who rises from his crouch, dropping the scissors into the Tesco bag's greenery."

"How is this possible," he says softly. Then, finding his voice, he shouts, "Ninurta? Is it you?"

The two friends slowly approach each other. Kate trails Mannu; Adad walks behind Ninurta. Mannu recognizes Adad, but Ninurta receives his full attention.

"It is me," Ninurta says, opening his arms wide.

As Mannu embraces him, Kate sees the knife in Ninurta's hand and screams Mannu's name.

Adad shouts, "Now! Kill him!"

When Ninurta's arms envelop the physician, he lets the knife slip to the ground and cries, "I would rather plunge a knife into my dear mother. I love Mannu like a brother. I will never do him harm."

Kate hurriedly retrieves the knife and drops it in her tote bag.

Looking up, she sees the other man, a hulking brute, pluck a fist-size decorative rock from a flower bed and swing his left arm toward Mannu's head.

"Look out!" she screams in English.

It is enough of a warning for Mannu to swivel at the waist.

The rock misses him but glances off of Ninurta's forehead.

As Mannu and Ninurta try to disentangle, both men trip and fall.

Adad still has hold of the rock, and as he raises it to strike Mannu again, Kate lunges at him with outstretched arms.

His body is solid as a tree trunk, and she bounces off. But the eunuch is enraged that a woman has dared touch his person. He invokes a curse and turns on her.

Ninurta has been stunned by the blow, and Mannu is first to his feet. He charges into Adad, toppling the eunuch and landing hard on his chest. Adad grunts like a trapped boar and bashes the rock into Mannu's back. Mannu yells in pain, rolls off Adad, and tries to wrest control of the rock.

If Adad had his usual strength, few men could have taken it from his right hand, but his left hand is no match for Mannu's fury. Using both hands to dislodge it, in a blind rage he smashes it again and again into the eunuch's face until the grunting stops.

"Oh, my God!" Kate says over and over. She forces her brain to switch to Akkadian. "We must leave. Now!"

Mannu looks in disgust at what he has wrought, drops the rock, and turns to Ninurta, who is struggling to his feet.

"Can you walk?" Mannu asks.

"I am able," Ninurta says. "Is he dead?"

"He breathes no more," Mannu says. "Why did he—?"

Kate grabs Mannu's arm and screams, "We must leave!"

"Do you have the plants?"

"I have them."

She pulls him toward the nearest exit and pushes at the doors, which are bolted shut.

" Oh, God," she says in English. "We can't stay till the morning. They'll find the body!"

There are large glass panels on either side of the exit doors. Kate fumbles for her flashlight, closes her eyes, and shatters one of the panes with the butt.

"I don't hear an alarm," she gasps in English, then knocks away jagged pieces.

"Come!" she shouts.

Mannu helps Ninurta through the panel, and she exhorts them to run.

A PAIR of night constables are microwaving snacks at the guardhouse near the Elizabeth Gate when a glass-break alarm at the Temperate House goes off.

"Not again," one of them says.

"You've had false alarms there before?"

"Twice last month. I asked them to look at the sensors, but they probably didn't attend to it."

"Still, we need to check it out."

"We can't bloody well ignore it, can we? Let me just have a bite of this while it's hot."

It takes five minutes to arrive at the glasshouse by golf cart.

One of them hops out and asks, "Which sensor was it?"

"South Entrance."

"Then why'd you let me go to the North Entrance?"

They bicker as they drive to the south end of the building, but as soon as they see the smashed panel, they curse and reach for their keys.

Unlocking the door, one hits the master lights, and the other shouts, "Kew Constabulary! Show yourselves!"

They creep forward on the walkway until one of them yells, "For Christ's sake! Call for an ambulance!"

KATE IS on the Great West Road toward London, checking the rearview mirror for police lights and muttering, "Stay calm, Kate. For God's sake, keep to the speed limit." Mannu is leaning over the seat to the rear, inspecting Ninurta's bruised forehead. Finally, she has the presence to ask, "How are there more of you here? Who was the other man?"

"This man is Ninurta. He is my friend," he says. "I am seeking answers."

"She speaks our tongue," Ninurta says, holding a hand to his head. "Who is she?"

"Her name is Kate," Mannu says. "She is helping me. Ninurta, answer her questions, for I, too, must have the answers."

The words pour through Ninurta's lips. He talks of a plot between Sin-shumu-lishir and Prince Ashur to poison Bel-ibni and deprive King Ashurbanipal of another heir. He tells Mannu that Kisir-malik, the chief exorcist, discovered Mannu's forbidden magic and learned how to perform the rituals. He speaks of being deceived into accompanying Adad under the guise of helping Mannu succeed. He hurriedly tells the story of arriving naked in this strange world about a kind Nubian, violent attackers, and the eunuch's injury.

"Are you saying Adad was sent to kill me so I could not save Bel?"

"Sadly, this is the truth. I think Adad would have killed me, too, had it not been for his injury."

"But he would be condemned to remain here," Mannu says.

"He planned to wait until you had the plants. He knew how to make the potion. Adad knew how to perform the ceremony. He would have returned alone to report his triumph."

Kate is listening as best she can, but Mannu and his friend are talking faster than she can process. All she can think about is getting home, getting to safety, and holding onto Mannu for every precious second.

"Did you find the cure?" Ninurta asks.

"Yes. I only pray I am not too late for her."

"What will you do now?"

"I will go to the house of Kate and brew the potion. I will conduct the ceremony. You and I will return to Nineveh."

Ninurta reaches over the seat and lays a hand on Mannu's shoulder.

"No, my friend. You will go alone."

"Have demons possessed your mind?" Mannu cries. "You cannot stay here. You do not know their tongue or their ways. You will be a soul lost in this terrifying world."

"No, Mannu, I will be lost in *our* world. My life in Nineveh is over. I am disgraced. Here, I have the Nubian. His name is Chinedu. I believe he loves me, and I believe I love him." Ninurta sees something and shouts, "Stop! Mannu's friend with bright hair. Please stop!"

Kate abruptly pulls to the curb. They are in Chiswick. It is nine o'clock at night, and the streets are lively.

"Why am I stopping?" she asks.

"There!" Ninurta says, pointing. "Taxi."

"You want a taxi?"

"Yes. It will take me where I want to go. I wish you the blessings of the gods, friend of Mannu. May you be rewarded for your kindness."

He opens the door, and Mannu follows to the sidewalk for a last embrace.

"Your clothes are stained with blood," Ninurta says, kissing him on the cheeks. "Leave before you are seen. Go now. Save Bel and find your happiness."

"I will miss you, my friend, my brother," Mannu says, tears streaming down his face.

"And I will miss you more than you will ever know," Ninurta says, turning away.

CHAPTER TWENTY-SIX

KATE IS STILL TREMULOUS AS SHE PULLS ONTO LANGHAM ROAD. IT'S just after ten, a notoriously difficult time to find parking on her block, and she has to go around the corner for a spot. Earlier, she texted Amrita a cryptic message that she needed the car until the morning. When Amrita replied, you ok? Kate answered with a thumb's up, a better option, she thought than a thumb's down.

She stops the engine and looks at Mannu who's been silent since they dropped his friend in Chiswick.

He turns his head and says mournfully, "I feel a great sorrow. I placed you in danger. I did not wish this to happen."

"The danger was not of your making," she says.

"Would that the gods curse me if you were harmed."

"I was not harmed," she says. "You protected me."

"I would gladly give my life for yours."

As he reaches to touch her face, she sees him wince.

"Your shoulder. You are injured."

"It is of no importance."

They walk in the cool autumn air past Victorian terrace houses with TVs glowing in front rooms. Kate glimpses her neighbors through parted curtains, people with wholly different lives, rooted in a slice of time called the present, whereas she——. But this isn't the time for metaphysical musings.

She reaches for Mannu's hand and says, "Do people walk this way in Nineveh?"

"Only lovers," he says, squeezing hers.

She stops abruptly at the iron gate to her front garden. A man is hunched on her steps. Her first thought is that it is Mannu's friend, but how would he know where she lives? She drops Mannu's hand to unlatch the gate, and the man looks up when it squeals open. He's got a small bottle of vodka wedged between his feet.

"Jeremy?"

"About fucking time," Jeremy says, slurring his words. "Chilly on the stoop." He stands, swaying. "Still here, I see. Man of the hour. How've you been keeping yourself, Kate."

"What are you doing here?" she says angrily.

"Waiting for you—what do you think? Wish I'd kept the key. Could've been nice and warm, like the old days."

Mannu tells Kate, "This is the man who came here."

Jeremy mocks him with some invented gibberish. "For Christ's sake, Kate. You haven't taught the poor bloke any English?"

"Leave," Kate says. "You're drunk."

"Little bit, yeah. So what? Can't leave, though."

"Why not?"

"Need to have a word."

She sees that Mannu is absorbing the tone of the conversation by the way he is setting his jaw.

"About what?" she says.

"This." He pulls a copy of *The Clarion* from his jacket and points to Mannu's photo.

Kate's expression reveals she knows nothing about it. It's not a paper she reads.

Jeremy giggles. "What? Haven't seen this? Oh, my bloody God. You really need to be better informed about your new beau."

Kate gets her keys out. "Come in, but only for a minute."

Mannu asks if she wishes the man to enter.

"He has a picture of you," she says. "I need to read what is written."

Kate lets Jeremy into the unlit sitting room and slides the Tesco bag of leaves behind the sofa.

"Late night shopping," Jeremy says, sitting in his old favorite chair and taking a swig from his bottle. "Very domesticated."

"Give me the paper," she says.

"Here, you go. Have at it. Thought I recognized you, mate," he says, wagging a finger at Mannu, standing beside Kate in the shadows. "Your face is one of the bits they didn't pixelate. You've seen the pixelated bits, haven't you, Kate?"

"Shut up," she says, turning on a table light to scan Graham Chapman's article. When she's done, she tosses it onto Jeremy's lap.

"What do you want?" she asks.

Jeremy has a good look at Mannu in the light.

"For fuck's sake," he says. "You're covered in blood. What the hell have you been up to?"

"It's nothing," Kate says, "and none of this is your business. I read the story. Now get out."

"I have concerns!" Jeremy shouts. "A woman I used to care for is harboring an undocumented migrant with blood all over him in her house—more than her house—because I saw his stuff in your bedroom. I'll wager the authorities would love to know what he's been up to, blood and all."

Kate's rage feels like a creature awakening inside her, clawing its way out. "Your time is up!" she shouts. "You don't have the right to come here and bother me. You gave that up when you brought another woman under my fucking roof! Get the hell out!"

Jeremy smirks and unscrews his bottle. "I have more rights to be here than he does. I'm a British citizen. What's he?"

Her body is no longer in her control. She feels her arm moving on its own and her hand grabbing his coat sleeve, yanking him up.

Jeremy says, "Hey, stop that," and slaps at her, missing her face and brushing her breast.

Mannu has been listening to the exchange, gleaning its meaning from intonations and facial expressions. When he sees this man lash out at Kate, he moves forward in two strides and grabs him by the face with one hand, squeezing his cheeks together. His grip is like a vise, and Jeremy's mouth opens like a hooked fish. He yelps in pain.

"Mannu!" Kate exclaims.

"I will crush him like an insect," Mannu says. "I will slay him if it is your desire."

"No! You must let him go. Please."

Mannu releases his grip, and Jeremy feels at his face with both hands.

"Christ, almighty! That hurt!" He springs up in terror and makes for the hall, tipping his bottle of booze on the floor. "That's assault!" he says. "You've fucking assaulted me!"

Kate follows him into the hall and watches him stumble out the door. She locks it and begins to cry.

She feels Mannu's presence behind her, and she lets herself go limp when he lifts her into his arms and effortlessly carries her up the stairs.

He lowers her onto her bed as gently as a feather drifting to the ground and strips off his modern clothes.

CHINEDU HAS HAD an awful time of it, and he looks every inch as bad as he feels. His eyes are bloodshot, and he's doubled over with cramps, drinking milk for an acid stomach.

He had never done anything like ditching a car, and after hours of driving around London, he had to ring his friend Abi.

"Why you calling me, Chinny? I don't want you calling me."

"I need your help."

"I haven't helped your ass enough?"

"I do not know where to leave the car. There are cameras everywhere."

"Reason you don't know, Chinny, is that you're not a villain. Last piece of help on this matter, then we're done. Here's where you go."

He found Abi's place, a bleak, undeveloped lot filled with fly-tipping debris and derelict autos behind Enfield's Meridian Water train station. Before walking away, he wiped away his fingerprints as instructed. Free of the vehicle, he boarded a London Overground train into town, and there, the loss of Ninurta finally hit him hard. An elderly black woman saw him crying, said he seemed like a nice young man, and hoped Jesus would help him through his troubles.

In the bath, he starts crying all over again and asks himself, "Why are you bawling like a child? You are a full-grown man. Forget him. You have had many men. Too many. There will be others. And you have all that money now."

He answers, "Because I love him. You understand? I know—first time for everything, but it is real. I will never love someone like that again. Never."

He's drying himself when there's a loud thud on the door. Then another.

He panics. It's the same thudding the Albanians made when they appeared.

Are their friends looking for them? Did they tell anyone where they were going last night?

Or is it the police? Maybe someone saw him ditching the car. Or maybe Abi turned him in for the murders.

He wraps the towel around his waist and goes to the door.

"Who is there?" he says weakly.

There's another thud.

There is no way to escape. He takes a deep breath, accepts his fate, and opens the door.

Ninurta is standing there, holding the paper with his address.

"Taxi," he says. "Ninurta go Chinedu."

Chinedu throws his long arms around Ninurta's neck and pulls him inside.

"My warrior! You have come back to me." He sees an angry mark on Ninurta's forehead, touches it, and says, "You are hurt."

They kiss for a long while before Chinedu asks, "Where is Adad?" He makes a cutting sign at the crotch. "The eunuch?"

"*Adad māt*," Ninurta says, sticking out his tongue and crooking his neck.

"He is dead? What happened? No, I do not need to know. As long as you are safe."

Ninurta says, "*Anni ewērum itta-ka adû.*" At Chinedu's quizzical expression, he says, "Ninurta, Chinedu," and pats the floor with his palm.

"You are staying?" Chinedu cries. "You are staying with me?"

Ninurta uses one of the words he knows.

"Yes."

KATE'S HAND is on Mannu's sweating chest, rising and falling with each breath. His hand finds hers, pressing it down, and she feels his heart rapping urgently against her fingertips. They turn their heads to look at each other. Words are unnecessary.

"*Ašāpēru,*" she says. I understand.

He gets out of bed, looks at the pile of clothes Kate bought him, and says, "I will not need these anymore."

She finds her robe.

"Tell me what you need?" she asks.

"A cooking pot, water, a fine cloth."

"That is all?"

"For the potion, that is all."

Kate gives him the largest pot in the kitchen, fills it a third way up per his instructions, and sets it on the electric stove. He has seen her cooking and knows the glowing rings produce the same result as fire. He empties the Tesco bag onto the kitchen table and asks for her scissors—an unknown word—by making a cutting sign with his thumb and forefinger. He sits at the table, naked, and tells her it is a good tool, better for the task than a knife. She watches him snipping the leaves from the stems, finds a second pair, and works alongside him until they have a mound of trimmed leaves.

When the water boils, Mannu scoops the leaves with his hands, drops them in, and stirs with a wooden spoon.

"I must clean my body for the ritual," he says. "When I return, I will prepare the potion."

269

She follows him upstairs and hears the shower running while she collects his bloody clothes for the wash.

She keeps busy to ward off the melancholy. She puts his clothes in the washer, feeds the discarded stems to the garbage disposal, and stirs the leaves. The vapors coming off the pot are elemental, and she can imagine herself in a steamy jungle.

He comes down with her bath towel draped over one shoulder, uninhibited by his nakedness. His hair is dripping wet, his beard natural and uncurled. A purple bruise is forming on the shoulder where Adad struck him; otherwise, his olive skin is unblemished.

He checks the pot he says, "It is ready to pass through a cloth."

He inspects her cheesecloth, folds it to make it finer, and approves her receptacle, a recycled pasta sauce jar. She lines her largest funnel with cheesecloth, and he pours the hot liquid until the jar is filled with the pale, greenish brew.

"I am ready for the ritual," he announces somberly. "I will perform it in your large room. I will need a jug of water to purify the space, a blank clay tablet for Nabu, and a sprig of ṣuṣū for Gula."

Kate doesn't know the word ṣuṣū, mutters, "Where's my damn phone," and runs upstairs for it. She comes down and tells him she doesn't have fresh thyme but has dried leaves. He sniffs the kitchen herb, pours a heap on a plate, and tells her it will suffice.

In the sitting room, he fashions a tablet from the remaining modeling clay, moves her coffee table so he has a circular space, and places the tablet, the thyme, and the jug of water around it. Kate lights a few candles.

"It is time," he says.

Kate fights the urge to sob. She doesn't want him to remember her that way. She bravely nods, fumbles with her phone, and puts it down.

Then, they walk into each other's arms and simply hold each other.

"The gods bought us together, and now they tear us apart," he says.

She squeezes him tighter. "I cannot bear losing you. If the gods are doing this, they are cruel."

"We are but their playthings," he says. "I will never forget you. You have shown me true love."

He releases her, and her hands slip from his back.

"I hope you can save her," she says.

"I pray I am not too late."

She watches him slowly position himself inside the circle. It's gone past midnight, and Kate's street is deathly quiet.

Mannu closes his eyes and breaks the silence.

O Nabu, scribe of the heavens, keeper of the tablets of destiny,
You who know the fate of all things, present and future,
Open the gates of time for your humble servant.
You lent me the wisdom of what has been written,
The knowledge inscribed in future stars.
You inscribed upon my mind the words of healers not yet born,
And guided my hands to save those who suffer.
By your hand, let the circle of time flow backward and forward.
And in this sacred circle, let the past and future converge.

Kate stands beside her dining table, gripping a chair back, fighting gravity. She is only half the room away from him, but it feels like half the universe.

Mannu opens his arms.

O Gula, mistress of life and breath,
Healer of body and soul, mother of physicians,
You granted me the cure I did not know.
You lead me through the veil of time to the land of distant healers.
To the gardens where unknown herbs grow,
And into the halls where learned healers practice.
By your hand, may the threads of fate be woven anew,
Allow your servant to return to Nineveh,
With the wisdom to cure Bel-ibni.

Kate's knees are softening. She has to hold the chair with two hands to keep from sinking.

Mannu's voice rises, filling her ears.

By the stars above and the earth below,
By the breath of life and the ink of destiny,
Let me pass through the rivers of time.
Nabu, Gula, open the path!
As I stand upon this sacred ground,
May my spirit travel beyond the reach of this age.
Seven are the stars that guard the heavens,
Seven are the gates that guard the unknown,
Seven are the healers who hold the knowledge.
By their hands and mine, may time bend,
May I pass through the seventh gate and return to Nineveh.

He finishes, but his chest continues to heave.

He reaches for the potion at his feet and takes three gulps from the jar.

He takes the jug, and as he rotates, he spills water onto the ground in a circle.

His eyes meet Kate's one last time, he drops the jug, and he is gone.

Kate takes small, fearful steps until she is over the spot he stood upon. She lies there, curled tightly, and doesn't move until sunrise brightens the room.

CHAPTER TWENTY-SEVEN

THERE IS A DISTRICT IN NINEVEH EAST OF THE PALACE COMPLEX, between the Shibaniba and Mushlalu Gates, where many of the city's artisans and blacksmiths live. It is crowded and noisy, with the constant ratatat of banging hammers and vocal hordes of children, thick as flies, scampering over the roofs of mudbrick houses and streaming through the narrow alleyways.

Apart from dead of night, the only time of relative tranquility is the early afternoon, when the sun is hottest, and laborers put down their hammers, step away from their looms, and take their meals.

One moment, Mannu-ki-Ashur, Chief Physician of Nineveh, is looking into the eyes of the woman he loves in the impossibly faraway city called Lon-don, and the next, he is in a small square with a few poor market stalls, surrounded by worker's huts. He inhales the pungency of woad and madder-root dyes, the smoky fires of the blacksmiths and bakers, the astringency of urine, and he knows: I am home. This is Nineveh.

He has little time to give full-throated thanks to the gods for delivering him. First, he must deal with his nakedness—not for modesty, but because naked men attract attention. He slips unseen

GLENN COOPER

into the nearest alley and searches for a clothesline. Partway down the smelly lane, he finds a hemp rope strung between two houses draped with indigo-stained linens drying in the heat. Among them is a damp dyer's tunic with blotches of purple and red that will never wash out. Mannu snatches it, puts it on, and runs barefoot toward the palace.

Although it is the quietest time of the day, there is a throng of people at the bronze gates of Ashurbanipal's palace, a delegation of merchants and officials from Babylon seeking an audience with the Vizier. Palace guards search them, one by one, for weapons, but Mannu is in no state to wait his turn. He goes around the gaggle and is about to enter the grand courtyard when a young guard moves to block him.

"You there. Where do you think you are going?"

Mannu puffs his chest and says, "I am Mannu-ki-Ashur, Rab Asû of Nineveh. I am going to my apothecary."

"Look at your tunic," the guard says. "Is this what the Rab Asû wears?"

"Look not to my tunic. I have been on a long and dangerous journey. Look to my face. I have seen you before, lad, and you have seen me. Now, stand aside. I must serve the King without delay."

He crosses the courtyard, enters the palace, and strides down familiar corridors he thought he might never see again. He wants to run, but his shabby clothes already label him suspicious. As it is, he draws curious looks from passing courtiers.

He barges through the doors to his apothecary, where one apprentice is sweeping the floor in a desultory way, and two others are tossing dice.

After momentary confusion, the apprentices snap to a panicky attention, and the oldest says, "Rab Asû! You have been missing! Everyone has been looking for you."

"As you can see, I am found. Listen to me well. I want you, the senior boy, to go to the chambers of the royal concubine and seek out the midwife, Tashmetum. Tell her she must come here immediately. Tell her only that she will understand the summons when she

274

arrives. And you two—bring me armfuls of stale bread from the bakers and a bushel of dates from the kitchens. And six clay pots. The largest you can carry. Fill the pots halfway with water, divide the bread and dates among the pots, mix them well, and place them in our courtyard under the shade of the date palm. Go, now—all of you. Run!"

Mannu goes to his private chamber, sheds the stained tunic, dresses in the tunic, robe, and slippers of his office, and sits on his bed. When he closes his eyes, all he can conjure is the sad, beautiful face of his woman with bright hair.

WHEN THE LAST of the Babylon delegation has been allowed to pass, one of the deputy commanders overseeing the operation, approaches the young guard manning the other side of the main gates.

"Guard, I saw you giving entry to someone who looked like a tradesman. Who was he?"

The guard snaps to attention. "Sir, that was no tradesman. That was the Rab Asû."

The superior officer is thunderstruck. "In a stained tunic? Are you certain?"

"Yes, Sir. I am certain. I have seen him before."

"Did you not know that the Rab Asû has been missing? And that the palace guard has been searching for him day and night?" The young guard answers fearfully, "I am sorry, Sir. I have been on leave for this past week, confined to barracks. Diarrhea, Sir."

THE SENIOR APPRENTICE delivers the midwife, Tashmetum, to the office of the Rab Asû. She is waiting there, bewildered, when Mannu enters.

"Rab Asû!" she cries. "Where have you been?"

"On a mission," he says. He sits, worried he might collapse if the tidings are bad. "Tell me—what is the condition of Bel-ibni? Is she alive?"

Over his heavy breathing, he hears, "She clings to life."

He lifts his hands to the heavens and says, "O Gula, great healer of the land, I give thanks with a grateful heart." Then, to Tashme-tum, "Tell me more."

"She is very weak. She rarely opens her eyes. Her breathing is rapid. Her skin is always hot. The exorcist comes and makes his spells. The diviner speaks of the omens. I see it in their faces. Every day could be her last."

"Does she take water, still?"

"With labor and perseverance, she does. I fill a beaker with water, hold her up with one arm, and use the spout to drip it in her mouth, a little at a time. Without that, she would have perished by now."

"Does the King come?"

"He comes to her bed every day, feels her belly, and weeps. He—"

There is a commotion in the apothecary, and heavy footsteps approach. Mannu's door is flung open, and the deputy commander of the palace guard enters with a squad.

"Mannu-ki-Ashur, by the order of the King, you are seized!"

King Ashurbanipal is in one of his private gardens, enjoying a midday meal with Queen Libbali-sharrat, when the Rab Shakeh, his chief cupbearer, whispers a message in his ear. The King abruptly rises.

"What is it?" the Queen asks.

"The Rab Asû has returned," he says.

"Come to offer his head?" she laughs. Then, dripping with acid, she adds, "How is your concubine? I forget to ask."

Mannu has seen Ashurbanipal in a rage, but nothing compares

with the look of madness when he tears into the throne room and fixes his eyes on Mannu.

"Mannu-ki-Ashur," he bellows. "Prostrate yourself before your Lord!"

Mannu obeys and lies flat on the cool, polished alabaster slabs.

"You have abandoned your sacred duties to the crown," Ashurbanipal bellows. "You have abandoned the afflicted woman, Bel-ibni. You have abandoned her unborn child—my heir! What do you say for yourself before I deliver you to the darkest hole in my palace and hold you until I decide upon the method of your execution?"

"King of the Universe, I did not abandon Bel-ibni. I have been on a mission to save her. I have found a cure."

"Rise," Ashurbanipal says, his eyes narrowing, "and explain yourself."

Mannu stands proud. "As Rab Asû of Nineveh, it is my sacred duty to heal the afflicted. As the Great King knows, Bel-ibni has been very sick. My strongest medicines did not help her. The best magic and rituals of your Chief Exorcist and Chief Diviner did not help her. Could I stand by and watch her die, or was it not my obligation to Your Majesty to do everything for her within my power?"

"What did you do?"

"I used forbidden magic. Black magic."

There were gasps among the gaggle of courtiers.

"This alone is punishable by death!" the King shouts.

"Compared to your welfare and the life of your future heir, my poor life is meaningless. I learned forbidden magic that sends a man traveling on the great circle of time. I made a perilous journey to a distant future in a strange and miraculous land called Lon-don. I—"

There is a disturbance as Sin-shumu-lishir and Kisir-malik run into the throne room, and Sin shouts, "Great King! Please stop! I will deal with this maggot!"

Word of Mannu's return had traveled quickly. Sin heard from a palace guard—one of his eunuch spies—and raced through the palace to find Kisir, spewing commands as he dragged the Chief Exorcist to the throne room.

"I will talk, and you will listen carefully to my words," Sin said, his sweaty feet sliding in his sandals. "Whenever I look to you, you will confirm that I have spoken the truth. If you value your head, you will obey me, Kisir-malik."

"Silence!" the King shouts. "I will hear from the Rab Asû."

Mannu glowers at the Chief Eunuch and turns back to the King. "A learned healer from this land called Lon-don taught me a cure, and I have returned to Nineveh to produce it for Bel-ibni. I prayed she would still be alive and the gods have been merciful."

"What is this cure? Is it a leaf? An herb? A seed?"

"None of these," Mannu says. "It is made from bread, dates, barley, vinegar, and water."

Kisir cannot suppress his laughter. "Your Majesty," he says. "These are mainstays of our diet. If this is a cure, everyone in Nineveh should be cured of whatever affliction they may have."

"The physician has lost his senses!" Sin shouts. "My King, please let me deal with him and free you from this folly."

Ashurbanipal raises his hand, calling for silence, and says, "Prove that you were in the future, Mannu-ki-Ashur. Show me the cure."

"My apprentices have begun making it. It will be ready in two days."

"If you want to live, you had better give me more proof than that," the King says, looking for his cupbearer. "Cupbearer, bring me strong wine, for I am much vexed."

"Here is proof," Mannu says, turning toward Sin. "I was not the only man from Nineveh in Lon-don. The chief deputy of Sin-shumu-lishir—Adad-ummi was also there."

"Chief Eunuch, is this true?" the King asks.

"It is a lie!" Sin says, his smooth face turning red.

"He was there, and he will not return," Mannu says, "because I slayed him."

"You cannot believe these rantings," Sin says.

"Then, where is Adad, Chief Eunuch?" Mannu says. "Bring him to us."

"He is not in the city," Sin says quickly. "I sent him to Kalhu on an important matter. When he returns, I will gladly indulge you, Chief Physician. If you are still alive."

"There is a man present who knows that Sin-shumu-lishir is lying and that I am telling the truth," Mannu says. "I know he is honorable. I am confident putting my life into his hands."

"Who is this man?" the King asks.

"It is Kisir-malik," Mannu says, pointing at his old rival. "He knows Adad-ummi is absent because he used the same black magic to send him on the circle of time to kill me."

Kisir looks like a man caught brazenly in the act of theft. He starts to say, "No. I—" when the King interrupts him.

"Chief Exorcist, did you practice black magic on Adad-ummi?"

Kisir looks to Sin, who stares at him with dagger eyes and shakes his head suggestively.

Kisir takes a step forward, gives Mannu a sidelong glance, and says, "My King, I was instructed by the Chief Eunuch to use the same ancient magic as Mannu-ki-Ashur to send Adad-ummi and Ninurta-sharru to find him. But I was told they would help him find a cure for your concubine and speed his return to Nineveh. I know nothing about a plot to kill him."

"Great King," Sin starts to say, but Ashurbanipal commands silence.

The King leans forward on his throne. "Why did Adad and Ninurta want to kill you, Chief Physician?"

Mannu chooses his words carefully. "Your loyal Chief Eunuch is not as loyal as you might think, Your Majesty. He sent Adad to stop me from curing Bel-ibni. Ninurta knew nothing of this. He was tricked into believing he and Adad would help me on my quest. Ninurta was to be killed, too. Sin wants Bel-ibni dead. More than that, he caused the wound that allowed demons to enter her body."

The King is gripping the arm of his throne so hard that his engorged arm veins appear as slithering serpents. "How was Bel wounded?"

Mannu says, "Adad buried a putrid piece of iron in her garden path. This, he confessed to Ninurta."

"Tell me why my loyal Chief Eunuch wanted Bel-ibni to die?"

Sin has thunder in his face and lightning in his eyes. Mannu turns to face him and says, "Because he acts in concert with your son, Prince Ashur, to deprive you of a new heir."

"No, My King, no!" Sin shouts. "He lies!"

Ashurbanipal rises from his throne and lifts his staff, commanding silence.

"I possess a gift from the gods," the King says. "I can see the soul of a man through his eyes, and I see that Mannu-ki-Ashur tells the truth and that Sin-shumu-lishir lies. Guards, seize the Chief Eunuch and use any method to extract the truth. And find out if there are spies in my city working on behalf of Prince Ashur."

As burly guards clamp down on the eunuch, he shouts, "No, My Great Lord, King of the Universe, I would never seek to harm—"

"Take him away!" the King bellows. "And seize the Chief Exorcist and pry the truth from his mouth."

"Your Majesty," Mannu says. "I am certain Kisir-malik is innocent. I believe him when he says he thought he was helping me to find a cure for Bel-ibni. She is very ill. The demons who torment her are powerful. They wish to drag her to Irkalla, where Ereshkigal awaits. Kisir-malik is a brilliant magician and healer. Bel-ibni will be best served by my new medicine and his magic spells."

Ashurbanipal takes to the throne again, has a large draught of wine, and says, "Very well. Work together to save Bel and my child. Mannu-ki-Ashur, where is Ninurta-sharru?"

"He chose to stay in Lon-don," Mannu says. "He found love there."

"They know love in Lon-don?"

"Yes, My King. Their world differs greatly from ours, but their people are the same. They live, and they love."

As he says this, he feels his heart aching.

"Mannu-ki-Ashur, tell me something of this city in the future."

"I will tell you this. I went to one of their temples. It is a sacred place where the people come to celebrate the past. And there, they celebrate you, My King. Your statues are displayed. Statues and carvings from this palace." He runs across the throne room and points to a large stone frieze. "I stood beside this very carving of you and the Queen. Far into the future, you are revered! And they revere your library. They have your tablets. They study them and learn our ways. I met a learned woman who devotes her life to you."

The King rises and says, "I am pleased we are well remembered. Now, come and walk with me, Mannu-ki-Ashur. I would hear more about this Lon-don."

CHAPTER TWENTY-EIGHT

Detective Sergeant Liz Warrington is only a few hours into a murder investigation, and she's already concluded it could be career-defining. She's two years overdue for a promotion to detective inspector, the rank she hopes to ride out until retirement, and this is the kind of high-profile investigation that will put her over the hurdle or leave her biting the dust.

She's spent the morning at the Kew Botanic Gardens, examining the battered body of the unknown male victim, checking on the progress of the crime scene investigators, meeting with the Kew constables who discovered the deceased, and requesting security camera videos.

On her return to the Twickenham Police Station, her boss, a DI who, painfully, is five years her junior, wants a briefing.

"No identification on the body?" he asks.

"His pockets were empty, Matthew."

"Fingerprints?"

"I scanned him on INKS. He's not in the database. And face ID's a bust because he no longer possesses one."

The DI leans back and mutters, "Wonderful. So, look, Liz, I'm the SIO on this. I'm already getting far more than the usual press inquiries. I mean, I could even write the bloody headlines. Hot House Horror: Faceless Body Found in Kew Gardens—that sort of drivel."

"I was thinking Bloom and Doom in the Botanic Gardens," she says.

"Right. I regret starting this," he says. "We're going to be in the hot seat on this one—oh, God, there I go again—so let's try and make fast work of it."

"They have a few CCTVs in the Temperate House—the greenhouse building where the murder happened. I'm awaiting the footage. I've also requested a fast-track postmortem."

"Excellent. Keep me in touch."

"Will do, boss."

She hears his feet hitting his desk before she's out the door.

She's having a sandwich at her desk when she gets an email from the Kew Constabulary with her requested CCTV files.

She shouts across the office, "Colin, could you come over here, please."

Colin Hayes is a newly minted, fresh-faced detective constable who hops to it.

"Yeah, boss. What can I do?"

"Let's look at some of the CCTV files, see what we've got, and divide and conquer."

He pulls up a chair and says, "Start with this one, I should think," smearing her screen with his finger. "Temperate House, South Wing."

"Yeah, go for the gold," she says. "We know the glass-break alarm went off at 9:49, so let's back up to 9:30 and play it forward —see what we shall see."

The camera is ceiling mounted, located at the midpoint of the South Wing and pointed toward the exit doors. Under the CCTV's night-vision, the greenhouse looks spectral, its glass and steel shell glinting faintly in black and white. Walkway fixtures cast faint pools of light, but most of the interior is cloaked in the shifting shadows of fronds and branches blurring together.

They slowly roll forward to the first hint of activity.

"There," she says. "Two figures in the bushes. Hunched over."

Several seconds later, they hear the first sound, a man calling loudly in a foreign language.

"What is that? Arabic?" she says.

Hayes shrugs. "Yeah, dunno." Then, two men appear on the walkway, their backs to the camera. One is broader and taller than the other. "Here we go," he says.

The hunched-over figures emerge onto the path, facing the camera lens, a man and a woman. The woman has short blond hair, and the man is a head taller with long hair and a full beard.

"Freeze that, will you?" she says. "Take the keyboard. I'm a computer idiot. He's not our victim. Mr. Faceless doesn't have a beard."

He moves his chair forward. "No worries."

"Okay, can you zoom in on their faces?"

"Yeah, can do."

"Freeze it, there. That's not bad quality for night mode," she says. "Print it, then keep rolling."

Hayes squints at the image. "I'm thinking maybe I recognize this bloke," he says. "But I can't place him."

"From where?"

"Can't really say. If it comes to me—"

He advances the video, and they can see the four people approach each other, conversing in the same foreign language.

Then, Warrington says, "Is that a knife in that one's hand?"

Two of the men embrace each other. Then, the woman screams something.

"What is that?" Warrington asks. "Play it back."

"Sounds like Manu," he says.

"What the fuck does that mean?" she says.

"His name? Like Manny or Manuel?" he says. He hits play again, and something drops from the man's hand, the one whose back is to the camera.

"He's dropped the knife!" she says. "And blondie picks it up, right there. And here comes trouble. The big guy picks up a rock. It's got to be the bloody one we found. He's left-handed."

They hear the woman scream, "Look out!"

"English," Warrington says. "Finally."

"Look at that!" Hayes exclaims. "He missed his target and hit his own guy."

"Freeze it," she says. "Yeah, look at the man he hit. He's got a beard too. So, the one who struck the first blow is the victim."

The two men who had been embracing tumble to the ground, and the large man swoops in with his arm raised. Before he can bring the rock down, the woman runs into him. She's repelled, but her companion gets up, bull-rushes the aggressor, and falls on him.

"Look at that," she says, standing up and pointing at the monitor. "He gets hit in the shoulder, then rolls off and fights for the rock. And boom, he's got it and goes tribal on our victim. Roll it back, then forward again in slow-mo."

She counts the blows to the face. "One, two, three, four, five, six. There it is. Rage overkill."

They hear the woman screaming, "Oh, my God," in English before switching to the foreign language. The perpetrator drops the rock where they found it. The woman picks up what looks like a bulging carrier bag, and they try the exit doors. The woman breaks a window at the end of the wing with an object from her shoulder bag, and then she and two men escape.

"God, I love CCTV," Warrington says. "Right. Get me a close-up of the carrier bag to see if there's any writing on it, make a few copies of the blondie and beardie shot, and get DC Aziz to tell us what they're saying. I'm going for a smoke."

When Warrington returns after not one but two cigarettes, the young officer is grinning broadly.

"What?" she says.

He holds up today's copy of *The Clarion*.

"It hit me when I saw the paper on Carter's desk—the place I saw the guy with the blond. It was in the news." He clicks on a file he left on her desktop. It's the front page of *The Clarion* from last week about the streaker in Piccadilly.

"Christ," she says, holding the CCTV closeup near the monitor. "It does look like him, doesn't it? Course, it could be someone else.

Here's what we do. Find out what happened to the streaker, and I'll get authorization from the Guv to disseminate the CCTV photo on Crimint throughout the Met. We can talk about releasing it to the public for assistance if it comes to that."

"Yeah, on it," Hayes says. "I had Aziz listen to the audio. He says it's not Arabic. Couldn't understand a word. And the carrier bag's from Tesco."

～

LATE IN THE AFTERNOON, Warrington calls the mortuary in Mortlake. She knows the autopsy won't have been done yet but she asks the forensic pathologist to see if the deceased had any distinguishing marks or tattoos.

"No ink whatsoever," the pathologist tells her, "but here's something reasonably distinguishing: he's lacking external genitalia."

"Come again?" Warrington says.

"To use the vernacular," the pathologist says, "no cock, no bollocks. From the look of him, it's not a recent occurrence. Your victim's a eunuch."

Warrington is about to spread this nugget up and down her command chain when she gets a call from the Richmond duty officer, telling her he's forwarding a call from an outside DS looking for the lead on the Kew Gardens murder.

"DS Warrington, this is DS Booth calling from Tottenham. We had a gentleman present himself to the station this morning to report an assault that allegedly occurred last night at an address on our patch. He said the man who assaulted him was the one in the news a few days ago, the streaker in Piccadilly Circus—"

"Fuck me," Warrington says. "Tell me more."

"We were planning to make contact with a woman who lives at the address where the assault occurred—the claimant's ex-girlfriend, who was present during the incident—when we saw your alert on Crimint."

Warrington makes wild hand gestures to attract her DC's attention. Hayes comes over, and she puts the call on speaker.

"Do you have names for the man and woman?"

"Our claimant said he didn't know the attacker's name. His ex's name is Kate Mayne. She's a lecturer at University College London."

"Look her up," Warrington whispers.

Hayes does a search and Kate's departmental photo pops out.

"Hello, blondie," Warrington says.

"Sorry?" Booth says.

"I'm on my way to Tottenham as we speak," Warrington says, throwing things in her bag. "We need to work with you on a coordinated response. I'll have my SIO call your guv to assemble an arrest unit."

"If you think he's armed, we can put SCO19 on alert," Booth says.

"I've no reason to suspect he has a firearm," Warrington says. "SCO19, TSG, local officers—I'll leave that to the guvs."

IT'S NIGHTTIME, and Kate is alone in the interview room at Tottenham Police Station with a very cold cup of tea. She's hungry, frightened, and trying to keep her composure from cracking under the strain.

When a dozen police officers arrived at her door that afternoon, she was under her duvet in a fetal position. Her pillowcase still had Mannu's scent on it. They did a cursory search of her flat looking for him, then requested she accompany them to the station for a voluntary interview. There, a very young-looking detective constable from Richmond informed her they had reason to believe she was a witness to a homicide. After his rather gentle line of questioning ran its course, he was replaced by a far edgier woman, Detective Sergeant Warrington. Finally, close to a breaking point, Kate invoked her right to a lawyer. At that, they informed her that while she was not under arrest, she was a material witness and was not free to leave.

The waiting game began.

Kate's father, the account he is, was his phlegmatic, efficient self and retained a criminal solicitor to attend the interview. As Kate sits in this godforsaken, drab room, waiting for the lawyer's arrival, thoughts fly through her mind like a swallow—zigzagging, skimming along the ground, then rising, then doubling back.

Did we leave any leaves in the Tesco bag?
What did I do with Ninurta's knife?
What happened to him after we dropped him off?
Am I going to be in horrible trouble?
What will they make of the jar of green liquid in my sitting room?
I had scissors and a flashlight in my bag. That makes it look like we were planning to stay past closing time.
How can I possibly go to work tomorrow?
Will they be able to find out we stole cuttings?
I don't have to worry about Mannu's tablet with the penicillin formula —they won't have a clue about cuneiform.

But over and over, she keeps coming back to this:

Mannu, Mannu, oh Mannu. Did you make it back to Nineveh? How will I live without knowing? How will I carry on without you?

CHAPTER TWENTY-NINE

"KATE, WE FINALLY MEET IN THE FLESH!"

Kate's solicitor is ebullient. Kate is not. It's a meeting she's been dreading, and she walked the last few yards to the restaurant with the halting gait of a condemned woman approaching the gallows.

Her lawyer is approximately her age, attractive in an athletic way, her dark hair cut severely in a square bob. The restaurant is a brasserie on Chancery Lane, packed to the gills with a smartly turned out luncheon crowd. Before menus are delivered, several diners greet Abigail with waves or swoop by to whisper something amusing.

"Honestly," Abigail says, leaning over the table as if confessing to a confidant, "I only come here because it's close to my office. It's more like a staff canteen than a restaurant."

Kate orders a glass of wine because Abigail does, and resigns herself to introductory chitchat.

"So, I don't know if you're aware of it, but our fathers are rather chummy."

"Are they?" Kate says.

"That's how we made the connection. They belong to the same country club."

Kate isn't sure this is the right thing to say, but she says if anyway. "Oh, God, I hate that place."

"I know! It's dreadful, isn't it?"

Kate has a suspicion that if she had professed her love for the club, her solicitor would have agreed it was wonderful.

"So, when you got in your jam, your father called my father for advice. He's a solicitor, too—commercial law. My dad replied that he happened to know the sharpest criminal lawyer in London."

Kate can already tell, that if given the opportunity, her father would swap daughters in a heartbeat.

Abigail adjusts her tone. "How have you been getting on? Keeping your head above water?"

"Trying to," Kate says.

"I'm sure you feel like you're in the maws of the legal beast. I hope you've been following my advice to leave all that to me and get on with life."

"It hasn't been easy."

"No, I'm sure not. Been able to get stuck back into your work?"

"Hmm. About that, I've been summoned to a meeting tomorrow morning with the director of my institute. They wouldn't give me a specific reason for it."

Abigail frowns, pursing her lips. Kate likes her shade of lipstick. "I see. We'll cross that bridge when we need to. I've got an education law colleague who's excellent on university matters. Deals with UCL regularly."

Once they've ordered off the menu, Abigail transitions to the business at hand.

"Right. I've been having an active dialogue with the Crown Prosecution Services on your case and I'm pleased to tell you that I think we can get to a speedy resolution."

"Resolution?" Kate says.

"I won't say it hasn't been tricky," Abigail says. "A man *was* murdered, so the CPS has taken an aggressive posture, and the police have been embarrassed by not being able to find your Dr.

Ashur. I understand that DS Warrington—that absolutely dreadful officer who interviewed you—has been pushing for a scalp—any scalp."

"You mean, me?" Kate asks weakly.

"You're the only one they can find. Dr. Ashur and the other mystery man have vanished without a trace. But, the CPS has reviewed your file and the good news is, they will not be filing charges against you for involvement in the murder of the other mystery man, the one *sans* genitals, as it were. They were persuaded by the CCTV evidence that you were an innocent bystander."

"That's good," Kate says. She's not fully relieved. She can tell there's more to come.

"No, that's *very* good," Abigail says. "That was the big one. It's behind us now. Also, I'm pleased to say that they won't be pursuing charges related to breaking and entry. They aren't completely satisfied that you didn't intend to stay beyond closing hours, but they are persuaded they can't prove your intent. So, another one in our column."

"Also, good," Kate says.

Abigail runs her finger around the rim of her wine glass, something Kate has never done. It feels out of a movie. "So, that brings us to the only sticking point."

"The plants," Kate says.

"The plants," Abigail repeats. "The CPS doesn't give a toss about a few clippings, but the director of the Royal Botanic Gardens has his knickers in a twist. He did a detailed inspection of their planting beds and found evidence of what you were up to. He sent photos to the CPS of the plants you decapitated or whatever it is they call it, and he's baying for blood. Wants to set an example. And the CPS is capitulating to a point."

Kate has a glug of wine. "To a point. What does that mean?"

"It means they insist on charging you with theft, specifically theft under Section 1 of the 1968 Theft Act. However, the monetary value of the stolen goods, to wit, the leaves and whatnot is small—it's not like you pulled things out, root and branch. The poor dears will grow back. To humor Kew Gardens, the CPS is bringing the mildest possible charge available, a charge which can be summarily charged in a Magistrates' Court. That means no jury trial or anything like that."

Kate feels quite ill. "Will I go to prison?"

"Oh, Lord, no. I've already come to agreement with the CPS that they will ask for a fine of five hundred pounds. They wanted a thousand, but I saved you some money. The magistrate hearing your case isn't obligated to accept this, but I know the chap and I'm almost certain he will. Oh, and you'll be trespassed for life from Kew Gardens."

"I never want to see it again," Kate says. "So, that's it?"

"That's it. Oh good, here's our lunch."

Abigail explains the next steps, then says, "Can I ask you something? For my own curiosity? Have you really not had any contact with Dr. Ashur since this incident?"

"None."

"You have no idea where he is?"

Kate half smiles. "No idea."

"All right, and this is your lawyer talking now—if he contacts you, you should advise him to go to the police. If you become aware of his location, tell me and I will contact DS Warrington. I don't want it to ever be said that you aided and abetted him. Understood?"

"It's not going to happen, but understood. Question for you—should I be telling UCL about my charges?"

"Nothing's official yet, so I wouldn't. Off the record, Kate, did you and Dr. Ashur have some sort of relationship?"

When Kate bursts into tears, Abigail passes her a pack of tissues and tells her she doesn't need to know more.

KATE HAS FINALLY AGREED to a night out with Amrita, but she regrets it almost immediately. It's a cocktail bar and kitchen in Haringey, near both of them, and the pickup vibe is not what she wants.

Amrita stirs her fancy drink and says, "Don't worry. I'll keep the flies from landing," and good to her word, she tells enough men to get lost that word gets out the two ladies in the booth are a lost cause.

"I thought it would do you good to have a few drinks, listen to the music, get out of your flat," she says. "And celebrate, right? That was terrific news your lawyer gave you today."

"I suppose so," Kate says.

"Then why do you look so miserable?"

"Do you have to ask?"

"You haven't heard a peep from him?"

Kate gets angry, then feels guilty for it. "I don't know why you don't believe me? He gone for good. He went home."

"I know, I know," Amrita says. "One second he's in your sitting room, the next he's in Nineveh. You're my best friend and I'll do anything to support you. But you keep asking me to believe in shit I don't believe in."

"I'm not going to do that anymore," Kate says wearily. "You know all the facts. Let's leave it at that."

"Deal," Amrita says. "Did you tell your father the good news about the CPS?"

"Not yet. I will, though. He's paying for my solicitor. It's hard talking to him. He makes it painfully clear every time he's on the phone how disappointed he is with me. The black sheep in the family has never been blacker."

"Oh, yeah. University lecturer's the black sheep. Quite the flock, the Mayne family."

"About that," Kate says. "I've got a bad feeling about my meeting with my director tomorrow."

"What's the worst that can happen?" Amrita asks.

"They fire me."

"That would be bad," the nurse agrees. "They can't do that, though. Can they?"

A couple of thirtysomething guys who haven't seen the serial rejections, saunter over and aggressively make their moves.

Kate slides out of the booth, tells Amrita she can't do this anymore, and heads for the exit. Amrita tells her to wait up so she can pay the tab, then finds her on the street in a puddle of tears.

"I'm sorry," Amrita says, throwing an arm around her. "I shouldn't have been pushy about getting you to come out. It's too soon. You've been through hell."

"I love him," Kate says through the sobs. "I'll never see him again. I don't even know if he's alive. It's too much."

"You're young, pretty, and smart," her friend says. "You will meet a terrific man one day who's not a couple of thousand years old."

At that moment, two drunk guys leave the club holding up their spectacularly drunk friend, who doubles over and throws up on the curb.

"You just won't meet him in Haringey," Amrita says.

THE DIRECTOR of the IoA is a professor of classical archaeology, well-regarded for his academics and administration. Kate knows him reasonably well but hasn't had cause to meet with him personally for quite a while. As she sits with him in the comfy part of his office, his avuncular countenance puts her somewhat at ease.

"So, Kate, I won't ask you how you've been, because I can imagine how difficult a time you've been having."

"I've had better fortnights," she says.

"Yes, I'm sure of that. I wanted you to come in so I could tell you how the Institute is coming down regarding the incident."

"Thank you," she says. "I haven't been thrilled about the uncertainty."

"Indeed. So, the Human Resources officer has been gathering facts. Am I correct in saying that the police have not charged you with anything at this point?"

"That's correct."

"I received the preliminary report from HR yesterday and I want to review it with you."

Kate is working on steadying her breathing. She gazes out his windows which afford a panoramic view of Gordon Square where the leaves are beginning to turn, and wishes she was anywhere but here.

"Before I do so, I wanted to ask you about the suspect in the police's homicide investigation. I believe you told Mona Perkins in HR that he was an Iraqi scholar named Dr. Mannu Ashur. No one in the Assyriology Department or the Institute has heard of this man. Are there details of his academic affiliations you could provide?"

Oh Mannu, she thinks. *Where are you?*

She says, "I mentioned his name to Mona shortly after the incident. Subsequently, my solicitor has advised me not to talk about him to anyone but the police."

"Oh, yes, I understand," the director says, slaying his hands. "No more about that, then. This is all new to us. We're not used to criminal investigations."

"Nor am I," she says. She decides to try to tilt things in her favor. "I am aware," she says, "that I am unlikely to be charged with the two most serious offenses, namely involvement in the homicide or breaking into the Temperate House."

He leans forward. "Oh, that is good news. What were the other offenses?"

"Only theft of plantings—leaf cuttings, actually."

"Oh, yes?"

"I might have to pay a fine," she says.

"But will they charge with theft?"

She swallows. "Potentially, yes."

"And I suppose you can't comment about why you or Dr. Ashur wanted these plants."

"My solicitor doesn't want me to talk about any of it."

"Yes, I see. Well, here's what's going to happen, Kate. You're a valuable employee, a real asset to your department. You're held in high regard. However, the university and the Institute believe this matter has done material harm to their reputation and the reputation of our students. Accordingly, we are suspending you with pay during the investigation. There will be a formal disciplinary hearing that will take place after the police investigation is complete. You will be allowed to respond to the allegations at the hearing and you may have legal representation at that time. If, as you say, you are charged with only something minor, I'm sure that will weigh in your favor concerning the final disposition of the matter. I'm sure this isn't the news you wanted to hear today, but there it is. You'll want to get with Saul Mazur to work through the short-term logistics."

KATE IS IN HER OFFICE, staring at the papers and manuscripts on her desk that, until recently, seemed to her like the most important documents in the world. She's had her meeting with Saul Mazur, who mercifully, kept it to the specifics of who would fill in for her seminars and which lecturers would take on the interim supervision of her doctoral candidates.

She's wondering what if any books, papers, or personal items she ought to take with her today and decides to just walk away emptyhanded. She doesn't want to be that person carrying a cardboard box down the lift. Her eyes get liquid thinking about when and if she'll be back, but those thoughts are soon trumped by thoughts of Mannu.

She thinks, *He risked everything for a woman he loved a woman he could never have. That's the noblest act I've ever seen. If I helped him save her, losing my job is a price I'm willing to pay.*

She's getting ready to walk away, when Wilson Banning inserts himself.

"Heard the news, Mayne. Bad luck," he says. "Sure it's going to go your way in the end."

"Thank you, Wilson," she says, shouldering her bag.

His tongue flips his lips, lizard-like, and he says, "I was thinking, as you're going to have more time on your hands, at least in the near term, whether you'd care to take in a show one evening? I was just perusing the West End offerings and—"

She looks at his puffy, pathetic face, imagines swearing at him with all the decibels she can muster, but quietly says, "I'd really like you to leave me alone. Could you do that, please?"

~

IT'S LATE, and Kate is bone weary. She's had a microwaved dinner and left the dishes in the sink, which she never does. She's had half a bottle of wine, which she never does. She wonders if she should tell friends and family, maybe her lawyer about her suspension, but doesn't have the stomach for it.

She's sitting in a tight ball on her sofa, knees pressed hard against her chest—no lights, no TV, no music. Langham Road is mercifully quiet—no cars, no dogs, no neighbors.

The streetlight sets her sheer curtains aglow, illuminating the little shrine she's constructed on a cleared-out shelf—his penicillin and her *Gilgamesh* clay tablets, the thyme for Gula, the blank tablet for Nabu, the purifying jug of water, and his half-filled jar of green potion.

She closes her eyes but doesn't want to fall asleep. She wants to remember every minute.

How did I go this long without realizing I've been emotionally stunted? How did I go this long without knowing joy?

She's been scared to do it, for fear of sending her off the ledge, but she can't resist hearing his voice. She pulls her phone from her jeans. She made an audio recording of his ceremony on his last night. Her finger has hovered over the play button countless times, and this time, she presses it.

O Nabu, scribe of the heavens, keeper of the tablets of destiny,
You who know the fate of all things, present and future,
Open the gates of time for your humble servant.

CHAPTER THIRTY

MANNU HAS SLEPT ONLY A FEW HOURS EACH NIGHT, AND HE sometimes dozes at his desk at the apothecary. He snorts himself awake when his senior apprentice knocks.

"Master, we are ready for you to perform the next steps."

Mannu rubs his face, rises, and goes to the next room to inspect the vessel of cloudy liquid the boy has passed through a square of linen.

"Let me see the cloth," he says.

The boy shows him the brown sludge left on the linen.

"Now the liquid."

He swirls the beaker it and gives it a sniff. The royal glassmakers have cast the largest vessels they have ever made—clear with flat bottoms and pouring spouts.

"Good," he says.

He has repeated the procedure every day and knows what to look for.

"Get me the vinegar."

Mannu adds the vinegar, little by little, until two layers form. He carefully pours off the clear upper layer, leaving the cloudy layer behind.

298

"Light the lamp. The big one," he says.

The boy does so by transferring a flame from a smaller lamp.

Mannu does not trust these last steps to the apprentice. He holds the vessel over the flame, heating the cloudy liquid, taking care not to let it boil. When half the water is gone, he rests his arm, then repeats the procedure until the liquid has halved again.

He tells the boy, "I will be at my desk. Inform me when the liquid is cool to the touch."

MANNU COMES in the chamber while Kisir is leaving. The two men give each other a collegial embrace. The room smells of the herbs Kisir burned during his bedside ritual.

Mannu kneels and wakes her gently.

"My Lady, it is time for your medicine."

Bel-ibni opens her eyes and which are no longer dull.

She smiles and says, "I do not like the way it tastes."

"Think not on the way it tastes," he says. "Think on the way you feel."

"I feel better," she says. "Every day, I grow stronger and my baby grows stronger. He kicks. Would you like to feel it?"

He is the only man besides the King allowed to touch her. He lays his hand on her swollen belly and laughs at the rough tapping.

"He will be a strong boy."

"Do you think so?" she asks.

"I do. Now, sit up straight and take your medicine."

"Will you walk with me in the garden when I am done?"

"I will."

"The King told me how you saved me," she says. "You were very brave."

He smiles and bows his head. "I did what any physician would do."

MANNU STAYS at Bel's bedside until she has slipped back to sleep. Leaving the palace, he squints at the strong, golden sunlight glinting off the limestone slabs of the vast courtyard. He is thinking of taking a walk through the districts and marketplaces that he and Ninurta used to frolic in as boys, perhaps stroll along the riverbank, feeling the long grasses against his palms, visiting the spot where Mannu the sapling found a wounded goat and redoubled his decision become a physician.

Mostly, he wants to be alone with his sadness. She is with him, day and night. The woman with bright hair will be in his heart until the day he dies.

He hears a commotion at the bronze gates. One of the palace guards is shouting at a crowd of people.

"You may not enter!" he yells.

Mannu makes out the screech of a woman arguing back, "We must see the Rab Asû!"

"The Rab Asû is a busy with royal duties," the guard shouts back. "He does not see the likes of you lot."

Mannu prickles at this. He is the physician of all of Nineveh. He will see any afflicted person who needs him.

He takes long strides forward until the crowd spots him.

"There he is! There is the Rab Asû!"

He says, "Guard, let them through. I will speak with them."

There are twenty, maybe thirty of them, mostly women. One of them, an old lady in a ragged tunic comes to the fore and says, "We found her in the alley behind my house. Wandering there, naked as a babe. I think there is something wrong with her. She keeps babbling the name of the Rab Asû. Her color is strange. We are scared she has *ummatu*—the plague."

The women push someone forward draped from head to toe in an old blanket.

Mannu reaches to pull the blanket back to see the afflicted one's face.

He sees the long, bright hair first.

"Kate."

Kate blinks at him. In dazed confusion, his face comes into focus, and she says, "You curled your beard."

His tears are flowing. "Yes. I did so."

As she feels his arms around her, she looks up and sees the ziggurats of the Temples of Nabu and Ishtar and the vegetation of the palace gardens cascading down the terraced walls.

"Nineveh," she says.

"You came," he says, raining kissing on every part of her face.

"It took me time to get the courage. I said your spell. I asked the gods to bring me to you. I drank your potion. I am here."

"Knowing that Nineveh will fall?"

"Knowing that whatever happens, I will be with you."

EPILOGUE

ROGER PARTRIDGE, IS IN HIS CURATOR'S OFFICE AT THE BRITISH Museum's Middle East Department, doing his correspondence, when there's a polite rapping at his half-open door.

"Come," he says, then looks up and says, "Oh, Mrs. Bedding-ton, what can I do for you?"

The retired security services official has been volunteering at the laboratory for years, meticulously sorting through the thousands and thousands of broken fragments of clay tablets from the royal library of Nineveh that the museum has stored away, uncatalogued, in racks of trays—the world's largest jigsaw puzzle.

She looks like a white-haired schoolmarm in her cardigan, blouse buttoned to the neck, and long skirt.

"I've been beavering away at that tablet with the poem, you know."

"I know you have. How long have you been looking for bits of it?"

"Oh, gosh. Almost as long as I've been here."

"Don't tell me you've cracked it?" he asks.

"I believe I have. Would you like to see? The glue has dried."

"Absolutely!"

He follows her to her station at the lab bench and looks at the small red tablet with diminutive cuneiforms, no larger than an egg yolk. Before reading it, he tries to count how many fragments she's pieced together.

"Thirty-three," she says proudly. "The largest was the size of my thumbnail, the smallest a fly's wing—lots that size. Someone in antiquity smashed it terribly. I imagine it was when Nineveh was destroyed, but you're the expert, not me. Anyway, it's been my baby and I'm dying to hear what it says. I only just found this good-sized middle bit. Without it, none of the lines were complete."

"All right," Roger says, adjusting the spot light. "Let's have a go. Akkadian first."

ina ūmi šaplûti itti nēmeqi ēšera
awīltu ša šēru ellu, kīma napšāti šanûti
tazzaz ana panīya, šulmu iddâk libbīya
kīma kakkab šamê ul ušēsi šubšudāya
ēpuš šemêšu ina qerbīya, ana dāriš
šumma šumšu: Mannu-ki-Aššur, asû ša Ninua,
ša napšāti ipuš ana šulmi

"That sounds lovely," she says.

"It is. It's quite beautiful," he says. "I'll have a go at translation."

In the days beneath wisdom, when the world was still,
She came—a woman of bright hair, like a soul not of this age.
She stood before me, and peace struck my heart.
Like a star of heaven she unsettled my dreams,
And I made her name dwell within me, forever.

He looks up and says, "It ends with a colophon."

If his name be sought: Mannu-ki-Ashur, physician of Nineveh,
who wrote this for the peace of souls.

"Gosh," she says. "It is beautiful. What do you think it means?"

"I don't really know, Mrs. Beddington," he says. He looks at the tablet again, scratches his cheek and says, "We'll need to have a think about it. Show it around. A poem. A vision. A dream. I'm not sure we'll ever know."

THE END

ABOUT THE AUTHOR

 Glenn Cooper is an internationally published thriller writer with over eight million copies sold in thirty translations. Many of his twenty novels have been top-ten bestsellers. Cooper has a degree in archaeology from Harvard College and a medical degree from Tufts University School of Medicine. He practiced internal medicine and infectious diseases before becoming a biomedical researcher and biotech CEO. He has also written numerous screenplays and produced three feature films. He draws on his experiences and studies to create fast-paced thrillers with historical, philosophical, religious, and scientific themes.

For more information visit his website:
glenncooperbooks.com

facebook.com/GlennCooperUSA

amazon.com/stores/author/B002L10BFU

bookbub.com/authors/glenn-cooper

goodreads.com/glenn_cooper

ALSO BY GLENN COOPER

The Cosmos Keys

The Silence of Flesh

The Physician of Nineveh